The verdict is in and

THE
TRIAL

'Incredibly clever and tense'
'A really addictive read'
'Looking forward to more!'
'An absolute delight'
'A fascinating insight into courtroom politics'
'Next book please!'
'A breathtaking courtroom drama'
'Entertaining, compelling and insightful'
'A rollicking good read'
'Gripping right to the last word'
'Please can we have more!'
'Wonderfully clever and entertaining'
'A thrilling story'
'Very cleverly written'
'Brilliantly entertaining'
'Deliciously good'
'Fast paced and full of twists and turns'
'A courtroom cracker'
'A must read!'
'I can't wait to read the next novel'
'Without a doubt one of the best books I've read this year'
'A great read indeed!'
'Very tense, suspenseful and unpredictable'
'Smart, snappy and intelligent'
'If you like courtroom dramas then this is a must'
'I was hooked from the first couple of pages'
'An excellent tale'

About the Author

ROB RINDER

THE
TRIAL

PENGUIN BOOKS

PENGUIN BOOKS

UK | USA | Canada | Ireland | Australia
India | New Zealand | South Africa

Penguin Books is part of the Penguin Random House group of companies
whose addresses can be found at global.penguinrandomhouse.com

First published by Century in 2023
Published in Penguin Books 2024
001

Typeset in 11.88/14.96 pt Fournier MT Std by Jouve (UK), Milton Keynes
Printed and bound in Great Britain by Clays Ltd, Elcograf S.p.A.

The authorised representative in the EEA is Penguin Random House Ireland,
Morrison Chambers, 32 Nassau Street, Dublin D02 YH68

A CIP catalogue record for this book is available from the British Library

ISBN: 978–1–804–94038–9

www.greenpenguin.co.uk

For Victoria Cohen

Prologue

It was the day he was going to die, but Detective Inspector Grant Cliveden didn't know it yet. The events of the morning had been strange, certainly, but now the sun was shining, he was striding down Fleet Street towards the Old Bailey and feeling quietly confident that everything would go his way. Athletically built, with the kind of good looks which, if not quite Hollywood level, were of soap heart-throb standard at least, DI Cliveden adjusted the gleaming buttons of his dress uniform and straightened his tie. At his level in the hierarchy, you didn't have to wear uniform for court appearances, but he always liked to, and his boss was more than happy to allow it. To him, being a police officer was a vocation, and a noble one at that, and he wanted the world to know the pride he took in his work. Of course, it also served to make him more conspicuous, and he became aware of a group of teenagers on a school trip who were excitedly pointing at him from across the road. He gave them a friendly wave. That documentary about his rescue of the late Queen from an attempted assassination must have been repeated on Channel 4 again; all the old royal shows had been getting a fresh airing since the monarch had passed away the previous September.

And, of course, his face had been splashed through a load of the memorial supplements too: a supporting character in a pivotal moment in royal history.

That was all a long time ago now though. Royal protection was his past; serious crime was his present and, God willing, his future. As he'd told Susanna Reid on the *Good Morning Britain* sofa when he was asked to talk through the police's new crime strategy, it was an honour to go from protecting one individual who represented the values of our great society to protecting society itself. He grinned as he remembered how her eyes had shone with admiration as he'd delivered his solemn vow of service; God, he'd always fancied her. The producers had fancied him, too, offering him a regular slot that they were going to call 'Good Cop Britain', or something. He'd turned them down, of course; policing was much more valuable.

Today he was due in court as the key police witness in another high-profile case – this one involving a nasty gang of teenage thugs. Thanks to the weapons and drugs he'd personally discovered during searches of the little shits' residences, he knew they had them bang to rights. The trial still had some way to go, but DI Cliveden was already mentally chalking it up as another win – well, four really, if you counted each of the defendants separately. That meant his personal tally for the calendar year had already hit fifty. He felt a shiver of pride – ever since he'd hit the headlines again last year, after recovering London's biggest ever haul of cocaine, he knew the public's eyes were on him. And he wasn't about to let them down.

The faces of his two children floated unbidden into his mind, as so often happened. He thought fondly of the school project his eight-year-old son Jamie had just completed, which his wife, Natasha, had shown him last night as she'd poured them big glasses of a crisp Waitrose Chablis. Jamie's class at Wimbledon Prep (£15k a year! What would DI Cliveden's younger self have thought of *that*?) had been asked to write about their heroes. Some of the kids had chosen popstars and footballers, Natasha had told him, but Jamie had written about his dad. 'My dad works hard to keep us safe and make sure the bad guys are off the street,' he'd written in his crooked eight-year-old's hand. DI Cliveden smiled to himself: yes, that was what he did – whatever the cost. It certainly beat being a hedge-fund wanker, like most of the other dads.

As the Old Bailey loomed into view, DI Cliveden rolled his shoulders back and glanced upwards. If he didn't know better, he'd say Lady Justice – or at least the twelve-foot golden statue version of her – was giving him an approving wink. It was a trip he'd made a thousand times before, but DI Cliveden didn't think he would ever get tired of arriving at the most famous court in the world, knowing that thanks to public servants like him, society's retribution would be dispensed to those lowlifes who deserved it.

He cut through the underpass where a ragtag group of friends and family of victims and defendants were gathered outside the public entrance, flashing a quick smile and relishing the ripple of recognition that went through the crowd as he bounded past. At the Lord Mayor's entrance he spotted a former colleague coming out, and couldn't resist giving her a wide Cheshire Cat grin as they crossed paths. The bosomy ageing female security staff who manned the door were always pleased to see him, and giggled and flirted as he put his wallet and keys through the scanner. He played along, asking after Dawn's son, winking at Brenda.

It was this easy warmth that not only endeared him to friends and colleagues but also made him a star – the nation's favourite policeman, called upon as a talking head for all issues of law and order, used in police recruitment campaigns, hailed in the press as a modern-day hero. Through the polished wooden doors he went, and down the marble corridor. A young court clerk he hadn't seen before, pretty, with soft blonde curls, hurried after him, pressing a coffee into his hands. 'You've just enough time to drink it, Inspector, before they call you!' the clerk said, blushing. He thanked her and continued towards the courtroom – pausing as, briefly, his vision swam. How strange. He wondered if he had time for a quick sit-down too. But no – he was summoned immediately to Court 3. Coffee in hand, Cliveden tried to ignore the strange sensation in his arms, the gnawing ache in his stomach. He must have gone too hard at the gym yesterday, he thought. He'd give himself tonight off.

Despite the odd sensation shooting through his muscles, Cliveden entered the courtroom with his usual swagger, drawing strength from the admiring glances of the twelve men and women of the jury. In the dock, four teenage boys, more baby-faced than he remembered, shuffled their feet and refused to look his way. The judge, a steely-faced woman he was not sure he had encountered before, fixed him with a cool stare. The stage was set – now for his star performance. He marched towards the witness box and stretched out his hand for the Bible. That's when he felt it – the sudden and inescapable knowledge that his body was failing. His face started to droop, his vision blurred. He grasped for the side of the stand, unable to breathe. He tried to call for help but all that came out of his mouth was a slurred moan. He clutched his chest and fell to his knees — aware of the commotion in court as a flock of barristers surrounded him, their cloaks flapping like bats' wings. As he collapsed backwards, his eyes fell on the Royal Arms, Britain's most potent symbol of justice, one last time. Then, everything went black.

1

On the steps of Bexley Magistrates' Court, pupil barrister Adam Green sighed and stuffed his bulging folder into his rucksack. It was starting to drizzle, making the pebble-dashed, utilitarian building look even more conspicuously depressing. The smeared glass double doors behind him swung open and two senior barristers, one middle-aged, male and portly, the other middle-aged, male and bald, came out. Either they didn't notice Adam or they pretended not to, because they didn't make any effort to halt their conversation about the declining standards in pupils.

Adam gritted his teeth, fished his phone out of his pocket, and tapped out a one-word message to his pupil master: Unsuccessful. It was a rather crude summing-up of the comedy of errors that had actually occurred, but how to put the full horror of Dale McGinn's conduct this afternoon into one text? He'd tell Jonathan about it properly at the party – or 'networking event', as everyone insisted on calling it – later.

It was already gone five, his bail application having been the last hearing of a typically busy day at the mags. Adam was exhausted and thought longingly of the IKEA bed at his grotty bedsit on Holloway Road. But that wasn't an option, because the party — or networking event — organised at chambers by the chief clerk, Tony Jones, was a three-line whip. And at this rate, Adam was going to be late.

He hurried past a scruffy row of pawnbrokers, takeaways and charity shops to the station, the April rain dripping from his short dark curls and soaking his cheap suit. He prayed to a God that he didn't quite believe in that he would start to get some better luck soon. Becoming one of two selected from 400 applicants to get a prestigious pupillage at Stag Court Chambers meant he'd used up quite a bit of luck already. And yet now he was here, it turned out that getting in was the easy part — staying was harder. Pupillage was essentially a year-long job interview for a coveted tenancy — a permanent spot at chambers — and he was already more than halfway through, without much to show for it. But after all the hard work, the debt, the sacrifices his mum had made, failure wasn't an option.

Breaking into a run, Adam reached the station platform just as a train to London Victoria was pulling in. Perhaps his luck was turning around after all. The train wasn't busy — at this time of day, commuters were all going in the other direction — so Adam got a seat: another sliver of luck. He picked up a copy of *The Sun*, its edges curled and grubby, which the seat's previous occupant had discarded. The first eight pages were dominated with the Grant Cliveden poisoning, just as they had been ever since the famous police officer had dropped dead in the Old Bailey a month earlier.

The press and public all seemed to agree on one point: there was only one thing worse than the murder of a police officer, and that was the murder of a police officer who was also a minor celebrity. Maybe 'celebrity' was the wrong word; Cliveden hadn't exactly courted the media's attention – he'd turned down *Strictly* 'at least four times', according to this particular breathless *Sun* write-up. But he'd nevertheless found a place in the nation's psyche, somewhere between national treasure and bastion of society. In an age of influencers and reality stars, Cliveden represented real heroism, duty and integrity; he had been, in short, everything the British thought their public servants should be. Adam had only been eleven when Cliveden had thrown himself between the Queen and that madman with a gun, but he still remembered how his own mother had wept at the grainy footage of the baby-faced officer prepared to make the ultimate sacrifice.

Adam flicked past the now-familiar picture of Cliveden surrounded by his adoring and extremely photogenic family, which had been splashed across every newspaper and television news bulletin. It showed Cliveden on an idyllic beach, barefoot, with his legs stretched out in front of him. His arm was around his wife, Natasha, her honey-blonde hair ruffled just so by the sea breeze, and the strap of her elegant white sundress slipping playfully from her slim shoulder. In their laps sat two cherubic children – Jamie and Arabella. All of them had deep tans, straight white teeth, and the kind of glow that looks like an Instagram filter but is really just a fortuitous combination of *Hello!* magazine, genes and money.

There were plenty of wizened and snaggle-toothed ex-cops who still managed to build media careers off the back of past triumphs, thought Adam (they'd all been wheeled out to write 'tributes' and 'analysis' to fill the endless pages of coverage of the murder). It would have been very easy for Cliveden to have done the same, and Adam admired him for instead remaining on the front line. Not content to rest on his laurels, Cliveden had moved to serious crime where he had cemented his reputation with a prestigious conviction rate and the recovery of enormous amounts of drugs. His death was, undoubtedly, a terrible waste – and the nation was howling for justice. Adam paused to look at the mugshot of the man charged with the murder: Jimmy Knight, an ex-con with a dead-eyed scowl that would give you nightmares. He wondered idly which chambers would get the defence case. As he flipped the page to find an incensed columnist raging beneath the headline IS LIFE IMPRISONMENT PUNISHMENT ENOUGH FOR HERO COP KILLER?, he didn't envy them the task.

The train crawled through the shadows of Battersea Power Station and at last into London Victoria. Adam caught the District line to Temple, from where he ran the final leg of his journey, through the winding lanes of Middle Temple, past the gothic splendour of the Royal Courts of Justice and up the flagged steps to his chambers, Stag Court. The noise hit him instantly as he pushed open the polished black door; the networking event seemed to already be getting out of hand. Solicitors from some of the city's top law firms were swigging Champagne with Stag Court's finest, spilling in and out of meeting rooms and up the stairs, laughing raucously.

No one seemed to notice Adam as he squeezed gingerly around the edge of the crowd, trying not to knock anyone's elbow. Catherine Jordan KC had a group of solicitors rapt as she narrated the dark tale of her latest rape defendant, which she'd nevertheless managed to turn into an amusing party piece. Adam was sweating, and it wasn't just because of his polyfibre shirt. He'd never been good at these sorts of things at Oxford.

The social awkwardness that had blighted his time at university had followed him into the real world, where he felt it even more acutely. It wasn't that people didn't want to come over to talk to him – his tall, broad figure, melancholic green eyes and angular cheekbones often drew people towards him. It was just that he never knew what to say. How he wished he could be one of those people who found this kind of thing easy – power pose, bank of anecdotes, honking laugh.

In one of the larger meeting rooms, Adam found a makeshift bar messily arranged on the glass conference table. Tony, the chief clerk and iron fist of Stag Court, had recently got rid of the blousy curtains and heavily patterned carpets that had adorned the chambers for decades in favour of corporate glass and all-beige everything, which Adam thought was an interesting choice for an office with a chronic red wine problem. He was flipping the cap off a bottle of Becks when he felt the back of his neck prickle, which could only mean one thing – she'd spotted him.

'Georgina, hi,' he said, trying to keep his tone as even as possible. His fellow pupil, Georgina Devereaux, was regarding him as a kestrel might look at a mouse, a slight smirk playing on her perfect rosebud lips. Privately educated, well connected, and extremely good at parties – and networking events – Georgina was everything Adam was not. That would have been fine, except that only one of them was going to get the tenancy spot at the end of their pupillage. And Georgina was the favourite – something she never liked Adam to forget.

'Finally decided to put in an appearance, have you? I thought you might need a little alone time after losing a simple bail application . . . again . . .' She pouted, sarcastically.

News travels fast, thought Adam.

'Well, it wasn't that simple, actually,' he said, trying to take away her sting with neutral friendliness. 'My client, Dale McGinn—'

'Oh, Adam, I don't actually want to hear about it!' Georgina cut in, with a laugh like tinkling glass. 'I just wanted to let you know that I'd already told Tony you'd be late. He wasn't very pleased, I can tell you . . .'

Damn, thought Adam. He had hoped he'd be able to sneak in under the radar and Tony would have been none the wiser. But that plan had failed to take into account the wolf in Reiss clothing. Georgina had already spotted someone more interesting and important than Adam and was looking past his shoulder, tossing her long auburn hair and setting her expression to 'flirty'. Adam took the hint and headed down the corridor to stash his bag in his pigeonhole, manoeuvring himself past a mass of bodies in Savile Row suits and pencil skirts. The door of the post room was shut, which was unusual, and as soon as he pushed it open, Adam realised why. There was Martin Norton KC, 'tactical acumen second to none' according to *The Legal 500*, proving that he had acumen in other areas too, if the expression on the face of his female companion was anything to go by.

Adam slammed the door shut – and kept his back to it when he spotted Tony storming down the corridor with a face like thunder. Shaven-headed and powerfully built, Tony looked like a bouncer and was about as intimidating as one too.

'You!' he barked at Adam, in his trademark gravelly Cockney. 'Pupil or not, I don't want to see any of my people standing around gawping when they could be building commercial relationships!'

Like 'networking event', 'building commercial relationships' was one of Tony's favourite new phrases. He'd left school at sixteen and had started making a living in the wheeler-dealer world of chambers in the 1980s, when clerks had needed to do little more than answer the phone and watch the money roll in. But his commercial instincts were as sharp as his suits, and he knew those days were long gone. Tony believed Stag Court needed to get corporate if it was going to survive, and was on a one-man mission to drag his creaking chambers into the brave new world.

Adam would almost have felt sorry for Tony if he weren't so scared of him. He knew the clerk had envisioned this evening as something of a glorified seminar, where London's highest-powered solicitors would politely discuss their legal specialisms and identify the best Stag Court barristers to take on their next lucrative cases. Sloshing Champagne and steamy clinches on the photocopier were definitely not what he'd had in mind.

'Where've you been anyway, Green?' Tony growled. 'I could not 'ave been clearer about the start time of today's event.'

'Er, yes, sorry about that,' said Adam, raising his voice in an effort to drown out the escalating grunts and moans coming from the other side of the door. 'I was held up at Bexley Mags because—'

'You must be mistaking me for someone who cares,' cut in Tony menacingly, one eyebrow raised. 'You'll have my full attention when – one – it pays, and – two – you've won. Now get out there and get schmoozing!'

As Tony barrelled off to browbeat someone else, Adam took a swig of his beer and scanned the corridor, trying to decide who would be the least intimidating solicitor to approach. He spotted Magda Frank, who'd instructed on a recent robbery case, but she was no fan of his since he'd gone to find their defendant's girlfriend in the magistrates' lobby only to have four women answer his meek call and a fight break out.

If only he could think of something clever to say. The person he actually wanted to talk to, Bobby Thompson KC, was standing a little removed from the crowd, sipping a glass of water with a haughty expression on his face.

Proud of his roots in the Jamaican community of working-class Birmingham, Bobby had come to the Bar when racism was casually deployed and widely accepted within the profession. Against the odds, he was now one of its leading lights, and it had been Bobby's incredibly inspiring speech delivered at Adam's school as part of an outreach scheme that had brought him here, to Stag Court. Adam had known, ever since what had happened to his dad all those years ago – but now wasn't the time to think about all that – that he'd wanted to do something that would make the world a fairer place. But it wasn't until Bobby and his talk on the urgency of creating a justice system that reflected the dignity of those who used it that a career in the law had seemed a realistic possibility. Hundreds of hours of study later, a ham-fisted attempt to make himself a whole new person, and a determined vow to keep the past in a box where it belonged, here he was, a pupil in Bobby's chambers. Surely now was the time to try some 'networking' that might actually matter?

'Do you think Bobby thinks it's weird, how much you stare at him?'

Rupert Harrington – sandy hair, rugby player's shoulders, charming dimples – nudged Adam in the ribs.

'I don't—'

'I'm only teasing, mate,' Rupert said, handing Adam another

beer. 'Here you go, you look like you need this. Let's go in the other room – not sure I want to be here for Martin's encore . . .'

Adam felt his shoulders relax as he followed his friend into the main lobby. Easy-going and good-natured, Rupert had the ability to put anyone at ease. As Stag Court's newest tenant, he'd become an invaluable source of guidance, particularly as he had been in Adam's shoes a year ago. It was Rupert who'd warned Adam not to follow chambers' official advice to 'ask any question, no matter how silly it sounds'. Rupert's sage riposte was: 'Only do that, mate, if you don't mind the KCs all saying, "He asked me a really stupid question six months ago," and deciding not to give you tenancy because of it.' Rupert got a vote on Adam's tenancy too, but he just wasn't the type to keep a running tally of follies and faux pas. As such, he was the only person Adam could speak (relatively) freely around without worrying that what he said might count against him.

'It's just as well there are plenty of criminal barristers here, because Tony might just commit a murder before tonight is out,' said Rupert merrily. 'I've been upstairs and there's a whole load of them in the stationery cupboard racking up lines on box files . . .'

'Well, I'd advise him to get someone other than me to apply for his bail,' said Adam, chinking his bottle with Rupert's. 'I've had another stinker today.'

'Go on?'

'So, my client has been done for a burglary at a betting shop, but he insists he didn't do it. His case is that it's mistaken identity – the culprit's on CCTV in a vintage red Man United top, and he tells me last week, that's not him. So today I'm all set to make the bail application, feeling good about it all, got my little spiel prepared — and then they bring him in. And you'll never guess what he's wearing.'

'What?'

'A vintage red Man United top.'

Rupert threw back his head and roared with laughter. Adam allowed himself a smile — but it didn't last long.

'Green!' The unmistakable reedy tones of Jonathan Taylor-Cameron, Adam's pupil master, were drifting imperiously over from the other side of the room.

'Godspeed,' said Rupert wryly, clapping Adam on the shoulder. Adam approached his bouffant-haired pupil master with some trepidation, wondering if he, like Tony, was about to admonish him for today's showing in court.

'So,' said Jonathan, arranging a crocodile smile on his boyish features. He was in his fifties but still retained his roguish good looks, notwithstanding the little paunch he'd developed in his middle age. 'How did we get on today?'

This was a first. The pupil master had generally shown next to zero interest in Adam's progress in his 'second six', the period of six months during which a pupil was allowed to represent their own clients in court, rather than simply doing the pupil master's donkey work.

'Well, it wasn't necessarily the verdict I'd have wanted, but—'

'No, no, no, I don't mean that,' Jonathan said, waving away Adam's words like a bad smell. 'I mean, how did you get on with the flowers?'

Adam had almost forgotten. Jonathan had rung frantically first thing that morning insisting there was an 'emergency' and he needed Adam to send flowers to his mistress, Allegra, as a matter of urgency.

'Oh, right, yes, that's all sorted,' said Adam. 'I wrote in the card "Never again, darling" like you asked . . .'

'Good, good,' said Jonathan. 'Did you add the bit about how I miss her milky thighs, or did we decide that was a bit much?'

Adam opened his mouth to answer, but didn't get the chance before their conversation was unceremoniously interrupted by Tony. The clerk's previous fury seemed to have passed, replaced with a fizzing, malevolent excitement.

'Mr Taylor-Cameron, Mr Green,' he said, his eyes glittering. 'Come with me. I've got you a big one.'

2

'Grant Cliveden.' Up in Jonathan's office, Tony delivered those two words with relish, grinning so broadly Adam could see his two pointy incisors. 'It's the biggest case of the decade, gentlemen, and it's come to us.'

Jonathan was flustered, not really taking in what Tony was saying – Adam could tell he'd been 'networking' with some gusto. Tony hadn't even given Jonathan the chance to sit down, and now the senior barrister shuffled papers onto the floor and sank into his dark leather swivel chair. Adam hovered awkwardly in the corner, by the newly painted coat of arms that Jonathan had enlisted him to commission during his first month of pupillage.

Jonathan's room was the one enclave of Stag Court that had escaped Tony's zealous purge of all things chintz. With its plaid wallpaper, moth-eaten velvet curtains, ugly lamps and dusty knick-knacks – including an alarmingly wonky taxidermy of Bitsy, a once-beloved childhood Jack Russell – it was the sort of room in which only a man who had spent his formative years at a fifth-rate boarding school could feel comfortable. The desk was littered with silver photo frames which faced Jonathan's chair. Knowing that he had at least seven children from his three marriages and multiple affairs, as well as several grandchildren, Adam had first assumed that the frames would contain photos of his brood. Having spent many long evenings in his pupil master's chair, drafting his briefs for him, he now knew better. Every single frame featured a photo of Jonathan himself – on the golf course, aboard a sailboat, at the races a few feet away from the then Prince Charles, or on the steps of the High Court with his most distinguished clients. The photos showing him celebrating court wins, Adam noted, were all at least twenty years old.

'Bloody hell, that's rather jolly, isn't it,' Jonathan bumbled, patting his perfectly coiffed hair. 'The murder of Britain's greatest living cop! I haven't prosecuted in a while but I'm sure—'

'It's not prosecution,' Tony cut in. 'It's defence.'

'Oh, for heaven's sake, Tony!' Jonathan banged his desk with his fists like an angry toddler. 'No way. That case is an absolute loser and everyone at the Bar knows it. I'm not doing it.'

'Sir, I'm sure I hardly need to remind you of the cab-rank rule,' Tony said evenly. A central tenet of the barristers' code, this ancient rule meant that a barrister had to take a case provided they were free to do so. 'Besides, the client asked for you specifically, apparently.'

Adam's mouth threatened to fall open at this revelation, and he clamped it quickly shut. He'd read enough about the case against the defendant, Jimmy Knight, to know that the evidence was damning. Knight had met with Cliveden shortly before his death and had bought him a drink – into which he'd allegedly slipped the poison. There was CCTV that placed him at the scene, and, if the press was to be believed, a history of bad blood between the two men. You'd think a defendant who found himself in such a serious hole would want a barrister who was supersharp, adaptable, ingenious and charismatic. As far as Adam could tell, Jonathan was none of these things.

'Look, I can understand why the boy would want a big name,' Jonathan blustered, without a hint of irony. 'But I haven't done legal aid criminal defence in years. Besides, I'm going to be far too busy with Kavanagh, and you know how valuable that fraud case will be to this chambers. You're going to have to get me out of it.'

'The Kavanagh case isn't until later this year, sir,' Tony said. 'You've more than enough time to do both.'

'I won't have it! This is unacceptable!' Jonathan was in full tantrum mode now, his face cherry-red, spittle spraying the desk in front of him. Tony merely raised an eyebrow, wandered over to the window, and looked out at the gloomy square below, letting the silence in the office brew ominously. Historically, clerks were meant to be the 'downstairs' to the barristers' 'upstairs' – but anyone who'd ever seen Tony with his barristers would know it was a lot more complicated than that.

'Please, Tony,' Jonathan wheedled to his clerk's bulky back, switching tactics quickly. 'It's a dud – please don't make me take it.' Tony turned around to face him, his expression an unreadable cliff-face in the office shadows.

'It may be a dud, sir, but the victim is a man for whom the King sent a personal message of condolence. Make no mistake, this is a case that will be on every newspaper and on every TV channel every day,' he said. 'And if we take this on, you know what else will be on every newspaper and every TV channel every day? Stag Court.'

'So that's your big idea, is it?' said Jonathan. 'Make us known as the home for the guilty until proven guilty? The chambers for losers and lunatics?'

'You're taking it,' snapped Tony. 'And, sir, with respect, I would not dream of telling you how to do your job, so perhaps you can refrain from telling me how to do mine.'

Chastened, Jonathan fiddled with his cufflinks.

'Fine. Tell me I've got a good junior at least.' Adam felt the corners of his mouth twitch. Jonathan might have accepted he was doing the case in principle, but he was already looking for a way to dump it on someone else.

'Slightly tricky situation there, sir,' said Tony brusquely. 'It's a legal aid fee, and let's just say the money is a little on the small side. So there's no junior. But you can use Mr Green here instead.' He gestured at Adam, as if he were a moderately useful cabinet. Adam felt the breath catch in his throat.

'Green?!' Jonathan was on his feet now, positively apoplectic. 'He's still a pupil! This is beyond the pale, Tony, it really is. You can't just give me some dead-end case, tell me it's going to be a media circus, and then expect me to do it with some garden-variety *pupil*.' The last word was venomously spat, and Adam wondered if Jonathan had noticed that he was in the room. Tony barely blinked at Jonathan's meltdown. 'I'm afraid, sir, that's just the way it is, and you'll have to make it work,' he said. 'I've heard Mr Green is progressing rather well, so I'm sure he will meet your – er – standards.'

Adam's emotions came thick and fast, falling over and crashing into each other. This case was a world away from the traffic offences and shoplifting charges that had made up the bulk of his work for the month that he'd been 'on his feet'. However much of a 'dud' it might be, it was still an Old Bailey murder trial, and that was exciting. It was the chance to really make his mark — although he would be working closely with Jonathan, which was pretty anxiety-inducing. Especially given that his pupil master had in no uncertain terms just written him off.

The verbal tennis match between Jonathan and Tony had moved on. Jonathan was now berating the chief clerk about how much work he had to do on the Kavanagh case. Adam's pupil master had spoken of little else for the last fortnight, ever since he had been engaged by his golf-course buddy, an obscenely wealthy businessman, to fight the complicated fraud charges against him. Victory in that particular case would mean an enormous payday for Jonathan, and you could practically see the pound signs in his eyes when he spoke about it. Adam had heard him boasting about how he'd be able to add a tennis court to his 'little place in France', as well as cover the next three years' worth of exorbitant school fees that he was still paying for his youngest daughter, Florence.

'So what I'm saying is, if I have to have Green for the Cliveden case, you should give him to me for Kavanagh too,' Jonathan was telling Tony, the mention of his own name snapping Adam from his thoughts.

'Deal,' said Tony, as Jonathan reached gratefully across the desk to his half-drunk glass of Champagne. 'And take it easy on that, sir — you've got a busy few months ahead.'

With that, Tony wrenched open the office door, and the raucous sounds of the party below assaulted their ears once more. Jonathan followed him out, grumbling loudly about how he would not be lectured to by a clerk on how much he drank. The door swung shut behind them, leaving Adam standing there in stunned silence.

The next five months of his life had just been bartered like poker chips, and he hadn't said a word. His opinion didn't matter, but how he performed in these two cases really did. It was five months that might make the difference between tenancy or disaster.

3

Phone call

'Hi, Mum.'

'Adam, you sound so tired! Are you eating properly?'

'What do you mean, this is just how I—'

'I was saying to Debbie at number forty-five only yesterday, "All Adam does is work, work, work, he doesn't eat, he doesn't sleep – I'm beside myself," but then I said to Debbie, "I suppose that's just what it's like being a partner."'

'Mum, I've told you so many times, I'm not a *partner*, I'm a pupil.'

'Pupil, partner, same thing – you're too old for me to be telling people you're still a student.'

'Well, that's not quite—'

'You're doing your own legal cases, aren't you?'

'Yes, but—'

'Big ones?'

'Actually, I've just got a really big one, Mum – you might have heard of it.'

'Oh, thank goodness. I've had to listen to Debbie banging

on and on about how her Angie has been made assistant manager of the Boots in Arnos Grove, so I could do with a bit of
ammunition.'

'So, you know the Grant Cliveden murder?'

'Of course! Oh, that poor man. And to think, after everything he's done for this country. I was reading about it in the
Daily Mail the other day – I know, I know you don't like it,
Adam, but it does have some good articles. Well, that Erica
Moss – you know, the columnist who's always having trouble
with her daughters – she was saying if you kill a police officer,
that should be the death penalty. And I know it sounds harsh,
but she's right. Cliveden, he was a hero. We can't just have
people going around, murdering police officers and thinking
they can get away with it, can we?'

'I'm on that case.'

'Oh, Adam! Well, I never! My little boy, on the biggest case
in the country! Just wait until Debbie hears you'll be putting
away our most-hated criminal! Do you think they'll put your
picture in the papers? If so, I have a lovely one from Pamela
Minsky's wedding. Don't let them use that dreadful one you
put on Facebook.'

'What . . . ? Actually – doesn't matter. I'm representing the
defendant.'

'The *what*?'

'Jimmy Knight. The man accused of murder. I – or really, my
boss – will be defending him, not prosecuting.'

'You're on the side of the *murderer*, Adam?'

'He's innocent until proven guilty, Mum. Didn't Grandad
always say how important—'

'I know about innocent until proven guilty, that's all very

well, but that poor man had a family, Adam. His poor children! Could you look them in the eye and say—'

'Mum. Come on. You, more than anyone, know that it's not as simple as that . . .'

'Oh, Adam. I'm sure you know what you're doing, but I thought when you said you wanted to be a lawyer you'd be making lots of money and doing lots of good and yet here you are, still up to your eyes in debt and trying to stop killers going to prison . . .'

'Everyone deserves a fair trial. Think how different things might have been if—'

'You're not eating, are you? That's what this is. You're not eating and you're not thinking straight.'

'I'm eating plenty—'

'You're not, because I was in your flat today—'

'You've been in my *flat*?'

'And the fridge was completely empty, unless you count a beer and some mouldy old yoghurts, which I don't, so I put them in the bin. What a mess it is in there, Adam. I've whizzed the duster round and given it a hoover but I'm going to have to drop you off some Cif for that bathroom. And I've filled up your freezer – now, to defrost the stew—'

'Mum, I know how to defrost food. And listen, you really didn't need to do that, remember that key is for emergencies only—'

'I despair, Adam, I really do. How do you think a nice young lady would feel if she calls on you and that's the state of your flat?'

'Luckily, Mum, there aren't any nice young ladies in my life so that's not really a problem.'

'No, Adam, that is *exactly* the problem! You're twenty-five, you've got to start thinking seriously about marriage. There hasn't been anyone, has there, since you broke up with that nice Rosie at Oxford . . . I know, I know, your nan wasn't thrilled that she wasn't Jewish but, Adam, we'd all rather you marry out than stay single forever! Judy has four grandchildren already and she's just told me there's a fifth on the way – how do you think that makes me feel? But anyway, I've got the details of a wonderful girl—'

'Mum, we've spoken about this.'

'Anna Goldberg – you must remember her mother, Lisa, who makes the fish balls for the synagogue? Anna's quite pretty, as long as she doesn't show her teeth when she smiles. She trained as a hairdresser, but she ran into a few problems with the customers at the hair salon, always saying the wrong thing, you know, so now she does dog grooming instead.'

'No. Mum, *no*.'

'Oh, Adam, what am I going to do with you? I hope this is all worth it – do you really think this Jimmy Knight character might be innocent?'

'It's not my job to decide if he's innocent, it's my job to listen to what he says and make sure he is fairly represented in court. Everyone deserves that.'

'If you say so, my love.'

'Mum, if I do well in this case, it could mean I get to stay on at chambers.'

'And that's what you really want?'

'More than anything.'

'Then I hope, for your sake, he really is innocent after all.'

4

'He's bloody guilty!'

Jonathan slammed his fist into his desk, making Jimmy Knight's solicitor, Nisha Desai, twitch. With Knight himself remanded in custody after entering an innocent plea at the magistrates' court, Tony had arranged a conference at chambers between Jonathan and Nisha so they could discuss the next steps. So far, it wasn't going well.

'Look, I know you think this is a hospital pass but have a little respect, yeah?' said Nisha with an accent and attitude infused with North London sass. 'We're either going to do it properly, or I'll take this case elsewhere. It's not too much to ask that you keep an open mind about our client, is it?'

Adam was warming to Nisha already. She was tiny – five foot tall, if that – with a frazzled air, hair piled chaotically on top of her head, and a stain on the lapel of her M&S blazer that looked suspiciously like baby sick. The middle of her brow bore a deep frown crevice, testament to the amount of dead-end legal aid cases she juggled, Adam supposed. Dealing with Jonathan's tantrum was probably the last thing she needed, but she was holding her own.

'OK, then,' said Jonathan, picking up one of the papers in front of him as if it were a rancid banana skin. 'Let's take a look at the things we need to keep an open mind about.' He perched his half-moon reading glasses on the end of his nose with a dramatic flourish. 'Our client is a career criminal who had his first conviction at the age of fifteen. From there he went on to keep his local police force and magistrates' court very busy indeed, with a varied portfolio taking in shoplifting, theft, marijuana possession and criminal damage. Ten years ago, at the age of thirty-seven, he expanded his operations into armed robbery, using a gun to rob a post office – *where he himself worked* – and stealing nearly ten thousand pounds in cash.

'So, Adam, you are an open-minded sort of fellow – how do you suggest we look favourably on this CV?'

Adam, perched on the swivel chair next to Nisha, had been furiously taking notes. His head snapped up, sensing the trap set by Jonathan. Luckily, he'd read the files so many times last night that he practically had them committed to memory.

'His earlier offences – the theft and drug possession et cetera – were all committed before he was twenty-seven. And he pleaded guilty to all of them, so that shows he has a record of copping to it when he's responsible. When the armed robbery occurred, he was working as a postman and he'd had no criminal record to speak of in the ten years before that. Crucially, he pleaded innocent – so maybe he really didn't do it and that conviction was just a big cock-up.'

'Nice try, but alas, wrong,' said Jonathan, with a sneer. 'Mr Knight has indeed protested his innocence for many years, but sadly the courts do not agree with him. He has exhausted the appeal process, to no avail, thanks to the incontrovertible

evidence against him, painstakingly assembled by the police.'
He turned the page over, his piggy eyes settling unpleasantly
on Nisha.

'Now, Ms Desai, enlighten us. Who was the lead officer in the
case that put Mr Knight behind bars for a decade?'

She sighed impatiently. 'It was Grant Cliveden.'

'Detective Inspector Grant Cliveden, the very same! The
police officer who carries the pride of the nation and dropped
dead in the Old Bailey less than two weeks after Mr Knight
finally completed his sentence for armed robbery. What a marvellous coincidence. Adam, I know you went to the kind of
grubby school where Latin was jettisoned in favour of comic-
book studies or similar, but can you tell me the meaning of *mens
rea*?' Adam felt a flash of annoyance. He knew Jonathan was
showboating for Nisha, but he never missed an opportunity to
remind Adam of the contempt he had for his background.

'Of course. It is the mental intention to commit a crime,' said
Adam, trying to keep his voice neutral.

'Clever lad, perhaps you *have* been listening to me after all,'
said Jonathan, with an ingratiating wink at Nisha, which caused
her to twitch again. 'So, would you say we have established a
clear motive for Mr Knight to want Mr Cliveden dead?'

'Yes, but that doesn't mean—'

'He actually did it? You're right, it doesn't. So now we come
to *actus rea* – or for those of us less versed in Latin – the guilty
act. Although, perhaps, looking at the prosecution's case, we
should say the guilty *acts*.'

Adam hadn't even met Jimmy Knight yet, but every loath-
some little smirk of Jonathan's, every performative little gibe,
made him root more for the accused. It felt a lifetime ago now

when Adam had heard that Jonathan Taylor-Cameron was going to be his pupil master and actually felt excited. Jonathan had decades of experience, a client list that read like a *Who's Who* of the British establishment, and a cheeky twinkle that had once made him a media star. But Adam had quickly discovered that all that was firmly in the past. Success had made Jonathan lazy, and Jimmy Knight's case was the sort he most hated, in that it would require a lot of work for almost no reward. That's why he was determined to make a mockery of the client he was supposed to defend, and it turned Adam's stomach.

He wondered what Bobby Thompson would say, he who had delivered such a stirring speech at Adam's school about how only in true equality could there be meaningful justice. In Bobby's words Adam had heard more eloquent echoes of his own grandfather, who had made his home in Britain after surviving the horrors of the Second World War in Poland. 'Never forget how powerful it is to be innocent until proven guilty,' he'd told him once. 'If they don't have to prove guilt, they can do what they like to the innocent.'

Before he could stop it, an uninvited memory pushed itself into Adam's consciousness. A phone ringing in the middle of the night, his little feet padding to the top of the stairs in dinosaur slippers. His mother, howling in pain, rage, grief, like a wounded animal.

Innocent until proven guilty was a luxury that Adam's father had never had. He squeezed the thought angrily from his mind and tried to focus on the case in hand.

Adam had to admit that for Jimmy Knight, things didn't look good. The prosecution was submitting in evidence searches made on a laptop recovered from Knight's home, which showed that in the ten-day period between his release from prison and Cliveden's murder, he had made multiple internet searches relating to the police officer. At the same address they had also found a burner phone: a cheap, prepaid mobile whose owner couldn't be traced. But the police were quite reasonably assuming it was Knight's, meaning that a text message sent from the phone to Cliveden, arranging a meeting at a Central London pub called the Old Nag's Head, was from Knight too. CCTV from the pub showed Cliveden and Knight meeting just hours before Cliveden died and having a drink together – the moment the prosecution were alleging that poison was administered. Their toxicology experts had given a small window in which they believed Cliveden must have consumed the poison: his meeting with Knight was bang in the middle of it.

'And then we come to the poison itself,' said Jonathan, with relish. 'Botulinum toxin – and here I have to applaud our boy's ingenuity. One of the most poisonous substances known to man. And yet it is available in most towns and cities across the UK, and many people will pay large amounts of money to have it injected into their foreheads.'

Botox. The variety of the poison used to kill Cliveden hadn't been made public yet, and Adam knew that as soon as it was, the already-slavering press was going to lose its mind. After all, death by Botox: it sounded mad. What could be more tabloid-appropriate than a poison that was routinely and safely injected into the faces of every actor, WAG and *Love Island*er? What could be more thrilling than discovering that a lethal dose, slipped into a drink, weighed less than one cubic millimetre of air?

'I really think there's something we can work with there,' Nisha interrupted. 'Botulinum toxin is tightly regulated and super expensive. Jimmy was out of prison for less than a fortnight – how on earth does he get his hands on enough of the stuff to kill someone? I know what you're saying about its wide availability, but it's not like you can just walk into a plastic surgeon's clinic and walk out with a lethal dose of Botox in your pocket. And when you meet Jimmy Knight, you're going to see that he's not exactly a frequenter of cosmetic clinics.'

'With respect, Ms Desai, I'm not sure it's going to be good enough to tell the jury that Mr Knight has never got Botox, so he couldn't possibly be guilty,' Jonathan said, rolling his eyes patronisingly.

'That's not what she's saying,' Adam blurted out, his cheeks reddening as he took the unusual step of contradicting his pupil master. 'It's that this doesn't add up. Knight is meant to be an armed robber – if he wanted to kill Cliveden, why would he choose poison? And why this poison? How could he possibly have planned and executed it when he's been in prison for a decade? Can he really be the only suspect in this case – or was he just the easy answer the police were looking for?' Jonathan narrowed his eyes, giving Adam a nasty stare. He didn't break his gaze as he addressed Nisha.

'Ms Desai, what does Mr Knight have to say about all this?'

'Not much, I'm afraid. I advised him to answer "No comment" in all his police interviews. To me he has confirmed that he did meet Cliveden, but insists they just drank and talked. He claims to have no knowledge of botulinum toxin and insists he is not responsible for putting it in Cliveden's drink.'

Jonathan turned back to Adam. 'And you believe him, Mr Green? That makes one of us at least. So, what are you going to do about it?'

'Even when the prosecution case is so strong, there are always weaknesses, right? We just have to find them, don't we?'

'No,' snapped Jonathan, and Adam could tell that whatever game they had been playing was over. 'Our job is to tell Knight to come to his senses and plead guilty. We're in full-life-term territory, but if he shows some contrition our boy might at least see the light of day before he dies – that's the best we can do here. Show Ms Desai out, please. I will see you both in the cells on Thursday morning. And, Green, try to remember that this is criminal justice, not *Murder, She Wrote*.'

Nisha stuffed sheaves of papers and her heavily chewed biro into a battered handbag as Adam stood to show her out. Once the heavy door of Jonathan's office had swung safely shut and they were out of earshot, Adam noticed Nisha breathe in deeply.

'Thanks for sticking up for me in there,' she said. 'I know it's a tough case. But my senior partner remembers Jimmy from when he was a little tearaway, and he said he always copped to stuff he did. This is different. If he says he's innocent, we owe it to him to put up a proper fight.'

'I know, and I'm sorry about him,' Adam said, jerking his thumb in the direction of Jonathan's office. 'He won't be like that when we meet Mr Knight – at least, I don't think he will . . .'

Nisha laughed hollowly. 'Nothing can surprise me in this job anymore.'

'Have you ever worked with Jonathan before?' Adam asked.

'Never,' said Nisha. 'I hadn't even heard of him to be honest – I don't think he and I do particularly similar casework. But he was the first person that Jimmy asked for. He said, "Get me Jonathan Taylor-Cameron," so I did – and here we are.' She grimaced. They'd reached the chambers' main entrance, where they stood and peered out at the April drizzle.

'Just what I need,' muttered Nisha. 'You think my hair's bad now, wait until it's been rained on.' She fumbled in the recesses of her cavernous bag for an umbrella. 'Listen, Adam,' she said, straightening up. 'Jimmy says he was framed the first time he went to prison. And if it happened before, it could have happened again. All we need to get Jimmy acquitted is to prove reasonable doubt. Yes, he had a motive. Yes, he met Cliveden. But could he really have pulled off that murder?'

This was exactly what had been bothering Adam ever since he'd read the files. 'But if Jimmy didn't do it, then who did?'

'That's the big question,' said Nisha, raising an eyebrow. 'And one I wish I had more time for. Sugar, I'm going to be late. I'll see you in court on Thursday!' Adam watched her go, handbag swinging wildly from her arm, rainwater splashing up her ankles as she bounded through the gathering puddles.

5

Shutting the heavy door, Adam headed back into the bowels of chambers, pausing to press his back against the corridor wall as Tony and two of his juniors stomped past carrying briefs tied with the distinctive pink ribbons that indicated they were defence cases.

There was a tiny office next to the cleaning cupboard, furnished with a random assortment of desks and chairs, which was allocated for pupils to use, and that was where he was headed. It wasn't much, but at least Adam usually had it to himself, as Georgina much preferred to do her own work perched on the end of the desk of her pupil master, Rory Parks – and he preferred to have her there too, if the constant peals of insufferable laughter that echoed from that particular room were anything to go by.

Adam planned to go back through Jimmy Knight's files. The case against their client was almost too strong. But there had to be something they were missing. Yes, Cliveden had got Jimmy locked up all those years ago – but would that really drive him to murder?

On YouTube, Adam clicked 'play' on a clip of an interview

with Grant Cliveden. It was taken from a documentary, *Queen and Country*, made about four years ago to mark the tenth anniversary of the attempted assassination of the then-monarch, which, as the Andrew Marr voiceover reminded viewers, had 'rocked the nation'. Cliveden was interviewed in lingering close-up, the George Cross pinned to his spotless dress uniform glinting in the soft studio lights.

'I just did what any officer in my position would do,' he said, with disarming modesty, as the footage rolled of him tackling a screaming gunman to the floor. 'I was doing my duty – I didn't even think about it.' There was something very human about Cliveden, Adam thought. None of the institutional stiffness with which some police carried themselves. No wonder the nation had fallen in love with him. He skipped the video on, past fawning royal experts, until he found Cliveden talking again. 'Look, that was one bad guy, who tried to kill Her Majesty,' he was saying, piercing blue eyes looking steadily at the camera. 'But there are thousands of bad guys out there, and they might not be attacking us in such an obvious way, but they are flooding our streets with drugs, with weapons. It's up to me to get them off the streets and into prison, where they belong.'

A voice calling out from a door half ajar made Adam quickly hit 'pause'.

'Is that you, Adam Green?' It was Bobby Thompson. Adam stopped the video and followed the voice to Bobby's room. With its beige carpets and executive drapes, it was to all intents and purposes the same as almost every other office in the building. Except for one thing – it was meticulously neat and tidy. Almost everyone else in chambers operated in a sort of organised chaos of tumbling stacks of box files and drifts of legal papers, family mementos competing for space with bulging notepads and piles of receipts. But every surface in Bobby's domain was serenely uncluttered, the very few objects all in the perfect place – down to the immaculate Apple laptop in front of him, and the three biros – red, black and blue – laid out in precise parallel beside it. It was a small oasis of calm – and on each of the few occasions he'd been called to Bobby's room, Adam had experienced a sense of ease which he rarely felt elsewhere in chambers.

'Hi, Bobby,' said Adam, with a genuine smile. 'Congrats on the Dobbs case – great result.'

Bobby waved the compliment away. 'We were lucky with the judge,' he said. 'Charlotte Wickstead – I've known her for years from the Treasury Counsel's room – just shows what can happen when you get a judge who sees an addict as a person, not a problem. Do you know much about her?'

'I don't think I do, actually,' Adam replied.

'Well, you should,' Bobby rebuked him, with a sharp look. 'She's been listed as the judge in the Knight case. *Do your research.*'

'Right, yes,' said Adam, chastened. He'd been so busy with Knight's paperwork, as well as the rest of his duties – writing skeleton arguments, pleadings and advices for various members of chambers, juggling the few clients he still had left, and, of course, managing Jonathan's romantic affairs – that this fairly crucial fact had passed him by. Bobby gestured at the computer in front of him and Adam moved closer to take a look.

'You're going to need all the luck you can get with that murder case, Adam,' Bobby said. 'Look at this – now, you'd expect this sort of thing from the tabloid rags, but this is *The Times*, no less.'

Adam scanned the offending article on Bobby's screen,

underneath the byline of a snooty-looking columnist with a bulbous nose and eyebrows as bushy as a hedgerow.

Hard times require hard choices . . . Pointless show trials are a luxury this country can no longer afford . . . When hard evidence is as conclusive as it is in the case against Jimmy Knight, is it not senseless to waste precious resources testing it in court?

'This is the sort of pigswill you're up against, Adam,' said Bobby. 'If your boy is going to get a fair trial, you and Mr Taylor-Cameron are going to have to fight for it.'

Adam nodded. He wished he could tell Bobby how little effort Jonathan would be putting in, but he knew it was inappropriate. At that moment a growing hubbub of voices, coming from down the corridor, indicated that chambers was emptying for the evening.

'They're all going to the Wig and Pen tonight,' said Bobby mildly. 'Go, you can catch up with them before they leave.'

'Oh, no, I've actually got some more reading I need to do, so I'll be here late anyway.' Bobby regarded Adam over the top of his laptop, his gaze direct and inscrutable.

'Do you know how chambers decides who gets tenancy, Adam?' he said. 'We all sit around and we talk about how you performed, and some people, like me, will remember the excellent advices you wrote, or maybe a few will have seen you on your feet in court and pinpointed some promise. But most of them will be going off a gut reaction: "What kind of bloke is he?" An impressive person around here isn't just one who walks the walk; you need to talk the talk too.'

Adam looked at the floor uncomfortably. 'I'd rather get ahead with my work – like you.'

'I don't need to impress them. You do,' Bobby said, and there was a new edge to his tone. 'Being an outsider is not a virtue, Adam, however much you may think it is.' As Adam stepped out of Bobby's office and into the corridor, he dithered. All he wanted to do was hole himself up in the grubby pupil room with his papers and notebook, but he knew Bobby was right. With a sigh he hurried back towards the front door, just as a gaggle of his colleagues – including, to his relief, Rupert, were spilling out onto the street.

'Adam, this is a nice surprise!' said Rupert warmly, which gave Adam instant anxiety as he recalled the many previous invitations he'd turned down. They fell into step behind Georgina, who was flanked by KCs Rory Parks and Martin Norton, and seemed to be holding court.

On hearing Adam's name, Georgina tossed her hair over her shoulder and gave him a sly smile. 'Sorry, Adam, I should have invited you,' she said. 'But I thought you'd be too busy writing Jonathan's acceptance speech for Most Hated Lawyer in Britain.' Rory and Martin both laughed uproariously.

'Ignore her,' said Rupert quietly, smiling. 'It's just a stupid joke because of some blog that went viral about the Cliveden murder today. People are saying that he doesn't deserve to have representation.'

'Great, another thing I've missed,' said Adam, rubbing his temples. 'Maybe the pub is a bad idea – I already feel like I'm falling behind with this case.'

'You need a drink,' said Rupert, throwing his arm around Adam's shoulders and steering him firmly towards the open doors of the old Victorian pub. 'So the only place you're going is the bar.'

It wasn't even six o'clock yet, but the Wig and Pen was already filled with Temple's great and good. Adam recognised a huddle of the clerks from the chambers next door in one corner, the instructing solicitor from a contract dispute Jonathan had done last month propping up the bar, and a Treasury Counsel barrister precariously carrying a bucket of wine and more wine glasses than she could comfortably manage over to a table of friends. Despite its traditional exterior, the inside of the Wig and Pen was a pastiche of trends from the last decade – globular chandeliers, geometrically patterned cushions and bright teal walls.

With none of the trendy industrial tables available, the Stag Court cohort hovered by the bar, Georgina shrieking with laughter at every lacklustre joke from her male superiors. Adam and Rupert clutched their pints of Camden Pale Ale and stood a little apart. Rupert seemed cheerfully oblivious to the giggling trainee solicitors who were sipping Prosecco and kept looking over at him; at least, Adam assumed they were looking at Rupert. They swigged their beer and Adam filled Rupert in on the disclosures in the Knight case.

'So, the prosecution expert says that the botulinum toxin must have been administered between ten and two hours before Cliveden dropped dead. And the meeting between Cliveden and Knight happened slap-bang in the middle of that window.' Rupert gave a low whistle. 'Bloody hell, Adam, things don't look good for your boy.'

'Well, not yet,' said Adam, taking a swig of beer with a half-smile.

'What have you got up your sleeve?'

'OK, have you ever heard of Botox being used as a murder weapon before? Literally, has that ever been a thing?'

'Not that I know of, no.'

'So it would be safe to say that the science around how long it takes to kill someone isn't exactly, well, an exact science.'

'You're getting an alternative expert.'

Adam shrugged. 'I've no idea if anyone else will tell us any different. But at the moment those timings are like a noose around Jimmy Knight's neck. He insists he didn't do it – and if he didn't do it, someone else must have had the opportunity to do it instead.'

'Yeah, I mean, Cliveden's whole job was putting bad guys away, right?' said Rupert. 'Knight can't be the only one with an axe to grind against him. It could even have been a republican nutter, still wound up about his big rescue of the Queen.' He gestured at Adam's empty pint glass. 'Another one of those?'

Adam nodded, and as Rupert turned back to the bar to order two more pints he felt in his pocket for his mobile phone. His breath caught as he saw the email notification flash up.

'There you go, mate,' said Rupert, handing him a frothing pint a few minutes later.

Adam held up the phone screen so Rupert could see and watched his friend's eyes quickly read the hasty email he'd just received from a certain Dr Alice Pettigrew.

Not sure about this window for the poison – happy to discuss. Come and see me. My PA, copied in, can set up a meeting.

Rupert's eyes met Adam's, and they smiled at each other. 'You might have a case to run after all, mate,' said Rupert.

6

It was a Thursday in early May, seven weeks since Grant Cliveden had been murdered, and with four months and seven days left until chambers took their tenancy decision. It was also the date of Jimmy Knight's plea and trial preparation hearing. In the three weeks since they'd been put on the case, Adam had thought of little else. Now, finally, it was about to properly begin. It was raining – again – and Jonathan refused to share his umbrella as he and Adam strode down Temple's warren of cobblestone streets and out into the cacophony of noise and fumes on Fleet Street.

'Legal aid have granted the money for an expert, and Nisha has agreed we should go for Dr Pettigrew. She's the leader in her field,' Adam was telling Jonathan. 'If she says the prosecution's poisoning window could be wrong then maybe it wasn't Knight. It could have been someone Cliveden met afterwards – who knows?'

Jonathan made a sniffy little sound of exasperation. 'We know Cliveden went from that pub to the Old Bailey – so are you suggesting that someone *within the Old Bailey* administered poison to a serving police officer, and no one noticed? Does that seriously seem likely to you?'

'I think we've got to explore it,' said Adam earnestly. 'Dr Pettigrew has offered to meet us – I really think she could be crucial to our case.'

'In a few hours' time there won't be a case, because Jimmy Knight will have changed his plea to guilty. That is our one and only job today, Adam – convince Knight that he is fighting a losing battle. We need to get him off our hands.'

Adam was about to argue back as the neo-Baroque splendour of the Central Criminal Court came into view, flanked by its modern extension – a blocky, armoured fortress known as the South Block. But the words died in his throat as he saw the rabble assembled there.

TV crews, reporters and photographers he had expected, and they had come mob-handed for the opening salvos in what promised to be the biggest case of the year. What he hadn't been prepared for was the crowd of wild-eyed protestors, who varied in age and appearance but all shared the same grimace of burning fury, their placards dipped end-to-end in self-righteousness.

A LIFE FOR A LIFE

KILL THE POLICE KILLER

KNIGHT MUST HANG

AFFRONT TO SOCIETY

As soon as they spotted Jonathan, the journalists who had been idly chatting among themselves sprang into action.

'Mr Taylor-Cameron, Mr Taylor-Cameron!'

'How can your client claim he is innocent?'

'Are you helping him lie in court?'

'Do you care that you're tormenting the Cliveden family?'

The throng of Dictaphone-wielding journalists dressed in the sort of outfits Adam had been shocked to hear his pupil master refer to as '*Big Issue* chic' pressed in on Jonathan, peppering him with questions. Jonathan didn't seem to notice the nastiness – only the cameras. However much he loathed this case, he had a narcissist's love of performing, and stages didn't get much grander than a murder trial at the Old Bailey. In the glare of the flashbulbs, Jonathan was positively preening.

The police officers outside the Bailey were doing a very lack-lustre job of keeping the crowd in check, which Adam suspected was not unrelated to the fact they'd lost one of their own. Even so, he and Jonathan managed to barge their way up the steps and into the lobby itself which, despite the metal detectors and security, still maintained its mythological air of scandal and slaughter. At Jonathan's insistence, and presumably for the bene-fit of the cameras, both of them were unusually already dressed in their white horsehair wigs and long black robes, which they'd normally have put on in the court's robing room. The capes bil-lowed around them as they paced down the Baroque corridor, lined with statues and crowned with vaulting painted domes. The whole place thrummed with activity – solicitors sweeping by dragging trolleys full of files, ushers darting in and out of courtrooms armed with clipboards, pale-faced friends and family there to support victims or defendants, with the desperate hope that justice would be served, whatever that looked like.

Maybe he was romanticising it, but Adam thought the air in the Old Bailey always felt thicker than the air outside – as if it was heavy with the reckonings of the past and the import of the present. Although they were only here for a plea and trial preparation hearing – which was little more than administra-tive theatre – the environment seemed designed to make every move seem steeped in meaning. Not that Jonathan had adopted much of the nobility of the surroundings.

'You know what would be even better than Knight changing his plea? If he tells us he did it but wants to plead not guilty anyway,' Jonathan was saying. 'How marvellous it would be to be conflicted. We'd have to drop the case immediately of course, then it would be up to some other poor sod to sort it out.'

They'd reached the cage door which led down to the subterranean cells where London's criminals had waited to hear their fates for centuries. Uniformed police officers let them through and led them down institutional steps which smelled vaguely of urine. Nisha Desai was already down there, hovering outside the metal door of the cell where Jimmy Knight was being held. Jonathan gave her a perfunctory nod.

'Let's get this over with then.'

A scowling warden clanged open the cell door, and the three lawyers squeezed into the tiny space, furnished with a bolted-down table attached to bolted-down chairs. Slumped on one of these, hands deep in the pockets of a suit that looked even cheaper than Adam's, was Jimmy Knight.

Having seen Knight's mugshot so many times in the papers, Adam found it a surreal experience to see him in the flesh. He was smaller and slighter than he'd expected, with bulging Popeye muscles but quick, intelligent brown eyes, which scanned the three of them quickly, appraising what he saw. Adam knew he was only forty-seven, but his lined and careworn face paid testament to a decade spent inside, and his close-cropped hair was flecked with grey.

The walls of the windowless room looked like they might once have been white, but were now yellow and peeling, dust and stale sweat hanging in the air. Adam felt a twinge of claustrophobia. It was always like this when he was in a cell with a client. It made him think of his dad's final moments – something he usually tried to forget.

Nisha made the introductions. 'Jimmy, this is Mr Taylor-Cameron and Mr Green, who will be representing you in court.' Knight said nothing, simply tilted his head back further to eye them with more menace.

'A pleasure to meet you, Mr Knight,' said Jonathan insincerely, arranging his papers fussily on the cracked table in front of him.

Knight didn't respond, so Jonathan ploughed on.

'As you know, today is simply an exercise in bureaucracy, and the trial has not yet started. There will be a judge, but no jury. Papers are served, a timetable is set – I don't need to tell you, you're an old hand. And it is of course your first chance to enter your plea. Now, we haven't had a chance to meet yet – but I am, of course, flattered to know that you've heard of me. Perhaps you know that they used to call me "the patron saint of hopeless causes". But your solicitor tells me you're keen to enter a not guilty plea – which is fine! Absolutely fine! And of course, that doesn't have to be final. Once we've got the papers we can discuss every option – decide to fight, or change our plea . . .'

'Hold on – change my plea to what?' Knight's eyebrows rose like two angry caterpillars.

Jonathan gave him a smooth smile. 'Well, to guilty, of course. It's murder, so you'd still get a life sentence, but the judge could set a minimum term, and that could be as little as twenty-five years. Think what a thrill it would be to get out on parole one day. Put in a guilty plea, and there's a chance you will get to sleep somewhere other than a jail cell before you die.'

A flash of dismay passed over Knight's face, and his head jerked round to catch Nisha's eye. That's when Adam saw it. Just below their client's right ear, a small tattoo of a black feather. He'd seen a tattoo like that before, but until this moment, he hadn't thought of it for nearly fifteen years. His grandmother had hated it, of course, but Adam's father had been proud of the feather he'd had inked on the inside of his wrist.

'A feather stands for freedom, Adam,' he had said, rolling up his sleeve to show his wide-eyed son. 'Every time I look down at this, I'll make sure I don't fall into any traps.'

Adam realised he was staring at Knight, who leaned back and slowly crossed his arms – clearly sensing a trap himself.

Jonathan's smile was faltering, his composure slipping. 'Mr Knight, you look like a man who doesn't mince his words, so I won't mince mine either. Never trust anyone who tries to butter you up – just ask my first wife. So I'll tell you straight – things are looking bad for you. I know everyone says, "Just have a go," if it's a murder case, but I'm not sure, in this instance, if . . .'

This was how it happened, wasn't it, thought Adam. Clever lawyers, too lazy or too busy or simply too cynical to fight for a client's innocence, tried to bamboozle them into sacrificing their freedom in the name of expediency. His mum refused to talk about it, but Adam was struck with the sudden realisation that this might have been what had happened to his dad right before he'd decided it would be better to be dead than to stand trial for a crime he claimed he hadn't committed. And it looked like it could be about to happen to Knight too.

All the muscles in Knight's face and arms were tensed, a

crouching tiger in a tiny cage. He took a deep breath; Adam willed him not to give in.

'I thought it was your job to listen to what I want to plead, and then plead it?'

Adam cheered internally as Jonathan flushed. 'Of course. But it is also my job to tell you everything – including the credit you get for showing remorse and entering a guilty plea as early as possible.' His tone was getting increasingly shrill, and Nisha seized the moment to intervene.

'Jimmy, why don't you tell Mr Taylor-Cameron and Mr Green what happened. In your own words.'

Knight nodded and rubbed his jaw. 'It's no secret that I ain't got a good word to say about Cliveden. That son-of-a-bitch framed me for the post office robbery – all that cash and the gun and whatever they found, it weren't mine. He planted it all there, I'm certain. But why – I ain't got a clue.'

It was a shocking accusation. Cliveden was a hero – what possible motivation could he have had for faking evidence in a random robbery?

'You lot won't know what it's like to spend what should be the best ten years of your life in a five-by-five-metre box, banged up with whatever lunatic or psycho they've decided to chuck in there with you,' Knight continued. 'But I can tell you it leaves plenty of time for thinking.

'And I did think about Cliveden, and what he did to me, a lot. I'll admit that. So yeah, when I got out I got online and I did some digging. And yes, I wanted to meet the sick bastard. Stupid, I know now, but it felt like something I had to do.'

'So you sent him a message telling him to meet you at the Old Nag's Head,' Nisha said.

'No – not me. That phone they found – it's not mine. Another plant. But an associate told me where he'd be, and don't ask me who that was because I won't tell you.'

'Now, come on, you expect a jury to believe that . . . ?'

'Look, I ain't denying I had a drink with Cliveden at the Old Nag's Head. How or why I came to be there don't really matter, does it? I didn't tell him who I really was and he didn't recognise me. But he told me enough that day that I got the answers I needed.

'Murder's not my style. If it was up to me, he'd be banged up, like I was. He needed to answer for what he did, but I'd happily have left that to the courts. So no, I can't say I'm sorry he's dead. But I'm not the one who killed him.'

Adam flinched involuntarily. Knight wasn't sorry Cliveden was dead? That was not the sort of thing the jury should hear. Jonathan had the expression of a man who had lost all interest. Before he even realised what he was doing, Adam found himself leaning forward to address Knight directly.

'Mr Knight, with respect – a police officer receives an anonymous message from an unknown number, and agrees to meet the sender alone, in a deserted pub. You just happen to be there, and he sits and has a drink with you. Why?'

Knight turned to look at Adam as if seeing him for the first time. He held his gaze, and Adam saw that behind the hard exterior there was a certain gentleness.

'You're very young to be a barrister, ain't ya?'

'He's just a pupil – a trainee,' snapped Jonathan.

'But he's asking the right questions,' said Knight, still looking at Adam. The intensity of Knight's gaze should have made Adam feel uncomfortable, but actually it just made him sad.

Knight must have spent years convincing the world he was tough, but Adam could see that right now, he was scared. This was a man who had spent ten years in hell, and now he faced going right back there, after less than a fortnight of breathing the fresh air of freedom. His expression was tinged with the quiet desperation of someone who knew his fate was almost certainly a foregone conclusion.

It was a look that Adam had seen before – and one that he would never forget. He had been ten years old. His father was crouched in front of him, grasping him by the shoulders, telling him everything would be OK and that he'd see him again soon. His eyes had been filled with that same desperate quality. Adam shivered. All those memories that he'd kept squashed in the darkness for so many years; now something about Knight had set them free.

'We don't have much longer,' said Nisha, looking at her watch. 'Jimmy, today is pretty straightforward. The charges will be read out and you'll be asked to enter your plea again. As it's not guilty' – Adam was sure he heard Jonathan tut – 'we will agree a date for trial and determine the issue of the case.'

'Well, quite,' spluttered Jonathan. 'The judge is going to ask me what the issue of this case is – what happened from our perspective – and so far I've got nothing. I have a proof here from Ms Desai' – he shook the paper, on which Knight's statement was written, huffily in his face – 'and all it really says on it is "Not me." That is not going to be enough. You don't have an alibi. You don't have anything I can run with. So, if you want this to go to trial you are going to have to do some serious thinking about what you want us to say.'

Knight shook his head. He seemed to have withdrawn into himself again, steeling himself for the impending ordeal.

The three lawyers got up to leave and Jonathan sighed theatrically. The cell door was unlocked by the warden outside and Nisha left first, followed by Jonathan who pointedly left his folder on the table for Adam to pick up. It meant Adam was a few seconds behind the others, and he had his hand on the door when Knight shifted in his seat.

'I know you were shocked, when I said I wasn't sorry he was dead,' Knight said. Adam realised he was talking to him. 'You think that makes me evil. But you wouldn't, not if you'd known Cliveden like I did. I might be the one in the cell, but if you're looking for evil in this story – it ain't me.'

For years, Adam had been desperate to believe his dad was innocent – despite everything that suggested otherwise. He realised, as he left the cell, he felt the same longing to believe Jimmy was innocent too. But this time, he would make sure it was proven.

7

The briefing with their client over, it was time for the lawyers to assemble in the courtroom for the hearing itself. Knight's warning echoed in Adam's ears as he hurried to catch up with Nisha and Jonathan. When he said there was evil in the story, he was referring to the real killer – wasn't he?

But then . . . Knight had claimed that no one had known Cliveden like he had. His claims about the police officer – that he'd framed him for a crime he hadn't committed – were inflammatory. Cliveden's reputation was impeccable; the many pages of newspapers and hours of TV coverage since his death hadn't found a single bad word to say about him. They'd presented him as a Croydon boy from modest circumstances, who'd dreamed of joining the police while friends and peers fell into street crime. He'd joined the Met as a regular bobby, excelling up the ranks at almost frightening speed before being hand-picked to be a royal protection officer. Why would he have risked a stratospheric career to frame a petty criminal who'd gone on the straight and narrow?

None of it made any sense. And yet, there was something about Knight that made Adam take him seriously. He hoped he wasn't being irrational – conflating Knight with another man close to his own heart, whom no one had believed. Adam was annoyed with himself – when he'd set his heart on a career in law, he'd promised not to let his own childhood memories cloud his judgement. But there was a voice deep inside him that he couldn't silence, saying it really mattered that at least *someone* was prepared to fight for Knight. Maybe, just maybe, if they could prove Knight's innocence, he'd be able to move on from what had happened to his own family all those years ago.

Nisha had hurried off to grab coffees, which left Adam and Jonathan standing in the ornate corridor outside Court Number One. Adam wondered if he'd ever get used to the unique splendour of this place, where it felt like you were constantly being watched by hundreds of eyes – whether it was Justice, Moses or Alfred the Great looking down from the imposing painted murals on the walls, or ancient kings glancing sideways from their statues.

Even though they were only there for a plea and trial preparation hearing, or PTPH, their case had been allocated the most notorious courtroom in the country, where the likes of the Kray twins, the Yorkshire Ripper, Dennis Nilsen and Ian Huntley had all been tried. The green leather benches of the public gallery would already be filling up with rubberneckers desperate to catch a glimpse of the man they assumed would be joining the canon of criminal infamy.

'If Jimmy didn't kill Cliveden, maybe there's someone else responsible,' Adam said to Jonathan, who, standing directly beneath a dome inscribed with TRUTH LEARNING ART LABOUR, was engrossed in his mobile phone. 'There's nothing on the defence case statement at the moment, like you said. But if we could find a credible alternative suspect . . . we'd be able to advance a positive case, wouldn't we?'

When he'd been considering who might want Cliveden dead, Adam had thought it would most likely be someone with a similar profile to Knight. A vengeful felon who had made the detective inspector their sworn enemy, or perhaps even a criminal kingpin who was sick of Cliveden's zealotry curtailing their business. How many of them felt as Knight did – delighted that Cliveden was dead and buried?

Jonathan grunted but didn't look up. Adam could tell he'd lost him. A sly glimpse told him that it wasn't Allegra who was the problem today but Nadine, whose WhatsApp messages appeared to be popping in faster than Jonathan could reply. Adam couldn't imagine having time for one girlfriend, but his pupil master seemed to find the energy for at least three – and a wife as well.

Clacking high heels sounded from the direction of the lobby, and Adam turned around to see another face he recognised from the press – Natasha Cliveden. She was tall, willowy and even more beautiful than her pictures. Dressed in immaculate charcoal cigarette pants, a crisp white T-shirt and a power blazer, with a Chanel handbag swinging from her arm, she could have been mistaken for a model heading to a casting. She was flanked by a burly, shaven-headed family liaison officer, or FLO, who stood outside the women's toilet like a bouncer while she dived inside.

Adam didn't know much about clothes, and even less about designer ones, but he knew enough to recognise that Natasha's were expensive. Which was strange, because even detective inspectors weren't on spectacular wages.

Maybe she had a high-flying career? Adam slipped his phone out and did a quick google – but no, Natasha was described as a stay-at-home mum. In the MailOnline article he was reading there was a picture he hadn't seen before showing Cliveden and Natasha grinning on a perfectly manicured lawn, an enormous mock-Tudor mansion looming in the background. The caption read: 'Precious Memories: the Clivedens at home in Wimbledon.' Adam's eyebrows knitted together. Scrolling down, he read how their two children, Jamie, eight, and Arabella, six, attended 'exclusive prep schools nearby'. The couple were living the kind of lifestyle even the top KCs in chambers might have found a bit out of reach. Maybe those infrequent *Good Morning Britain* appearances paid more than he'd thought.

Looking up from his phone, Adam noticed that the FLO had been joined by a female police officer, who was probably only a few years older than Adam. She wore owl-like glasses, sensible shoes, and had her light blonde hair pulled back neatly in a bun. Adam caught the broad vowels of a Yorkshire accent as she and the male FLO discussed the ongoing building work at Westminster Coroner's Court; they were clearly colleagues, which made her an FLO too.

He was about to try again to extract Jonathan from his furious texting, when Natasha Cliveden emerged from the toilets. Her face suddenly congealed like old milk. '*You!*' she exclaimed in a furious rasp. Her laser eyes had settled on the female FLO, who flushed.

The stand-off reminded Adam of two urban foxes he'd seen fiercely eyeballing each other when he'd walked home last night. The FLO hadn't said anything, but the atmosphere had changed so dramatically that people further down the corridor had sensed it in the air and turned around to look. Someone had to retreat, and it was the FLO who dipped her red face and hurried away, without saying a word.

'Are you all right, Mrs Cliveden?' her FLO was asking her, as she breathed heavily, nostrils flaring. 'Do you know PC Owens?

'Sorry, it's nothing, I – oh . . .' stuttered Mrs Cliveden, lowering her lashes as perfectly formed tears started leaking from her pretty blue eyes. 'It's just being here, all of this – I can't bear it.' The FLO patted her awkwardly on the arm, and the two of them headed towards the courtroom.

It was a bizarre exchange. Adam glanced at Jonathan to see if he'd caught any of it, but he was still engrossed in his phone. 'Jonathan, did you catch that?' said Adam.

'Who? What?' said Jonathan, finally looking up from his phone with the disorientation of a man waking from a deep sleep. Adam sighed.

Nisha was back, carrying three cappuccinos – 'Sorry, the queue was enormous' – which they didn't have time to drink as the hearing was about to start. Jonathan admonished her loudly when an usher instructed them to put the coffees in the bin, as they weren't allowed in court. Just before he headed into Court Number One, Adam paused. Not for the first time that day, he felt like he was being watched, and this time he was pretty sure it wasn't just the paintings.

He looked over his shoulder and squinted down to where the grand staircase was. There, hovering with one hand on the banister, he saw her. The blonde FLO. She was with a group of people of various ages who he assumed must be a victim's family she was chaperoning.

But she wasn't looking at them. She was gazing down towards Court Number One, as if hoping that if she stared hard enough she might be able to see through the door. Her expression made Adam think once more of the foxes he'd seen on his walk home. Watchful, wary, ready to strike.

8

Even the most hardened criminal would have struggled not to feel a shiver when shown into the notorious enclaves of the Old Bailey's Court Number One.

With its ominously dark wood panelling, vaulted ceiling and austere white walls, the Edwardian room seemed to have been designed with the sole purpose of intimidating the accused with its malevolent grandeur. There were no windows – the entire world reduced to what was contained in this room. The judge's seat was less chair and more throne – made of carved wood and upholstered with establishment green leather, placed below a looming wooden sculpture of a portico.

Like a cross between a Jacobean theatre and a Puritan chapel (which perhaps it was, thought Adam), the courtroom and its hushed sense of ceremony reminded its occupants that matters heard here were often very literally a case of life and death. The ghost of past defendants, who ranged from the diabolical to the pathetic, gathered in the corners, like invisible spectators. It was here that many unhappy souls had been sentenced to death, and latterly life imprisonment – with acquittals vanishingly rare.

At Oxford, Adam had read a treatise by Sir Patrick Hastings, a distinguished barrister who was briefly Attorney General in the 1920s, who had described this courtroom as reeking 'of misery and squalor . . . No human feeling could possibly exist within its walls, no hope, sympathy, nothing but indifference.' He'd always thought of those words on the rare occasions that he had sat at Court Number One's hard wooden tables which faced the jury benches. This was a place where reputations were ruined, truths twisted and fates finalised. Humanity didn't come into it.

Today the public gallery, which floated above the amphi-theatre of the court, affording its occupants a bird's eye view of the judicial theatrics, was predictably packed. Among the sea of faces, Adam spotted Mrs Cliveden, now a picture of compos-ure alongside her minder-like FLO.

'Jonathan, old chap, how are you?' It was Edward Lowe KC, First Senior Treasury Counsel, and the prosecutor in this case. The CPS were bringing out all the big guns to make sure Knight went down, and guns didn't get much bigger than the most senior member of the most elite unit of prosecuting law-yers in the country, who took only the most serious and com-plex cases.

'Edward, how nice to see you,' said Jonathan, in a tone that suggested it was anything but. 'It's been a while – are you still buzzing about on that ridiculous bike of yours?'

Lowe met Jonathan's bitterness with an affable smile. 'I am indeed – and the nippers are big enough to buzz about with me now! How's your Florence getting on?'

As Jonathan flailed around trying to say something meaning-ful about a daughter he'd packed off to boarding school aged eight, Adam observed Lowe, whom he knew by reputation but had never met. He certainly looked like a man who spent a lot of time outdoors on a bike, with his trim figure and healthy colour. The wig and gown, which could make many men look ridiculous, actively suited Lowe, making him look like some kind of ceremonial superhero. Although he was about twenty years younger and ten times more astute than Jonathan, he wore his accomplishment lightly. Jonathan hated being in the presence of people who outshone him, and was doing his very best to sneak in jabs at the younger man. But Lowe was just so nice it was impossible to land a blow.

'Oh, I do apologise, I don't think we've been introduced.' Adam realised Lowe was talking to him, waiting for his response with a pleasant smile.

'I'm Adam Green, I'm a pupil at Stag Court,' he said. 'Pleased to meet you.' As usual, Adam had to fight all his instincts not to reach out to shake Lowe's hand. That was one of his most gauche mistakes in the early days of his pupillage, which had made Jonathan rant and rave about his lack of propriety (which Adam had felt was a bit rich even then). By tradition, barristers never shook hands, based on the fiction that everyone at the Bar already knew and trusted each other.

'Call me Ed,' said Lowe warmly. 'You're straight in at the deep end with this one, aren't you?' They were interrupted by the judge's clerk, who was setting out jugs of water on the legal benches. 'Oh, Raquel, you angel, I'm absolutely gasping.'

Raquel rolled her eyes at Lowe. 'Now don't take the piss or my hand might slip and that lovely robe will get all soggy.'

With her brassy blonde hair and power curves, Raquel had the look of a love child between Jessica Rabbit and Bet Lynch. Unlike most women in court, she'd eschewed the usual sensible low block heel in favour of towering stilettos with red soles – extra impressive, as she had to be on her feet all day. Of course, Jonathan was immediately enthralled. 'It takes a lot of work to look that deliberate,' he said under his breath to Adam, with a wolfish smile.

'I don't think we've had the pleasure,' he said greasily, addressing himself to Raquel. 'Jonathan Taylor-Cameron, for the defence.'

Raquel raised a plucked eyebrow. 'Are we going to save everyone a lot of trouble with a once-in-a-blue-moon situation and a guilty plea to murder?' she said.

'If only that were true,' said Jonathan loftily.

A flash of annoyance passed over Raquel's face, and she looked officiously at her gold wristwatch.

'The defendant will be shown in any minute – be ready,' she snapped, and hurried off to switch on the rest of the microphones, leaving Jonathan gaping like a fish.

'All rise!' The buzz from the public gallery fell instantly silent as Raquel announced the arrival of the judge. There was a scraping of chairs as the court got to its feet, and then, like a magician emerging from a puff of smoke, the judge appeared – Charlotte Wickstead.

The effect she had on the court was instantaneous. The officials she worked with regularly, like Raquel, seemed to radiate a strange pride as she caught their eyes, nodding her thanks graciously. Meanwhile, the press and public galleries fell silent, in instant thrall to her irresistible charisma. She was like no judge Adam had ever seen before. He had seen plenty of ancient, grumpy old duffers who looked like they'd been exhumed to sit on the bench, with their rheumy eyes and wiry nose hair, some of whom pointedly radiated general disdain for anyone below their exalted status. But Judge Wickstead was young, glamorous, with high cheekbones and long red nails. Every wisp of hair was tucked neatly under her wig, giving the impression that the icy white curls were her own. As she took her seat her back remained perfectly straight, and she rearranged her black robes so that they fell just so. Her hazel eyes scanned the room, her face completely unreadable.

Lowe stood to deliver the preliminaries – introducing himself and his 'learned friends' who would be providing the defence. Adam had finally got round to a quick google of Judge Wickstead, and knew that she and Lowe likely knew each other very well – although you wouldn't know it from the formal way they addressed each other. Until her recent appointment as a judge, Wickstead had held Lowe's current post, and the two of them must have worked closely together in 'the Room' – the hallowed chamber which served as Treasury Counsel headquarters in the Old Bailey.

'Are you ready to proceed, Mr Lowe?' Her voice was as pure and clear as crystal.

'I am, My Lady.'

'Please bring in the defendant.'

A rattle of keys and the creak of wooden benches, as the spectators in the public gallery craned to get a good look, heralded the arrival of the star of the show: Jimmy Knight. He was a powerfully built man but he looked small between the two hulking security guards he was handcuffed to. They showed him into the dock, which was raised several feet above the floor and encased in bulletproof glass. With the judge's podium sitting directly opposite, and arranged to the same height, Knight and

Judge Wickstead would spend the trial sitting eye-to-eye. Many defendants found this uncomfortable, but not Jimmy Knight by the looks of things. He showed not an ounce of nervousness.

Raquel cleared her throat. 'Can you confirm your name for the court?'

'James Robert Knight.'

'Mr Knight, you were charged with murder. That on the thirteenth day of March 2023, you poisoned Detective Inspector Grant Cliveden with the intention of causing his death. How do you plead – guilty, or not guilty?'

'Not guilty.' There was a murmur from the public gallery. There'd been much speculation in the press as to whether a full trial would go ahead – but those two words confirmed that journalists would get the blockbuster court showdown they all secretly wanted.

The judge nodded curtly and made a note. 'Please be seated.'

Everyone sat, except for Lowe, who remained on his feet. 'My Lady already has the case summary and will know that it is the Crown's case that the defendant, James Knight, poisoned the victim, Grant Cliveden, between the hours of 11 a.m. and 1 p.m. on 13 March, causing Mr Cliveden's death some hours later at 2.42 p.m. in Court Three at the Central Criminal Court, London. The evidence we wish to submit in support of this trial is as follows . . .'

Lowe ran through the witnesses he intended to call, including Reg McNally, the landlord of the pub where Knight had met with Cliveden, and Gary Parker, an old cellmate of Knight's who would testify to his preoccupation with Cliveden. He would also call one of the barristers who'd seen Cliveden collapse in court; his wife, Natasha Cliveden; and, of course, their star witness, the pathologist who had carried out the post-mortem and would testify to the time of poisoning.

Then there was the digital evidence. Searches from Knight's computer, the text message exchange with Cliveden, and CCTV footage from the pub where the two men had met.

The physical evidence numbered just one single exhibit: the Nokia burner phone that had been recovered at Knight's property and had been used to contact Cliveden.

The judge looked up, sphinx-like. 'Is that all?' she asked.

'Yes, My Lady.'

'No evidence of the vessel the poison was administered in, vials it was transported in, et cetera?'

Lowe looked uncharacteristically flustered. 'That is correct, My Lady. Unfortunately none of those items have been recovered.'

The judge made the tiniest incline of her head.

'And no DNA evidence linking Mr Knight to the poison?'

'Again, by the time the suspect was arrested it was not possible to recover anything of value.'

'I see.' The judge made a note, letting the silence in the court hang ominously.

Finally, she lifted her head again. 'Is there anything else you wish to add, Mr Lowe?'

'No, thank you, My Lady, other than to note that I have furnished the defence with a list of both the used and the unused material.'

The 'used' material was all the evidence that Lowe had listed, which the prosecution would present at trial, and the 'unused' was other material uncovered in the investigation that had been discarded, as relevant to neither the defence nor the prosecution case. In legal aid cases, such as this one, the defence only got paid to read the 'used' material. So you had to trust the prosecution and assume that 'unused' basically equated to 'useless'.

'Very well,' said the judge. 'The date of the trial has been set for 30 August – does either party have any difficulties with that?'

Just under four months from now. Adam did the calculation in his head and realised that if it was a two-week trial, it would finish literally days before chambers voted on whether to give him tenancy or not. There was no getting away from the fact that his performance would be completely forefront in their minds.

With both Lowe and Jonathan agreeing to the date, the day's housekeeping was complete and court was dismissed. Jonathan, Nisha and Adam went back down to the cells for another conference with Knight, with Jonathan sighing theatrically the whole way to underline how little he wanted to be there. Adam felt grateful for Nisha, who remained remarkably buoyant.

'That was pretty promising if you ask me,' Nisha told Knight, who was slumped expressionlessly in his bolted-down chair as before. 'The judge wasn't impressed by the prosecution's lack of physical evidence. She made that very clear.'

Nisha was right. The judge couldn't tell a jury whether to convict or acquit, but their final summing up could be a powerful tool. It was the last thing the jury heard before they deliberated and could subtly push them one way or another. If the judge was on their side, so much the better.

'Less promising is the sheer volume of other evidence against you,' Jonathan said to Jimmy. 'It's all going to be very difficult to explain away. Listen,' he said, his voice dropping conspiratorially as he leaned forward on the table. 'If you did it, just tell us. We can build a much better defence if we know exactly what we're dealing with.'

Adam and Nisha both stared at Jonathan, open-mouthed. Nisha's bird's nest of hair seemed practically to bristle with fury. Adam knew exactly what Jonathan was trying to do. If Knight admitted he was guilty, the whole legal team would become conflicted, which would mean that they could no longer represent Knight if he wanted to continue to enter a not guilty plea. Jonathan had daydreamed out loud about this eventuality earlier on – but it was a cheap and nasty trick to try and lure Knight into getting them dismissed.

'You know what, there is something I should tell you,' said Knight, and he leaned forward too, so that his face was just inches from Jonathan's. The senior barrister licked his lips in anticipation – like a dog waiting for a treat.

'You are my brief. You do as I say. And I say – I. Am. Innocent.'

Jonathan flung himself back in frustration.

'With respect, Mr Taylor-Cameron,' Nisha cut in, 'our client has been crystal clear from the start. He wishes to plead not guilty – end of story.' She was seriously annoyed, Adam could tell, and although she caveated her statement 'with respect' he could tell any respect she'd had for Jonathan was long gone.

'How do you explain the dead body in the middle of the Old Bailey then?' said Jonathan petulantly. 'Hours after you met with the victim – who you freely admit you hated – he just drops dead and you had nothing to do with it?'

'I didn't kill him,' said Knight. 'So someone else did.'

9

'It's just so *unfair*! We're window dressing the *Titanic*!' Jonathan and Adam were outside the Old Bailey, Jonathan lighting his third cigarette on the trot. Nisha had huffily excused herself, but Jonathan wanted to do some chain-smoking and foot-stamping before he and his pupil went back to chambers.

'Did you see how many people there were in the gallery today? And that's just the PTPH,' Jonathan railed. 'The whole world is going to be watching while we go in to fight one of the most robust cases ever produced by the CPS armed with little more than outlandish conspiracy theories.

'And what a load of horseshit from Tony, saying this boy asked for me personally. He loathes me, and let me tell you, the feeling is mutual.'

Jonathan's rant was interrupted by the shrill ring of his mobile. He looked at the number on the screen and blanched, immediately answering it.

'My dearest darling one, yes, I got your messages, I was just tied up, that's all. No, I'm not avoiding you . . . You know how much you mean to me!'

Jonathan wandered away, still whispering implausible excuses to whichever of the women in his life was currently giving him an earful. His pupil master might think it was unfair to get stuck with Knight, but Adam thought the really unfair thing was that Knight was stuck with Jonathan. He'd assured Nisha that Jonathan would at least pretend to be on their client's side when they met, but he'd behaved worse than he could ever have imagined. It had sickened Adam to see his privileged pupil master try and outwit the client who was relying on him; someone less streetwise than Knight could easily have walked into the trap.

Something else was bothering Adam. Nisha had said Knight had asked for Jonathan personally – but why? He hadn't defended in a murder case for years, and his reputation was as musty and moth-eaten as Bitsy the taxidermy Jack Russell.

Now that the case was underway and legal aid was granted, it would be very difficult for Knight to switch barristers. He'd have to go in front of the judge and persuade her he had a very good reason for needing new counsel. But he hadn't even asked Nisha if it was possible. What had he said to Jonathan, in their conference just now? 'You are my brief.' He'd seemed pretty certain about that.

Adam was pulled from his thoughts by raised voices from around the corner – and the word 'Cliveden'. Curiosity piqued, Adam shuffled to the end of the wall and peered round it. To his surprise, he spotted Natasha Cliveden's FLO and the young blonde police officer from before – having a heated discussion.

'Look, it's your business and I'm not going to pry but there's obviously bad blood, so you need to stay away,' the bearded officer was saying crossly. 'I can't have you upsetting Mrs Cliveden like that.'

'Ray, I'm just trying to do my job,' the other FLO replied,

with obvious frustration. 'My new job, by the way – which I wouldn't have if it wasn't for her husband . . .' Her voice trailed off bitterly.

Ray folded his arms. 'You need to watch your tongue, Owens,' he said, sternly. 'You might think you're better than the rest of us with your degree and your fast-track scheme, but don't go thinking you're too good for this. You couldn't cut it in serious crime, and if you're not careful, you won't cut it in family liaison either. You're lucky that I've kept quiet so far about the things I've heard about you . . .'

Owens put her head in her hands. 'I'm sorry, Ray,' she said, softly now. 'I didn't mean to offend you – I know family liaison is valuable work, and I'm so grateful for the opportunity. It's just that I'm under a lot of pressure because of, you know . . .'

Ray's body language had softened. 'Look, you've just got to be patient. And steer clear of Mrs Cliveden, yeah?'

Adam was straining so hard to surreptitiously listen to their conversation that he hadn't realised Jonathan was back, his mobile phone still cradled under his chin. He clicked his fingers imperiously at Adam and gestured for him to follow. Reluctantly, Adam abandoned his eavesdropping. He had no idea what the two FLOs were talking about, but he'd heard enough to know that he'd not been mistaken by what he'd seen before. This Owens, whoever she was, had history with Cliveden – and his wife knew it.

They set off back towards chambers, Adam loaded down like a packhorse with Jonathan's briefcase, the trolley of files and his own rucksack, while Jonathan strode ahead, whispering into the phone all sorts of promises that Adam knew he'd never be able to keep.

They hurried through the cloisters of Lincoln's Inn, passed the squat fortress of Temple Church and across the flagstones of Pump Court, in the shadow of its magnificent Christopher Wren buildings. Adam's arms were aching by the time they got to Stag Court – where they found Tony waiting ominously on the steps.

'OK, petal, I've got to go now. Lots of kisses. No, I won't. I promise. Yes. Bye. Bye. Bye.' Finally, he hung up the phone, to be met with a glare that could melt metal from Tony.

'Didn't you get my messages?' the clerk hissed.

'Er, no, I was on a business call . . .'

'Kavanagh is here.'

Jonathan looked like all the wind had been knocked out of him. He had the expression of a naughty boy who'd been caught with his pants down – which he probably had been, on more than one occasion.

'Here – now?!'

'Waiting in your room – and you know how he hates to be kept waiting.'

10

Adam had never seen his pupil master in such a state of skittish anxiety as when he heard mention of Kavanagh's name. Jonathan patted his coiffed hair constantly and fiddled with his cufflinks as they hurried through the chambers corridors to his office.

'Charles and I go way back, actually. I'm sure he won't mind waiting for a couple of minutes,' Jonathan muttered, more to himself than to Adam.

'He's a wonderful fellow, you know. Very – ah – forthright, but that's what makes him such an excellent businessman. Now you mustn't say anything, Green, because Charles really doesn't suffer fools. It's why he came to me for this case, because he knows I will get the job done, without any nonsense. Just like I do on the golf course, if I do say so myself.

'It's an outrage that he's facing any charges at all, but those ghastly snowflakes at the CPS can't bear anyone who is successful and not afraid to show it. All Charles wanted to do was make cancer medications more affordable for the NHS – that's why he was importing them from abroad. How was he to know that there were such wicked people within his supply chain? He had no idea the medicines were useless, or dangerous. And now he's being prosecuted for fraud, when he acted in good faith. It's enough to make one despair.'

They'd reached Jonathan's office door, where he turned to Adam and pulled back his lips in a horrible grimace.

'Anything in my teeth, Green?'

'You're all good.'

'Excellent. Now, remember what I said – not a *word*.'

'Got it.'

Jonathan threw open the door, throwing his arms wide at the same time.

'Charles!' he beamed. 'What a wonderful surprise!'

A squat little man, almost as wide as he was tall, was engulfed in Jonathan's own chair like a gremlin. He had greased-back hair, stubby little fingers and a deep tan, offset by the whitest – and widest – collar Adam had ever seen. He wasn't smiling.

'I wouldn't have thought it was a surprise, for a client paying as much as I am to want to see his lawyer briefly,' he said quietly. Jonathan's smile faltered. 'Long lunch, was it?'

'Nothing like that, I can assure you,' burbled Jonathan, forced to take a seat in the chair usually meant for clients, seeing as Kavanagh had so presumptuously colonised his own territory. 'Just a hearing for another case – we got held up.'

'Another case?' said Kavanagh, his voice like silk. 'I thought I had your – now, how did you put it? – *undivided* attention?'

Jonathan looked ashen. 'Oh, you absolutely do have my undivided attention, of that rest assured, dear Charles!' he stuttered. 'Your case is of the utmost importance to me, the very utmost.'

Kavanagh picked up a pen and started lazily doodling on the papers in front of him. Jonathan and Adam both watched the pen. He was drawing all over Nisha's submissions for the Knight case. Jonathan swallowed.

'You say it is of the utmost importance to you, Jonny, but I really don't think you understand what that means,' said Kavanagh, in a sort of gentle sing-song, as if he was talking to a child. 'It is of the utmost importance to *me*. If I lose, I will lose my business, my whole life's work.'

'Well, actually, Charles, it's a lot more serious than that,' Jonathan cut in helpfully. 'If you lose you could go to prison.'

Kavanagh gave Jonathan the kind of look that could turn someone to stone. Two pink patches of embarrassment rose in Jonathan's cheeks as Kavanagh let the silence drag.

'You think I'm going to prison?'

'Well, I, er, I didn't mean—' Jonathan began, his voice practically shaking with terror. And then, to Adam's astonishment, Kavanagh threw back his head and gave a great bark of laughter. And it didn't stop. Just when you thought he was going to stop laughing, he kept going.

Jonathan and Adam nervously joined in, not really knowing what they were laughing about, until Kavanagh's mirth abruptly stopped.

'I'm just messing with you, Jonny,' he said, to Jonathan's obvious relief. 'We all know it won't come to that.'

Adam was struck by how effectively one person could control the weather of a room. Jonathan was smiling again, the wind back in his sails.

'Well, Charles, as you know, my door is always open,' said Jonathan. 'But I understand we have a meeting in the diary for

Friday with your solicitors to go through the latest developments and discuss our strategy.'

'Oh, I really would feel much better if we could discuss this now, not Friday,' said Kavanagh, pleasantly.

There was a split-second pause, where Adam could almost see Jonathan mentally calculating everything else he was meant to do today, before he recovered himself.

'Of course, of course.' He seemed to suddenly remember Adam was there. 'Green, go and fetch Mr Kavanagh a black coffee with two sugars.'

Kavanagh seemed to notice Adam for the first time too, and he gave him a benevolent smile.

'Come now, Jonny, I wouldn't expect an up-and-coming young legal star to wait on me hand and foot. I'm perfectly happy with this,' he gestured at a strange green concoction he had in a plastic bottle, which was making an unpleasant ring on Jonathan's antique desk.

Jonathan glared angrily at Adam, as if the exchange were his fault.

'How rude of me not to introduce myself,' Kavanagh went on, still addressing Adam. 'I'm Charles Kavanagh, CEO of Invicta Medical Supplies and Jonny's favourite client,' he said, holding out his hand.

'Adam Green, I'm a pupil here,' he replied, as Kavanagh took his hand in a vice-like grip.

'Pupil, eh?' said Kavanagh with a grandfatherly chuckle. 'Hope you're not learning all of Jonny's bad habits. I'm joking, Jonny, I'm joking,' he added, holding up his hands.

'So, Adam, has Jonny here told you I'm one of the country's biggest drug dealers?' He took a swig of his radioactively green drink. 'Ha – not that kind. I import medicines. And Jonathan – that's what really worries me,' he turned back to his barrister, rubbing his forehead. 'Not the prison term, or the business collapse – but all the thousands of patients who will go without vital, life-changing medicines if they get me for this. We've got to win, for their sake.' He looked out of the window, studied pensiveness on his face.

'Adam, get a pad, take notes, please,' said Jonathan curtly. 'Charles' – his tone was conciliatory now – 'I think we're a long way from that point. We will be mounting an extremely robust defence.'

'First you want him to be a waitress, now he's a secretary?' said Kavanagh with an eyebrow raised. 'Adam, you look like a bright lad,' he continued. 'Say the NHS has a problem – a big, expensive problem – whereby they need to import certain medicines from abroad but lack the wherewithal to do it themselves. Then, say someone has a business, and that business is to buy those medicines from third parties, facilitate the import, and sell them to the NHS at a fair price. And then, say some of those medicines the business provided – a tiny percentage – have fraudulent paperwork, and turn out to be faulty. Who would you say in that scenario was at fault?'

Adam swallowed. It wasn't a pretty picture. 'Well, it would depend. But . . . the third-party suppliers? The business was let down by them.'

'Exactly, Adam, exactly,' breathed Kavanagh. 'And my God, do I hate to be let down.'

Jonathan cleared his throat. 'The prosecution is going to run the case that you were aware of the problems with the certifications,' he said. 'It's worse than we thought – because initially they were just accusing you of not taking proper steps to prevent the fraud happening.

'I think, however, it gives us greater scope to prove them wrong. They delivered the boxes of papers today – it's what they call unused material – and based on what your solicitor has informed me, we should be able to put together evidence that will blow the prosecution case out of the water.'

Adam scribbled notes as instructed. Only clients with deep pockets could afford to pay lawyers to sift through unused material, especially if it was a fraud case like this, where the paperwork alone could total many thousands of pages.

'Sounds like a big job, but I'm sure you'll be billing handsomely for it!' said Kavanagh. 'Jonny here stands to pay off his mortgage *and* his kids' school fees if he pulls this one off. It's a big pie – so don't let him stop you taking a slice.'

Adam tried to smile back, though his stomach twisted. Every friendly word from Kavanagh was another hammer blow to his working relationship with Jonathan.

'Right, well, I better let you boys get back to all your *other little cases*,' sneered Kavanagh, slapping his thighs. 'Although, Jonathan – do you have that amended contract that we discussed? If I could have it now, it would really put my mind at rest.'

'Of course, I'll fetch it for you right away,' said Jonathan, shooting Adam the blackest of warning looks as he exited the office.

'I suppose it will be you who ends up going through all those boxes of material,' said Kavanagh casually, when they were alone. 'And I've got to warn you – the police took a hell of a lot!'

'Probably, but I don't mind,' said Adam. 'It will be a privilege to work on such a prestigious case.'

'It certainly will,' said Kavanagh, and he reached out and grabbed Adam's wrist. There was a sudden darkness in his eyes, and the temperature of the room dropped drastically. 'Just remember who you're working for.'

11

Phone call

'Mum, I can't talk now, I'm on my way to a meeting.'

'You can't spare five minutes for your dear mother?'

'OK, yes, yes, I've got five minutes. How are you, Mum?'

'Well, I've still got that problem with my back, and I've had a bit of a cough, very strange-coloured mucus coming up. The doctor said it was nothing and it would clear up on its own when I saw him yesterday, but I'm not convinced so I've made another appointment to see him tomorrow, just in case.'

'Tomorrow? Don't you think – Never mind.'

'Are you still doing that case where you're defending the police killer? It's all gone a bit quiet now in the papers, hasn't it, so I wondered if they'd dropped it.'

'No, it's just that the trial isn't for a few months so we've got time to prepare. And, Mum, I've told you, you shouldn't simply assume he is the killer, because isn't that exactly what happened when—'

'All right, all right, I'm sorry, Adam.'

'I mean, it's like with Dad, isn't it, Mum? Everyone was saying he was guilty, but—'

'Oh, it was shocking about the poison, wasn't it? Aren't they calling your man the Botox Butcher now?'

'Yes, they are, but that's actually very prejudicial, Mum.'

' "Very prejudicial"! Aren't you Mr Fancypants these days.'

'Not really, Mum . . .'

'Well, if the case isn't for a few months then you must have some time on your hands, so why don't you come back to Southgate for a weekend – no, a week! Anna Goldberg is dying to meet you. I could set it up—'

'Sorry, Mum, things are actually still really busy. I'm on this fraud case, and my boss wants me to go through all these boxes of paper trying to build our defence, and then I'm still doing my own cases too. Actually, this will make you laugh . . .'

'Go on?'

'Remember Gloria, the prostitute I've defended a few times before, a real character?'

'Oh yes, although I don't like you mixed up in all that. She's the old girl, isn't she, about seventy-five – you said she's the kind that Wayne Rooney would like.'

'Yes, I've had to go to Thames Magistrates' three times now when she's been arrested for soliciting. Always gets off with a fine and she's happy.'

'She'll never learn that way, will she?'

'But this week, I get the call, and she's been arrested for shoplifting.'

'That's a bit different!'

'It is. So I said to her, "Gloria, are you off the game?" And she says, "Yes, I am, as a matter of fact." I said, "Why's that?" And she said, "The stairs." '

'Oh, poor woman. I quite understand, what with my back and all. Once you get to our age you just can't be doing with going up and down all day, I said that to the caretaker at work, and especially not if you make an effort and wear a nice pair of shoes, which you know I always do.'

'Maybe you and Gloria have more in common than you think, Mum.'

'Oh, stop it, Ad. What am I going to do with you? Are you eating? What did you have for your dinner last night?'

'OK, Mum, I've really got to go. Love you.'

12

As well as Gloria's shoplifting case, Adam had defended two burglars, a drunk driver and an indecent exposure that week. He was working flat out now that he was two months into his second six, and was desperately hoping it would be enough to secure his tenancy. The late nights prepping for cases, followed by the long days defending them, left him with very little time for anything else. He couldn't remember the last time he'd seen his university friends, and he'd had to cancel on a mate's birthday drinks last weekend because he'd needed to make up lost time working on the Kavanagh case. But amid it all, the client he couldn't get out of his mind was Jimmy Knight.

They were still waiting for the meeting with the poisoning expert, Dr Alice Pettigrew, which kept getting pushed back because of her teaching commitments. With months until the trial, Jonathan seemed unconcerned about the delay, but Adam was itching to get on with building their defence case. And at the moment, they didn't have one to run. All they had was Knight's assertion that it wasn't him.

But ever since the PTPH, and their rushed, cryptic conversation in the cells, Adam felt certain Knight had more to tell them. He'd petitioned Jonathan relentlessly, trying to get him to agree to a visit to Belmarsh, but his pupil master had consistently refused.

'Do you know how much we are being paid for this case?' Jonathan said indignantly. 'If we add in a traipse over to the bowels of South-East London we will not only be working for free but we might as well pay the state for the privilege of doing it.'

'Look, you keep saying yourself that we need a better defence case statement,' said Adam. 'Can't I get Nisha to set up a visit, and I'll go, without you?'

Jonathan met his question with undivided indifference, so Adam took it as a yes. Nisha, however, was even more exasperated by his request.

'I only went to see him last week. Is this really necessary?' she asked Adam on the phone. 'You've no idea how much work I've got on at the moment . . .'

'That's OK, I can go on my own,' Adam said. It wasn't usual for barristers to visit clients in prison without the solicitor present, but this felt important – and Nisha was so overwrought she might just agree to it.

'Fine, OK,' she eventually agreed. 'I'll set up the visit. Is Jonathan OK with this?'

'Yes,' Adam lied. He knew Jonathan would much prefer him to be sifting through Kavanagh's papers, and he'd have found it highly unusual that he was off to Belmarsh without Nisha. But this might be the only way to get the answers he needed.

As he made the grim fifteen-minute walk from Plumstead station to the prison, with traffic screaming alongside him on the A road, Adam wondered if Knight could be worth all this effort.

The clock was ticking until chambers voted on Adam's tenancy, and spending half a day on a potential wild goose chase in this godforsaken corner of South-East London probably wasn't the best use of his time.

But if he was honest with himself, this wasn't just about Knight anymore. Every time a newspaper, Jonathan, his mum – especially his mum – made an assumption about his client's guilt, his urge to prove his innocence became more profound. He wasn't sure how he'd got into this mess – the whole point of doing law had been to stop those old wounds aching so badly. But instead, he found himself thinking about them more than ever.

At the visitors' centre, Adam joined a long queue of lawyers and prisoners' families being processed through a seemingly endless parade of prison security. Passports were scrutinised, fingerprints scanned, bags confiscated, photographs taken and databases updated.

Through each successive steel-bound door there was an extra layer of security – metal detectors, sniffer dogs, a full body scan looking for hidden drugs or mobiles tucked into the most unlikely of orifices. Adam had forgotten he'd have to hand over his own phone, and as he dropped it into the Ziploc bag proffered by a white-gloved screw, he felt a cold sweat of panic. He'd told Tony that he was just popping to Highbury Mags – he hoped the clerk wouldn't try to get hold of him.

A final heavy door was rolled back and Adam – along with his herd of fellow visitors – were shown into a putrid-smelling corridor. Apart from the smell, the first thing to hit him was the wall of noise. From all angles came the assault of metallic clanging – pounding feet and slamming gates. But this was just the bassline to the hundreds of screaming voices, which seemed to reverberate and amplify around the bare, peeling walls.

There was no time to adapt to the sensory overload, as prison guards frogmarched the crowd through another gate and into the visitors' rooms. Here the lawyers were divided from the family and friends, and shown through a further barred gate, and into separate meeting cubicles. Adam took his seat at the bolted-down table, and nervously laid out a notepad and pen in front of him.

Finally, the prison guard clanked the door back open and showed in the prisoner – Jimmy Knight.

'I wondered when you'd come.' Knight was smiling at Adam, the cheerful expression at grotesque odds with the two enormous bruises that bloomed across his eyes like hideous violet peonies.

'Mr Knight – Jesus. What happened?'

'Oh, this?' Jimmy gestured at his battered face. 'The perks of being "high-profile".'

'Don't take this the wrong way, but I thought being accused of killing a cop wouldn't make you totally unpopular in a place like this?'

Knight's expression darkened. 'Cliveden wasn't an ordinary cop.'

The door to their cubicle opened again, the same blank-faced guard looming in the doorway. 'You've got thirty minutes,' he said, and slammed the door shut.

Knight chuckled. 'Typical Belmarsh hospitality.'

'Have you reported your attack?' Adam asked, still distracted by Knight's battered face. 'I can help you escalate it, if you—'

'No,' Knight held up his hand. 'You forget I've done a decade inside already. Believe me when I say that will only make things worse.'

'OK, if you're sure,' said Adam. 'How are you – otherwise?'

'How do you think I am?' Knight snorted. His eyes cast around the room. 'Your boss not with you then?'

'Er, no,' Adam said, shifting uncomfortably. 'And if you don't mind – it would be good if you didn't mention that I came without Nisha.'

'I see,' said Knight, leaning back in his chair. 'So this is off the books. What brings you here then, Adam Green?'

Adam was impressed he'd remembered his name. He knew his best tactic was just to be honest. 'There's so much about your case I don't understand,' he said. 'It feels like you're leaving so much out. I want to make sure you get the best defence you can – but I can't do that when I don't have the full facts.'

The playful light that had been dancing in Knight's eyes just a few moments ago went out.

'What do you want to know?' he said surlily.

'Why did you want to meet Cliveden in the first place?'

'He ruined my life.'

'You mean by . . . framing you?' Adam tried to keep the tinge of doubt out of his voice. He'd read so many profiles, watched so many clips of handsome, straight-talking family man Cliveden – and he still didn't understand how or why that could have happened.

Knight shook his head. 'I know what you're thinking: my life was ruined long before that happened, and now I'm just looking for someone to blame. But it ain't like that.'

'What is it like?'

Knight took a deep breath. 'OK. I come from a shit family, in a shit part of the world, and I turned out to be a little shit. What a huge fucking surprise. My old man knocked us all around, nearly killed my mother more than once. I saw things – heard things – no kid should have to. That crunch as his fist hit her nose – he broke it so many times she lost count. I remember one day when I was not much older than seven holding the flesh on her scalp together while we waited for the ambulance.'

Adam tried not to let his nausea show on his face, as Knight ploughed on.

'When she wasn't getting battered, she drank. And she were always thirsty, so my brothers and I, we were always hungry. It was down to us to clean up her sick and piss and blood and try not to listen when she told us she wished we were dead. I'm not telling you that to make you feel sorry for me. Just to explain.'

'Explain what?'

'Why I ended up on the streets. Thieving, running drugs for the older lads. I was a career criminal before I was old enough to take my GCSEs – which of course I didn't bother with. The rozzers caught up with me a few times – you'll have seen my record. I was good at it, but I hated it. I knew I was going to end up in prison eventually, or dead.'

'So you stopped.'

'Yes. I stopped. I was twenty-seven. Just young enough for a fresh start. I went back to college, got some qualifications. Got a job – a real job. And . . .' Knight tailed off. He rubbed the feather tattoo on his neck thoughtfully, and Adam thought of his dad, working endless hours at the bus depot. 'One pound of your own is worth fifty of someone else's, Adam,' he always used to say. Adam tried to banish the memory from his mind and focus on Knight, who seemed equally lost in his own thoughts.

'And then you get arrested for armed robbery . . .' Adam prompted him.

'Yes.'

'But you didn't do it?'

'Of course I didn't fucking do it. Why would I blow up my life like that? It was the post office I worked at that got robbed – who'd be that fucking stupid? I thought it was just a terrible mistake when they arrested me. Then they started saying they'd found a load of the cash in my house, then the gun. And I knew it was no mistake at all.'

'So you were framed. Why?'

'That's a question I asked myself for the best part of ten years. I kept going over and over it – why would the police want me banged up? I wasn't causing anyone any trouble, I'd gone straight as they come. But that was the mistake I made. Because *it wasn't about me.*'

'What do you mean?'

The door of the cubicle banged open; it was the guard. 'Five minutes!' he barked.

'Short half an hour,' said Knight ironically.

Adam tried to rewind. 'What do you mean, it wasn't about you?'

Knight sighed, and Adam noticed his eyes glance up at the camera he hadn't realised was watching them, blinking in the corner of the cell.

'There are paths it's better for you not to go down,' he said, eventually. 'It's better if I don't say no more.'

'What are you talking about?' said Adam, exasperated.

Knight leaned across the table towards him. 'Do you really think that I could have pulled off Cliveden's murder, Adam?'

'I've told you, I believe you.'

'I don't care what you believe. It's what the jury believes that matters. I just need you to prove I didn't do it. You can do that, can't you?'

Adam didn't have time to reply before the guard came in to officiously put Knight back in handcuffs. As his bruised and battered client was led away, Adam was sure that he winked at him. He'd come for answers, but all he'd got were more questions.

13

Jimmy Knight had urged him to prove that he couldn't have committed the murder. And a week later, as he arrived at the University of York, that was exactly what Adam hoped Dr Alice Pettigrew would help him to do.

The poisons expert was expecting Jonathan Taylor-Cameron, and if she was disappointed that it was fresh-faced Adam who turned up on his own, she didn't show it.

'Jonathan sends his apologies,' Adam explained. 'He got called to an emergency hearing at the last minute. I'm here as his junior.'

'No matter,' smiled Alice, a tall woman with an angular brunette bob and horn-rimmed glasses. Wearing stylish wide-legged trousers and a loose beige blazer, she was waiting for him outside the Brutalist grey chemistry block that housed her office. 'Shall we walk and talk? It's such a beautiful day.'

The truth was that Jonathan had flat-out refused to come, despite Adam's best efforts to persuade him. 'I can count on one hand the things I would go to "the North" for,' he had told Adam humourlessly. 'And this isn't one of them.'

Adam was still convinced that Dr Pettigrew could be a key

witness, so he'd got the two-hour train to York anyway. He was glad of the excuse to stretch his legs as they strolled along the concrete walkways that surrounded the university's man-made lake, where newly hatched ducklings and goslings took their tentative first swims in the May sunshine.

'So how much do you know about botulinum toxin, Adam?' Dr Pettigrew asked, with a professor's instructive tone.

'Not loads,' admitted Adam. 'I know it's super poisonous, that the Nazis considered it as a weapon of war. That it's now mainly injected as a means to treat certain medical conditions, and to improve cosmetic appearance. But as a murder weapon – I'm stumped.'

Dr Pettigrew laughed lightly, as they paused to admire a pair of elegant black swans. Adam had found her not in a directory of expert witnesses but by trawling through academic papers relating to poisons. Hers, entitled 'Fatal Attraction', had caught his eye for its unusually thorough look at the function and uses of botulinum toxin.

'I couldn't believe it when I got your message saying that's what had been used to kill that police officer,' she said. 'It's incredibly difficult – and extremely clever.'

She reached in her pocket, and threw a handful of crumbs into the lake, which were immediately set upon by a frenzy of water-fowl. Adam noticed that she had perfectly normal laughter lines around her eyes – she clearly didn't partake of the substance she'd spent so long studying herself.

'Botulinum toxin is one of the most powerfully toxic sub-stances in the world. It is seven million times more toxic than cobra venom.'

'Bloody hell.'

'Bloody hell indeed. The bacteria that produces the toxin, *Clostridium botulinum*, has been killing people for centuries. In the 1790s botulism, which is the food poisoning it causes, was identified in people eating tainted sausages. Thankfully we've moved on from then in terms of sterilisation and food storage, so food-borne cases are rare, but they can still be serious if untreated. Between five and ten per cent of people who contract botulism die — although the greatest risk is to babies.'

'I'm guessing our murderer was confident he had a better than five to ten per cent chance.'

'Right,' nodded Dr Pettigrew. 'But why, I can't quite figure out. You see, there are very effective medical interventions for botulism. You wouldn't expect someone to die until several hours or even days after their first symptom. And the symptoms are so distinctive, that allows plenty of time for medical intervention, which would almost certainly save a victim's life. So in this case, I don't see . . .' She trailed off, her eyes fixed on a flock of goslings fighting over the final crumbs.

'Could it be because of the size of the dose?' Adam said.

Dr Pettigrew turned back to him. 'Well, your victim certainly had a big dose. The toxin works by attacking the nervous system. It prevents signals from the nerve cells reaching the muscles, effectively leaving the muscles without instructions, and therefore paralysed.

'Imagine if your muscles stop working. The early symptoms are going to be drooping eyelids, slurred speech, blurred vision — all those basic muscle functions that we take for granted start failing. But if the toxin reaches the respiratory system, that's when you're in real trouble. Because if the muscles that control your breathing stop working, that's it – you will simply suffocate. But this – it was so sudden . . .'

Adam shook his head. 'It's mad that people inject this stuff voluntarily.'

'Well, not really,' said Dr Pettigrew, dodging out of the way of a group of chattering students bearing hockey sticks. 'The Botox that's used cosmetically contains such a tiny amount of toxin, and is injected into very specific sites, so its effects are localised. It is still very safe.'

'But it can't be that safe if it caused the death of Grant Clive-den,' Adam pressed.

'True,' said Dr Pettigrew. 'But there were two unusual things to take into consideration. First, that in his case the toxin was ingested, not injected. Second, the autopsy report you sent over shows very high levels of the toxin detected in the victim's bloodstream. I won't bore you with the maths, but it's far more than you'd find in bottles used for cosmetic procedures, which are themselves tightly regulated. Botox comes in a powder form, in little glass vials, and practitioners then reconstitute it using a saline solution before they inject it. And after it's mixed with the solution, it's only viable for twenty-four hours. I've no idea how your killer got their hands on the toxin in the first place, but if they were getting it in Botox form, they'd have had to do some serious stockpiling. One possible theory is that they tampered with a large number of vials, then combined them into a lethal dose – say, in the form of an ice cube that could be easily slipped into a drink.'

None of this fitted with Jimmy Knight, who had been released from prison just ten days prior to the murder – and certainly wasn't an expert in such complicated science.

'I'm guessing it's not that easy to get hold of Botox, even in those small quantities you describe,' he said.

'Right,' said Dr Pettigrew. 'Botox is just a brand name, and they're one of a very small number of companies who are legally allowed to manufacture botulinum toxin. Licensed brands are prescription-only drugs. Although beauticians can administer the injections, they have to be trained and legally their clients must first have them prescribed by a doctor who has seen them for a face-to-face consultation.

'Anecdotally, however, there is a growing black market for Botox, with unlicensed products being doled out by practition-ers who bypass the usual prescribing process. There is a chance your murderer could have got hold of such a product, in a higher concentration.'

Adam had been furiously making notes in his phone, and he paused now as a thought struck him. The police officer Emma Owens, standing in the Old Bailey corridor, tensed with a mys-terious fury.

'If the police were to discover someone selling unlicensed botulinum toxin, would they seize it?'

'Undoubtedly,' said Dr Pettigrew. 'As we've seen, it can be very dangerous in the wrong hands.'

They'd reached a bridge that looked out to the bizarre space-ship type structure which constituted the university's Central Hall, and they paused for a moment to take it in.

'This must have been someone who knew what they were doing, who understood the science and what it would take to administer the lethal dose,' said Adam. 'It wasn't as simple as just getting a syringe full of the stuff and putting it in a drink.'

'That's my conclusion too,' nodded Alice.

'I just don't know how my client could have pulled that off, on his own,' said Adam. 'The prosecution toxicologist reckons that the poison was administered within ten to two hours before the victim's death. Is it possible that isn't correct?'

Adam knew it was a long shot. Even if the window was increased, he'd gone back through the police reports of Cliveden's last movements and he could see scarce other opportunities for a poisoner to strike. But if they could just move the window of suspicion slightly away from Knight's meeting with Cliveden, they could introduce reasonable doubt.

Dr Pettigrew nodded. 'There's a reason I asked you to come all the way up here,' she said. 'I wanted to speak to you face-to-face.'

Adam was confused. 'Why?'

Dr Pettigrew looked away uncomfortably. 'I don't like to openly criticise the work of my colleagues in the toxicology community,' she said. 'So this isn't something I'd have wanted to say over email. But in my professional view, that window can't be guaranteed. This death is so highly unusual. And then you have to take into account how each human body presents so many variables, and the effects of ingesting this toxin in this form and quantity are so under-researched.'

'OK . . . so what sort of window do you think we are looking at?' asked Adam, scarcely able to believe what he was hearing.

'It would be impossible to conclusively say when the poison was administered,' said Dr Pettigrew. 'But I think it would be in a much bigger window – and it could have been less than half an hour before. What's really relevant is when in that period the victim ate – or drank.'

Adam let out a low whistle. So Cliveden could have been

poisoned by someone within the Old Bailey just minutes before he died.

It was a dark thought, but it was better news than he could ever have hoped for. Jimmy Knight couldn't possibly be the only suspect now.

14

The train back to London seemed to crawl as it got closer to its destination. Dr Pettigrew had never been an expert witness before, but she had agreed to give evidence in Jimmy Knight's case. Adam was dying to discuss what she'd told him with someone else, but neither Jonathan nor Nisha was picking up their phone. Nisha, he assumed, was busy – Jonathan, presumably, was simply screening his calls. He wrote up everything Dr Pettigrew had told him and emailed them instead, and by the time the train reached Peterborough he had a dashed response from Nisha: Ta – on way to Pentonville. Will read later. Still nothing from Jonathan.

When the train finally reached King's Cross, Adam hopped on a bus heading towards chambers, hoping to catch his pupil master there. It was a Monday, and that meant Mrs Taylor-Cameron had choir practice, and Jonathan usually seized the opportunity to stay late in town and meet Nadine, Allegra or God knows who else. It was quite shudder-inducing, Adam thought, to have such an intimate understanding of his boss's sex schedule – but perhaps it would be useful on this occasion.

Alighting on Holborn, he had just cut down Shoe Lane

towards Stag Court, when he felt a tap on his shoulder and wheeled round to see a familiar, smirking face – Georgina. Just what he needed.

'Are you going back to chambers?' she said. 'Because you can't use the pupil room. I've got a load of CCTV evidence I need to go through and I asked Tony specifically if I could have it.'

Adam shrugged. 'Fine.'

'Think I'm going to be pulling a late one,' she said, self-importantly. 'This CCTV evidence has just come in, and I think I can use it to build a great case for my boy. You see, he was wearing white trainers . . .'

Adam tuned out as Georgina launched into a long-winded story about some teenager who had supposedly set a pub on fire with a gang of his mates. But Georgina thought that a glimpse of his shoes on CCTV from further down the road showed that he wasn't there at the exact moment of arson – or something like that. Adam wasn't really listening, but was instead just waiting for the inevitable barb aimed at him which would come at the end of her story.

'So, yeah, it's probably, like, the most serious case I've done on my own and it really feels like one I could actually win, you know? Guess you wouldn't know what that's like . . .' Bingo.

Adam took it on the chin. 'Have you seen Jonathan today?'

Georgina pulled a face. 'I try to avoid him . . . God, he gives me the creeps. You know all the female silks can't stand him. Do you think Catherine and Fiona will hold it against you when they come to vote on your tenancy – the fact that you're his pupil?'

It was a thought that hadn't occurred to Adam before, but he knew immediately it would now be joining the rich ledger of things that kept him awake at night.

They had reached chambers, where Tony stuck his head out of the clerks' room to growl at them. 'Green – there's a bail ap for you tomorrow morning in Highbury, I've emailed you the details. Devereaux – you've got another paedo case. Indecent images allegedly downloaded, I should say. Brief coming over now.'

Georgina grimaced playfully at Adam, and if he didn't know better Adam would have said she was attempting to bond with him. 'The fun never stops, does it?' She was already skimming through her emails on her phone as she stalked away towards the pupil room.

'Tony, is Jonathan still here?' Adam asked.

Tony grunted. 'Think he's just about to leave.'

Adam didn't need telling twice. He took the stairs two at a time, only to almost collide with his pupil master, who was coming in the opposite direction.

'Jonathan, hi. Did you see my messages, about the poisoning expert? It's brilliant news for our client – and she'll testify!'

'Yes, yes, I got your little email. Very good,' said Jonathan, as Adam fell into step beside him.

'Good? You'll use her then?' Adam had been braced to have an argument with Jonathan about this, given how much he'd resisted lifting even his little finger to build Knight's case. But here he was being remarkably sanguine.

'Of course. It will be good to look like we've at least tried. But let's not get carried away: we both know this isn't enough to save our punter.'

'Well, sure, but it's a start – if we can show that the police investigation didn't properly take into account other suspects, and that they forced the evidence to fit . . .'

Jonathan rolled his eyes wearily. They'd reached the front entrance, and Adam went to follow him to continue their conversation. But his pupil master stopped him, his hand on the door.

'Where do you think you're going?'

'Well, I can walk with you to the Tube. I really think—'

'No. You're staying here. You've been out all day and I'm not having you neglecting the Kavanagh files. I've billed him for four hours work today and so that's what you're going to deliver.'

Adam's heart sank. It had been a blessed relief to get a whole day away from the intimidatingly enormous number of cardboard boxes that had been sent over by the prosecution in the Kavanagh case, but he should have known better than to hope Jonathan would let that slide. It was already gone six – he was going to be there well into the night.

'OK. I'll see you in the morning, I guess?'

'Make sure you write an inventory of what you've gone through so I know you've done it,' Jonathan snapped, and flounced out.

Adam sighed and headed down the steps to the basement room where the boxes of Kavanagh's unused material were being stored. They didn't fit anywhere else – there were too many of them. The investigation into Kavanagh's alleged fraud had produced a tsunami of paperwork, years and years' worth of invoices and orders, licensing reports and customs declarations. The used material alone numbered nearly 15,000 pages, but that was a drop in the ocean compared to the rafts of total evidence the police had seized. Kavanagh, and by extension Jonathan too, was convinced that it would be possible to prove from the unused material that he had acted completely in good faith, and that he was in fact a victim of fraud himself.

But that was going to be a long old process. On one particularly soul-crushing day Adam had counted the boxes – there were twenty-three. And each box held something like 4,000 pieces of paper – which meant the total number of pages wasn't much short of 100,000. Jonathan had theatrically come to 'help' on the day the boxes had arrived, pulling out pages at random and flourishing them in the air while holding forth about how meticulous Kavanagh's record-keeping was, and what this said about his status as a first-rate man of business. But Adam knew that the bulk of the filing, reading and reporting would be down to him. He wearily pulled box five towards him and forced his eyes to focus.

The sheer time, effort and manpower that was going into fighting Kavanagh's case was such a sharp contrast to the cursory effort that was being given to Knight's – at least by Jonathan. If real justice was this expensive, was it really justice at all? Something Adam had forgotten came back suddenly in crystal-clear focus: fiddling with one of those little biros attached to a ball-bearing chain as his mother pleaded with a grim-faced bank manager. 'Please, I know my credit score is bad, but my husband, he's been arrested . . .'

And yet here he was, giving up his evening to truffle for treasure on behalf of a millionaire; although who said Kavanagh didn't deserve justice too?

A couple of hours later, Adam was struggling. He yawned and stretched, realising he was long overdue a coffee. He climbed the stairs and walked along the quiet corridor of the deserted chambers. With a stab of annoyance he noticed the bar of light sneaking under the closed door of the pupil room, which advertised Georgina's continued presence. It wasn't enough that she outdid him at everything else – now she was working harder than him too.

In the little kitchen by the loos, Adam flicked the kettle on. There was a fancy coffee machine as well, but he preferred the comforting taste of watery Nescafé.

Although he was trying hard to concentrate on the Kavanagh case, he couldn't stop his thoughts drifting back to Knight. Waiting for the kettle to boil, he pulled out his phone and saw an email had just popped in from Nisha in response to his note on what Dr Pettigrew had told him. Brilliant Adam!!!! Just what we need, it read, but Adam could feel his earlier optimism ebbing away. Like Jonathan had said, on its own, Dr Pettigrew's evidence wouldn't be enough.

Adam refreshed his Google search on the name 'Jimmy Knight'. It had become a bit of a nervous tic for him – every time he had a spare minute he'd check the internet for the latest coverage, most of which centred around their client's presumed guilt.

His mum was right, things had calmed down a bit in recent weeks – there was a High Court libel battle between two ageing soap stars which had captured the rapacious public appetite for messy legal scandal instead. There weren't any new results since he'd checked yesterday, but he flicked through the latest. Knight's mugshot, which had once held a look of pure evil, now just seemed sad to Adam. He was in such a mess, early mistakes had snowballed, and now he was facing life in prison. You couldn't see the tattoo in the picture, but Adam's mind went to the feather on Knight's neck, and what his dad had said it stood for. He wondered if it held the same meaning for Knight – freedom, now just out of reach.

Sipping his coffee, he scrolled past the spittle-spraying opinion pieces and the reports of Knight's initial arrest and first appearance at the magistrates'. As he went further back, Adam realised he'd never seen any report of Knight's initial conviction for armed robbery. Would the internet go far enough back?

On page nine of the Google search, he found it – a short write-up in the *Croydon Advertiser*. MAN JAILED FOR GUNPOINT ROBBERY OF POST OFFICE. The sub-postmaster was quoted talking about the life-altering impact his terrifying ordeal had had on him, and the judge's final remarks describing the robbery as a 'wicked act' were duly reported. The article concluded: 'Father-of-one James Knight, 37, of Eastney Road, was sentenced to ten years in prison.'

Father-of-one?

Adam knew Knight's file like the back of his hand. It had been diligently prepared by Nisha and was supposed to cover everything about their client, including his family set-up and personal life. But nowhere did it mention that Knight was a father.

Which meant that during the conversation they'd had at Belmarsh, when Knight had revealed the most personal details of his upbringing, his history of crime and his new life, he'd left out something crucial. Why would he keep such a significant part of his life from them?

15

'Enough for another cup in there?'

Adam started – it was Bobby Thompson. It was long gone 8 p.m. and he'd had no idea he would still be there.

'Sure,' he said, spooning a scoop of Nescafé into a grubby Sports Direct mug. 'You're here late.'

Bobby raised an eyebrow. 'So are you. And so is your fellow pupil. I'll tell you the same as I told her – it's not the quantity of hours you put in, but the quality. No one's going to be impressed by presenteeism.'

Adam almost retorted that Bobby only knew they were both working so late because he was there so late himself, but thought better of it.

'It's the Kavanagh case, the unused,' he explained instead. 'There's just so much of it, and quite a tight schedule, so Jonathan is keen for me to bill a set number of hours on it each day.'

'I bet he is,' said Bobby, the corner of his mouth twitching into the ghost of a smile. 'Perhaps he's right. Quite often the answer is there in the bits the other side reckons aren't worth bothering with.'

Bobby took the coffee wordlessly and went to plug his

headphones into his phone, making it clear he considered the conversation with Adam over. He wasn't one to bother with social niceties; it was one of the things that Adam both admired and feared about him. But he needed the older man's help.

'Can I ask you a question, Bobby?'

'Adam, I'm very busy . . .'

'What do you do if you realise your client is hiding something from you?'

Bobby looked at Adam sharply. 'Clients hide things from us all the time. But we deal in the truth. All we can do is urge them to be as honest as possible with us, so we can get them the fairest possible outcome. What do you think your client is holding back?'

'It's Jimmy Knight – he's got a kid. I found it in an old news report from his first sentencing. I don't know why he's never mentioned it to his solicitor before. I know it sounds weird but I can't help but think it's relevant.'

Bobby stirred his coffee. 'How old was the news report?'

'Well, it's from ten years ago. That's when he was first jailed for robbery.'

Bobby remained silent, still stirring his coffee. Adam finally saw the obvious answer that he, of all people, should have considered straight away.

'Maybe he's not a dad anymore?'

'If a client is being cagey, there's usually a good reason. If you want honesty from him, be honest in turn about what you know. And remember what I've said before – *do your research*.'

Back in the basement, Bobby's words ringing in his ears, Adam couldn't concentrate on Kavanagh's deathly-dull papers anymore. He switched on his laptop, and fired up the cuttings service chambers used for news articles too old for the internet.

SEARCH: \<James/Jimmy Knight\> \<son\> \<daughter\> \<robbery\> \<Croydon\>

He yawned as he peered at the results. Not much at first, but then, there it was. A more detailed report in the *Evening Standard* about Jimmy's sentencing.

'Reg McNally, representing James Knight, argued in mitigation that Knight had sole custody of his ten-year-old son, Marcellus.'

It was a helpfully unusual name. Marcellus Knight, thought Adam, there can't be too many of those. Sure enough, when he punched the name into Facebook only a handful of profiles came up, most of them in America. He clicked on the one whose network was listed as 'St Thomas Catholic High School, Croydon'.

The profile picture showed a skinny lad with the same soulful brown eyes as Jimmy Knight, posing surlily by a graffitied wall. But there had been no activity on the page since February last year, when it had been flooded with messages from friends. Variations on 'Rooting for you Marc – please please just pull through,' 'Sending so many thoughts and prayers mate,' until the most recent messages, which said things like 'Fly high angel' and 'Always in our hearts.'

Adam's stomach clenched. He put Marcellus Knight's name into Google, and discovered that shortly after his nineteenth birthday he'd been the victim of a hit-and-run, suffering catastrophic injuries. He'd survived in a coma for just over a fortnight before he'd died. The driver had never been found. In reports of the death, Marcellus was described as an 'aspiring barrister', who was taking a law degree at the City Law School.

Adam pushed the laptop away from him. Hit-and-run — that horrific phrase never ceased to make him feel sick. His dad's hands on his shoulders after the officious knock at the door, 'Everything will be OK,' the clink of metal on metal as the police led him away in handcuffs. He'd never seen his father again.

He stopped the slew of memories with a flat palm to his forehead. No wonder Knight hadn't mentioned his son. Being separated from your child, accused of something you insisted you hadn't done — it was enough to make a man do desperate things, as Adam knew too well. The difference was Knight had lived — but his son had died. Barely a year before Knight was due to walk free. Maybe it didn't really matter, but Adam couldn't help wondering — had Marcellus believed in his dad's innocence?

Knight was a closed book. But here, finally, was a clue to what was going on inside. It wasn't clear how Marcellus's death was connected to Knight sitting in a cell in Belmarsh awaiting trial for murder, but Adam thought at the very least it could be a way through to understanding their mysterious client better.

He needed to know more — to talk to Knight. But he'd only just got away with the last trip to Belmarsh, and he didn't dare pull the same trick again. Looking around at the piles of Kavanagh boxes, he knew the chance of Jonathan allowing him a day to go to the high-security prison so soon after his last visit were slim to zero. And given that Knight had so studiously air-brushed Marcellus's existence last time they spoke, the chance of him being open and honest about it seemed unlikely too.

So who else could he speak to instead? He cycled back through the open tabs on his browser, to the original cutting about Knight's first sentencing. He just needed the name of the barrister who'd represented him then, who should know the details of Knight's initial conviction – and might even be able to give some context about his relationship with Marcellus. Ah, there it was – Reg McNally.

Where had he seen that name before?

He put Reg's name into the online law directory and saw that he'd been called to the Bar in 1989, which meant he'd probably still be practising.

But he wasn't, because he'd been disbarred – later in the same year he'd represented Jimmy Knight. The reason was listed simply as 'misconduct'.

Adam stared at the entry, desperately trying to place where he knew that name from. Reg McNally . . .

He flung open the box file where he'd put the Knight brief and leafed frantically through its pages. And there, in black and white, on the list of witnesses, was the name he recognised.

Reg McNally – landlord, the Old Nag's Head.

Knight's old barrister had been there at the very moment he was accused of poisoning his old enemy. And no one seemed to have made the connection.

16

Adam was waiting on the steps of chambers early the next day, when Tony came into view, clutching a coffee in a cardboard cup and a bacon roll. It was one of those bright blue mornings of early summer which promised heat, birdsong and the smell of freshly cut grass – even in this most urban of enclaves. Unable to sleep, Adam had walked to work and had been here since not long after seven; he'd already watched the cleaners come and go.

'What the hell are you doing here so early, Green?' said Tony gruffly, shifting the coffee cup under his armpit as he fiddled in his pocket for his keys.

'I've got something to ask you, Tony,' said Adam, eagerly, following close behind the chief clerk, who didn't bother to hold the door open behind him.

'That may be so, but I've not had my breakfast yet,' grumbled Tony, flicking lights on as they made their way along the corridor. 'Put it in an email, son, like everybody else.'

'It's not that kind of question,' said Adam, following Tony into the clerks' room. 'It's about someone who was at the Bar, ten years ago.'

Tony grunted, sinking into his chair and emptying three sugars into his coffee. 'Don't sound like my problem, Green.'

Adam changed tack. 'It's just – everyone says you know more than anyone about the Bar. That you never forget a face and you're more reliable than *The Legal 500*. I know you're really busy . . .' – he ploughed on, ignoring the fact that Tony was now unfurling his copy of that day's *City A.M.* – '. . . but I think it sometimes gets overlooked that you're, like, chambers' greatest asset, and I didn't want to make the mistake of not going to you first.'

Tony looked up, his face if not softened then at least beginning to defrost. 'Flattery is a cheap trick, Green,' he said. 'But I'm not too proud to admit it works on me. Go on then . . . What do you want to know?'

Adam grinned guiltily. 'OK, so, I came across the name of a barrister who was struck off in 2013, but there was no explanation of why – and I think it could be relevant to my case,' he said. 'So I wondered if you knew anything about him. He was called Reg McNally.'

Tony gave a low chuckle. 'Now that's a name I've not heard for a while,' he said. 'But yeah – I know Reg all right.'

Adam couldn't believe his luck. He'd been hovering awkwardly, but now he excitedly pulled up a chair next to Tony. The name Reg McNally had been whirling round and round his sleepless mind all night. Now perhaps he was about to get some answers.

'Do you know why he was struck off?'

Tony chewed his bacon roll thoughtfully. 'Well, if I remember right, what they got him for in the end was accepting money direct from clients,' he said, through a mouthful of bread. Adam knew that was a big no-no — barristers were paid by solicitors, who engaged the advocate on their client's behalf. 'But it went a lot deeper than that. He was in cahoots with one of the big gangs that were running the cocaine trade in London at the time. Knowingly helping them run false defences in court. And he got banged up for money laundering too, after he was disbarred.'

Adam marvelled at the clerk's encyclopedic knowledge of events from a decade ago. But what Tony was telling him was troubling too. He was determined not to lose faith in Knight's innocence — but if he was innocent, why had he had such a dodgy barrister? And why had he ended up at his pub, all those years later? He was about to ask Tony more, but realised the older man was lost in his memories.

'Reg weren't a bad lad, you know, before all that,' Tony said, spraying crumbs liberally. 'But he was one of them that attracts trouble. And he was a bit too fond of the jar, if you know what I mean.'

'So you knew him then?' said Adam, intrigued.

'Oh, yeah,' said Tony. 'Anyone who drank round Temple in the nineties knew McNally. That man spent more time in the pubs than he did in court. Actually, hang on . . .'

He set down his coffee and went to a filing cabinet in the far reaches of the office, where he rooted around in the bottom drawer. 'Yep, I thought I still 'ad these . . .'

Tony emptied a plastic wallet of faded Polaroids onto the desk in front of Adam and fanned them out, searching through them. Adam immediately spotted Tony in several of them — albeit with a bit more hair and a couple fewer chins.

''Ere you go,' he said at last, tapping a stubby finger on a gloomy photograph clearly taken in a pub. Three grinning young men with arms draped around each other's shoulders, one of them instantly recognisable as Tony, all wearing near-identical boxy pinstriped suits and wide ties.

'Which one is McNally?' said Adam, scanning the other two faces.

'Oh, he ain't one of them – that's Nipper Elliot and Greg Gregson, two clerks I came up with. That's McNally, there.' Tony tapped a figure in the back right-hand corner of the photo, who Adam hadn't noticed at first. The man sat alone at a small table, whisky glass in front of him, pale face turned slightly away from the camera. The flash bounced off a beautiful gold watch he wore on his left wrist, illuminating the shadows under his eyes. There was something about the slump of his shoulders and the drooping corners of his mouth that spoke of an unnamed sadness.

'I thought I 'ad a better one of him, but maybe not,' said Tony, turning back to his heap of photos. 'He was never too happy if the camera came out, come to think of it. Reckon he wanted history to remember him at fancy parties with the flashy Oxbridge types, not down the Old Nag's Head with the clerking rabble. He was a Cockney lad, like the rest of us, but he didn't like that one bit. Why he got himself into so much bother, I suppose, spending money he didn't have, trying to keep up with a crowd that didn't want him anyway.'

Tony tailed off, still staring at the old photo clutched in his hands, memories crowding out his words.

'So you've not seen him since those days?' Adam prompted.

'No,' said Tony. 'Nasty business. Everyone knew by then he was mixed up with some very unpleasant types, so we kept our distance. I heard he took over his old man's pub when he got out the slammer, something he swore he'd never do. But no one drinks there anymore, not after everything that went down. Best to leave that shithole to the unlucky tourists who take a wrong turn.' Tony let the photo drop from his hands, back onto the pile of old faces and grungy pubs. 'What's all this got to do with you, anyway?'

'McNally is a witness in the Cliveden murder,' said Adam. 'The prosecution say Knight poisoned him in McNally's pub.'

Tony stared at him in astonishment. 'That's where it happened? The Old Nag's Head?'

'Yes, and then I was doing some research on Knight's previous conviction, for robbery, and the barrister in that case was McNally! It's too much to be a coincidence, don't you think?'

The expression on Tony's face had closed, like a slammed door. He started shuffling his pictures back into their folder.

'Like I said, Green, McNally was trouble,' he said. 'And by the sounds of it, he still is. Maybe it's a coincidence, maybe not. But if he's involved somehow – remember there's nothing more dangerous than someone with nothing more to lose.'

Adam felt a chill, which was at odds with the peaceful warmth of the day. 'I need to talk to him,' he said, more to himself than to Tony. 'Do you still know how to reach him?'

Tony looked at Adam with barely contained contempt. 'Thought you had a degree from Oxford, Green,' he said. 'You don't need me to tell you where to find that old soak. Now get out of here and get to work – you're not paid to stand around gassing, are you?'

Adam knew there was no point in arguing. Dismissed, he headed towards the pupil room, mentally calculating when he could fit in a visit to the Old Nag's Head among the traffic offence and shoplifting cases he had today. He'd hoped McNally would tell him about his client's past, but now his mind was racing with what he could tell him about Knight's present predicament. And if he couldn't . . . Well, Jimmy Knight still had a hell of a lot to explain.

Not for the first time since he'd seen his Facebook profile last night, Adam found himself thinking of Marcellus Knight.

If he'd lived, he and Adam wouldn't have been far off in age. Had he started looking into his dad's crime once he was old enough to understand the enormity of what he'd been accused of? And if he had discovered that his father's barrister was corrupt – in the pocket of criminals – what had he made of that? Had he concluded Jimmy must be guilty, or had he kept faith in his innocence, against the odds?

Adam chided himself for seeing parallels between his client and his own past. It wasn't the same, because Knight had kept fighting to clear his name. He hadn't given up, accepting guilt by default. If only Adam's father had done the same. But he was gone, leaving behind him an impenetrable wall of silence. No one in his family – least of all his mother – wanted to talk about the trauma that had exploded their lives like a nuclear bomb. Manacled by shame, the questions that needed asking were left unsaid, until they'd almost forgotten what they were.

Adam breathed a heavy sigh. This case was getting under his skin. And if McNally meant trouble – then he was just going to have to risk it.

17

Phone call

'Adam, you won't believe what Brenda Hoffman has gone and done now. She's dyed her hair red! At her age! Can you believe it? I said to Judy, "Judy, what on earth does Brenda think she looks like?" And Judy said, "At her age? Can you believe it?"'

'I don't think I even know who Brenda Hoffman is, Mum.'

'Of course you do! Brenda! Big Brenda, from Walford Road. Very unhappy marriage – comfort-ate. But she's done Weight-Watchers now, and credit where credit's due, she really does look well. I said, "Brenda, you'll have to give me some of those slimming recipes!" And actually there's a lovely one for spaghetti bolognese where instead of spaghetti it's courgette, and instead of bolognese it's just, well, seasoning. I'll make it for you next time you're home.'

'Er, can't wait.'

'What's that noise? Where are you?'

'That's just the traffic – I'm on my way back from Thames Magistrates' Court. I was representing this man who was arrested for shoplifting, but I've got him a conditional discharge.

That means he's released and there will be no further action unless he commits another offence.'

'Oh, well done, Ad. I bet the gentleman was pleased with that.'

'He was actually. So pleased that he went immediately to the shop next door and nicked me a box of chocolates.'

'How nice. You wouldn't think of a criminal having such lovely manners, would you?'

'Well . . .'

'Are you eating properly, anyway? What did you have for your lunch?'

'I haven't actually had time for lunch yet today but I'll just grab—'

'You haven't had lunch yet? Adam, it's two-fifteen! That's it, I'm getting the bus to yours and I'm bringing you enough soup for a week, you can take it to work in that nice flask Grandma got you for your birthday, with the cats on . . .'

'Mum, please don't put yourself to that trouble, I've got to work late tonight anyway so I won't be there. The prosecution in the Knight case are disclosing their evidence today.'

'You work too hard, Adam.'

'Mum, can I ask you something?'

'Anything, my love.'

'Do you still wonder? About what was going through Dad's head that night?'

A pause.

'Mum, are you still there?'

'Yes, but Adam, you know that I don't like to—'

'It's just this case, and the fact no one believes Jimmy Knight either, and I just wonder what might have happened

116

if someone had tried, you know, really *tried*, to clear Dad's name . . .'

'It's ancient history, Adam. It can't do any good to rake over all that now.'

'Mum—'

'Adam love, I've got to go, or I'll be late for the Ladies' Guild.'

'I didn't mean to upset you, it's just—'

'I've really got to go, Adam . . . Don't forget to eat.'

18

It didn't get easier to watch.

Adam rewound the CCTV footage, and pressed 'play' again. Saw the figure of Grant Cliveden stagger in the witness box, grasp his chest. There was half a second of shocked delay before the other occupants of the court were on their feet. An usher was the first to reach the witness box, fumbling with the door before he half pulled, half dragged the stricken police officer out and helped him lie down on the floor. The barristers were next, two KCs and their juniors, flapping in alarm, while the clerk rang desperately for an ambulance. Even the defendants were on their toes in the dock, alarm just about visible on their blurred faces as they craned to get a look. Then the unmistakable glacial figure of Ms Justice Charlotte Wickstead, proffering a glass of water to one of the crouching barristers who held it to the dying police officer's lips.

The CCTV had no sound, so the whole scene was like a grim tableau from a silent movie. By the time the paramedics came rushing into the courtroom just minutes later, the clerk was hurriedly ushering the jury out of the room. They jostled with each other and peered anxiously over shoulders, towards where Cliveden was lying, quite still.

Adam pressed 'pause'. He'd watched it enough times to know what happened next. The paramedics' efforts were in vain — the short sequence ended with Cliveden's body being removed in a zipped body bag. The courtroom emptied, leaving only Judge Wickstead there alone. The angle of the CCTV made it impossible to see her face, but those who were there that day said that even her usual steely composure was disturbed. Talk around the Bar was that this was the reason she'd been so determined to sit on the case where Cliveden's alleged killer would be tried.

'The prosecution will open with that, for sure,' said Rupert, from over Adam's shoulder. He plonked a brimming coffee by Adam's elbow. 'Real emotive stuff. Get them to focus on the brutality of the death.'

'I'm sure you're right,' said Adam. 'I don't think it helps or hinders our case one way or another, though — all it does is show that Cliveden was poisoned and died at the Old Bailey, which we already know.'

They were in Jonathan's room — without Jonathan. It was two days since the disclosure of used material had been made, three days since his conversation with Tony about McNally, and Adam already had three notebooks worth of questions, suggestions and lines of inquiry for the case. He had drafted a defence case statement, stating that Knight was not responsible for the murder — and that there were other suspects who would have motive and opportunity to carry out Cliveden's murder.

Trying to get time with his pupil master to discuss it, however, had been predictably difficult. It was Friday afternoon and Jonathan had left at three, so Rupert had kindly agreed to take a look at some of the evidence to give Adam a second opinion.

'Where is Jonathan, anyway?' Rupert asked, examining the golfing trophy that was acting as a paperweight on his desk.

'Well, his wife thinks he's visiting his daughter at boarding school in Rugby. And his daughter thinks he's been urgently called to Edinburgh on business.'

'So he's with his mistress?'

'No, she thinks he's in hospital with gallstones.'

'So where is he really?'

'With his girlfriend, of course. They've got some kind of Tesco Clubcard deal on a Marriott near Swindon.'

Rupert snorted. 'I don't know how you put up with it . . . So he hasn't seen all this yet?'

'Bits. But he was a little distracted, you know . . .'

'So what else have you got?'

'There's this,' Adam tapped a stack of papers, which was topped with a photograph of an old Nokia mobile sealed in an evidence bag. 'This is the burner phone they recovered from Knight's address.' He flipped the page. 'And these are the messages they found on it. Just one number is saved – it's Cliveden's. On 12 March – the day before he dies – this message is sent from the phone.'

Rupert squinted as he read the message. 'Well, that doesn't make a lot of sense.'

He was right. Adam had been over and over the message but it seemed to be in some sort of code.

D/d aeries & blanco. Easy win. Can meet to discuss.

'And this next is Cliveden's reply?'

'Yep – he writes, "Who is this?" Not "What on earth are you talking about?" so it must make sense to him.'

The reply from Knight's phone was just as cryptic.

A friend of J. He said to tell you S699 – you'd know what it meant.

'Well, at least someone knows what it meant,' joked Rupert.

Cliveden had written back: When and where?

Burner phone: Old Nag's Head, Bouverie Street. Midday. Come alone.

Rupert looked up. 'And that's it?'

'Yes,' Adam nodded. 'That's the sum total of phone data the prosecution has released. It's why I'm suggesting that on our defence case statement we ask for all the extra evidence from Cliveden's phone to be handed over, because we just don't have enough information at the moment. Whatever that stuff means – "aeries", "blanco", "J", "S699" – it was enough to convince Cliveden that he should meet this unknown person.'

'And does the prosecution have a theory on that?'

'I don't know – maybe they won't bother. All that really matters to them is that Knight said enough to Cliveden to lure him into a meeting. But I think this exchange doesn't just tell us about the person who sent the messages, it tells us about Cliveden too. What does he think this meeting is all about? That could be the key to understanding who would want to kill him and why.'

'So what's your boy saying? Can't he shed some light on it?'

'He's saying it's not his phone. He didn't send the messages.'

'That would be a bit more believable if he hadn't then shown up at the Old Nag's Head exactly as planned.'

Adam nodded. 'Right. He claims someone he knows told him where Cliveden would be. But he won't say who, and I don't know why.'

Rupert's brow furrowed. 'Was there anything else on the phone?'

'There were three calls to this number,' said Adam, tapping a phone number halfway down the page. 'Two the night before the murder, and one the morning of. And yes – we've looked it up, but it's unregistered too.'

'And your boy can't help with that either?'

'Still insists the phone's not his. It is helpfully free of prints – someone knew enough to wipe it – but it was still found in the flat where Knight was staying, alone. Anyway, Knight did turn up to the meet, early in fact.'

He cued up the next file of CCTV – the footage taken from the Old Nag's Head. He was about to press 'play' when the door of Jonathan's office was pushed open abruptly.

'Rupes! There you are. Rory is legit doing my head in today – no, I can't go into it, you'd just die. But I wondered if you could be a total darling and reach me down the Smith and Hogan text-book in the library? Oh, hi, Adam.'

'Hi,' said Adam, rather grumpily. Of course Georgina had 'Rupes' running around after her like a manservant.

'I will in a minute, just going through some CCTV with Adam right now,' said Rupert mildly.

'Ooh, juicy!' exclaimed Georgina, bouncing round the desk to peer over Adam's shoulder. 'This is the Botox Butcher, right?'

'It's the evidence for Jimmy Knight's trial, yes,' said Adam stiffly.

'Well, are you going to show us or not?' Up close the scent of Georgina's sweet perfume and minty chewing gum was strangely hypnotic.

Adam pressed 'play'. The footage shot in the pub was of much worse quality than the Old Bailey CCTV – the lens smeared and the movement jerky. But Jimmy Knight was still instantly recognisable when he entered the pub not long after it opened, at 11.15 a.m. He went straight to the bar, where he ordered what looked like a whisky, and downed it in one. He seemed to exchange a few words with the barman, before he went to sit at a table in the corner, furthest from the camera.

'God, what a weirdo,' Georgina said. 'Look how he's just staring into space – not looking at his phone or anything.'

'He didn't have a phone with him,' Adam explained. 'Or at least, the police weren't able to triangulate any data placing a phone connected to Knight at this pub.' He glanced at Rupert. 'Strengthens the argument that the burner phone wasn't his.'

'Or weakens it,' said Rupert. 'Because it suggests he knew the police would run those tests.'

They watched in silence for the long ten minutes in which Knight sat perfectly still, eyes fixed on the middle distance. If it wasn't for the movements of the barman polishing glasses in the foreground, you'd think the camera was broken.

'How long does this go on for?'

'Wait – yes, here we go.'

Knight had got up from his seat, and headed towards the door, where he stood, as if waiting for someone. The camera was angled in such a way that you could see he was by the door, but not what he was looking at. After about ten minutes of him standing like a statue at his sentry post, he returned to his table and sat down. Three and a half minutes later, Cliveden entered.

'There he is – does he recognise Knight?' said Rupert excitedly.

'It's hard to tell – but I don't think so,' said Adam. 'Look how they shake hands, like they've never met before. You'd think that if Cliveden realised this is a guy he put behind bars he might not look so comfortable.'

The men chatted briefly, before Knight rose again and went to the bar. He ordered, and then, for a split second, looked directly at the CCTV camera. The barman pulled a pint, then filled up a glass with what looked like Coke, before placing them on the counter in front of Knight. Then he turned to his till.

'This is the moment, right here,' breathed Adam. 'This is when the prosecution says he slipped in the poison.'

All three of them craned closer, so their faces were just inches from the laptop screen. They watched as Knight angled his body over the two glasses, in such a way that they were momentarily invisible to the camera. Then he straightened up, just in time for the barman to turn back.

'I mean, you can't really tell . . .' began Rupert.

'No, wait, it gets better,' said Adam. The barman was handing Knight his change, and as he did so, his sleeve caught the pint of Coke. It almost fell, and in the fumble both the barman and Knight reached to catch it. Again, Knight's broad shoulders blocked the view of exactly what happened to the drink, but when he turned around, he had both glasses safely in his hands and full to the brim.

'Something could have—'

'Exactly,' grinned Adam. 'If you accept that Knight had the chance to slip something into Cliveden's drink, then you have to accept that the barman did too. Because this footage isn't conclusive. I've slowed it down and zoomed in, and no matter how you do it, you can't see for sure if he does or doesn't put something in the drink.'

Georgina raised an eyebrow. 'Is that the best you've got?'

'Well, it's a start, isn't it? All we've got to do is create reasonable doubt.'

'OK. I'm not sure a jury will see it that way.'

Adam knew she was just trying to wind him up, but it was working. His blood temperature was rising, and he struggled to make sure the volume of his voice didn't rise too.

'The so-called poisoning isn't *actually* on camera. That means everything else is circumstan—'

'Circumstantial, yes. But you have to admit the circumstances are pretty damning.'

'Well, I'll just have to hope for a jury with a better grasp of the standard of proof than you—'

'WHAT ON EARTH IS GOING ON HERE?' It was Jonathan, standing in the doorway, tweed jacket flapping open and overnight bag in hand. 'This is *my* room, not some kind of . . .' He cast around for the right insult. '. . . junior common room!'

'Sorry, Jonathan, we've been going through the Knight material,' said Adam as the three of them scrambled to their feet. 'We've actually made some good progress. There's loads of ways we can build a strong case – I can go through it now with you if you like.'

Jonathan sighed theatrically and started rifling through one of his filing cabinets, ignoring what Adam had said.

'We wouldn't have been in here if I'd known you were still around,' Adam added hurriedly. 'I thought you were gone for the day.'

'I was,' said Jonathan peevishly, finally pulling something blue and shiny from the cabinet with a flourish. 'I forgot my Clubcard.'

He turned on his heel and flounced out, while Rupert stifled his laughter, leaving the door swinging open behind him.

Adam waited until he was out of earshot. 'But there's another thing you should know about this guy – the barman,' he said, pointing at the paused footage. 'He's not just a random person. He was Knight's barrister, in the armed robbery case a decade ago. Which was right before he got struck off – for corruption.'

'*What?*' Rupert and Georgina exclaimed in unison.

'Surely it can't be a coincidence, can it? And he doesn't mention it in his police statement – and neither did Knight.'

'Have you tried to talk to him?' Rupert asked.

'I've tried,' said Adam. 'I've been down to the pub every day and evening since I found out – it's only a ten-minute walk from here. But every time it's been completely shut up.'

'Almost like the guy doesn't want to be found.'

'Right,' said Adam, nodding.

Georgina was deep in thought and, for once, it didn't look like she had anything sarcastic to say.

'If they put him on the stand and that comes out in court, it could go either way,' Rupert said. 'Yes, he could be seen as an alternative suspect – but it could also suggest a conspiracy, with Knight at the middle of it.'

'I know, and that's why I've got to talk to him,' said Adam. 'One way or another, he's hiding something. Tony reckons he was tangled up with a load of gangsters back in the day, laundering their money and fixing their cases. Who's to say he hasn't gone from enabler to killer?'

'Bloody hell, that's quite a theory,' said Rupert. 'Look, your best bet might just be to show that he's not a credible witness because of his past . . .'

'That won't be enough,' said Adam. 'Because almost everything he's going to say in his testimony is right there on CCTV anyway. I need to get to the bottom of how the hell he is involved – and if he had a reason to want Cliveden dead and Knight fitted up.'

'Adam, this sounds really dangerous,' Georgina cut in. 'You should leave that sort of stuff to the police. And if they didn't think it was a line of inquiry worth pursuing then—'

'Georgina, it is our *job* to ask questions!' Adam exploded, surprising himself with the force of his outburst. 'We can't just accept everything we're told: Knight looks guilty and the police think he's guilty so therefore he bloody is. There is a known criminal associate at the middle of the case and no one seems remotely interested in why, so don't you dare tell me that it's too dangerous to bother with. You know what's really dangerous? Getting a fucking useless lawyer who's happy to condemn you for a crime you didn't commit, just because to do anything else looks too much like hard work.' He slammed his hands down in front of him. As he caught his breath, he saw that both Georgina and Rupert were looking at him with alarm.

'Adam, mate, Georgina's just trying to help,' said Rupert tentatively.

'Yeah, right,' said Adam, starting to feel uneasy with how he'd lost his temper.

Georgina's face was flushed. 'Oh, fuck you, Adam,' she said, turning on her heel. 'Do what you want – I don't care.' She slammed the door of Jonathan's office behind her.

Rupert was still regarding Adam nervously, concern written all over his face.

'Are you all right, mate?' he said. 'I know pupillage can be intense, and with this case on top of everything else . . . If it's all getting too much, then—'

'It's not too much,' said Adam, quickly. 'I'm sorry, I was out of line. I'll apologise to Georgina. It's just . . . I really care about this case.'

'I can tell,' said Rupert. 'And passion is good. But a good lawyer doesn't get personally involved. Try and keep some distance; listen to your head and not your heart and all that.'

Adam nodded as Rupert clapped him on the shoulder. As his friend headed back to his own room, Adam put his head in his hands and turned back to the evidence.

Don't get personally involved.

It was too late for that.

19

'Don't you think it's strange, though?' It was Monday and Adam had been obsessively reading and rereading the computer and mobile phone evidence against Knight, and rewatching the CCTV until his eyes strained. So much for Rupert's advice to try and switch off from the case. He had to admit that McNally would have needed extraordinary sleight of hand to have managed to put poison in the drink, but his bizarre connection to Knight was still playing on Adam's mind. He'd spent most of his weekend in a Pret just down from the Old Nag's Head, watching to see if anyone came or went, but nobody had and the pub had remained resolutely closed.

Meanwhile, Jonathan had spent the weekend . . . Well, Adam would rather not think about it. All he cared about in this moment was getting his pupil master to listen to him.

Jonathan barely looked up from his briefing notes. 'What's strange?' he snapped. He was reading up on the Kavanagh case. They were in the barristers' mess at the Old Bailey, nominally having a meeting about Knight's case before they headed into Kavanagh's pre-trial hearing, but so far Jonathan had shown only monumental disinterest in Adam's impassioned review of the evidence.

'That Reg McNally was only interviewed as a witness, not as a suspect, when he'd had exactly the same opportunity to poison Cliveden as Jimmy did. And arguably a motive too.'

'You said yourself, the CCTV shows that he would barely have had the chance.'

'OK, but it's still weird that the police didn't even consider it, especially given his past. And don't you think it's also strange that we have so little idea about what else Cliveden did that day? We don't know who else he called or texted in the twenty-four hours up to his death, or even who he might have met.'

Jonathan looked up at last and sighed. 'Do I think it's strange that once the police found the killer they stopped looking?'

'*Alleged* killer—'

'No, I don't think it is remotely strange. *They* know, *I* know, even *you* know that no one else could have done this. Knight's case is a farce, and I'd rather not spend any more time than absolutely necessary thinking about it. Today I need your total focus on the only client who really matters – Mr Charles Kavanagh.'

Jonathan drained his coffee and looked at his watch. 'Charles will be here in twenty minutes. Show time!'

Reluctantly, Adam trailed his pupil master up the stairs from the mess to the robing room. Female barristers had a separate robing room, so the male one – which was long and rectangular, lined with benches and hooks – had that distinctive smell of testosterone common to football dressing rooms and school PE changing rooms the world over. It was where briefs pumped themselves up before a big case and calmed themselves down afterwards. It was also, crucially, the epicentre for Old Bailey gossip.

Adam shuffled over to his own locker, while Jonathan loudly greeted two ruddy-faced associates. Adam noted with disgust that it was Hugh Montgomery and Brian Flynn, two men he would put in his top five most-despised senior barristers. Well, Montgomery was all right, he supposed, if you didn't mind his honking laugh, raging sexism and fondness for extolling the virtues of foxhunting at any given opportunity. But Flynn – his was the sort of face that was set in a permanent sneer, and he was known for bullying his way through trials with little regard for victims, families or, indeed, normal moral standards. And, Adam remembered with a sting, he'd once overheard Flynn make the sort of insidious antisemitic remark that could be shrugged off as naivety – but really, really wasn't.

Adam put his head down and fiddled with his collar as the three men greeted each other with lots of noisy cries of 'old boy' and slaps of shoulders. They quickly fell into the usual offensive banter about their cases – Montgomery had an 'easy' rape defence in which the victim was 'just a common tart', while Flynn was defending in a gang murder case, or 'natural selection', as he called it.

'Anyway, what about you and the Botox Butcher?' Flynn said eventually, his eyes glittering with mischief. 'How does it feel to have to do some heavy lifting again?'

Jonathan huffed and puffed. 'I've been stitched up like a prize kipper with that one,' he said. 'But between you and me, chaps, there are a few gaps in the prosecution's case, so all is not lost.'

Adam's ears pricked up. He knew Jonathan was just showing

off to his mates, but it was the first time his pupil master had admitted any kind of interest in making the case a success.

'Breaks one's heart, doesn't it,' said Flynn, his voice dripping with sarcasm. 'A police officer, a public hero – a *family man* no less.'

'Well . . . Cliveden was a family man in the way that *you're* a family man,' Montgomery quipped, giving Jonathan a knowing wink.

'Oh, really?' Jonathan said with what sounded like admiration.

'Just ask Raquel in the clerks' office.'

The three men snorted with laughter like naughty schoolboys, and quickly descended into an innuendo-heavy analysis of Raquel's various 'assets'. Adam didn't want to listen to their lewd jokes, but his interest had been massively piqued. If it was true that Cliveden had been unfaithful, and the tabloids found out, they'd have to choke back their sentimental drivel.

The tannoy system crackled into life: 'All parties in The Crown versus C. Kavanagh to Court Twelve please.'

Jonathan was suddenly serious again. 'Green!' he bellowed at Adam, as if summoning a dog. 'Gentlemen.' A slight incline of his head bid his friends farewell.

As pupil and pupil master strode to Court 12, Adam tried to engage Jonathan in a conversation about what he'd just heard.

'Do you think it's true about Cliveden and Raquel? Should we talk to her?' he said.

Jonathan looked at him sharply. 'You shouldn't eavesdrop. Nasty, common habit.'

'I'm sorry, I didn't mean to, but—'

'No buts. You absolutely will not talk to Raquel. In fact, I forbid it. She is the clerk of the judge in our case, and for heaven's sake, you are a barrister – or at least pretending to be.'

'But I really think—'

'*Enough!*' Jonathan's face was white with rage. 'We are here for our client Mr Charles Kavanagh and not for your ludicrous conspiracy theories.'

Adam relented. He'd pushed too far. Every time he fought for Knight he was alienating his pupil master that much more. And that meant Jonathan's valuable vote for his tenancy was getting less and less likely.

But there was no time to apologise, because Jonathan was already slapping on an expression of lurid sycophancy and opening his arms wide to greet his 'dear Charles'. Kavanagh, who looked like he might have dunked his hair in a vat of cooking oil that morning, was accompanied by a statuesque woman dripping in diamonds, who was about a foot taller and twenty years younger than him.

'And Oksana, how wonderful to see you again,' said Jonathan, planting a kiss on her hand. 'Let's get this over with, shall we?'

He ushered the pair into court, shooting a black look over his shoulder at Adam as he did so. It was a warning, and Adam heard it loud and clear.

Adam took his place on the bench behind Jonathan, alongside Kavanagh's flashy-looking solicitor, in an expensive suit and enormous Rolex, who looked at him as if he'd rolled in fox poo. The court rose for the judge – stone-faced Mr Justice Aubrey Palmerson – and the hearing began. It was a technical case and there were many parameters to be discussed between defence and prosecution ahead of the trial, each more boring than the last. Adam felt his eyes droop, but for once Jonathan seemed fully absorbed – and even looked to be making a decent fist of things, springing to his feet frequently with the energy of a particularly eager cocker spaniel.

His pupil master's bouffant hair seemed to quiver with excitement, and it was a good forty minutes before Adam realised what a golden opportunity he had. Nothing could distract Jonathan now – least of all the absence of his pupil. So Adam got quietly to his feet, bowed to the judge and tiptoed out of the chamber, on the pretence of going to the bathroom. Jonathan didn't even give him a second look.

The Old Bailey was a labyrinth, and Adam was not yet confident that he knew all of its secrets. But he chanced it on a back staircase down to the second floor, where he knew the clerks had their empire.

Just as clerks were crucial to the smooth running of the barristers' chambers, courts would not function without their own engine room of clerks. They managed all the crucial administration, ensuring everyone was in court when required as well as organising the judges' diaries and managing their time like fussy parents, recording pleas and verdicts, jury notes, rulings, orders and sentences. And long after the judges went home, they still beavered away on the paperwork in their mysterious realm where organisation and efficiency were king.

It wasn't usual for a barrister to find themselves in this place, and Adam proceeded tentatively along a gloomy corridor of closed office doors, until he reached a hatch in the wall that acted as a makeshift reception. He peered in – the small room directly behind was deserted but for one occupant, a woman about his age with freckles and soft blonde curls, stirring a cup of herbal tea.

'Hello, sir!' she said brightly. 'Are you lost?'

'Er, no, I'm looking for Raquel.'

'She's not here, I'm afraid, she's in court. But I work with her – maybe I can help? I'm Abi, by the way.' She smiled at him guilelessly, and Adam felt the jolt of nervousness he always got around pretty girls. He resisted the urge to run.

'My name is Adam Green, and I'm on the Grant Cliveden murder trial. I'm representing Jimmy Knight.'

Abi's eyes widened. 'That's a big one! You're very young to be doing that, aren't you? You must be really good!'

Adam blushed. 'Well, I'm just a junior. And I'm trying to find out some extra information about DI Cliveden.' He realised he needed to tread carefully. 'Just in the interests of the case. From what I understand, he was a regular at the Bailey and quite – er – friendly with some people in the clerks' office?'

Abi took a sip of her tea. 'Well, I wouldn't really know about that. I only started working here about a week before he died. So I'd never met him before that.'

'I see,' Adam tried to hide his disappointment. 'Has Raquel ever spoken about him? Were they friends, do you know?'

Abi thought for a minute. 'I guess we have spoken about him – but then everyone in the country has really, haven't they! But they must have been on friendly terms, yes. Because otherwise she wouldn't have got him that coffee.'

'What coffee?'

'Ah, sorry, I should have said! It's really sad actually – it was the day he died. Raquel had just been to Costa, and she'd got a couple of coffees – I said, "Oh, thank you, but I don't drink coffee." ' She gestured at her camomile tea. 'And Raquel said, "I've just seen DI Cliveden arrive" – he was the police witness in our drugs case, so I knew who he was even though I'd not met him. She said, "He always likes a flat white – can you run down and give it to him?" So I did, and he was so charming, and very handsome . . .' Abi trailed off, a wistful look in her eye. 'It's funny to think, isn't it, that less than an hour later he was dead? Just absolutely tragic.'

Adam was astonished. She didn't know what she was saying, but Abi had just revealed that Cliveden's possible lover had had a drink delivered to him – right before he'd dropped dead from poisoning.

'So if they were friends, Raquel must have been quite upset by what happened,' Adam remarked.

'Sort of, I suppose,' said Abi. 'She was definitely shaken. And she said something about how we should be thankful for those people who will stop at nothing to keep us all safe, which I thought was a lovely tribute. Anyway, did you want me to pass on a message to Raquel?'

'No, that's all right, thank you.' Adam's mind was racing. 'I'll try and catch her another time – but thank you, you've been really helpful.'

As he walked down the corridor he couldn't stop thinking – when she'd praised the people who would stop at nothing to keep others safe, had Raquel been talking about the victim – or the killer?

20

Adam knew he should go back to court, but he needed time to think. Instead of taking the stairs back up to the third floor, he wandered aimlessly towards the canteen, half wondering whether he might have a cup of tea and a KitKat. There was a 'dining room' for advocates on the fifth floor, but Adam much preferred the hustle and bustle of the brightly lit public cafe, where court staff, police, members of the public and bailed defendants were all equal. It was ruled with an iron fist by squeaky-voiced Filipina matriarch Divina, who would often tell you that the jacket potato was available but without any beans, cheese or even butter – and expect you to be grateful anyway.

With most courtrooms in session, the canteen was unusually quiet – save for Divina's cheerful rendition of Diana Ross's 'Upside Down'. But to his delight, Adam spotted a familiar figure at a table near the window – Rupert.

'Hi, mate!' he said, hurrying over and pulling out the spare chair. 'You won't believe what I've just heard. So I was in the robing room with JTC, and he's chatting to a couple of those dinosaur KCs, and—'

'Adam—'

'—they start saying this stuff about one of the clerks – like, alluding that she's been having an affair with Cliveden. So I go down to the clerks' rooms and—'

'Adam!'

'—I get chatting to this junior clerk and she says—' Adam broke off abruptly. Standing over him, looking pointedly at the chair he was sitting in, was the FLO PC Owens, holding two cups of coffee.

'Adam, this is Emma,' said Rupert, hesitantly, his cheeks a little pink. 'Emma, this is Adam: he's a pupil at my chambers.'

There was a pause as the three of them assessed the awkwardness of the situation. From Rupert's manner, and the fact Emma had rather bright lipstick on, Adam surmised that he had crashed some kind of date.

'I'm in your seat, aren't I?' said Adam to Emma, because he didn't know what else to say.

'Just grab another chair, Ad,' Rupert said hurriedly, before Adam could excuse himself. Classic Rupert, thought Adam – he'd have so hated the idea of making the situation briefly uncomfortable that he'd accidentally made it long-term uncomfortable instead.

As Adam pulled a metal chair from under the nearest table, Rupert explained how he and Emma knew each other. 'Emma's the FLO on the infanticide case I told you about,' he said. 'It's been a bit of a gruelling one actually, so we just thought we'd have a bit of a catch-up . . . And, anyway, here we are.'

Rupert grinned at Emma, who gave a tight smile, her eyes flicking to Adam. If she recognised him as a witness to the incident with Natasha Cliveden a few months ago, she didn't show it. She wasn't wearing her glasses, and without them Adam noticed how clear and green her eyes were. He could see why Rupert was stumbling over his words a bit.

'It's cases like these that make you appreciate how hard it is being an FLO, and how valuable the work is,' Rupert gabbled on, desperately resisting any kind of clumsy silence. 'Em's been with the grandparents of the little lad who died. They're really lucky to have you with them; some of the stuff that came out today — it breaks your heart.'

'I'm just doing my job,' said Emma modestly, her voice warm with broad Yorkshire vowels.

'How long have you been an FLO? Is it what you always wanted to do?' Adam asked Emma, even though he knew the answer.

She shifted a little in her seat. 'Not too long actually — about eight months,' she said. 'Before that I was on the serious crime squad.'

'Serious crime?' Adam feigned surprise. 'Then you must have known Grant Cliveden. I'm defending in that case.'

Adam didn't think he imagined the shadow that passed over her face. 'Yeah, I knew him,' she said shortly.

'Did you? My word!' said Rupert. 'You never said! What was he like? It feels like we all know him now, he's in the papers that much, but how surreal — and sad — it must have been for those of you who actually *did* know him.'

'I guess,' said Emma, fiddling with the lid on her coffee cup. 'He was a bit more . . . complicated . . . than the papers would have you believe.'

'So you worked directly with him?'

'Yes — he was my supervisor.'

Adam was watching her closely. She wasn't comfortable with where this conversation was going, that was for sure. But Rupert seemed to have put it down to grief.

'I'm sorry, it must have been such a hard time for you,' he said, twitching as if he was about to grab her hand, then thinking better of it. Changing the subject instead, he went on: 'Serious crime must have been an exciting place to work. Catching crooks and all that. How come you decided to move?'

Emma gave a wry smile. 'It was exciting – for a bit. But I guess I just thought we were catching the wrong crooks. Anyway, family liaison is valuable work, as you say.'

'And you're really good at it,' said Rupert firmly. The conversation moved back to the case they were both on, and Adam used the opportunity to go and order himself a coffee. He knew he should be getting back to court, but the chance meeting with Emma Owens was too good to pass up. He still didn't understand what had happened between her and Natasha Cliveden – or why she could not bring herself to say a single nice thing about her former boss now that he was dead.

When he got back to the table, Rupert and Emma were talking about the Hoxton Three, a murder trial that had made waves at the Bar lately because of how extraordinarily long it had lasted.

'I'm telling you, total numb bum after that one,' Emma was saying. 'And I was only in court for twenty-six days – the poor jurors were there for sixty!' She and Rupert both laughed.

Adam sipped his coffee and did a quick mental calculation.

'So you were FLO for the victim's family, in the Hoxton Three?'

'Yes, that's right,' she said, jovial and friendly now that they weren't talking about Cliveden. 'It was a fascinating case, but thank goodness the family got justice after sitting through all that.'

'Didn't that case sit all through March?'

'It did, yes.'

'So you were here the day Cliveden was murdered?'

There was a pause – Rupert looked at Adam quizzically. 'I'm sorry, Emma, Adam has a bit of a one-track mind at the moment – I'm sure he didn't mean to bring up anything that would upset you.'

'It doesn't upset me,' Emma said defiantly, but her tone was cold now. 'And yes, I was here. We passed each other on the way in – I could never have imagined what was about to happen.'

It was Rupert's turn to look surprised. 'You must have been one of the last people to see him alive! I'm so sorry, Emma, I had no idea – we shouldn't be making you relive all this.'

'It's all right, honestly,' Emma said, recovering herself, and even managing a slightly unconvincing smile in Adam's direction. Rupert expertly steered the conversation on, and within minutes the two of them were having an impassioned discussion about their mutual love of Labradors.

It was Adam's cue to leave. They were so deep in conversation they barely acknowledged him when he said he had to get back to court, and Adam hoped his friend would forgive him for how bullishly he'd interrupted their romantic tête-à-tête. But he was glad he had, because now he knew two crucial facts: Emma Owens had a history with Grant Cliveden that she'd rather keep secret – and, more importantly, she'd been there just before he'd died.

21

Phone call

'Mum, it's Adam. I haven't heard from you for a few days, so just checking you're all right. I know you're probably busy with work and bridge and keeping an eye on the neighbours, ha-ha. But you know what? You were right about that new bathroom cleaner you left. It does smell nicer than the usual kind, and you wouldn't know it was cheaper. Yes, that's right – I cleaned my sink. Miracles do happen.

'I hope you're not upset because of what I said about Dad the other day. I guess this case I'm on has just got me thinking about the unfairness of it all. I know everyone said that the fact he took his own life before he could stand trial was evidence of a guilty conscience. But you never really believed that, did you?

'I know you hate talking about it. And I promised I was going to put it behind me too. You're right, it's in the past, and he's not around to tell us what really happened. But I guess I'm wondering . . . maybe it's not too late to fight for the truth. Just because it looks like there's one obvious answer, it doesn't mean that if you dig a little deeper then . . . I don't know. Maybe we need to talk about it? I was so young, but if there's anything you can remember that we could use to clear his name . . . that's got to be worth a try, don't you think?

'Anyway . . . give me a call when you get this. Love you.'

22

'People don't murder each other because affairs go wrong,' Jonathan boomed. They were in the courtyard outside chambers as Jonathan smoked a cigarette. 'Trust me. And they don't murder each other because of unsuccessful working relationships either – otherwise you might be dead.'

It was the same circular conversation they'd been having for days, ever since the prosecution had come back to deny their request for the release of extra data from Cliveden's phone.

Adam was trying to persuade his pupil master to put in a section 8 application, which would ask the judge to overrule this decision and give them access to the victim's text messages and phone records.

'Jonathan, we say in our defence case statement that someone other than Jimmy killed Cliveden. But at the moment we don't have anything that proves that.'

'My point exactly!'

'But the phone records – they could fill in the gaps. Everyone thinks Cliveden is a hero, but there's so much about him we don't know. What was going on with Raquel? With Emma Owens? And his wife – she was acting weird too, wasn't she?

And what did those text messages from the burner phone mean to him? And why did he go to the pub? Then there's the fact that Knight's old barrister, who just happens to be a disgraced associate of organised crime, was manning the bar in the pub where he was allegedly poisoned . . .'

'Well, that we can maybe use. If the police didn't know about it, then potentially they didn't do their job properly.'

'We need more,' said Adam. 'There's a lot that doesn't stack up.'

'Trashing the victim is not generally a very good strategy, Adam,' said Jonathan curtly.

'I'm not saying we need to trash him. But we need to understand him at the very least,' Adam said. 'There's the hearing tomorrow – I've already drafted the section 8. This is our last chance to get a look at that stuff on Cliveden's phone.'

Jonathan shrugged. 'I'm not going to the hearing, so you can do what you like. Knock yourself out.'

Adam blanched. 'You're not . . . going to the hearing?' Tomorrow was the final hearing before Knight's trial, and he had assumed Jonathan would be leading it. It was practically unheard of for a pupil to represent a client accused of murder, alone – even if it was just a hearing.

'I've got lunch with Kavanagh,' said Jonathan, tossing his cigarette butt on the ground and grinding it with his heel. 'You're on your feet, aren't you? No reason you can't give it a go, seeing as you so clearly believe you know best in this case.'

Adam felt his face turn from white to red. 'I don't mean that . . . I really think—'

'It's not up for discussion,' said Jonathan, looking at his watch. 'Now, you better run along – don't you have some scrubber in

Westminster Mags you're meant to be representing?' He gave Adam a wolfish smile.

Adam looked at his own watch – it was later than he'd thought. He was due in court in an hour defending a drugs offence. He took off quickly towards the Tube station, breaking into a jog once he was out of Jonathan's eyesight. If he rushed, there was time for a quick pit-stop at Caffè Nero – where he'd be able to email that section 8 application just in time.

He couldn't believe his pupil master was abandoning his responsibilities in Knight's case. If Jonathan had wanted Adam to lead the hearing on his own, couldn't he at least have given him more than twenty-four hours' warning? Luckily Adam had spent so long trying to convince Jonathan to apply for the unused material that his arguments were well rehearsed. But it was looking more and more like Jonathan wanted Adam to fail – and that would not bode well for his chances at tenancy.

The next morning, Adam was at the Old Bailey early, clutching print-outs of his section 8, knowing that these sorts of applications sometimes got lost in the creaking system. He tried to silence his jangling nerves as he hurried along the bustling corridors and down the staircase that led to the cells, nodding to the police and security guards who opened various gates and doors. As the natural light faded, to be replaced with the institutional glow of fluorescent strip lighting, he realised he had another valuable opportunity – the chance to speak to Knight alone again. He hadn't done so since that snatched meeting in Belmarsh a few weeks ago. This could be his last chance to persuade him to expand his proof of evidence, which was Knight's official version of events to be used in court. At the moment it was flimsy and unconvincing – but Adam was sure some more of Knight's secrets could flesh it out.

A final door was opened and Adam was shown into a tiny cell, so small a Shetland pony would have struggled to turn around in it. Knight filled half of the space, the bruises on his face mercifully less livid than they had been before, though still lurking like ominous shadows. He nodded briskly at Adam.

'Where's Taylor-Cameron?'

'I'm really sorry, he's not coming, he sends his apologies,' said Adam, setting his file down on the grubby table between them.

A look of disquiet floated over Knight's face like a cloud. 'I thought this guy was meant to be the best,' he muttered.

'Who told you that?' Adam asked, but Knight just shrugged. The shutters were coming down once more.

'Look, Jimmy, we don't have much time,' Adam said. 'So I'm going to get to the point. I know there are things you're not telling me, and I think that's a mistake. The prosecution's case is strong, and it's not much of a case for you to just say, "It's not me." We – I – need to know if there's stuff that's going to come out, or anything that can help your defence. So I'm going to ask you again: is there anything else you want to tell me?'

Knight snorted, but his expression didn't change. 'Everything I have to say is in that document already,' he said. 'I told you before, Adam – there are things you just don't need to know.'

Adam pushed the heels of his hands against his eyes in frustration. There was one card left to play.

'I know about Marcellus, Jimmy.' He looked up, his eyes searching his client's stony face for some sort of poker tell.

Knight nodded; there was no hint of shock, no jolt of emotion. 'Then you know how dangerous it is to ask the wrong questions.'

'Hang on – are you saying Marcellus's death is linked to all this?' He could barely fathom what he was hearing.

'I'm saying you're a smart lad, Adam,' Knight growled. 'So be smart, OK?'

The door banged open, a uniformed guard stood there, bearing handcuffs.

'Case called,' he said gruffly. 'Sir, you better get to court. We're to take the prisoner up.'

Adam gave Knight one last desperate glance. Knight gazed back at him steadily, a hint of kindness in his eyes. He shook his head. Whatever secrets he was still keeping, Adam would not be getting them today. Whether it was for his own protection, or for someone else's, he couldn't figure out.

But there was one question that he sensed would answer all the others. Who had killed Marcellus – and why?

23

They weren't in Court Number One today – they were in Court 14, a dismally institutional box with a scabby carpet and wood panelling in a headache-inducing shade of varnished orange. When Adam arrived he saw that the security guard had been overzealous and it did not look like the court session was going to start any time soon. The prosecution team hadn't yet arrived, and apart from the court officials only Nisha was there. She was shuffling papers frantically in between trying to do up the buttons of her cuffs.

'Have you been down to the cells to see Jimmy? I meant to but the nanny was late, then the Tube was a state and I ran out of time . . . But it should be pretty straightforward today, shouldn't it? Where's Jonathan?'

'He, er, got caught up,' said Adam, wondering why he kept covering for his lazy pupil master. Nisha's brow furrowed and her face made clear exactly what she thought of a KC who sent his pupil to do his work for him.

The *click-clack* of high heels heralded the arrival of Raquel, the court clerk. Adam's adrenalin started pumping. He wondered if he should defy Jonathan and seize this opportunity to talk to her about Cliveden. He was so distracted he barely heard what Nisha was asking him.

'Sorry, Nisha, what did you say?'

'I said, "Did you get the section 8 application in on time in the end?"'

'Yes, I did. Fingers crossed we get what we need.'

Raquel was fiddling with the recording system just in front of them, wearing a skin-tight leather skirt. When she turned around, her expression was severe.

'You've submitted a section 8?'

'For Cliveden's phone communications, yes,' Adam said, smiling pleasantly.

'Well, there's no point doing that,' Raquel snapped. Adam was taken aback. Sure, he was just a pupil, but even so – it was irregular for the court clerk to be telling a barrister how they should run their case.

'I think there's a strong argument it will aid our case,' he said evenly.

'She won't grant it,' said Raquel sharply. 'Judge Wickstead, I mean. There's no way she's going to be convinced that's a good idea, so there's no point riling her up by asking her.'

'With respect,' Nisha cut in, 'how would you know what the judge will or will not do, before you've even heard our arguments?'

Raquel was flustered now, but she tilted her chin up defiantly. 'I am with My Lady day in and day out – I know how she thinks about things,' she said. There was something possessive in the way she spoke about Wickstead, who clearly had a way of invoking loyalty – Adam had observed that in the way all the court officials responded to her. 'And you won't get legal aid to read it, so it's in your interests just to drop it.'

The prosecuting barrister, Ed Lowe, and his junior had arrived and Raquel took her cue to strut off, fussing over the prosecutors like a mother hen. If Adam hadn't been nervous before, he was now. It was nerve-wracking enough having to handle this hearing alone without Raquel telling him he was an idiot too. Sensing his anxiety, Nisha nudged him lightly.

'Don't listen to her. Moody cow doesn't know what she's talking about,' she said, reassuringly. 'You've got this, Adam.'

It was a mercy to have some support at least. Ed Lowe came over and they exchanged pleasantries. Adam tried to concentrate on whatever the Treasury Counsel was saying about triathlons, but it was hard when his breathing was as frayed as an old rag and his legs felt like jelly. Ed barely raised an eyebrow when Adam revealed that he would be representing the defence alone, with his pupil master absent.

'You'll be fine, mate,' he said, gently. 'Just work out exactly what you need to say, say it, and then stop. Good advocacy is about keeping it simple.'

Adam nodded. Had he just learned something more valuable in five minutes with Ed Lowe than he had in ten months with Jonathan? But that was why Ed was in 'the Room' – Treasury Counsel headquarters, where only the very best survived – while Jonathan was skipping court for lunch with his old golf buddy.

'All rise!'

Judge Charlotte Wickstead swept in, her black robes billowing around her like a witch's cape, carrying a folder in crimson leather that was the same colour as her perfectly painted lips. She took her seat and looked at the faces in the room turned towards her one by one. When she looked at Adam, it felt like a laser was dissecting his insides. Finally, she turned to Knight, who had just been shown into the dock. But her gaze didn't linger on him, and she quickly turned to Lowe and asked for his submissions. As Lowe got to his feet and eloquently started to make various points of order about witnesses and timings with practised ease, Adam rehearsed what he was going to say over and over again in his mind. He felt almost like he had left his body – surely that couldn't be him, defending alone, in an Old Bailey murder trial?

Finally, Judge Wickstead called the defence, her voice as smooth as buttercream. Adam got unsteadily to his feet and tried not to wilt in the midst of her razor stare.

'Adam Green for the defence, Your Honour,' he said. He caught Nisha's eye, and she gestured for him to speak up. 'You will have seen my section 8 application. Having received the schedule of unused material, the defence argues that we need disclosure of all communications to and from DI Cliveden's phone in the three months preceding his death.'

Judge Wickstead looked down at the printed application in front of her, and let the silence stretch just a little too long as she read it. Adam was about to open his mouth to say something else when he remembered Ed Lowe's sage advice. Say what needs to be said, then shut up. He glanced over his shoulder at Knight, behind the bulletproof glass panelling of the witness box. He was watching Wickstead, his face inscrutable.

'Mr Green, I understand you are very – forgive me – green,' she said. 'But you must surely know that the prosecution is only obliged to serve material if it clearly could support your case, and as yet, we don't know what that case actually is.'

Adam tried to swallow his nerves. 'Your Honour, I appreciate that this is a very unusual state of affairs. We have not yet given a full statement setting out what our client's defence will be, but it is our submission that, given Mr Cliveden's line of work, in all likelihood there are other parties who wished him ill. I seek his phone records to establish whether he was in touch with anyone else who may have had both motive and opportunity to poison him.'

The judge's red lip curled. She was looking at him as if he'd just executed a stinking turd on the courtroom floor.

'That sounds rather like a fishing expedition to me, which is exactly why the prosecution has already denied your request. No doubt the police disclosure officer has already diligently gone through all of that material and deemed it irrelevant. I am not minded to rule to overturn that decision on the basis of your extremely vague hunch.'

Adam's heart sank. It had been a long shot anyway – but Raquel had been right. Even making the request had been enough to rile the judge, and that wasn't going to help them at all. Raquel faced the court with her back to the judge and gave a little smirk in Adam's direction that said, I told you so.

Wickstead lifted her pen, as if about to rule. Then she stopped and caught Ed Lowe's eye.

'However,' she went on, 'I doubt it would harm the prosecution's case for you to have a look at this material, especially as it is unlikely to be served as part of the prosecution case – so you won't get paid for it under legal aid. What do you say, Mr Lowe? You and I both know what it's like to have difficult cases – and Mr Green here does seem extraordinarily keen to apprise himself of as much context as possible . . .'

'He does, Your Honour.'

'I am not going to rule that he has the right to see these phone records, but Mr Lowe, surely it would not harm your case if Mr Green was to be granted access? Perhaps he could see merely the past thirty days' worth of communications rather than ninety, which would reduce the photocopying burden on the prosecution. And of course, there will be no legal aid budget to cover this, so Mr Green will not bill for his time in reading anything you disclose.'

'Your Honour, I see no reason why that can't be done,' Ed Lowe replied nonchalantly. 'I'd be happy to arrange for the relevant material to be sent over.'

'Thank you, Mr Lowe, that is a great help – as you know, we have a limited time allotted for this trial and I don't want it to get interrupted by any last-gasp disclosure applications.'

Adam hardly dared to believe it. The judge had deemed he didn't have a legal justification for seeing the phone records, but then she'd charmed the prosecution into letting him see them anyway! He turned to Nisha, who gave him a jubilant thumbs-up.

Suddenly, there was a commotion at the front of the court. Raquel had turned pale as if she was going to pass out, and she motioned at the judge to excuse herself before quickly hurrying from the court. Adam had never seen anything like it, but Judge Wickstead acted like nothing had happened. Lowe took his cue from her and ploughed on despite the dramatic exit of the clerk.

As proceedings came to a close, Raquel had still not returned and it fell to the usher to step in and dismiss the court.

'Well done,' Nisha murmured as Judge Wickstead stalked

from the room. 'That wasn't cut-and-dried – but thankfully we've got a prosecutor with a healthy dose of decency.'

She was right – and Adam knew that without Lowe's inherent sense of fair play he may not have got what he wanted. Adam said a quick thank-you to Lowe, who promised to send him 'pages of stuff to bore you with' by the end of the week. He was desperate to see where Raquel had gone.

While the other lawyers dawdled, Adam darted out of the courtroom in the direction he assumed the clerk had fled, promising Nisha he would call her later. He looked up and down the marble-tiled corridor, where columns of light poured in from the upper windows. It was deserted – but then he spotted it. A tiny shaft of sunshine by the fire door, suggesting someone had recently opened it and gone through it.

Adam hurried over and pushed it gently open. There was Raquel crouched on the fire-escape steps, head in her hands, looking like she might vomit at any moment.

She started in fright when she noticed him.

'You,' she said, or rather spat.

'Hey, I just came to see if you're all right,' said Adam carefully. 'Do you want me to fetch some help?'

Raquel fiddled with a strand of bottle-blonde hair and sighed. 'I just needed some air,' she said heavily. 'You'll understand soon enough why I'm upset.' She looked up at him, and Adam saw that her mascara had been smudged by tears.

'I don't follow . . .'

'That phone stuff you want. Some of it – well, it's private. It shouldn't be out there. And it's irrelevant – you heard what Lowe said.' She sounded more like she was trying to convince herself than Adam.

So the rumours had been right, Adam thought. Raquel and Cliveden must have had some sort of relationship – and she knew that texts between the two of them would be part of the evidence seized. But why was her reaction so visceral?

'Look, if what you're worried about is personal communication, and it's not relevant, then there's no reason for it to come up in court,' said Adam. He couldn't help but feel sorry for this woman with her gaudy shell cracked right open, the tender, vulnerable being inside laid bare. 'But it's my job to do everything I can to build my client's defence.'

'I don't know why you're bothering,' Raquel retorted. 'Everyone knows Jimmy Knight is guilty. You won't convince a jury otherwise.'

'But I've got to try.'

Raquel got to her feet, dusting down her leather skirt.

'You do what you've got to do,' she sighed. 'But do one thing for me, OK? Remember there are two sides to every story.'

24

It didn't take long for Adam to work out why Raquel had been so keen for the unused material to remain unused.

Among the text messages Cliveden had received in the thirty days before his death, no less than 304 of them had been from her. They started out innocuously enough.

I miss you x

No reply.

Three hours later: Don't you miss me? x And a close-up photograph of a rather spectacular pair of breasts, barely contained in a lacy red bra.

No reply.

Forty-five minutes later: a missed call from Raquel.

Just checking you're still alive! Let me know you're ok big boy x

A reply from Cliveden: I told you never to call me in the evenings. I'm with N and the kids.

Sorry sorry! I just got worried – I thought you were ignoring me. See you at the usual place tomorrow?

No reply.

Four hours later: Night, baby. Can't wait to see you tomorrow. I've got a special treat for you ... xxx

The next day, 1.47 p.m.: five missed calls from Raquel.

I'm going to hope you've got a good excuse for keeping me waiting for 45 minutes . . . but I can't wait much longer. Got to get back to work. I'll let you make it up to me another time x

No reply.

Four more missed calls.

Grant, what's going on? Why are you ignoring me? Maybe I'll have to check with your wife that you're ok.

Reply from Grant: Everything's fine – just tied up at work.

Ok . . . as long as you're alright. I can't help feeling something is up. We need to talk properly, give me a call when you can xxx

The messages continued in this vein for pages and pages. Raquel trying desperately to get Cliveden's attention, him mainly ignoring her, occasionally batting her away when she started to get too cross or mentioned his wife. She'd often send him sexy pictures – Adam would turn the page fast, cheeks reddening – and he'd reply with the bare minimum: the heart-eyes emoji.

Then, on 12 March, the day before Cliveden had died . . .

Raquel: You absolute piece of shit. I should have known better than to let you use me. How dare you. I bet Natasha would love to hear about how you've been fucking me for nearly a year, how when you said you had to work on her birthday we were making love over and over in the back of your car, how you said she doesn't satisfy you in bed. I bet your kids and your colleagues and all your family and friends would just love to know what a great guy Grant Cliveden really is.

Cliveden:	You think you can ruin my life? Just try. I will burn yours to the ground.
Raquel:	I'm not the one that's married hun.
Cliveden:	You forget that I know about Liam's little marijuana mishap. Would be awful if that caught up with him.
Raquel:	Leave my son out of this.
Cliveden:	What a terrible waste it would be if he got a drug charge. Would lose that uni place he worked so hard for. All because his dear old mum couldn't keep her legs closed and her mouth shut.
Raquel:	Are you threatening me?
Cliveden:	Are YOU threatening me?
Raquel:	You are scum. You will regret this.
Cliveden:	Babe, I'll ALWAYS regret the day I stuck it in an old slapper like you.
Raquel:	Fuck you.

And that was it. Adam had read and reread the exchange, trying to get his head around this whole new version of Cliveden that was coming to life on the page. The devoted family man, for whom duty was sacrosanct, transformed into a philanderer who abused his position as a police officer to blackmail his scorned mistress. Adam knew Jonathan was right when he said it wasn't a good strategy to trash the victim in court, but after all the fawning one-dimensional media tributes, he wished the jury could see Cliveden's true colours.

Adam looked up from his bundle, at his pupil master, whom he'd just presented with the new disclosures. For the first time, Jonathan looked fully absorbed in the case. He was lingering on a page that showed Raquel, her face cropped out, posing coquet-tishly in a sheer black negligee.

'See? It wasn't just a love affair gone wrong,' Adam said. 'Clive-den was threatening to have Raquel's son arrested. She's a single mum. Who knows what she would have done to protect him.'

Jonathan nodded slowly, his eyes still on the picture.

'Either way, it shows a whole new side to Cliveden. If this is how he treats someone he's slept with, he could have had any number of enemies. And there's more,' said Adam, gently extri-cating the bundle from Jonathan's sweaty paw. The older man looked up at him in childlike bewilderment, like a toddler who had just had his favourite toy confiscated. Adam flicked quickly through the pages to what he wanted to show him.

'Look, here. Remember how the prosecution's case is that Knight made numerous searches relating to Cliveden? I asked Lowe for the full breakdown of the searches on Knight's com-puter in the days before the murder, and it's true, he really did google the hell out of Cliveden.'

Adam ran his finger down the long list of searches Knight had made about the victim, and the various news articles he'd read about his convictions, accolades and promotions.

'But look. That wasn't all he searched for.'

Jonathan squinted at the document. ' "Cheap used cars London . . ." "Changing a parole appointment . . ." "Away tick-ets Millwall . . ." An Amazon order for *The Mysterious Affair at Styles* by Agatha Christie . . . I don't really see the relevance of any of these.'

'This one,' said Adam, pointing. 'He searched for "Emma Owens Metropolitan Police corruption".'

'So?'

'Emma Owens is the FLO I told you about! She used to work with Cliveden, left the serious crime squad in mysterious circumstances, then pitched up in court on the same day he died. She was the one Natasha Cliveden had an altercation with before the PTPH.'

Jonathan's brow furrowed and he flicked back through the pages.

'So you're saying he was having an affair with her as well? Are there pictures of her too?'

Adam shook his head, exasperated. 'No, I don't think it's that. It's something that happened when they worked together. Knight clearly thinks Cliveden is corrupt – he thinks he framed him. Maybe he got some intel while he was in prison that Emma Owens was also involved?'

'And what did he find?'

'Nothing. I've tried doing the search myself. There's almost nothing relating to Emma Owens on the internet full stop.'

'So how do you explain this so-called altercation with the wife?'

Adam sighed. 'I can't. But there's definitely something going on. And that puts two women, both with an axe to grind with Cliveden, at the Old Bailey on the day he died. And neither of them were investigated as possible suspects.'

'But that's all they are – possible. Not credible. Not like our boy, who was the prime suspect with good reason.'

Adam felt like he could scream. 'This could be enough to get the case thrown out! The police didn't investigate properly, and—'

'*Opportunity*, Adam, *opportunity*!' bellowed Jonathan, and Adam found himself splattered with flecks of his pupil master's spittle. 'There is only one person in this scenario who can be placed with the victim, giving him something to drink. Those women can have all the motive in the world to kill him, but they didn't have the opportunity.'

'Raquel sent Cliveden a coffee. I think we should request the CCTV from the corridor outside the court where he died – if it shows him drinking it, then—'

Jonathan slapped his hand on the desk with sudden ferocity, stopping Adam in his tracks.

'Green, which of us has more than thirty years of experience?'

'Well, you . . .'

'And which of us is King's Counsel?'

'You.'

'So which of us is best placed to decide how this bastard case should be run?'

'It's just that—'

Jonathan banged the desk again. 'Do not try me, Green! I don't want to hear any more from you today unless it's to tell me you've found a smoking gun in the Kavanagh files. Now get out!'

Adam was shaking as he left the room. He couldn't understand why every time he came up with something that might help their case, Jonathan did not want to hear it. He clearly thought Adam was overreaching and forgetting his place, but he was just trying to help. All he wanted to do was get their client justice.

Adam headed to the tiny kitchen down the corridor and ran himself a glass of water. He gulped it down, splashed more water on his face, then ran himself another. It had been a while since he'd left her a message and he still hadn't heard from his mum – which was practically unheard of. And the longer he didn't hear from her, the more entwined Jimmy Knight's case and what had happened to his father became in his mind. Giving up on Jimmy would feel like giving up on his dad all over again. He downed another glass.

When he turned around, he saw Bobby Thompson standing in the doorway of the kitchen.

'Everything all right?'

Adam was suddenly painfully aware of how strange he must look, his fringe and face dripping with water, puddling onto his shirt.

'Yes, fine, thank you,' he said. 'Just . . . one of those days.'

Bobby moved quietly past Adam and ran his own glass of water. He let the silence stretch until Adam felt compelled to fill it.

'There's stuff in the papers from the Knight case which I think suggests our client could be innocent,' he said. 'But Jonathan isn't so sure.' He almost instantly regretted it. This case was making him so stressed that he'd started to forget that literally anything he said in chambers could be held against him when it came to the tenancy decision.

But Bobby nodded sagely. 'Frustrating, isn't it,' he said. 'Playing the system. Having to tiptoe around when you just want to bulldoze in there. But listen. I've been a bulldozer in my time. And it doesn't always work. Especially not for those of us that don't naturally fit in.'

Adam stared at Bobby. Surely the man who had made such an impassioned speech about how justice relied on those outside the establishment being willing to fight it wasn't telling him to put up and shut up?

'It just feels like everything is stacked against our client,' he sighed. 'I remember you saying once that the law was the best way to repair something that was unjust. It's what I really want to believe too. But right now, it doesn't seem that way.'

Bobby turned to look at Adam, and his expression was severe. 'The law is not a weapon, Adam,' he said. 'It is an arena. And it's up to you to find a way to box clever. Just because you're not getting your own way straight away, it doesn't mean the system is at fault.'

'No, that's not what I meant,' protested Adam weakly, sensing he'd made a horrible misstep. 'It's just that everything I try seems to hit a dead end, and Jonathan is, well, he's great, but I'm not sure we quite agree on . . .'

Bobby held up a hand to stop his frantic burbling. 'Are you a lawyer who specialises in excuses? Or one who finds solutions? Because I know there's only one kind I want in my chambers.'

And with that, Bobby strode back to his immaculate office, leaving Adam with cold water trickling down his neck, a sinking feeling in his stomach, and a new angle to explore.

25

Not for the first time, Adam found himself wondering if his actions would come back to bite him. It was the day after his conversation with Bobby and he was back in the Old Bailey, climbing up the back stairway, taking the gaudily carpeted stairs two at a time. He hadn't told anyone where he was going, and as far as Jonathan knew he was down in the basement working through the Kavanagh boxes. Bobby hadn't exactly told him what to do, but he'd told him what wouldn't be tolerable – sitting back and letting this case fall apart. Adam was going to fight. He was going to find a way through the brick walls. He'd do whatever it took.

At the clerks' corridor Adam hurried past several closed doors, trying to keep his footsteps as light as possible. He didn't want another run-in with Raquel. Not yet, anyway.

Finally, he reached the open hatch, and to his relief Abi was there, tapping away at her computer. When she saw him, two pink spots of pleasure rose in her face.

'Oh, hello again!' she said, a broad smile lighting up her pretty features.

Adam knew he should probably try flirting, but he literally

didn't know how. Instead, he settled for a rather stiff: 'Hi, how are you?'

'Oh, you know, just busy, busy!' said Abi. 'What brings you back here again? Are you still looking for Raquel?'

'Er, no,' said Adam hurriedly. 'That's all sorted. I just wondered – do you guys have access to the CCTV in the corridors? That I could potentially look at, as evidence?'

'I think so,' said Abi. 'You have to make a request to security for it, but you can do that via the clerks' office.'

'OK – how long does that take?'

Abi shrugged. 'Hopefully not too long. A week maybe? Fill out the form now and I'll do what I can to get it sorted as quickly as possible.'

'OK, great, thank you,' said Adam, taking the form she offered him and scribbling down the relevant details.

Abi watched him closely. 'You're really passionate about what you do, aren't you?' she said.

Adam looked up, surprised. It felt like the first time someone had properly noticed him in a long time. 'I guess, yeah,' he said. 'I always wanted to be a lawyer – so I feel like I've got to give it everything.'

Abi sighed. 'You're lucky. I wish I knew what I wanted to do. All I know is it's not this!' She gestured around the tiny cubicle and laughed.

There was something about her that put Adam at ease. Maybe it was her accent – she spoke just like all his mates at home in Southgate.

'I'm still training, you know,' he said. 'I'm not a real barrister yet. And I don't know if I'm going to make it. I've got to do well in this case, and even if I do – well, it might annoy more people than it impresses. And I'm not sure my face fits anyway.'

'Everyone has to start somewhere, don't they?' said Abi brightly. 'Raquel says that Judge Wickstead's rise in the legal world is proof that anything is possible if you work hard enough.'

Adam assumed she was referring to the fact that it was so shamefully unusual to see such a young female among the judges. Wickstead ignored the old hierarchies in her interactions with court staff, and the clerks loved her for it. He realised that he had no idea about her background, but perhaps she was an outsider too. It was a comforting thought.

'I'd be happy just to pass my pupillage for now,' Adam told Abi, smiling.

'I'm sure you'll do great – and if this CCTV is going to help, I'll make sure you get it nice and quick. Hey . . . why don't you write down your number?' She blushed. 'Just so I can let you know as soon as it's ready.'

It was only on the way back down the staircase that it occurred to Adam that Abi's desire for his number might not have been purely professional. But, then again – surely not? She was so lovely, with her radiant smile and easy manner, and he was just . . . weird and awkward.

The question of her possible interest in him preoccupied him as he exited the Old Bailey and followed the side street down to Fleet Street. The ancient thoroughfare that had once been the bustling home to London's newspaper empires was now just a soulless high street, with a few family-run barbers squeezed in amid the Prets and Superdrugs. But Abi wasn't enough to drive from his mind his current obsession – trying to catch Reg McNally at the Old Nag's Head. Instead of continuing on towards chambers, Adam peeled left after City Thameslink station, and down Bouverie Street, just as he had almost every day since he'd discovered that McNally had been Knight's barrister.

The Old Nag's Head was positioned far enough down the street that few tourists would accidentally wander in. You'd have to know it was there – and even if you did, Adam wasn't sure there were many reasons you'd make the effort. There were bars on the grimy windows, which had such a thick coating of dust and city dirt that you could barely see in. Ancient peeling posters advertised the fact that the pub had shown the World Cup – in 2006. Two of the letters from the pub's tired signage were missing – so that the casual observer might think it was the OL NAG'S H AD.

As he drew closer, Adam thought the pub looked dark and shut up as usual. But he decided he'd better go right up to the door, just to double-check. And thank goodness he did, because once he was there he could see that the door was missing its usual heavy lock. A dangling sign on the frosted window pane read OPEN.

Hardly daring to believe his luck, Adam stepped inside.

The pub smelled of stale cigarettes and drains. The light was so gloomy that it took a moment for his eyes to adjust. The fraying carpet was covered in stains, and mismatched chairs crowded around rickety tables. Wires dangled naked from the speakers inexpertly mounted on the wall, trailing over posters for pub quizzes and open mic nights that had been and gone many years before. The whole place felt unloved – and it was deserted.

Adam gingerly approached the boxy wooden bar which dominated the room. There must be someone here, surely?

There was a twitch — Adam jumped, thinking it was a rat — but then a figure moved forward out of the shadows and he saw that it was a man with a rat's face. Pinched features, greying skin spattered with liver spots, straggly hair and as dusty as his pint glasses. Incongruously, he was wearing a three-piece suit — which, although undoubtedly it had seen better days, like its wearer, was nevertheless beautifully cut.

Although he'd only seen him on the CCTV footage and in the shadows of Tony's photograph, Adam recognised Reg McNally instantly.

'What can I get you?' McNally said, with a leer that showed yellowing teeth.

'Just a pint of lager, please,' said Adam. 'And . . . whatever you're having.'

'Very kind,' the barman said. He poured Adam a pint, stopping just short of the full measure, and then filled up a glass of sticky-looking lemonade for himself.

'You don't drink?'

'Not anymore.' Reg took a sip and belched unpleasantly.

Adam took a swig of his own pint and wondered how he should play it. He'd been so desperate to meet McNally, he hadn't properly considered what he would say to him once he did. Looking around desperately for inspiration, his eyes settled on an old photograph propped up against grimy gin bottles, showing an older man, also rat-faced, with a young boy, perched on the same bar.

'Is that you?' Adam asked, pointing.

Reg eyed him suspiciously. 'It is, yeah, me and my old man.

169

Always swore I'd get out of this dead-end trade, and yet here we are.' He gave a hollow laugh that echoed around the decaying pub. Adam smiled back uneasily, only to be met with a cold, hard stare.

'But you didn't come in here to ask me about my family history, did you?' McNally added softly.

Adam played for time, Tony's warnings about McNally being a man with nothing to lose ringing in his ears.

'I know an old friend of yours, actually,' he said. 'He, er, recommended this place.'

'Not true,' said McNally shortly. 'I don't have any old friends – certainly none who would tell a nice lad like you to come here.' He was leaning on the bar now, every sinew of his body strained with malice.

'Tony Jones,' said Adam quickly, while McNally looked at him blankly. 'You used to drink together, years ago. He's the chief clerk, in my chambers.'

'Oh, I see what this is,' said McNally, leaning back and crossing his arms. As he did so, his sleeve rode up and Adam noticed the same gold watch that he'd worn in Tony's Polaroid – a relic of his better days.

'So you're a little baby barrister, are you?' said McNally, looking him up and down with beady eyes. 'And let me hazard a guess – you've got something to do with the murder trial I somehow find myself caught up in.'

There was no point hiding his hand any longer. Adam nodded. 'I'm representing Jimmy Knight, the defendant.'

'How sweet,' said McNally. 'So you thought you'd come down here, try and draw me out with talk about the good old days, I'll reveal some vital clue that somehow the police missed, and you'll be able to heroically prove your client's innocence. A lovely idea, but take it from an old hand, pal – it doesn't work that way.'

Adam flushed. He'd thought he was being clever but McNally had seen right through him. But he wasn't prepared to let the mercurial old fox outwit him that easily.

'Maybe I already have my vital clue, as you put it,' he said, with more confidence than he felt.

'What's that, then?' said McNally, feigning boredom as he picked up a filthy old dishcloth and started to polish glasses.

'That you represented Jimmy Knight ten years ago.'

The dishcloth in McNally's hand fell still for a split second before he recovered himself and carried on.

'I've no idea what you're talking about,' he said.

'Oh, I think you do,' said Adam. 'You must remember Jimmy Knight. I mean, he was here, just a few months ago – you recognised him, right? He's the one who said he was framed for armed robbery. You defended him. And then ten years later, the police officer he says planted the evidence ends up poisoned – after visiting *your* pub.'

McNally put down the glass, and started to pace up and down behind the bar. If it weren't for his shabby appearance, it would have been easy to imagine him in wig and gown, limbering up to deliver a fatal blow to the opposition's case.

'All very interesting,' he said, a strange smile playing on his chapped lips. 'But tell me, my learned friend, what are your submissions to the court? Because I put it to you that if it were true that I previously represented your client, and if it were true I was aware of the ill feeling he bore the victim, the fact that he met the victim in my pub does not aid his claim to innocence.

In fact, members of the jury would be forgiven for concluding the exact opposite.'

Adam knew McNally was trying to wrongfoot him, but the way he came alive as he played at being a barrister told him he must miss his old profession.

What a fall from grace it had been.

'It might not be relevant if it wasn't for the fact you got struck off for your involvement with criminal gangs,' Adam said, and watched as McNally's bonhomie instantly fell away. 'So yeah, I'd think the jury might find that element pretty interesting. Maybe they'd think that you'd got so desperate that you graduated from laundering money to doing other work for your old paymasters – like finishing off the top police officer who was on their tail. And that maybe you lured Knight here too, because you were the only person who knew that suspicion would instantly fall on him. Those would be my submissions to the court.'

He downed the rest of his pint, and stood up. He hadn't meant to get into a fight with one of the key witnesses – but then, he hadn't counted on how patronising McNally would be.

The barman was glowering at him. For all his bravado, he was rattled. 'Be very careful what you're saying, pal,' he said.

Adam rolled his eyes, heading for the door. 'If you won't give me straight answers now, we'll just have to wait until cross-examination,' he said. 'I'll see you in court.'

His hand was on the filthy door handle, when McNally called out behind him.

'You asked me if I recognised Knight,' he said. 'The honest answer is, I didn't. It was ten years ago – and there are some pretty compelling chemical reasons that I don't remember much from those days. But you never asked me if I recognised Cliveden.'

Adam turned around slowly. 'Did you?'

McNally's rat eyes glittered. 'Now he's what I call a regular.'

It didn't make sense. Cliveden, a regular in this dive? Adam looked around, taking in the dusty surfaces and the broken light fittings. Cliveden was wealthy, clean-cut, high-flying – famous, even. The pub seemed the opposite of his natural environment.

'Cliveden was a regular here? What was he doing in a place like this?' Adam asked. 'No offence,' he added hurriedly.

'None taken,' Reg said. He was taking his time, peeling Adam with his cunning gaze, weighing up what was in his best interests to reveal and conceal. 'You might not like the, ah, decor, but for a lot of my customers, it's helpful to meet in a place that puts off outsiders. Due to the nature of their business, if you understand me.'

Adam felt a twinge of revulsion. 'So you're saying this is a pub for criminals?'

'I said no such thing, you did,' said Reg, but there was that yellow grin.

'OK . . . so if this is where gangsters hang out, was Cliveden here to catch them?'

Reg laughed like a hyena.

'Right, that wouldn't make sense . . . because if he was regularly coming here to nick people, then no one would ever come.' Adam was thinking aloud. 'So that means . . . he was here to meet with them? But . . . why?'

Reg was still studiously concentrating on his pint glasses, wiping them down with the old rag.

'I couldn't possibly say,' he said. 'Although, as you so kindly mentioned earlier, I do have some experience with one particularly powerful gang. They are men of simple demands. They need to know what their rivals are up to. Where there may be a stash of drugs or weapons that they can steal. And most importantly, they need to stay out of jail.'

Adam's mind was racing. 'The sort of help that could only be provided by a senior police officer.'

After all this time fumbling around in the dark, Reg had finally shed some light on the mystery at the centre of their case. Adam couldn't believe he hadn't seen it before. Cliveden wasn't just a cheat, and he hadn't only framed Jimmy – he was bent.

'You've got to say all this on the stand,' he said to McNally.

'Say what?' he said, with mock naivety.

'Mr McNally, please,' said Adam. 'An innocent man could go to prison for murder.'

'Who said Jimmy Knight is innocent?' said McNally. 'Like you said – if it wasn't him, suspicion might fall elsewhere. And we wouldn't want that, would we?'

It was a warning. If they pushed him on the stand, McNally would have no qualms about doing whatever it took to stop the finger pointing at him. Adam simply nodded, and stepped out through the door.

As he left the pub and headed towards Fleet Street, Adam thought he caught a movement behind him, in the corner of his eye. He spun round – no one was there. All this talk of gangsters and conspiracies – it was making him paranoid.

26

'Do you just, like, not care about tenancy?'

Georgina was standing in the chambers lobby, hands on hips. The late-afternoon sunshine streaming through the window made her auburn hair look like spun gold, but the expression on her face was far from angelic. This was the last thing he needed.

'Jonathan thinks you've been in the basement, but I know you've been gone for hours, and it's lucky *he's* been gone so long at lunch or he'd definitely know you've been sneaking off without permission.'

Adam sighed. He'd apologised to Georgina after his outburst last month, but the battle lines were still well and truly drawn between them. 'It's really none of your business, Georgina.'

'I'm trying to help you, Adam!' she insisted.

There was no way that was true. Georgina's games were often too complicated for Adam to work out, but he knew enough to assume she didn't have his best interests at heart.

'OK, well, thanks, but I don't need your help,' he said churlishly.

'Oh, really? Do you not?' said Georgina, her voice rising. 'Because if you don't need my help, maybe I shouldn't have bothered getting your client a coffee and making excuses as to why neither you nor Jonathan can be bothered to be on time for your own meetings!'

Adam was instantly tense. 'What client?'

'Mr Kaven, or something.'

'Kavanagh? He's here? There's no meeting in the diary . . .'

'Yes, Kavanagh, that's right. And he doesn't seem too happy. I showed him up to Jonathan's room.'

Adam hurried up the stairs, panic rising in his throat. This was obviously part of Kavanagh's MO – turning up at chambers just to keep an eye on his lawyers and hoping to catch them off-guard. If it was a power move, it was working.

As Adam entered the room, he could feel the temperature drop several degrees. He was used to seeing Kavanagh with his mask on, his sociopathy lurking just beneath the surface. But today there was no attempt to hide his anger.

'So, Jonny's sent his lackey again! Aren't I paying for the real A-Team!' He was pacing back and forth.

'I'm sorry, Mr Kavanagh, I don't think Jonathan realised you were coming in today,' Adam said lamely.

'Well, he should realise that if I'm not getting updates, if I'm not hearing that you boys have come up with some major break-throughs, then of course I'm going to come down here and find out what the *hell* is going on!' Kavanagh's anger was like a hurricane, and Adam knew it could easily floor him.

'We're working really hard on it,' Adam said, trying to hold his nerve. 'There's a lot of material to go through, but we are assessing it all methodically and building the case—'

'I know there's a lot of material to go through,' snapped Kavanagh. 'Which really does make me question why you'd be doing anything but going through it. The girl with the great rack who brought me the coffee tells me you're running around town on this ridiculous policeman murder.'

'It's just a very busy time,' said Adam. He realised immediately it was completely the wrong thing to say.

'A very busy time, is it?' said Kavanagh, softly. He came right up to Adam, until their faces were just inches apart. Adam could smell the stale coffee on his breath. 'I would have thought a little Yid like you would be smart enough to follow the money. And there's no money in that fucking murder.'

Adam's cheeks went hot. It wasn't the first time he'd heard that kind of insult, but this really stung. He'd made it to chambers; he was inside the establishment. And yet he still wasn't immune to this sort of dirty gibe. It left him lost for words.

Kavanagh stepped back. 'Tell Jonny I'm waiting for his call!' he barked, heading for the door. 'And get back to work – or I'll end your career before it's even started.' He slammed the door behind him.

Adam was reeling. It took a minute for his breathing to return to normal. Eventually he stumbled down the stairs, to the basement, and started rifling through papers. Numbers and codes swam in front of his eyes. He did his best to make sense of them, swallowing down his hatred for the man he was working for.

He was so distracted he wasn't sure how much time had passed when he was joined by an unexpected visitor: Rupert.

'Hey, man,' Rupert said, handing him a mug of tea. 'Thought you might need this. Georgie said you've had a bit of a rough one.'

Adam scowled. Georgina just couldn't help revelling in his misfortune, could she?

'Thanks — but honestly, I'm fine,' he said. With both of them so busy with their own caseloads, and Rupert having just been away in Manchester for a trial, it was the first time Adam had seen him properly since bumping into him and Emma Owens at the Old Bailey a few weeks ago. 'How are you? Hey — I hope I didn't make things awkward for you and Emma that time. I didn't mean to overstep the mark with the Cliveden stuff.'

'Oh, no, that's totally cool,' said Rupert.

'So, are you two dating or something?' Adam asked.

Rupert grinned. 'Yeah, we're something,' he said. 'It's going great with her actually. She's really fun. Not into all the usual dinner-and-cocktails kind of stuff. We went kayaking near Walthamstow Marshes at the weekend.'

'That's great,' said Adam, but he felt uneasy. Rupert didn't know about the search on Knight's computer relating to Emma. Now that Adam knew Cliveden was corrupt, and that Knight had been searching Emma's name in the same context, he was even more suspicious as to whether she could be involved in the murder.

'She's actually been asking a fair bit after you,' Rupert went on. 'She's pretty into that case you're working on, I guess cos she knew that Cliveden guy. Wants to know what you're up to — I'm like, "He works so hard, I never see him!"'

'Right,' said Adam, but he found it hard to smile back at his friend. This was all very weird. Was Emma only getting close to Rupert so that she could keep tabs on Adam?

'Hey, you going to be here much longer?' Rupert asked. 'Fancy going for a quick pint?'

Adam surveyed the mess of paperwork on the floor in front of him. He knew he should stay and put some hours in, but he was still so shaken by Kavanagh's vicious words, he knew there was no way he'd be able to concentrate on it now.

'I was just about to call it a night actually,' he said. 'So yeah, a pint sounds great.'

'Good stuff,' said Rupert. 'I've just got a couple of emails to send, so I'll meet you in the lobby in ten?'

'Sure.'

Adam shuffled papers into boxes, then wandered back upstairs. He went into the pigeonhole room to see if there were any new briefs for tomorrow. There was a dull-looking plea and trial preparation hearing, which he was just about to flick through when he noticed what had been lurking underneath it. An envelope, addressed with spiky black handwriting: FAO ADAM GREEN.

Intrigued, Adam picked it up and tore it open. Out fell two folded sheets of paper. Written on one, in the same distinctive scrawl, was a message: WOULDN'T WANT THESE IN THE WRONG HANDS.

His heart quickened as he unfolded the first piece of paper. It was a photocopy of an old family photograph, three people he instantly recognised. With trembling hands he unfolded the second sheet, already knowing what it would be. It was another photocopy, this time of a newspaper cutting he hadn't seen for years . . .

27

Adam dropped the papers and envelope like they were on fire. He hardly dared think of the consequences if this information was to fall into the wrong hands, as the note put it, while he was working on a case that had the spotlight of the entire national media trained upon it. He'd never told anyone at chambers what had happened with his dad – and although he believed deep down that his father was innocent, he knew most people wouldn't see it that way. He imagined with horror the disgust of his chambers colleagues and the sharp retorts of Nisha, who'd think he had turned their case into a circus. But mostly he feared the humiliation his mother would have to endure all over again. It was his job to protect her – and this scandal getting dredged up for the world to pick apart was his worst fear.

It was another threat, that was for sure. And this one didn't come with mutually assured destruction, like McNally's did. Someone thought he was asking too many questions, and they wanted him to stop.

'Adam? You ready?' Rupert called.

'Coming!'

Adam scrumpled up the papers and the envelope and stuffed

them right to the bottom of his bag. When he emerged from the post room, he had just about stopped his hands from shaking.

As they walked to the Wig and Pen, Adam found it hard to concentrate on Rupert's good-natured chatter about football. Rupert was an Arsenal fan, and never missed an opportunity to rib Adam about the latest Spurs defeat. Usually Adam would give as good as he got, but the envelope, and its unsettling contents, were all he could think about. Who had sent it?

Once they were sat down with their pints, Adam tried to focus on what Rupert was saying, while attempting to drown out and ignore the disturbing images that were crowding his brain. McNally's cruel sneer, Kavanagh's racist insult, the envelope bearing a long-buried secret. Without warning, he thought of his mum's silent tears as she'd stood by the side of his father's grave over a decade ago in the wrong part of the Jewish cemetery. She still hadn't called him back, had she?

Rupert was talking about Emma again. 'I'd pretty much given up on meeting someone in real life, you know,' he said. 'I thought it was Tinder or nothing. Then bang. You wouldn't think it was possible to fall for someone when you're in the middle of a child murder case but . . .'

Adam attempted to smile and say the right thing, but the subject of Emma Owens made him feel even more disconcerted. There was so much he wanted to ask – and so much he should say. But how? It was the first time he'd felt awkward around Rupert, and he didn't like it. His allies at chambers were thin on the ground; it didn't seem fair that Emma Owens and her strange connection to the Cliveden case had come between them. Rupert didn't seem to notice, keeping up his jokey banter about Adam's enduring singlehood.

'You could clean up on Tinder, mate — no, seriously, you could!' he boomed at Adam, over pint number three. In the end, Adam let Rupert create a profile for him, just to keep the conversation on neutral ground. When the barmaid finally called last orders, he was almost relieved.

Rupert was heading to Blackfriars but Adam decided he'd go along to Embankment to get on the Northern line. It was a warm, still summer night, one where the vast deluge of London's lights hadn't quite been able to drown out the stars. He ducked away from the human soup of High Holborn — still bustling with tourists, city workers and drunks — and entered the silent world of the inns of court. He hurried along deserted alleyways and across hushed squares, but even along this familiar route he couldn't stop the hairs on the back of his neck prickling. Every few minutes or so he would stop suddenly, and wheel around to find that no one was there at all.

It's just paranoia: that envelope has got under your skin, Adam told himself firmly. But though he knew he was being ridiculous, he couldn't shake the feeling he was being followed. It was exactly the same sensation he'd had when he'd left the Old Nag's Head.

He quickened his pace, turned onto Middle Temple Lane, then immediately peeled off under the archway that led to Middle Temple Gardens. But instead of hurrying through, he stopped in its shadows, and held his breath. And that's when he heard the sound — footsteps.

'Who's there?' he called into the darkness. There was no answer — but the footsteps stopped dead.

Adam was suddenly very aware of his own breathing, which was ragged in his throat. He peered out from his hiding place, and could just about make out a hooded figure in the half light. Whoever it was, they weren't about to scarper.

Summoning every ounce of his courage, Adam stepped back out onto the lane. At the same time, the figure, which was smaller and slighter than he'd anticipated, moved forward into the puddle of light cast by the gas streetlamp. As they did so, they lowered their hood, and a flash of blonde hair caught in the glow. It was Emma Owens.

28

'You!' Adam didn't know whether to be relieved or horrified.

'Don't freak out,' Emma said. She sounded incredibly nervous herself. Adam wondered if he'd be able to outrun her – he was taller, but with her police training, she was probably fitter.

'What the hell are you doing here?' he shouted. 'Are you following me?' He looked desperately up and down Middle Temple Lane, but there was no one else coming.

'I am, yes, but it's not what it looks like,' Emma insisted.

Adam stepped back as she stepped forward, to maintain a healthy distance between them. 'You're up to your neck in the same corruption Cliveden was. You're getting close to Rupert to keep tabs on me. And once you realised I'd found out more than you bargained for, you thought you'd try and blackmail me with stuff about my family!'

'Blackmail?' Emma's facial expression was one of genuine concern. 'I don't know anything about that . . . but if someone is sending you a warning, then – Adam, you could be in real danger.'

He noticed how she kept looking up and down the lane too, as if terrified that someone was about to come round the corner.

He realised she was even more scared than he was, and it calmed him down.

'So what do you want?' he said, as his heart rate started to return to a more normal pace. 'And why couldn't you have sent me an email, instead of creeping up on me in the dark?'

'This isn't the sort of thing you can put in an email,' said Emma, her voice low, eyes still flitting this way and that. 'There's something I need to tell you – but not here.'

'Where, then?'

'Follow me – but don't walk near me.'

Emma pulled her hood back up and set off at a rapid pace through the archway and towards the gardens. Adam floundered for a second – this was his chance to sprint for the Tube. But curiosity got the better of him.

Minutes later they were by Middle Temple Gardens. The immaculate lawns were fenced and locked at this time of night, but it didn't seem to deter Emma. She upturned a bin, and stood on it to hoist herself up the fence, before dropping down onto the soft green turf on the other side.

'What the hell are you doing?'

'Come on – just trust me!'

Adam didn't think she'd given him any reason to do so, but something told him to follow her anyway. He took a running jump and scrambled up the fence, before half leaping, half falling down to join her.

Inside the garden it was even darker than on the street outside, and the air was thick with the scent of lavender. He tried to keep up with Emma as she strode towards the darkest spot in the centre of the gardens, furthest from the fence. At last, she came to a stop and spun round to face him, her face barely visible.

'You're right about the corruption – but you're not right about me,' she said.

'You had to follow me in the dark and do some light breaking-and-entering in order to tell me that?'

'Yes – because it's dangerous. Those men Cliveden was involved with – they'll stop at nothing.'

'How would you know?'

'Because I've seen it in action. I was working with him, when I found out how deep in he was. He was the gang's most valuable asset.' She rubbed her temples. 'O K . . . I need to explain this properly.'

She pointed to a bench. 'Look, it's a lot to take in. You better sit down.' Adam tentatively did as she said while Emma kept pacing. When she started to talk, her voice was low and nervous.

'I was so excited when I got assigned to Cliveden's team in the serious crime unit. Obviously, he was a total legend, and not just the stuff with the Queen – within the Met he was known for doing some of the most cutting-edge policing, with an incredible conviction rate. I was only nine months into my training and it felt like getting called up to the big league.'

Adam thought about the day he'd got the call to say he'd won a spot at Stag Court as a pupil and knew exactly what she meant. He wondered if he'd ever feel like that again.

'At first, it was great. Really exciting – we were going on these big raids every other day, finding these massive stashes of drugs and weapons and cash. And Cliveden was brilliant to work for – everybody loved him. Because he was making us all look good. He just seemed to have this almost like, sixth sense, of where we should hit next. Of course, later I found out it wasn't a sixth sense at all,' she added bitterly.

'What do you mean?'

'This is how I think it works. Whoever he was working for, they had their own intel on what their rivals were doing. They knew when there were going to be big shipments of drugs, for example, or where they'd hidden their stash. But this organised crime group – gang – whatever you want to call them – they didn't want to risk out-and-out warfare by just hitting up their rivals. So that's where Cliveden came in.'

Adam nodded. So far, it was tallying with what McNally had said.

'Cliveden sweeps in, seizes the stash. He gets to look good to the bosses, meanwhile the gang's rivals are weakened. And I think that's how it worked for a bit. But then he started getting greedy. He stole drugs from crime scenes and he'd sell them back to his paymasters at knockdown prices. They must have loved it because their profit margins would be massive.'

'And Cliveden?'

'He was getting seriously rich. You've seen the papers. That beautiful mansion, his kids in private school, all these exotic holidays. It was kind of like a running joke on the unit, how much cash he had. But no one really minded because he always got the drinks in at the end of a shift.'

'Come on, you're telling me a bunch of detectives didn't think there was anything suspicious going on?' said Adam incredulously. 'They must have known. They were turning a blind eye, because everyone was riding on the coattails of his success.'

'No. It's not like that,' said Emma fiercely. 'Those officers in serious crime – they're good people. They work bloody hard, they're brave, they want to protect their communities. Look, Cliveden went on telly from time to time. You think your average bobby knows how much that pays? I guess everyone just assumed his wealth came from other sources that they didn't really understand. And it hardly seemed like a big deal, when we were making such a serious difference by disrupting organised crime. Or so it seemed.'

'OK, fine,' said Adam. 'So how come you figured out he was up to something?'

Emma turned away – her face which had briefly been visible in the starlight fell back into shadow. She ignored the question.

'What you need to understand is that the rest of the unit . . . I respected them as police officers, but that didn't change the fact they didn't like me. I didn't have an easy time. They didn't like the fact that I was on the fast-track scheme, they didn't like that I was Northern, they didn't like that I was female. They didn't trust me, and they made that clear. It didn't bother me really – it's been like that my whole life in the force.'

Adam frowned. 'What does that have to do with—'

Emma cut in. 'Only Cliveden was good to me – he took me under his wing. So I was close to him, all right? He was my role model, everything I wanted to be, and he knew it. God, he had me fooled. I shouldn't have been so blind, so fucking stupid. I could have acted sooner. But I didn't, and I've got to live with that.'

There was genuine pain in her words. Adam could empathise; having everything you believed in suddenly crumble into dust was incredibly hard to come back from.

'But you did do something – eventually?' he prompted her.

'Eventually, yes,' said Emma, choked with self-loathing. 'When I look back on it now – I can hardly believe how cocky Cliveden was. He must have assumed I was so focused on my career, so personally loyal to him that I wouldn't say anything. So anyway, what happened was we were on a drugs raid, with a whole armed response team. We turn up at this big abandoned barn out by the canal in Essex. It's deserted so Cliveden tells the armed unit to wait outside and it's just me that goes in with him. At the back there are these two big bags like they'd keep animal feed in, and inside them are twenty-four big blocks of white powder. I counted. I'm holding the police camera to photograph them for evidence, but Cliveden says, "No, put the camera away." And I'm like, "Why?" And he says, "We'll do it later. Just go and wait outside." And I know that's against all the protocol but I do. And when I come back in, there are only twenty blocks. I've no idea how he did it but he took those drugs, I'm sure of it.'

'So what did you do?'

'Well, at first I didn't want to believe it. I didn't say anything there and then, just took the pictures and did my job. But later, when we were driving back to base, I confronted him. I said, "Boss, I'm sure there were twenty-four blocks – but we've only recovered twenty." And he said, " You must be mistaken." I said, "No, I'm really certain." And that's when it got scary. He whacked the blue lights on, started driving super fast. And the whole time he was shouting at me, saying he hopes I'm not accusing him of what he thinks I'm accusing him of. I was terrified.'

'It sounds like you didn't have much evidence.'

'No. But I had seen enough. And it was almost like, once I had seen that, everything else just fell into place. The money, his hit rate – it all made sense. Cliveden was corrupt. So I decided to do some more digging. Not that he made it easy for me. After the day at the Essex barn, I found myself stuck on desk duties pretty much the entire time.'

'What did you find out?'

'I started to look into Cliveden's conviction record. It's so celebrated that I don't think anyone had ever really questioned it. But when you get down to the details, there's a strange pattern. It's always the same. Some guy with a relatively low-key criminal record of minor offences suddenly gets done for something massive. And inevitably, these guys have no serious links to organised crime, so that's where the trail stops. Case closed. I became convinced Cliveden was framing them, to take heat off the people who were paying him.'

'So what did you do?'

'I took it to the anti-corruption command. What else could I do? It was my duty, as a police officer. I gave my statement, and they seemed to take it seriously enough, but then I didn't hear anything more for weeks. I was starting to get nervous, thinking nothing was going to come of it.'

'So they didn't follow it up?'

'Oh, they followed it up all right. Just when I'd all but given up hope, they turned up at serious crime to do a raid. On the whole unit. All our desks and our cars and our lockers were searched. And you'll never guess what they found.'

'What?'

'Two blocks of cocaine. Tests revealed they were from the same batch as the drugs seized at the Essex barn that day. There was just one problem. They were found in *my* police-issue vehicle.'

'*What?*'

'Yep. I mean, it's pretty obvious Cliveden or one of his crew must have planted them. But that was the end of my career in serious crime. They moved me to family liaison, and there's supposedly an investigation ongoing into whether I'm actually guilty, but I'm not holding out much hope. There's a good chance this is the end of my career in the police full stop. And if I get struck off for corruption, who is ever going to believe what I've got to say about Cliveden?'

'You've got to try at least – you need to get the truth out th—'

'I can't.' Emma cut him off quickly, and her voice was shaking. 'If it was just my career I stood to lose, then fine. But the day after the anti-corruption raid, my parents up in Wetherby got a visit from a group of masked men. They forced their way into the house, smashed things up, urinated all over the carpet. My parents were petrified. Then they took Cassie, our old collie, and slit her throat in front of them.'

'My God.'

Emma's voice was trembling. 'Yeah. So maybe you can see why I'm not so keen on anyone knowing I'm talking about this. You said you got a warning? Well, I got one too. And I listened.'

Emma had been right – it was a lot to take in. Adam felt a chill.

'I saw you – with Cliveden's wife at the Old Bailey. What was that all about?'

Emma sighed. 'She thinks I made spurious allegations about her husband and tried to ruin his career. As does almost everyone else connected to the police. You may have noticed that I'm a bit like a bad smell.'

'Why are you telling me all this?'

'Because you're in danger. I know you want to do right by your client, but pit yourself against these people and you won't win.'

There was something still bothering Adam. How had Jimmy Knight known about Emma Owens?

'Do you know Jimmy Knight?'

Emma looked at the floor.

'No. But I can see why he'd want Cliveden dead.'

'He didn't do it.'

She didn't respond.

'Emma – you could say all this stuff about Cliveden on the stand. We're trying to show that others aside from Jimmy would want him dead. Based on what you're saying, he could have loads of potential enemies.'

'That's not a good idea. I'm serious,' said Emma curtly. She pulled out her phone, looked at the time. 'I've got to go. Don't follow me straight away.'

Adam stayed on the bench as Emma headed for the fence at a gentle jog. As he watched her retreating back a thought occurred to him.

He ran after her and grabbed her elbow just before she was about to scale the fence.

'You said you don't know Jimmy Knight – but did you know his son, Marcellus?' Adam whispered, Emma's warnings about discretion ringing in his ears.

Emma shook his hand away.

'I can't talk about that,' she hissed.

And with that, she clambered over the fence and dropped back down into the street, and disappeared into the night.

29

Phone call

'Mum! I'm really glad you called.'

'Oh, Ad, I had to. I've just read the most shocking news.'

'What? Has someone been around asking questions? Did you get a note too?'

'A note? No, Adam, I'm talking about an article in the *Daily Mail* today. Scientists have done a study, and they've found that single men are thirty-two per cent more likely to die young than married men. Thirty-two per cent! And I said to myself, "You've got to call Adam, because he might not know that he's literally putting his health at risk."'

'Mum, that is ridiculous.'

'It's not ridiculous, Adam, it's science!'

'OK, well, I guess it's a risk I'll just have to take for now.'

'You can have a read of it yourself. I cut the story out of the newspaper and I'm going to post it to you this afternoon. And just in case it brings you to your senses, I've popped a photograph of Rachel Silver in there and her mother's phone number, because she really would be a lovely match. Now, she's thirty-four, but that's really not too old to have your first baby these days – all the career girls are doing it.'

'So I haven't heard from you for weeks and then you finally call me to tell me I'm going to die unless I immediately marry some random Jewish girl?'

'Oh, don't exaggerate, Adam – we just kept missing each other.'

'I was worried, Mum! I upset you, didn't I? Because of what I said about Dad.'

'Adam, you know what I've said before. There's no point going over and over what happened. You'll drive yourself mad. The best thing for all of us is to move on . . .'

'I know, Mum, and I'm sorry. I really thought I had. But ever since I've started representing an innocent man who's falsely accused, it's brought it all back. I feel like unless I can prove for certain that Dad wasn't behind the wheel that day, I might never stop wondering about it.'

'Adam, he was your dad. Do you really think he could have killed that little girl? I've told you before, we believe in him and that's all that counts.'

'I'm just sick of not having any answers, Mum! Believing isn't enough! You can't stand up in court and say, "This guy seems like a good bloke, so I *believe* he didn't do it." You need facts, and we don't have any, do we? Dad never got a fair shot. A good lawyer could have proved it wasn't him, surely?'

'Maybe. Maybe not. We'll never know.'

'What makes you so sure he didn't do it, Mum? Because if you know something, then . . .'

'Adam, if I could wave a magic wand and get rid of the shame and stigma, I would. But I've told you – there are some questions that just can't be answered, and we have to live with that.'

'I don't know if I can do that anymore, Mum.'

'Oh, Ad. It'll do you no good to dwell on the past. Don't let it define you. You've got to look to the future now – you're going to be a top barrister! Your dad would be so proud. Your big trial must be starting soon, isn't it?'

'Yeah, in two weeks.'

'Well, that's come round quickly. Have you booked a haircut? Do you have enough shoe polish? Would you like me to come over and make up some packed lunches for you to take with you?'

'Thanks, but definitely not.'

'I'll be glued to BBC News when that's on, Ad. I'll be keeping an eye out for you! Make sure you look nice and smart.'

'Ha-ha, OK, Mum . . . but when you hear about the evidence, just keep an open mind, OK?'

'I'll try, Adam.'

30

A fraught journey back from Highbury Mags, where Adam had been defending in a harassment case, saw him make it to Belmarsh just in time to join Nisha and Jonathan for a meeting with Knight. Through the rigorous security they went, only for Adam's phone to start ringing just as he was about to hand it over, prompting a poisonous glare from Jonathan. Adam glanced at the screen as he pressed the red button: a number he didn't recognise. If it was important they'd leave a message.

It was two weeks until the trial and they were shown into the same cubicle that he and Knight had used during his first visit. This time it was even more crowded, with Nisha and Jonathan squeezed around the scratched table too. August was sweltering – evidenced by the two enormous sweat patches bleeding from beneath Jonathan's armpits – and it felt almost impossible to breathe.

Jonathan had spent the whole walk down to the cells complaining about how he should be at '*la maison*', as he insisted on calling his house in France. Nisha, who had drawn the short straw, was sitting on the same side of the table as Jonathan, leaning as far away from him as her bolted-down chair would allow.

'Jimmy, what you need to remember is that it's not even what you say, so much as how you say it,' Nisha was saying. 'Your tone, your posture, eye contact, even the way you hold your hands – that can all impact whether the jury believes you or not.'

Jonathan yawned theatrically. Nisha tried to ignore him and ploughed on.

'Try and keep your answers simple. Don't hesitate. And stick to what it says in your statement – nothing more, nothing less.'

'OK, so—' Knight began.

'Nope!' shouted Jonathan, suddenly rousing himself. 'Not going to happen!'

The other three all stared at him.

'What are you talking about?' Nisha said, her face congealing.

'He's not going on the stand,' said Jonathan, as if Knight weren't in the room. 'There's no point. He has nothing to say.'

Nisha blinked in bafflement. 'With respect, that's a bad call. The judge will make a section 35 ruling and advise the jury they can draw a negative inference from his refusal to give evidence. Why on earth wouldn't you want him on the stand?'

'Because of this.' Jonathan turned to Knight. 'Mr Knight, why were you in the Old Nag's Head at half past eleven on 13 March?'

Knight grunted. 'I wanted a drink.'

'And had you arranged to meet Mr Cliveden there?'

'No. We both just happened to be there.'

'Even though you had spent the previous evening googling Mr Cliveden?'

'Yes.'

'And even though a phone containing a text message arranging a meeting with Mr Cliveden was found at your property?'

'It wasn't my phone.'

'And yet you and Mr Cliveden arrived at a similar time at the exact pub prearranged in said messages?'

'Yes.'

Jonathan threw up his hands theatrically and addressed himself to Nisha again. 'See? He has literally nothing to add to our case. We can't put him up there.'

'With respect, Jonathan' – Adam had come to recognise this phrase as a tell that Nisha was on her last nerve – 'they're going to think he has something to hide if he doesn't take the stand.'

'They're going to think he has something to hide if they hear his so-called evidence!'

Jonathan's double chin quivered with self-righteousness, while Nisha's hair bristled angrily. 'Besides, if our case is simply that it wasn't Mr Knight – which it still is, by the way, in the lack of anything remotely stronger – logically, we can't call him.'

'We need to humanise him!' said Nisha shrilly. 'It doesn't matter that he doesn't have anything to add – the jury might like him, as a person, an innocent man caught up in a nightmare. Unless they hear him speak, he's just a monster in the dock, which is exactly what the prosecution wants.'

'Nisha, you're talking like a trainee. You know that's not how things work.'

'Jonathan, please,' Adam intervened. 'Putting Jimmy on the stand is the only way for the truth to come out. Cliveden's corruption, how he framed Jimmy – all of it.'

'How is that relevant? And where's the evidence that any of that is true?' asked Jonathan, turning his crackling antagonism on Adam. 'So far the only people accusing Cliveden of anything inappropriate are his scorned lover and an alcoholic ex-barrister struck off for misconduct. Oh, and the defendant himself. Hardly cut-and-dried, is it?' he added witheringly.

'But—'

'He's right.' It was Knight this time, his voice quiet and steady. Nisha, Jonathan and Adam had been so wrapped up in their own argument they had almost forgotten he was there. 'A jury didn't believe me before, and they won't believe me again.'

'Jimmy, they will believe you, if you just tell the truth, without leaving bits out,' Adam said, turning to the older man, and he could hear the desperation in his own voice. 'This is your shot at justice.'

But Jimmy just shook his head.

'So what's your grand plan, if you're ruling out hearing from the actual defendant?' asked Nisha, her voice dripping with scorn.

'I'm going to rely on our old friend reasonable doubt,' said Jonathan, spreading his hands. 'The CCTV doesn't clearly show Mr Knight administering the poison. We have an expert who says the poison could easily have been dispensed before or after the window in which Knight and Cliveden were together. And with Mr Knight's rather unconvincing version of events, that is the best we can do really.'

'That is not going to be enough!' Nisha exploded. 'The jury is just going to think, If he didn't do it, then who did?'

'That is not our question to answer,' said Jonathan curtly.

'But there is evidence that others could have had motive, and opportunity,' said Adam. 'There must be a way we can introduce that, to give the jury something solid to focus on?'

'Absolutely not,' said Jonathan. 'The case we are going to run is purely scientific. It is not for us to prove who else could be responsible. All we will do is show that the prosecution's science is flawed. We're calling other witnesses so I can make an opening statement, and I'll use it to remind the jury that the burden of proof rests squarely with the prosecution. And then all we need to do is posit the question "Can it be proved for certain that Jimmy Knight did it?" And hope for the best.'

Jimmy had slumped in his chair. He might not have wanted to give evidence, but he seemed unconvinced by Jonathan's strategy too. Adam had one last card to play, and he'd been hoping he wouldn't have to do it in front of Nisha and Jonathan. But the way this conversation was going, he had no choice.

'Jimmy, why did you search for the name Emma Owens on your computer the night before the murder?'

Jimmy shrugged. 'Dunno. Was she selling a used car? I was looking for a car at that time.'

'She's a police officer who accused Cliveden of corruption. Did you know that?'

Jimmy's poker face didn't flinch. 'Maybe it's a different Emma Owens.'

Jonathan and Nisha were already gathering their papers with a bad-tempered air, disregarding this strange tangent.

Adam was certain that Knight was lying to them. But he still had no idea why.

31

With one week to go until the trial, Adam was in the stuffy pupil room at Stag Court redrafting pleadings for Jonathan. He couldn't help but notice that recently he had been sent far less of his own work by Tony. Meanwhile, Georgina had never been busier. Although he was grateful for the extra time to spend on Jimmy Knight's defence – and, of course, the intimidating number of documents in the Kavanagh case – Adam worried about what it said about his chances of getting tenancy. The decision on who got a spot at chambers was getting closer and closer, and if the chief clerk considered Georgina his go-to pupil then things didn't look good for Adam.

It wasn't the only thing playing on his mind. Ever since the mysterious envelope had turned up in his pigeonhole, Adam hadn't been able to stop obsessing about who could have sent it – and what they planned to do with the information they'd dug up. Could it be someone who knew he was on to Cliveden's corruption, and was determined it stayed hidden? Or the real killer, who was afraid he might succeed in clearing Jimmy Knight's name? Either way, he felt like he was getting tantalisingly close to the truth. But at what cost? A wave of nausea passed over him as he imagined again what would happen if his long-hidden family scandal was let loose again. His mum had told him to leave the past where it belonged. Well, it seemed like he might not get a choice in that.

August was getting hotter and hotter, and London was like a cauldron. Sweat dripped down Adam's neck and puddled around the collar of his sticky shirt. It was the non-iron kind from M&S (left in his flat by his mother during another un-authorised visit while he'd been out at work) but somehow it still conspired to crumple in the inescapable heat.

His swirling thoughts were interrupted by his phone buzzing with a text message. It was a number he didn't recognise, but he was grateful for any momentary distraction from the legal problems that were making his head spin. He swiped it open.

Hi lovely, happy Thursday! Nearly the weekend, woohoo – gonna be a scorcher – do you have any plans? It's Abi here from the clerk's office at the Old Bailey. Just to say that CCTV footage you asked for came in. I'll be around until 5. Maybe we could grab an iced tea lol? X

This felt like progress. With everything that had happened lately he'd totally forgotten about the CCTV Abi had promised to get him. He should have had it a long time ago, but better late than never. If it showed Cliveden drinking a coffee supplied by Raquel, it would be impossible to argue that she wasn't a cred-ible suspect. That could be enough to get those text messages between her and Cliveden submitted in evidence – or even get the case thrown out completely.

On my way over – will pick you up a drink. Adam.

Ten seconds later her reply popped in. Yippee! Though we could go to a cafe if you prefer? Whatever is easier! See you soon xx

Half an hour later Adam was hurrying down the now-familiar clerks' corridor, armed with two iced teas from Pret – one lemon, one raspberry. Abi beamed when she saw him coming. She looked far less ruffled by the heat than he did. The formality of the Bailey seemed extra cruel on scorching days like this, but Abi looked effortlessly cool in a pretty sleeveless silk blouse, her jacket slung over the back of her chair.

'This is so nice of you!' she said, taking the raspberry one. It was the exact shade of pink as her lip gloss, Adam couldn't help but notice. 'I didn't mean for you to get one, I thought we could have gone out . . . but maybe next time?'

Adam realised he'd made a faux pas, and awkwardly sipped his tea. 'Ah, sorry. I thought . . . I didn't realise . . .'

'No, this is lovely, honestly!' said Abi hurriedly. 'You're probably really busy anyway, so . . .' They gulped their tea through straws, avoiding each other's gaze.

'So, the CCTV?' he said at last.

'Oh! Yes,' said Abi, beckoning for him to come round to her side of the desk. 'I've got it here, hang on . . .'

She opened up Outlook and tapped something into the search box. If she had it in an email she could have just forwarded it to him, so she must have wanted to see him . . . The thought of that made Adam more nervous than the prospect of what was on the film itself.

'Here it is,' said Abi, loading up the video. 'I haven't actually watched it yet . . .' She hit 'play'. Adam craned over her shoulder to watch.

'Oh, gosh, my hair looked terrible that day,' murmured Abi, as the video showed her walking down a marble-floored corridor towards Court 3, a cardboard Costa Coffee cup clutched in her hands. Her hair looked perfectly fine to Adam – nice even. The wooden double doors about midway down swung open and Cliveden appeared, his swaggering figure now familiar to Adam, having pored over the rest of the CCTV from that fateful day. In the video, Abi quickened her pace, and soon fell into step beside Cliveden. The pair exchanged a few words and Cliveden took the coffee, the megawatt smile he flashed Abi visible on CCTV.

'So sad, isn't it?' Abi said softly as her CCTV version turned her back and walked away. Cliveden took a brief look after her, then turned back towards court, coffee in hand – and everything went black.

'Hang on – what happened?' Adam said frantically. He grabbed the mouse, tried to refresh the feed – but it was over. 'Where's the rest of it?'

'Oh, that's all there is!' said Abi. 'Sorry, I should have mentioned it . . . Security said the tape was corrupted, so they were only able to recover some of it. The rest is lost.'

'But it doesn't show whether he drank the coffee or not!' exclaimed Adam. 'Abi, think back . . . Do you have any idea whether he did?'

Abi's brow furrowed. 'Why would that matter?' she asked. 'You don't think the coffee has something to do with his death, do you . . . ? Hang on, you're not saying that *I* might have had something to do with it, are you?' She was looking at him with alarm, her warmth all gone.

'No, not you, Abi. I don't know, maybe Raquel . . .'

'*Raquel?*'

'Well, I'm not sure, but—'

'Hang on, you roped me in to help investigate my boss, without telling me?'

'It's not like that!'

'Why on earth would you think Raquel has anything to do with this?'

'Why would you think Raquel has anything to do with what?'

The distinctive squawk came from behind Adam. He turned around slowly, his stomach sinking. Raquel herself stood at the open hatch to the clerks' office, hands on her hips, her nostrils flaring.

Adam didn't know what to say. Abi looked at him nervously, but he knew there was no way she was going in to bat for him.

'Hi, Raquel,' she said tentatively. 'Adam just wanted to see some CCTV footage from the day of the Grant Cliveden murder. He's got some, ah, concerns about that coffee you gave me to take to him. But I'd had no idea that's what he was thinking until just now – honestly, I was trying to be helpful!'

Raquel took a deep breath and her eyes flashed with anger.

'Abi, give Mr Green and me some space, please.'

'Yes, of course,' said Abi, flustered, picking up her iced tea and hurrying from the office, her face burning.

'I had a feeling I hadn't seen the last of you,' said Raquel coldly, once they were alone. 'Do you care to explain yourself?'

She was wearing a skin-tight grey skirt suit that accentuated her curves, with the top of a hot pink bra just about visible under her white shirt. Adam recognised the lace from one of the pictures she'd sent Cliveden. She was close enough that Adam could smell her perfume. Could she be a killer? Adam wondered. She certainly had the composure.

'Abi's telling the truth,' he said. 'I asked her to help me take a look at some CCTV from the Old Bailey on the day of the murder, but I didn't tell her why.'

'Well, well, have a gold star for gallantry,' said Raquel sarcastically. 'So why did you want to see this CCTV?'

Adam gulped. He decided he had no choice but to be honest.

'I'm trying to establish whether anyone else would have had the motive and opportunity to kill Grant Cliveden. And, um, after I read your texts . . .'

'You thought that maybe I slipped a bit of Botox into his flat white,' Raquel sneered. 'Tell me, Adam, have you, a pupil barrister, been able to find any evidence for your little theory that the top detectives at Scotland Yard missed?'

'I certainly find it interesting that the crucial bit of CCTV seems to be missing – or deleted,' stammered Adam.

Raquel threw back her peroxide hair and laughed, a throaty cackle that went right through him.

'Adam, which fancy law school did you go to?'

'Er, Oxford.'

'And at Oxford, what did they say about the admissibility of "interesting" information that is in no way related to the facts of your case?'

'Well, it would probably depend on the individual—'

'No, Adam,' Raquel interrupted him, holding up her perfectly manicured hand. 'I may have left school at sixteen, and I may be a single mum, and I may have had an affair that I regretted. But I know this – whatever you think you know, you're not going to be able to use it. So get it out of your head. And don't you ever, ever again think that you are better than me.'

Adam was about to protest that he didn't, but thought better of it – this was Raquel throwing him out of the clerks' corridor with the same fizzing fury as Peggy Mitchell ejecting a rogue punter from the Queen Vic. Just when he'd thought he'd found Jimmy an escape route – they'd hit another maddening dead end.

32

'Now remember, the media are going to be out in force tomorrow,' said Jonathan, flipping shut his box file. He, Adam and Nisha had just concluded a bad-tempered final conference ahead of Jimmy Knight's trial. Adam had decided not to tell them about Raquel and the missing CCTV, because Jonathan had expressly forbidden him from talking to the judge's clerk and he'd not been able to produce anything useful anyway. Meanwhile Nisha, who now openly rolled her eyes at whatever the KC said, had fought again for Jonathan to call Jimmy to give evidence, which he had again refused.

'So do you think we should draft some kind of press statement, about how our client is innocent?' said Adam, eagerly.

'Oh, God, no,' said Jonathan, witheringly. 'I just mean I need to leave early to go to Trumpers for a haircut.'

'Well, I'm glad someone's got their priorities right,' muttered Nisha as she and Adam watched Jonathan leave, with a surprisingly buoyant spring in his step for a man who had just admitted the case they were fighting was 'utterly hopeless'. She turned to Adam. 'Please tell me you're at least going to be working on this tonight, and correcting the many, many factual inaccuracies in his opening statement?'

Adam nodded. It was going to be a late one. He couldn't remember a time when he had felt as nervous as this. Even the night before his pupillage interview hadn't been as bad. At least then it was only his own fate at stake, not someone else's.

Once Nisha had gone, Adam shut himself in the pupil room with the legal documents. He corrected and redrafted as he had promised he would, then looked over the evidence for what felt like the thousandth time, desperately trying to spot something that could help them, knowing that it was hardly possible he'd have missed it by now. Rereading the transcript of Jimmy Knight's police statement, he wondered if Jonathan was right about not putting him on the stand. It was full of evasions and 'No comment' – hardly a convincing rebuttal of his guilt. If they were going to convince the jury that Knight wasn't the killer, it was going to be a seriously uphill struggle.

Adam wanted so badly to believe in Jimmy Knight's innocence – and the power of the British justice system to vindicate it. He saw an image in his mind of Jimmy's face, eyes round and pleading, asking: 'Do you really think I could have pulled it off?' It morphed and merged into his father's face – 'It's all just a silly misunderstanding, Addy – you'll see . . .'

Adam quickly distracted himself from those thoughts. Old ghosts weren't going to help now. Then there was a soft knock at the door. It was Bobby, his silk KC's gown folded neatly over his arm.

'I just wanted to wish you luck tomorrow,' he said, to Adam's delight and surprise. 'Not everyone has failed to notice how hard you've worked on this case – and I hope it will pay off.'

Adam noticed how he'd said 'I hope' rather than 'I'm sure'.

'Thanks, I'm pretty nervous,' he admitted. 'Do you ever get used to that feeling?'

Bobby chuckled. 'I'd hope not,' he said. 'We barristers, we need the fear. Our clients stand to lose their greatest gift – freedom – if we fail. So if we didn't feel those stakes in our bones, then we'd be little better than trussed-up actors putting on a show.' Adam thought of Jonathan, off to Trumpers, his main thought of how he'd look in the newspaper pictures. 'Embrace that fear, Adam,' Bobby went on. 'It's your most valuable asset.'

Adam opened his mouth to reply but was interrupted by the shrill sound of his phone ringing. He quickly switched it to silent.

'Sorry, that'll be my mum,' he told Bobby. 'I'll ring her back later.'

'Is she calling to tell you to polish your shoes?' Bobby asked.

Adam was astonished. 'How did you know?'

Bobby just laughed. 'She's right, you know. If you look the part, you'll feel it too. Mums are smarter than we give them credit for.' He tapped his nose and then he was gone.

Adam reached for his phone, thinking he'd call his mum back while he remembered. But it hadn't been her. It was that unknown number again, the one that had tried to call while he was at Belmarsh, and hadn't left a message. He frowned – first he'd had an anonymous threat left in his pigeonhole, now he was getting calls from a random mobile number – could they be connected? Adam decided against returning the call. He had enough to worry about already.

*

The day of the trial dawned muggy and grey. After weeks of sunshine, the weather had finally broken, dry summer air replaced by murky drizzle. Adam lay awake waiting for his alarm, listening to the mice that shared his Holloway Road flat scuttle around in the dark. When at last it was an acceptable hour, he dressed quickly in a carefully ironed shirt, smart wool trousers, and, of course, freshly polished shoes.

The agreement was for Adam and Nisha to meet Jonathan at chambers, then they would get a cab to the Bailey together. Adam had hoped that this would mean they could review the day's order of business together one last time, but he knew that really it was because Jonathan liked the idea of lackeys walking behind him carrying his bags as he swept into court.

Although it was early when they called the taxi, most members of chambers were there forming a sort of guard of honour, to see off the trio to what would be the set's most high-profile case of the year.

'Don't mess this up,' said Tony gruffly, shaking Jonathan's hand at the door. Adam glanced upwards and saw Georgina leaning over the upper banister, next to her pupil master, Rory. 'Good luck,' she mouthed. It was impossible to tell her tone but Adam scowled, assuming it would be sarcastic as usual.

None of them spoke during the short cab ride to the Old Bailey. Jonathan pulled out a small mirror from his pocket and preened this way and that, his hair even more bouffant than usual. Nisha sighed and took out her phone and started texting furiously – no doubt about Jonathan, Adam thought. It meant he was the only one to spot the enormous mob of media blocking the street as they approached the court.

If he'd thought the crowd outside the first hearing had been big, this was something else. Photographers jostled on step-ladders to get the best view, TV crews used enormous micro-phones to barge each other out of the way, reporters lingered with notepads in their hands and pens in their mouths. There was something of a carnival atmosphere – they all knew this story would be leading their front pages or evening news bul-letins, and they were going to enjoy it.

'It's going to be hard to get much closer than this, mate,' said the taxi driver.

Nisha and Jonathan peered out of the windows and then all of a sudden a prison van came into view from the opposite direction.

The effect on the journalists was instantaneous. They rose as one, a flock of starlings taking flight, swarming around the van, yelling and banging and snapping their cameras. The jovi-ality of moments ago had disappeared and suddenly they were snarling with the rage of their readers and viewers, practically pushing the van over with their combined strength. The court security team tried to hold them back, and the van made its way slowly through the teeth of the vast metal gates which led down to the Bailey cells.

'Oh my days, they're not going to hold back, are they?' said Nisha. Adam thought of Jimmy in that claustrophobic tin can, reverberating with thunderclaps of hate as reporters banged on its side, and wondered how on earth he was feeling. He doubted he'd be feeling confident.

'All right, chaps, let's get this show on the road,' said Jona-than as they alighted from the taxi. 'Adam, carry the bag – and try not to look like such a wet weekend . . .'

Trailed by Adam and Nisha, Jonathan swept through the

crowd and up the Bailey steps. 'Good morning, gentlemen, ladies!' he greeted the members of the press warmly, unperturbed by their looks of disdain. Inside the Great Hall there were even more journalists, these ones with accreditation to sit inside the court itself, but the atmosphere was more subdued, as if the solemnity of the building had dampened their blood lust. Adam let his eyes drift upwards to the vaulting cupola above their heads, on top of which the golden statue of Lady Justice was perched. He hoped she was watching over them today.

'Jonathan, good morning!' It was Ed Lowe, crossing the black-and-white marble floor towards them, tanned face grinning. Jonathan managed only a sour grimace in return. 'Feeling confident?'

'Perhaps not as confident as you,' answered Jonathan archly. 'Now, as much as I'd love to stay and chat about open-water swimming or whatever nonsense you're up to these days, I've got to go and see my client . . .'

He gestured to Adam and Nisha, and they headed towards the cells. Even Jonathan seemed to be taking this seriously at last. He had his game face on.

Adam felt the tension grow with every security check, until at last they were ushered into the same tiny, foul-smelling cell as last time. Jimmy Knight was waiting for them – and to Adam's surprise, he was smiling.

'Here we go then,' he said, looking at his legal team. Jimmy was dressed in a navy suit, his grey tie knotted perfectly. Adam had become accustomed to his world-weary face with its eyebags and lines, but today Jimmy looked remarkably well rested. The jittering anxiety that had infused their previous meetings was gone, to be replaced with a quiet confidence. Adam couldn't understand it.

'Good morning, Mr Knight,' said Jonathan, taking his seat. 'Today should be relatively straightforward, with jury selection and opening statements. We don't get down into the nitty-gritty until tomorrow. Now, I must ask you, is there anything further you have remembered that you think I should know, as your brief?'

Jimmy shook his head. 'We're good to go.'

Jonathan patted his carefully coiffed hair. 'Now, Jimmy,' he started, tentatively. 'I don't wish to offend you. And I will act on whatever your instructions are. But if you do want to change you plea . . .'

'I don't.'

'I merely wish to remind you that it's not too late.'

'It's "not guilty" all the way.'

Jonathan sighed. 'Very well. You have my word that we will do our very best.' For once, Adam believed him.

'We'll see you up there, Jimmy,' smiled Nisha.

They got up to leave while Jimmy remained seated.

'It's the same judge, isn't it?' Jimmy asked suddenly. 'The woman, from the first hearing?'

'Yes, Charlotte Wickstead,' said Jonathan. 'Is everything all right?'

'Oh yes,' said Jimmy. 'I think it's going to be fine.'

'That's the spirit!' said Jonathan insincerely.

The door clanged behind them.

'Poor fellow's lost his mind,' muttered Jonathan, as they ascended back towards Court Number One.

33

'All rise.'

They'd all taken their places in the courtroom, like pieces on the chess board ready to play. Raquel was the ringmaster, as usual, but her eyes flashed daggers at Adam. He noticed how she'd poured no water for the defence.

Judge Charlotte Wickstead swept in, regal in her black silk. She settled herself on her throne, folding her robes around her like wings.

'Can I remind everyone to please switch off their phones?' Raquel was addressing herself with matriarchal hauteur mainly to the press benches and the packed public gallery, but there was a ripple around the whole court as everyone checked theirs was on silent. Adam noted with amusement that even the judge took out hers: a large iPhone with a bright pink cover decorated with pictures of pugs. It seemed so out of kilter – a hint of daytime telly in a Proust novel.

The air of anticipation grew as bailiffs spoke into walkie-talkies – the defendant was about to be brought in. At last, the figure they'd all been waiting for arrived – Jimmy Knight, handcuffed to two security guards. As he was led up to the bulletproof dock, he didn't hide from the hostile glares that ricocheted around the court, or the whispered murmurings that swirled around him. He held his head high. There was a sudden noisy sob and Adam spotted Natasha Cliveden, flanked by her FLO and a slightly dowdier version of herself that he took to be her sister. She was dressed in a tasteful silk charcoal shirt dress, a tissue clutched in her hand.

'Now, before we begin, I shall address the Crown's bad character application, namely that the defendant's previous convictions be submitted in evidence to the jury,' the judge said, addressing the two KCs. Jonathan sighed theatrically; he'd told Adam earlier there was no way this one would go their way.

'Although this issue has arrived rather late in the proceedings, which is unfortunate, I am going to allow the submission of the defendant's armed robbery conviction, as this has been widely reported and the fact of his imprisonment is materially relevant to essential issues in the case, namely the timeline of events,' she said. 'But I will not allow further submission relating to other offences.'

Jonathan stared. He got slowly to his feet. 'Thank you, Your Honour,' he said, in puzzlement.

Nisha jabbed Adam in the ribs. 'Big call, that one,' she said. 'Prosecution won't be able to paint Knight as just some career criminal now – first bit of good luck we've had!' Adam smiled back, as the judge motioned to Raquel to bring in the potential jurors.

Sixteen men and women, all different ages and states of obvious reluctance, were ushered in. Raquel bossily told them that the court would require twelve of them to sit as jurors, and if they were not available for the trial they would have to explain themselves to the judge. For her part, Charlotte Wickstead scanned their faces as if she could see into their souls, before turning back to Jonathan and Ed.

'I have not heard your submissions on this subject, but given that the case concerns a victim who was a serving police officer, I requested that all jury panel members complete a questionnaire in advance,' she told the two silks. 'The court will exclude any person who works or has worked within the police, or who is related to anyone who has. Were there any other categories of person that you would argue should be excluded?'

She looked beadily down at Ed and Jonathan, who both stood to say that they would not. Ed did a better job than Jonathan at keeping any surprise he felt off his face at this unusual invitation.

Adam hadn't expected jury selection to take so long. Unlike in America, advocates in the UK didn't get to cross-examine jurors and object to their selection if they believed they were biased. Twelve jurors were selected at random from the possible sixteen, but any of them who didn't want to give up two weeks of their life to sit on the case – and there were several – were able to make their case to the judge to be excused. She didn't let anyone off lightly, grilling them on why they thought their small business, or holiday, or job was more important than their civic duty. In almost every case, she concluded that they must sit anyway, to their obvious discontent. Only one person was able to prevail: a streetwise woman of about thirty who described in her sassy East London accent how she needed the time to revise for her upcoming accountancy exams.

'I'm working all hours as a cleaner right now to pay for the course,' she said. 'I can't afford to fail. This is my one chance to change things, for me and my family,' she told the judge. Wickstead inclined her head and dismissed her.

'Jesus, this isn't *The X Factor*,' murmured Jonathan to Adam. 'How come she's letting that miserable girl off but she wouldn't excuse the fellow who needs to go to his sales conference? This is the problem with women judges – they think with their heart, not their head.'

Adam tried to ignore him, but Jonathan's restlessness was spreading around the court. The press and public were eager for things to get started; they had come for a spectacle, not death by admin.

Eventually, the judge was satisfied with her jury – eight women and four men. The public gallery heaved forwards, in anticipation of some action finally getting underway. But the judge simply looked around airily and announced: 'Let's break for lunch.'

Raquel stood to dismiss the court, then tottered out after the judge, throwing Adam one last filthy look over her shoulder as she did so.

'Decent start for you lot!' said Ed Lowe, wandering casually over to the defence bench. 'Didn't see her stopping the previous convictions.'

Jonathan sniffed. 'Doubt it makes much difference,' he said. 'The jury will know he's been behind bars anyway so the details are fairly irrelevant.' He wasn't going to give his opponent an inch.

Ed turned to Adam. 'I should have given you a health warning with that "unused" by the sound of it,' he said chummily. 'I heard you had a bit of a run-in with Raquel – never a good idea . . .'

Adam's stomach churned. He knew Ed was just trying to be

friendly, but he'd really dropped him in it with Jonathan. His pupil master was staring at him with unrestrained spleen.

'Excuse me, Edward; my pupil and I need to have a word in private,' Jonathan said, through gritted teeth.

He turned on his heel and stalked out of the courtroom, with Adam hurrying to keep up with him. Once they were out in the Great Hall, Jonathan grabbed him roughly by the elbow and dragged him into an alcove beneath a painting of Alfred the Great.

'What does Mr Lowe mean, that you had a "run-in" with Raquel?' he hissed.

Adam swallowed nervously. 'Well, I didn't mean for it to happen, but I was in the clerks' corridor . . .'

'What the *hell* were you doing there?'

'I was following up a lead, and like I said, I didn't plan on speaking to Raquel but I ran into her and we got onto the subject of the text messages, and so it just sort of happened,' Adam finished lamely.

Jonathan drew himself up to his full height. 'Am I to understand that against my express wishes you have gone to the clerk of this court, with ludicrous and extremely personal accusations, and not only that, you have kept it from me?' His words were like bullet shots, and they sprayed Adam with spit.

'Jonathan, she sent Cliveden a coffee, right before he died!' Adam said. 'She had motive and opportunity. That was why I was in the corridor. I was trying to check the CCTV to see if it showed he'd drunk the coffee – but the CCTV is missing!'

'*What?*'

'I know it sounds far-fetched, but if Raquel did it then maybe she arranged for the footage to be wiped.'

'I have half a mind to kick you off this case for good, Green,' said Jonathan, and Adam felt his stomach clench. The idea of not seeing Jimmy's case through to the end was too awful to contemplate — let alone what it would mean for his chances at tenancy.

'I should have told you what I was doing — I'm sorry, Jonathan,' he pleaded. 'But Dr Pettigrew is going to say that Cliveden could have been poisoned in a bigger window, so I wanted to show that the police haven't considered who else could have done it.'

'How many times do I have to tell you, we are lawyers, not detectives!'

'I know, I know,' said Adam. 'But if we're just trying to create reasonable doubt . . .'

Jonathan was silent for a moment, and Adam could sense the cogs in his brain whirring.

'And who else knows about this?' he said.

'The missing CCTV? I think only Raquel — and one of the junior clerks, Abi. And I guess whoever in security sent it to Abi.'

Jonathan was breathing heavily, his nostrils flaring.

'Keep it that way, for now,' he said. 'I can't work out if you've done enough to kill our case — or save it.'

34

After lunch, the jury were brought back and sworn in. The judge looked at them sternly.

'I must remind you,' she said, 'that you must not be prejudiced by anything you have read or heard so far about the defendant. Or, indeed, the victim.'

A few of the jurors looked over at Knight, who sat impassive in the witness box. He ignored them, staring straight ahead.

'All right, Mr Lowe.' She gestured to her erstwhile colleague that he may begin. A hush went round the court as the prosecutor got to his feet. He arranged his papers on the lectern with a couple of precise movements, then turned to the jury, looking each of them in the eye in turn.

'In the afternoon of 13 March this year, a fit and healthy police officer dropped dead in this very court building. His name was Grant Cliveden, and he was not just a public servant but a much-loved colleague, a devoted father, a cherished husband and a dear friend to many. His loss has left a huge hole – in the Metropolitan Police, in his family, and in our society at large.'

Adam had to hand it to Lowe – he was good. Methodically

putting the victim central to the jury's mind, using restrained language to convey the enormity of the crime.

'To witness a man of just forty-three die in the prime of his life was appalling. But to then discover that this was no freak accident, but a deliberate and callous attack, is unspeakable. You will hear that post-mortem tests show that Grant Cliveden was poisoned, murdered with a substance that is seven million times more toxic than cobra venom. The botulinum toxin that he unwittingly ingested shut down his nerve cells one by one, until finally even his respiratory system was unable to cope. Even as his body desperately needed air, the muscles that enabled him to breathe simply stopped working. Grant Cliveden effectively drowned, on his knees in the Old Bailey. It would have been a desperate, terrifying and painful death.'

Lowe paused after he'd finished and let the court process the horror of what he had described. Everyone in the room was silent, rapt. The jury were in the palm of his hand.

'But who would want a man like Grant Cliveden, a pillar of our community, dead? The answer was surprisingly easy to discover. It was this man you see before you in the dock. His name is James Knight.'

Lowe shifted attention from himself, from his tale, to the dock. In it, Jimmy sat upright, to attention, like a soldier.

'The accused is not a man like Grant Cliveden. On the moral spectrum, they sit far apart. And James Knight loathed him for it. You will hear, ladies and gentlemen of the jury, how within days of his release from prison Knight began to plot the murder of the man he believed had put him behind bars. You will hear digital evidence that speaks to his obsession with Grant Cliveden. You will be shown phone records, which reveal how he lured Grant Cliveden to his death. And you will watch CCTV, which captured the final, fateful meeting between the victim and the accused.'

Some of the jury were taking notes — others were too engrossed in Lowe's spiel to look away. Lowe carefully described events at the Old Nag's Head, concluding that this was the moment when Knight slipped the poison into Cliveden's drink.

'Just hours later, that poison had the effect that the accused knew it would have. Natasha Cliveden lost a soulmate, Jamie and Arabella Cliveden lost a father, and Britain lost a hero.

'Ladies and gentlemen, the bravery and sacrifice of our public servants is something we rightly hold sacrosanct in this country. No one has the right to trample on that. But you will see, in the course of this trial, that James Knight believed that he did. Without remorse, he killed Grant Cliveden.'

Lowe sat down. The atmosphere in the court was electric. No one said a word, but no one had to. The silence did all the talking. It was only broken by the judge, shuffling papers and pouring herself a glass of water, apparently unmoved by Lowe's efforts.

'Mr Taylor-Cameron, would you like to proceed?' she asked Jonathan before Lowe's words had too long to settle. The defence rarely made an opening statement, but if they planned to call witnesses other than the defendant, it was permitted. Jonathan's decision to give a statement was partly strategic, but mainly down to the fact he didn't want to miss a chance to show off in front of such a huge audience, Adam supposed.

Jonathan got theatrically to his feet, lightly adjusting his wig.

'Ladies and gentlemen of the jury, my learned friend tells an enchanting story. But that is all it is — a story.'

In court, Jonathan's voice sounded even plummier than it did in the outside world. His mouth was set in a smug little pout, his eyes darted around — not fixed on the jury but checking that everyone else in the room followed him too. Adam wasn't sure it was doing him any favours.

'James Knight isn't a hero like Grant Cliveden. He's not handsome or eloquent or engaging; he has few friends; he's been in prison. All this makes him an easy person to blame. But just because he *seems* like the guilty party does not mean that he *is*.'

Adam groaned internally. This wasn't the opening statement they had prepared. Jonathan was ad-libbing, and from the confused expressions on the jury's faces, they didn't quite understand why he was being so dismissive of his own client.

'You are being asked to decide whether James Knight murdered Grant Cliveden *beyond reasonable doubt*. For this reason you must study the evidence — or lack thereof — extremely carefully. You will see that the prosecution has failed to show if or how James Knight procured this highly regulated poison. That they have failed to recover any DNA linking him to the crime. Although they will make much of the meeting in the Old Nag's Head, the CCTV footage does not conclusively show that James Knight poisoned Grant Cliveden. In fact, you will see that there is very limited CCTV altogether — almost as if it was cherry-picked to tell a very particular story.

'You see, James Knight's face may seem to fit this crime. But the facts don't fit the theory.

'The defence will be calling witnesses and producing hard,

scientific evidence that show that this is the case. Now, this is not Miss Marple. It is not for the defence to tell you who committed this heinous crime. But the burden of proof lies with the prosecution, and they must prove absolutely, incontrovertibly, that Jimmy Knight was responsible. And I am afraid that science will thwart them in this task.

'Ladies and gentlemen, if you have even a shred of reasonable doubt about Mr Knight's part in this crime, then you must acquit. I put it to you that by the end of this trial, you will have far more than a shred.'

Jonathan gave a self-satisfied little nod and sat down. As opening salvos went, it wasn't dreadful – but it had dwelt rather a lot on how unappealing Jimmy Knight was. Adam looked over at Nisha, who had her head in her hands.

'OK, then,' said the judge, pursing her lips. 'I think we will leave it there for today. Court will reconvene tomorrow at ten a.m. sharp.'

Once Jimmy had been led out in handcuffs and the judge had left in a swirl of silk robes, the volume in the court became almost unbearably loud. Post-match analysis among punters, press and court officials had begun. But Adam, Jonathan and Nisha looked at each other and realised they had nothing to say.

'Let's just go and say goodbye to Jimmy, shall we?' said Nisha.

They traipsed down to the cells, where they found Jimmy, pacing up and down.

'I think the important thing to take from Mr Taylor-Cameron's speech is that he focused on the reasonable doubt,' said Nisha, her eyes flashing towards her loathed colleague. 'I don't think the jury will really remember all that stuff about you seeming guilty.'

'Oh, stop worrying, it's all part of the plan,' said Jonathan, his face mischievous. 'However careful the judge was in choosing the jury, it's unavoidable that they have preconceived ideas about Mr Knight. Might as well acknowledge the elephant in the room.'

'Yes, that's what she was doing, isn't it, with all her instructions,' said Jimmy, more to himself than anyone else. His face was dancing with a strange, frantic energy. 'Making sure no one thought I was guilty from the off.'

'Charlotte Wickstead has a reputation for impeccable fairness,' said Adam gently. 'She'll make sure there's a level playing field, I'm sure.'

The guards came to load Jimmy back into the prison van, and the trio of lawyers took their leave. Nisha was rushing to make nursery pick-up, and Jonathan said something vague about going for a drink at his club, which Adam knew was usually code for having yet another lady on the go.

He looked at his watch. It was only just 5 p.m. – court had concluded nice and early. He dithered on the steps of the Old Bailey, then went back inside. If he was lucky, Abi would still be there. Raquel should still be with the judge concluding today's administration, so he thought he might get the chance to find the junior clerk on her own and apologise. He wasn't quite sure what he would say, or if there was any point – she hadn't responded to any of his texts – but it was worth a try.

Making the now-familiar journey up to the second floor via the back stairway, Adam rehearsed his speech: he should have told her the truth from the start; he'd never meant to get her in trouble; he'd love to make it up to her by taking her for an iced tea, properly this time. But when he got to the entrance to the corridor, he found it blocked off.

'Closed for cleaning, I'm afraid,' a rotund woman in a blue tabard told him. 'But if you go through the cafe, you can get in from the other side.'

Adam thanked her and followed her directions. Approaching the corridor from the other end, he realised how close it was to the locked door of the security office, which he hadn't seen before. That must be where they oversaw the CCTV. He made a mental note to ask Jonathan if it was worth speaking to them about the missing footage of Cliveden with the coffee.

He made his way down the clerks' corridor, to the open hatch of Abi's office. Except it was closed. She must have left for the day. Adam was half disappointed, half relieved. Perhaps this was a sign. Someone like Abi wouldn't be interested in a loser like him anyway.

Adam went back out the way he had come, taking his time. He turned the corner that led to the security office, and that's when he saw it. A figure he recognised, coming out of the door and shutting it tight behind them.

Not for the first time, he wondered what on earth Emma Owens was up to.

35

Phone call

'Oh, Adam, I've just seen you on the six o'clock news! Have you watched it? I suppose you're not home . . . but don't worry, it's recorded on Sky Plus so you can watch it any time. Maybe it's on that player thingy too . . .'

'Er, thanks, Mum, but I'm sure it's probably just a two-second glimpse—'

'That's two seconds more than most people have been on national news! I've already had Judy round to watch it, and Penny, and Mike and Ruth, Brenda has Pilates tonight but she said she'd call in on her way back . . .'

'Oh God, Mum, why do you have to be so embarrassing?'

'Embarrassing? What's embarrassing about being proud of my only son? Now, the only thing I would say is that you're not smiling, and your face really does transform when you smile, so that's something to think about for tomorrow.'

'You think I should be grinning as I walk into court to defend in a murder trial?'

'Well, not grinning exactly, but maybe you could just try and,

I don't know, smoulder a bit . . . Who knows what single girls might be watching.'

'MUM.'

'Your boss is a bit of a dish, isn't he? Although he really needs to rethink that hairdo – all a bit OTT if you ask me.'

'Ha, OK, I'll pass that on.'

'Did you get my message the other day?'

'Er, no, sorry, Mum – did you leave it on my voicemail?'

'That's OK, I thought you probably didn't. It said your mailbox thingy was full or something but I tried to leave one anyway.'

'I don't think that works, Mum.'

'Well, clearly not. Anyway, it was just to say – I'm sorry, for getting upset about you trying to talk about your dad. Of course you've got questions. You were so young when it happened and I've just always tried to protect you. I sometimes forget you're a grown man now.'

'I know, Mum. And I'm sorry too. I know how hard you've tried to move on.'

'I'm sorry, Adam. I wish I could – but I just find it so hard . . . even to think of it now . . .'

'It's OK, Mum. Honestly. We should talk properly about it though, don't you think?'

'Maybe . . . Why don't you come home at the weekend?'

'I can't – we're in the middle of the trial . . .'

'Oh but, Adam, it's the synagogue rounders tournament to raise money for the roof repairs, and rabbi was just saying we need more young people to even out the teams, so I was going to put your name down.'

'Actually . . .'

'Oh, and they're doing a buffet after, which is the perfect time to introduce you to a few of the young ladies – just wait until they hear you've been on the telly! I wonder if there's a way to get a Sky Plus recording onto a DVD so I could bring it with me . . .'

'Seeing as you needed a step-by-step guide for sending an emoji to Judy, I'm going to hope that's an empty threat.'

'Don't underestimate your mother, Adam!'

'Seriously, Mum, it won't be this weekend, but if I come, can we talk? There's just so many questions—'

'Adam, darling, that's the doorbell ringing, it will be Brenda. I've got to go. Let me know about the rounders. Love you.'

36

Ed Lowe kicked off the second day in court by showing the jury
the CCTV of Cliveden's last moments. There were audible
gasps from the jury as they watched the police officer falling
to his knees and helplessly grabbing at his throat. Adam had to
admit that blown up to such grotesque proportions and shown
on the big screen, it looked even worse than he remembered
from seeing it first time around.

'I'd now like to call Jade Evans.'

Jade was a junior barrister, who had been in court that day
and was one of those who'd rushed to Cliveden's aid. She had
a round, trustworthy face and wore her braided hair tied back
neatly in a bun.

Under Ed's questioning, Jade described how Cliveden had
been called as the police witness in the case she was defending, where the four young men were accused of possession
of a variety of drugs and weapons. She said he'd entered the
court shortly after half past two, and then once in the witness box had become 'suddenly and visibly unwell'. Jade and
her fellow barristers had rushed to his aid, but he'd seemed
unable even to speak, and as they'd helped him from the

witness box they'd realised he was also struggling to breathe. They'd tried to give him a glass of water but he'd started to choke. An ambulance was called – 'by the usher, I believe' – but, Jade said, 'it was too late'. Concluding her testimony, she wiped a single, stoic tear from beneath her dark eyes. Ed sat down, looking pleased. As well he might, noted Adam. He'd set the scene perfectly.

Jonathan bounced to his feet. 'Ms Evans, would you say that Mr Cliveden was in his usual good health when he entered the courtroom?'

Jade frowned. 'I'd never met him before, so it's hard for me to comment on his "usual health".'

'Very well, let me rephrase. Did he seem unwell when he arrived?'

'Not noticeably, no.'

'And was he consuming any food or drink as he came into the courtroom?'

Jade's frown deepened. 'As my learned friend must know, eating and drinking is forbidden in the courtroom.'

'But, for the benefit of the jury, it is allowed elsewhere in the Old Bailey building?'

'Yes.'

'So it is possible that Mr Cliveden was eating or drinking shortly before he was called at half past two?'

Ed Lowe was on his feet. 'Objection – the witness cannot be asked to speculate.'

The judge nodded. 'I agree. Mr Taylor-Cameron, please keep your questions to facts the witness can reasonably comment on.'

'My apologies, Your Honour. No further questions.'

The jury looked nonplussed, but this was good, thought Adam. Jonathan was attempting to establish early on that there were other potential opportunities for Cliveden to have been poisoned. And given his focus on what Cliveden was doing right before he entered the courtroom, he was preparing the ground for revealing that the CCTV had been deleted. Although the judge had overruled his question, the point had been made.

Adam looked down at the list of witnesses to see who was up next and inwardly groaned. Any marginal gains they'd made were about to be immediately lost.

'I'd like to call Natasha Cliveden.'

Cliveden's statuesque wife rose from her seat at the side of the court and made her way to the witness box. She glided in with the elegance of tall reeds swaying in the breeze. As Raquel swore her in, Adam studied the two women. Today Natasha was dressed in a pale blue shift dress and navy blazer, with a string of egg-shaped pearls wound around her neck — a look that was classic and yet somehow, on her, looked fresh. Her honey-blonde hair was swept effortlessly to one side, her lips painted the perfect shade of rosy nude. She had no idea she was reciting her oath to her husband's mistress, of that Adam was convinced. She barely seemed to notice Raquel, a woman at least fifteen years her senior, whose yellowish highlights, clinging skirt suit and towering Mary Janes were so at odds with Natasha's chic presence. For her part, Raquel maintained admirable composure. If she was thinking in that moment of the terrible things the man they'd shared had said about this woman, she didn't show it.

'Mrs Cliveden, I know this will be very difficult for you,' Ed Lowe was saying, his voice a new octave of solicitous concern.

He somehow addressed Natasha directly while still keeping half an eye on the jury. 'Just take your time and answer my questions as best you can.'

Natasha nodded, regarding Lowe demurely from beneath long Bambi eyelashes. A balled tissue was clutched in her hand.

Lowe asked her a series of sympathetic questions about Cliveden's personal and professional lives. No, he didn't have any enemies, she confirmed, and he didn't seem to be under any particular stress – no more so than you'd expect of a police officer of his rank. He'd never received any threats on his life or been in any kind of trouble. Grant loved his job, she said, fighting back tears, and he knew the risks involved – but he'd always been so careful.

Adam wondered if Lowe had worked out the exact angle he needed to tilt his head in order to signal maximum compassion – because it was locked at forty-five degrees as he listened to Natasha's faltering words.

'Let me take you back to 13 March, the day that Grant died,' Ed went on. Natasha gulped and dabbed her eyes some more. 'When was the last time you saw your husband?'

'It was at home, at about eight,' Natasha said. 'I was leaving with the kids for school. Grant's shift was starting a bit later that day so he was still in the house.'

'And had Mr Cliveden told you what his plans were for that day?'

'He told me he had to be in court that afternoon,' she said. 'And that he would be home about seven.'

'So he didn't mention this meeting in the Old Nag's Head, which we now know he had arranged the night before?'

'No, but he wouldn't generally tell me the ins and outs of what he'd be doing at work,' Natasha said.

'So that tells you that the meeting was, in Grant's eyes, a work engagement?'

'Yes.'

'And he had no cause for concern about the person he was meeting?'

'He definitely didn't seem worried or stressed,' Natasha said. 'He was laughing and joking – I can remember him holding Jamie upside down by his ankles . . .' Her voice choked, and she pressed a trembling hand to her mouth.

'I am sorry, Mrs Cliveden,' said Lowe. 'But this is important. Did your husband give you any reason whatsoever to suggest that he was worried about or indeed frightened by the meeting he had arranged that day?'

'No, none.'

'And had he ever mentioned the name James Knight, or Jimmy Knight, to you?'

'No, never.'

'Thank you, Mrs Cliveden,' said Lowe. 'Now, this may seem off topic, but it is relevant. Did you see your husband eat or drink anything that morning?'

Mrs Cliveden shook her head. 'He was doing the twelve-eight diet, we both were, because we were meant to be going to Mauritius in April,' she sniffed. 'It means you are only allowed to eat and drink between the hours of twelve and eight, so no, he wouldn't have had anything other than water.'

'Thank you, Mrs Cliveden. No further questions.'

'Mr Taylor-Cameron, do you wish to cross-examine the witness?' the judge asked.

When they were preparing the trial, Jonathan had insisted that cross-examining a grieving widow would be a bad look. He was already flipping through his box file and getting ready for the next witness, but something had struck Adam. He thought of Natasha and Emma Owens confronting each other all those weeks ago, and the white-hot fury that had twisted Natasha's perfect features. And then Emma, coming out of the Old Bailey security office. He scribbled a quick note and handed it to Jonathan. His pupil master read it, his brow furrowed.

'Mr Taylor-Cameron?' the judge repeated.

'My apologies, Your Honour,' said Jonathan, getting to his feet. 'Yes, just a few brief questions.'

He looked down at his note, and then up at Mrs Cliveden, who was making desperate eyes at her FLO, who had no doubt told her she probably wouldn't face cross-examination. Adam held his breath. He couldn't believe that Jonathan had agreed to act on his suggestion – but then, he supposed his pupil master could never resist the chance to revel in the sound of his own voice.

'Mrs Cliveden, had your husband ever had problems with any of his work colleagues?'

'His work colleagues loved him.'

'Of course, there is no doubt that your husband was extremely popular. But were there any individual cases where Mr Cliveden experienced conflict at work?'

Natasha paused, fiddling with the tissue in her hand.

'People were jealous of him,' she said quietly.

'Jealous, you say?' said Jonathan, eyebrow raised theatrically. 'And what problems did this cause?'

'It didn't cause problems, not really,' said Natasha. 'Except for a few months before he died, there was one very bitter individual who made some very nasty allegations. She was trying to ruin his career.'

'And what were these allegations?'

'That he'd been breaking police rules,' said Natasha. 'Like he was bent, or something.' The jury were visibly interested now, some of them leaning forwards, the note-takers among them scribbling furiously. 'But that was all disproved,' she added hurriedly. 'The troublemaker was shown to be just that – a troublemaker. And she had to leave the department.'

'I see,' said Jonathan. 'So when you told my learned friend earlier that your husband didn't have any enemies, that wasn't quite true, was it?'

Natasha looked startled. 'That was just a silly work thing,' she said. 'There was no truth in what she said.'

Jonathan pulled an exaggerated confused face. 'I didn't ask if it was true, Mrs Cliveden,' he said. 'I merely wish to establish that there may be others who would have a motive to kill your husband, other than my client – who has not been linked to the crime by any DNA evidence.'

They were on a roll. The jury were engaged, alert. They'd all seen *Line of Duty*, and this talk of bent coppers had them hooked. He scribbled another quick note to Jonathan – 'Ask her about their money.'

Jonathan took the folded paper, read it, but shook his head. Adam leaned forward, trying to implore him with every sinew of his body.

'No further questions, Your Honour.'

'Are you sure? Do you wish to consult with your junior?' said the judge. She was regarding Adam with interest.

'No, thank you, Your Honour.' Jonathan sat down, shooting Adam a stern look. He clearly thought pursuing the mysterious source of the family's wealth would be too much like 'trashing the victim'. Ed Lowe was on his feet immediately.

'Mrs Cliveden, are we to understand that your husband spoke openly to you about the allegations this individual had made against him?'

'Oh, yes.'

'And did he consider this person to be a threat to his personal safety?'

'Absolutely not.'

'Do you believe this person wanted your husband dead?'

'No!'

'No further questions.'

Natasha had retained remarkable composure for the duration of her testimony, but the moment it was over it was like whatever life raft she had been clinging to suddenly deflated. She dropped her head to her hands and started weeping great wracking sobs, her whole body shaking. As her sister and her FLO helped her from the box, practically holding her up as she wailed like a wounded animal, the jury shifted uncomfortably in their seats. Adam wondered what they'd remember from her testimony – that Cliveden had been accused of corruption and had an enemy within the police force, or simply that she was a woman broken by the heart-stopping grief of losing her husband?

As if she could read his mind, the judge waited until Natasha had been shown from the courtroom, then addressed the jury.

'It is difficult not to be affected by the sight of such terrible

238

grief,' she said. 'But I must urge you not to let it cloud your judgement. Your task here is to dispense justice, not sympathy, and it is essential that remains your focus.'

Adam caught Nisha's eye, and she was half smiling. This trial was already going in directions they couldn't have dared hope for.

37

Adam slept restlessly that night. As soon as court had been adjourned, he'd asked Rupert for Emma Owens's number. His friend had been confused as to why he'd wanted it but had texted it to him anyway. Adam had tried to call Emma multiple times – he'd wanted to ask her what she'd been doing in the security office and also to explain what had happened in court that day. But Emma had never answered. Perhaps it was no surprise. After all, if she'd been talking to her colleague, Natasha Cliveden's FLO, or had read any of the many online reports of the trial, she would know they had insinuated she could be a murderer.

On the third day in court the prosecution's star witness was Gary Parker, who had shared a cell with Knight for four months in late 2021 and early 2022. Adam wondered how on earth he'd been compelled to give evidence – grasses had to be the least popular people in prison.

Before Parker was sworn in, the judge issued a reporting restriction to the press preventing them from identifying him. The prisoner twitched nervously in the witness box, eyes darting all around the courtroom. Parker was in his mid-thirties, but was as short and slight as an eleven-year-old boy, with angular features and acne-scarred skin. His dark suit was inevitably too big for him, and no one had bothered to help him do up the cuffs of his voluminous shirt. A nervous tic saw him regularly pull back his lips so his gums and a set of broken, wonky teeth were on show.

Lowe began his questioning. Parker confirmed he was serving an eight-year sentence for burglary – his fourth stint inside. He went on to describe the rooming arrangements at Pentonville, whereby prisoners were randomly moved around between cells and given new cellmates a few times a year. That was how he had ended up bunking with Knight. In the dock, his former cellmate grimaced.

'And how would you describe Mr Knight, as a cellmate?' Lowe asked.

'Decent. He was pretty quiet, kept himself to himself. Didn't cause no trouble or attract none. That's all you really want inside.'

'You say Mr Knight was quiet – but he started to open up to you, did he not?'

'Yeah, like I said, for the first month or so I barely got a peep out of him. But that's not that unusual – there's some fellas who wanna play the game, prison politics and all that, talk all day to anyone who will listen. Then there's others who just want to keep their head down and try to pretend all this ain't happening. And I thought he was that kind of fella, you know?'

Adam suspected Parker himself probably fell into the category of 'talk all day to anyone who will listen'.

'Anyways, that all changed when he got the news his son died.'

In the dock, Knight's jaw clenched.

Lowe looked down at his notes. It didn't matter that Knight had tried to keep this detail secret; the prosecution had found out anyway. 'This is Marcellus Knight, who died aged nineteen in February 2022, the victim of an unsolved hit-and-run.'

'Yeah, that's right. Jimmy was very upset, as any father would be. Him and his kid, they were tight. Before Jimmy got banged up it was him who had sole custody of the boy cos his ex was a junkie. And all them years he was inside, his kid came every week. That was the only time I ever saw Jimmy smile, on visiting day.'

'So how did his demeanour change after the death of his son?'

'Jimmy was angry. Like, really angry. Punching the walls of the cell, smashing stuff up. And he started doing mad shit, like at lunch one day he flipped the tray of one of the worst gang-bangers in there for no reason, and that's just asking for a whole world of trouble.'

'And how did Grant Cliveden's name come into it?'

'Jimmy blamed that Cliveden bloke for the whole thing. He started going on and on about how Cliveden had framed him and he'd never be inside if it weren't for him. And he said – and I remember this is the phrase he used – that when it came to his kid, Cliveden had "blood on his hands".'

'And what do you think he meant by that?'

Parker shrugged. 'I suppose just that if he weren't inside, he would have been there for his kid and he wouldn't have been there at the wrong place and wrong time.'

'And did Mr Knight express a wish to harm Mr Cliveden?'

'He kept saying, "He has to pay for this." He wanted revenge, that is for sure.'

'You have spent a significant proportion of your life in prison, Mr Parker. Is it usual for prisoners to have such strong feelings about individual police officers?'

Parker's lips peeled back in a grotesque grimace. 'Most of the lads, they hate the rozzers full stop. All of 'em. But I doubt many can remember the name of the cop that nicked 'em. I wouldn't have a scooby who did me. So yeah, it was unusual to hear Jimmy chatting on about this Cliveden, like it was all his fault. For him, it was personal.'

'Thank you, Mr Parker, your testimony has been most illuminating. No further questions.'

As Lowe took his seat again, Adam looked over at Knight. It was the first time in the trial he'd shown even a hint of emotion. Until now he had looked completely unruffled by events, but now his jaw was working in furious agitation. Adam wasn't surprised Parker's testimony had got to him — it was a major blow, from someone he must at one time have trusted.

Jonathan rose to his feet.

'Mr Parker, did you ever hear Mr Knight make specific threats to kill Mr Cliveden?'

'Not, like, a plan or nothing, but what he meant was clear.'

'So did you report this to the authorities?'

'No, but like I said, it's not like he'd said anything pacific . . .'

'Specific, Mr Parker. Either you thought Mr Knight wanted to kill Mr Cliveden, or you didn't. Which was it?'

'I thought he wanted to kill him, but, no offence, you don't really get what it's like to be doing bird. Wouldn't be a good look for me to be going around grassing on my cellie.'

'But that's exactly what you're doing now, is it not?'

'That's different.'

'Different how? Is it different because this time you've been offered something in return?'

Ed Lowe was on his feet. 'Objection, Your Honour! This question is prejudicial.'

The judge paused. 'I disagree. It is material to the case. Mr Taylor-Cameron, you may continue.'

Jonathan smirked. 'Have you been offered anything in return for your testimony today, Mr Parker? And may I remind you that you are under oath.'

Parker's lips were working overtime as he gurned and twitched in discomfort. 'They said it would look good for my parole,' he finally admitted. 'I've got the hearing next month, so I wanted to be helpful.'

Jonathan grinned, scenting blood. 'Are you an honest man, Mr Parker?'

More writhing and twitching. 'I am being honest today.'

'That wasn't the question I asked. You have pleaded not guilty to your previous . . .' he glanced down at the brief Adam had painstakingly prepared '. . . eleven convictions, all of which you have conclusively been found guilty of. To give just one example, when you were caught driving without insurance you tried to claim it was your twin brother behind the wheel, even though you do not, in fact, have a twin brother.'

There was a small snigger of laughter from the jury. Parker squirmed.

'I will admit, yes, that in the past I have sometimes been less than one hundred per cent truthful.'

'What an interesting way of putting it,' said Jonathan. 'But with that being so, why should we believe you now?'

'I'm just trying to do the right thing,' mumbled Parker, but the wind was gone from his sails.

'No further questions.'

Adam sneaked a look at Knight. His poker face was back, and as Parker was led from the witness box he stared straight ahead, his eyes fixed on the judge.

38

The conclusion of Parker's testimony also brought the court proceedings to a close for the weekend. After a quick conference with an agitated Jimmy in the cells – 'Thank fuck the judge made Parker reveal he's only doing this for his own stinking gain' – Jonathan, Adam and Nisha headed to the Wig and Pen for a quick drink. If you'd asked him on Wednesday morning what the mood on Friday night would be, Adam would have guessed commiseration rather than celebration – but in fact, the team found themselves in remarkably good spirits. Jonathan downed a pint of Guinness in an unfeasibly quick time, and excused himself – much to Adam and Nisha's relief. No doubt he had several other 'social engagements' to fit in before his wife-imposed curfew.

'You know, he's actually turned out to be much better in court than I expected,' said Nisha after Jonathan left, taking a swig of her second gin-and-tonic. 'A born show-off, I guess.'

Adam smiled. 'Yeah, I know. It's just all that pesky "preparing" and "listening to the client" that he hates.'

Nisha cackled. 'But in all seriousness, it could be going a lot worse,' she said. 'We've had a couple of important calls go our way and that's made all the difference. But next week is going to be much tougher.'

Adam nodded. 'The scientific evidence.'

'Yes, and the phone and computer stuff. That's much harder to counter. Jimmy hasn't been able to give us a proper explanation himself. Oh, shit.' She was staring at her phone. 'Nav has to work late, I'm going to have to go and relieve the nanny – sorry, Adam.' She drained her drink. 'You must have, like, mates to meet? A hot date or something?'

'Yeah, right,' laughed Adam, and Nisha looked at him strangely. 'But honestly, it's fine! Have a great weekend – I'll see you on Monday.'

Adam had most of his pint left so he found a stool at the bar and sipped his drink slowly. It was still early and his veins were coursing with the adrenalin of the day in court; he certainly wasn't ready to go home yet. He pulled out his phone and wondered whether he should see who was about. It had been ages since he'd seen any of the guys from Oxford – but he'd skipped so many plans recently he doubted they'd want to meet up spontaneously. Maybe Rupert was about – or even Georgina? But if he asked he could imagine her saying she'd rather spend her Friday night sticking pins in her eyes than drinking with him.

He was still staring at his phone wondering what to do when it lit up with a text message alert. He almost fell off his stool when he saw who it was from: Emma Owens.

I'm at your chambers. We need to talk.

He texted back: I'll be there in 10.

However he'd thought he'd be spending Friday night, it wasn't this. Adam downed the rest of his pint and power-walked to Stag Court. Emma had been so paranoid about speaking to him before that she'd made them break into a locked garden in the middle of the night, but now she'd just strolled right up to his office – what was she playing at?

He got his explanation within minutes of arriving at chambers – where he almost ran into Rupert, coming out.

'Oh, hey, Adam, what are you doing here?'

'Um, just got some papers to pick up. What about you?'

Rupert sighed and rolled his eyes. 'Few bits of work to finish off before the weekend. Em's here actually – we're meant to be going out for dinner when I'm done. I'm just running to the offie to get us some beers to keep us going – you want anything?'

'No, you're all right – thanks, though.'

He hurried down the corridor and let himself into Rupert's small room. It was the sort of environment that would give his mother an immediate heart attack. Every surface was covered in avalanches of paperwork, books were stacked upside down and back to front on shelves, a jumble of dirty shoes and a bulging gym bag had been tossed willy-nilly around the desk. Discarded takeaway boxes were near the bin but not quite in it, banana peels sat on top of open briefs. It was no wonder that Rupert always held his meetings with clients in the conference room.

In the middle of all this chaos sat Emma Owens, arms folded. It was the first time Adam had seen her out of police uniform, and she suited the green tea dress covered in daisies she was wearing instead. But her face was like thunder.

'You didn't take me seriously, did you?'

'Emma, I don't know what to think with you. Have you been tampering with CCTV at the Old Bailey?'

'*What?*'

Emma got to her feet, and Adam thought she was about to run out of the room. But she simply went to the door and locked them in.

'We don't have much time. I've sent Rupert to the off-licence but it's not that far.'

Adam eyed the locked door warily, as Emma sat down again.

'I was in court today,' she said.

'Were you? I didn't see you.'

She shrugged. 'There are ways of not being noticed. Anyway, what do you think was the most important thing the prison informant said?'

Adam was still thrown by Emma saying she'd been there. Hadn't he studied the faces of everyone in the public gallery – how could he have missed her?

'Um – that Knight never actually said that he had a plan to kill Cliveden?'

'No,' said Emma. 'It was about Marcellus.'

'Are you going to tell me then? Like you said, we don't have much time . . .'

The tension was sliced through by the vibrating sound of a phone.

'Is that yours?' said Emma, annoyed, as Adam scrambled to silence it. That strange number again – who was trying so hard to get hold of him, but not hard enough to leave a message? It was starting to get weird now.

'Sorry, sorry.' He switched it off. Perhaps he should block the number – if it was the person who'd left the note in his pigeon-hole trying to intimidate him further, he wanted nothing to do with it.

Emma glanced nervously towards the window. 'According to Gary Parker, Knight said Cliveden had blood on his hands when it came to Marcellus. And I believe he was right.'

'You mean . . . Cliveden killed Marcellus?'

Emma looked at her feet. 'Look, I didn't know Marcellus was going to come up in the trial. I hoped he wouldn't, because this is really hard for me to talk about – you'll see why. But I think you need to know.'

Adam bit his lip. He noticed that Emma was shaking. She took a deep breath.

'Marcellus found me. He was a law student, and he sent me an email saying he wanted to talk to me for his dissertation, which was about the interaction between the justice system and the police, or something. And I was part of this outreach programme in the police, so it was the sort of thing I got approached for from time to time. Anyway, I bought it. I agreed to meet.'

Adam didn't want to interrupt her. She was stumbling over her words, which he knew was what happened when you kept a secret locked away long enough.

'We met in this old greasy spoon near his uni. Straight away, I knew, this kid was something special. He had that South London slang thing, and style-wise he wasn't much to look at, but he was super smart, switched on. He was asking me all these incisive, direct questions – kind of like he was a barrister. I was impressed. But it quickly became clear that we weren't really there to talk about his dissertation.'

'He wanted to talk about his dad.'

Emma nodded. 'He told me his dad was a victim of a major miscarriage of justice. And the way he spoke about his dad, you could tell he just idolised him, you know? He never knew his mum, so for as long as he could remember, it was just him and his dad, against the world. His dad could fix anything, he said. Knew everything there was to know about football. Made him work hard at school, was tough on him when he misbehaved, but so proud of even the tiniest of achievements – like a swimming badge, or a good mark on his homework or something. His dad had never let him down, not once. And then when Marcellus was ten, his dad got sent to prison. Losing him was the toughest thing he'd ever had to go through. But he never once doubted that his dad was innocent, just like he said he was. That's why Marcellus wanted to be a lawyer. He wanted to clear his dad's name.'

'And that's why he wanted to talk to you.'

'His story was incredibly moving. I asked him, "How did this miscarriage of justice come about?" He replied that his dad was framed, by a corrupt police officer who'd planted evidence. And that police officer was Grant Cliveden.'

She paused, took another deep breath. 'I was shocked, naturally. I said something like, "That's my boss," and Marcellus said, "I know." That's when I realised this meeting was no accident.'

'He wanted your help?'

'Exactly. He said no one believed that Cliveden could be responsible, and he needed help proving that he was corrupt. He needed a whistleblower on the inside, basically.'

'Why did he come to you?'

'God, I wish I knew,' said Emma bitterly. 'Maybe because I was young and he thought I'd be more likely to take him seriously? Maybe because I have some bullshit profile on the outreach website saying I got into policing to give a voice to the voiceless and to protect justice at any cost? Maybe he was just going to try anyone who worked with Cliveden, until someone agreed to help. I don't know why he trusted me. But I wish he never had.'

'So what did you say?' Adam asked, although he could guess the answer.

Emma looked away. She couldn't meet Adam's eyes.

'Look, you have to understand – I was so new on the job back then. I was naive. Some kid contacted me out of the blue and asked me to set fire to everything I'd worked towards, for years. I didn't want to believe that what he was saying could be true. I couldn't afford to.'

'You turned him down.'

'I told him he'd got it all wrong. Said I worked alongside Cliveden and I'd never known a police officer with such impeccably high standards. I said I understood why he would be so desperate to believe his dad was innocent, but sometimes emotion can distort the truth. And I told myself that was true too.'

'So what changed your mind?'

Emma put her head in her hands. 'I thought I was doing the right thing.'

She'd clearly got to the part that she found most difficult to tell. Adam was quiet, letting her compose herself. She kept her hands clamped to her forehead as she continued.

'So I went back to work, and I tried to put what Marcellus had told me out of my mind. I was totally convinced it was nonsense. Then I started to worry – what if he keeps making trouble, and it comes out that he met with me and I didn't say anything? So I decided I better tell Cliveden.'

'Oh, shit.'

Emma nodded grimly. 'Like I said, I was naive. I was ambitious. I was totally fucking stupid. So I went to Cliveden and said, "Look, this is probably nothing, just some mad conspiracy theory, but there's this kid, and he's poking around, saying you framed his dad." And Cliveden looked at me sharply and asked for his name. So I told him. And a week later – a *week* later – Marcellus was dead.'

'So you're saying . . .'

'That Cliveden killed him, or arranged for him to be killed? What do you think? The timing was more than a little coincidental. I wouldn't have known about it at all because it didn't make national news – the deaths of kids like Marcellus rarely do. But I happened to be on a callout in Croydon and I saw a report of the funeral in the local paper. And, Adam – I can't describe to you how I felt.'

She was crying now, tears running silently down her cheeks.

'I couldn't stop thinking about that sparky kid, who got into law school despite all the odds being stacked against him. Who was driven by love, and a sense of what was right, and paid the ultimate price.'

'It's not your fault,' said Adam, awkwardly. He didn't know whether he should try and comfort her.

'It is,' said Emma thickly. 'If it wasn't for Marcellus, I could still be like the rest of the morons in this country, believing Cliveden was the next best thing to Superman. But after Marcellus died, that's when I started looking for signs that Cliveden was corrupt. And you know what? Every single thing Marcellus told me was right.'

Emma dried her eyes and looked directly at Adam. 'So when

I say you're in danger digging into this case, I don't mean it lightly. They could kill you.'

'Cliveden is dead . . .'

'But his paymasters aren't.'

Adam was aghast at what she was telling him. 'Have you not tried to report this? You could have brought Cliveden to justice, when he was still alive!'

'You think I didn't try?' Emma said, angry red spots rising on her cheeks. 'When I went to anti-corruption command about Cliveden, I told them I thought he was also involved in Marcellus's murder. It sounded so wild the officer I was speaking to actually suggested that I might need some time off for stress. And you know what, planting that cocaine in my vehicle was the smartest thing Cliveden could have done. Once they found that, no one took anything I said seriously – especially the stuff about Marcellus, which they thought was crazy anyway.'

Adam was thinking fast. 'So Jimmy must have suspected the same thing you did – that Cliveden was the killer.'

Emma sighed. 'All I know is that Marcellus died trying to clear his dad's name, so I have a duty to carry on that work for him. I'd say Jimmy Knight has the strongest possible motive for murdering Grant Cliveden. But if there's a chance that this is another miscarriage of justice, I don't want to stand by and let it happen. So yes, I was at the Old Bailey security office, and I was looking at CCTV. But only because I thought – I hoped – it might prove Jimmy didn't do it.'

'And what did you find?' Adam asked eagerly.

Emma opened her mouth to answer, but there was a rattle at the doorknob.

'Em, are you in there?' came Rupert's voice. 'Why've you locked the door?'

Emma looked at Adam in a way that let him know the conversation was over.

'Oh, shit, is it locked? Sorry I didn't realise . . .' She went to the door and opened it. Rupert stood there, a case of beer in his hands.

'What the hell are you doing in a locked room – with Adam Green?'

39

It was lucky that Rupert wasn't the jealous type, because he was fairly easily persuaded that there was an innocent explanation to the door being locked, with the girl he was dating and his male colleague on the other side.

Even so, it was clear Adam wasn't welcome to stay and share the beers. He made his awkward excuses and left, fearing that Rupert was looking at him slightly askance as they said good-bye. That was just what he needed, Adam thought. Rupert was the only solid vote he thought he had in the tenancy decision and now even that might be in peril.

Adam's weekend passed in a blur of sleepless nights and gruelling hours spent at his desk, poring over the technical details of the evidence they expected to hear in court at the beginning of the week. He tried to do a couple of hours on the Kavanagh boxes too, because their difficult client was still peppering both him and Jonathan with aggressive emails asking for progress updates. On Friday night he had made a mental note to ring back the mystery number that kept calling, but whether it was the lack of sleep or the sheer amount of work he was trying to cram in, he completely forgot about it.

Meanwhile, he couldn't put what Emma had told him from his mind. Had Marcellus been murdered in cold blood because she'd tipped off Cliveden? If so, didn't that give Jimmy Knight an even stronger motive for wanting the police officer dead? For the first time, Adam started to have doubts about their client. He also found himself spending a lot of time lurking by his window, peering down at the street below and thinking about the envelope that had been left in his pigeonhole, turning over questions in his mind that he'd barely allowed himself to think about for years. Was he being watched, even now?

By the time Monday morning rolled around, Adam's every last nerve was jangling.

'Big weekend, was it?' Nisha said, when she saw the shadows under his eyes and his trembling hands as he sipped his Costa coffee outside Court Number One. Adam shook his head. Jonathan seemed not to notice at all.

The morning of day four in court was taken up with the evidence from Knight's computer, which wasn't really his computer at all but had been lent to him by a cousin. First the cousin was reluctantly brought in to confirm his loan of the device. Then a police I T expert explained the process of harvesting the data from the computer in painstaking detail, before going into what their findings showed. Finally a 'digital psychologist' was called, to give their professional opinion that Knight's search pattern showed 'obsessive tendencies' and a 'one-track fixation' with the victim.

Jonathan spent their morning conference raging that the expert witness represented a wishy-washy profession with no basis in science, but he failed to land any blows during cross-examination. The psychologist – a lean, serious man with a perfectly bald head – was reasonable and persuasive. As far as the jury would be concerned, the computer had spoken – and what it said was damning.

It was a crushing morning. But Jonathan seemed to shake the disappointment off like a dog emerging from a muddy bog – 'I mean, what else could we expect?' – while Adam felt the setbacks deep in his bones. Last week's triumphs were a long time ago now – and he wondered if the jury even remembered them at all.

'And it's only going to get worse,' muttered Nisha, as the judge adjourned court for lunch.

She wasn't wrong. By the time they returned to court in the afternoon, the temperature had reached unbearable levels. Although they were into September, the heat of earlier in the summer had returned with a vengeance. With no windows and little ventilation, Court Number One felt stickily oppressive. The jury were restless, prickly with heat, and visibly unhappy to be in their mahogany pen. The public gallery was noticeably emptier, with the hardy spectators who remained fanning themselves with their order papers.

Into this cauldron stepped Detective Chief Inspector Paula Brook, wearing a dark blue two-piece, her greying brown hair pulled back into a neat bun. She was the officer who had led the investigation into Cliveden's murder. Adam wondered, as she took the witness stand, whether it played in Brook's mind that Cliveden had been doing exactly what she was doing now when he met his end.

Lowe eased her in by asking about her career – twenty years with the Met, many of them spent leading high-profile murder inquiries – and how her unit had been put in charge of this investigation. Brook explained that she had been assigned the case because she hadn't known Cliveden personally – though she admitted that she had of course known him by reputation.

'And can you explain how you came to arrest Mr Knight?' Lowe asked.

'Certainly. Once the lab had established that the cause of death was poisoning, and the fact that poison was likely to have been administered within the previous forty-eight hours, it was then a case of tracing DI Cliveden's movements prior to his arrival at the Old Bailey shortly before 2.30 p.m. Examining his phone, we were able to establish that he had arranged a meeting at the Old Nag's Head via communication with an unknown number. CCTV recovered from the pub revealed that the meeting did go ahead, and that there was an opportunity for poisoning. The number used to arrange the meeting was unregistered, but triangulation data placed it at a property known to be occupied by James Knight. Face recognition experts were able to identify Knight as the same man who had met Cliveden in the Old Nag's Head. We were then able to obtain a warrant to raid Mr Knight's property, where we recovered evidence that linked him to the crime.'

She was a good witness, thought Adam. She answered Lowe's questions with helpful detail, while always remaining on topic. That's what experience got you.

'And what evidence was recovered?' Lowe was asking.

'We recovered a laptop, details of which I believe have been presented to the jury,' Brook said. 'And a prepaid phone – the same one which had been used to contact DI Cliveden.'

Lowe paused and held up a Nokia phone in a sealed plastic bag, which he then handed to the jury.

'I believe you are referring to exhibit 7B, which I have now presented to the jury.'

'Correct.'

'And this phone had only been used to contact one number?'

'Well, it only sent texts to one number. And that was to Grant Cliveden.'

'You refer to the fact this phone was also used to make and receive calls?'

'Only made them, in fact. Three calls, two on the evening before the murder and one on the morning of, to another unregistered number. Unfortunately, we were unable to determine who those calls were to.'

It was one of the things that was bugging Adam too – who were those three calls to, and why were they made? They had hit a complete dead end in following that one up, and it seemed the police had too.

'Very well,' Lowe was saying. 'Let us focus on the text messages. Members of the jury, I would now like to refer you to document 7C in your bundles,' Lowe said, flipping his own ring binder to the relevant page. 'As it is short, I will read aloud to you the exchange between the two numbers. "7B" refers to the phone you are currently looking at, "GC" refers to Grant Cliveden's phone.

'7B: D/d aeries & blanco. Easy win. Can meet to discuss.

'GC: Who is this?

'7B: A friend of J. He said to tell you S699 – you'd know what it meant.

'GC: When and where?

'7B: Old Nag's Head, Bouverie Street. Midday. Come alone.'

Lowe paused, letting the jury catch up with him. Then he addressed Brook again.

'Chief Inspector, can you explain to us what "D/d aeries & blanco" could mean?'

'We believe it is in reference to a drug drop,' said Brook. ' "Aeries" and "blanco" probably refer to heroin and cocaine.'

'Only probably?' asked Lowe. He really was even-handed to a fault, thought Adam – even if it harmed his own case.

'Street slang is very fast-moving,' Brook demurred. 'But d/d is a known code for a drug drop, and cocaine generally goes by words connected to white – hence blanco.'

'All right. And what about "a friend of J" – do you know what that refers to?'

'We have not been able to establish that. But in context, it could mean a criminal informer known to Cliveden.'

'And "S699"?'

'We were unable to establish the meaning behind S699. But we are confident that it was familiar to DI Cliveden, as it persuaded him to proceed with the meet.'

'Based on your understanding of these messages, what do you think DI Cliveden's intended purpose was in agreeing to this meeting?'

'It seems quite clear,' said Brook. 'DI Cliveden believed that he was in contact with a potential informant, who had information about a forthcoming drug drop that would enable his unit to disrupt serious criminal activity. Under his duties as a detective, he was compelled to investigate it.'

'So the messages sent from 7B were, in essence, a masquerade – to arrange a meeting with Cliveden without revealing the true purpose?'

'We believe so, yes.'

Lowe moved on. He got Brook to describe their arrest of Knight and his subsequent interview, a tape of which had already been played to the jury, in which he answered 'No comment' to all questions.

'So to recap, Chief Inspector: during the course of your investigation Mr Knight has never denied that the phone used to contact DI Cliveden, and found in his property, was his?'

'He has not.'

'And he has not denied that he was the one to use said phone to contact DI Cliveden?'

'He has not.'

'And he has not denied that he met DI Cliveden at the Old Nag's Head, shortly before midday on 13 March 2023?'

'He has not.'

'Thank you, Chief Inspector. No further questions.'

There was a hush in court after Brook's damning evidence. Jonathan seemed barely to notice it, and began his cross-examination immediately.

'Chief Inspector, is it also true that Mr Knight has not *confirmed* that the phone is his, that he used it to contact DI Cliveden, or that he arranged the meeting?'

'That is fair to say – he has not confirmed those facts. But they are reasonable assumptions to make,' she said, unflustered by his shouty question.

'There seem to be rather a lot of assumptions in your testimony,' said Jonathan.

He was right, but Adam wasn't sure it was playing well with the jury. They'd warmed to Brook's quiet authority, and now Jonathan was pompously shouting her down he could see several of the jury – especially the women – bristling.

'Could there be another reason Cliveden agreed to meet this so-called fake informant in the pub?'

'There may be other interpretations of the messages, yes. But I have told the court our best assumption based on expert analysis by my team.'

'You say that J "could" be a criminal informer working with Cliveden. Is there any evidence that this is the case?'

'Details and identities of informants are classified. It is not information we had available to us, but as I explained, the context makes it quite easy to assume a meaning.'

'There you go again, assuming!' Jonathan roared, and Adam saw a female juror cringe. 'And is it normal for a police officer to meet an unknown source alone?'

'Guidance is to work in teams of at least two,' said Brook. 'But on this occasion DI Cliveden obviously deemed the operational need was best served by him attending alone.'

'And if a police officer was to decide to conduct a covert meeting alone, would it be usual to have back-up stationed nearby?'

'It would be, yes.'

'And on this occasion, did DI Cliveden have back-up?'

'We don't believe he did, no.'

'And had he informed any of his team about what he was doing?'

'No, he had not.'

'Is this not highly irregular?'

Brook's cheeks were burning but she remained steadfast. 'It may be, but I am not here to comment on DI Cliveden's adherence to due process. I am here to comment on my own investigation into the accused.'

'Chief Inspector, I put it to you that the so-called evidence you have presented here today is a fairy story,' said Jonathan bombastically. 'You have no idea why Cliveden met with Jimmy Knight, and you have failed to carry out police work that would have established real facts. Is this not true?'

'Obviously, I don't agree.'

'No further questions.'

Adam knew what Jonathan was trying to do – he wanted to throw up smoke and mirrors, discredit the police while not really offering an alternative narrative of his own. But the danger with that strategy was it could be confusing for the jury. They certainly looked confused.

Ed Lowe was on his feet. He was obviously annoyed with how Jonathan had treated his witness. 'I just have a few further questions, Your Honour – this won't take long.'

The judge's eyes flicked to the clock. She'd been ready to adjourn. 'Very well.'

'If the text messages were to have a completely different meaning to the one you put forward, does it change the fact that Mr Knight met with DI Cliveden and had the opportunity to poison him?'

'No, it does not.'

'And does the fact that DI Cliveden came alone, without back-up, in fact make it even more likely that Mr Knight would have had the opportunity to poison him?'

'Yes, it does.'

'I think that's all that is actually relevant here. Thank you, Chief Inspector.'

40

'I take it all back about Jonathan,' groaned Nisha, as they filed out of the Old Bailey that afternoon. 'If I've ever said a single nice thing about his performance in court — strike it from the record.'

For his part, Jonathan huffily told Knight during their conference in the cells that he was 'playing without any cards'. He clearly knew it had gone badly — they all did. Knight sat slumped in his chair, expressionless.

'What do you expect me to do?' Jonathan ranted. 'You were there. You haven't explained why.'

Knight didn't reply.

The annoying thing was that Jonathan hadn't been miles off the mark with his cross-examination. The police *had* made assumptions, and there were a lot of unanswered questions about Cliveden and Knight's meeting. But his bullish style had turned off the jury. And the trial wasn't about Cliveden's corruption — much as Adam wished it was.

'They're showing the CCTV tomorrow,' said Jonathan, nostrils flaring. 'Anything else you want to add, before you send me up shit creek without a paddle again?'

Knight shook his head. 'It was just a drink. That's all.'

'Utterly convincing,' said Jonathan witheringly, and flounced out of the cell without saying goodbye.

The next morning, their fifth day in court, the KC didn't even bother to go and see his client in the cells before the day's session began, so Adam and Nisha met Jimmy alone. 'Could be another rough day today, Jimmy,' Nisha warned him. 'But the defence case starts soon. Just try and stay focused on that.'

'What do you think, Adam?' said Jimmy, giving him a piercing look. Adam hadn't told Jimmy what he had found out about Marcellus, but he felt like the older man somehow knew he'd made the discovery. 'Is it going to be OK?'

Adam shivered. His father's last words to him before he'd been dragged from their home in handcuffs rang again in his ears. 'Everything will be OK.' Less than three days later he'd been found dead.

'I don't know, Jimmy,' he said, honestly. 'All we can do is fight your case, as best we can.'

Anxiety gnawed at Adam's stomach as he took his place on the defence bench, behind Jonathan. Once the jury had filed in and everyone had risen to greet the judge, Lowe began.

'Today, ladies and gentlemen of the jury, you will see footage of the meeting discussed in court yesterday. It took place shortly before midday on 13 March 2023 in the Old Nag's Head, a pub on Bouverie Street, which is about ten minutes' walk from the Old Bailey. If you turn to document 19 in your folders, you will find a map marking the location of the pub.

'The meeting was between the accused and the victim. During the course of this meeting, the prosecution alleges that the accused poisoned DI Cliveden. I ask that you watch closely, although we will replay it and pause at certain points. OK, Tom . . .' Lowe gestured to the officer in the case. 'Let's begin.'

The blurry footage played. Jimmy entered the pub, downing a whisky at the bar, and took his seat, sitting and waiting, then standing and loitering by the door. Adam noticed that the judge had leaned right forward, chunky glasses he hadn't seen her wear before perched on her nose, her eyes screwed up in a squint as she studied the footage rolling on the big screen.

'OK, Tom, we can whizz it forward here, I think,' said Lowe. 'Mr Knight stands by the door for nine minutes and thirty-three seconds, and yes, if you start it again here, he then goes and sits back down at the same table. And then three minutes and forty-five seconds later, DI Cliveden arrives.'

The footage showed the two men shake hands, then Cliveden sat down, and Knight went to the bar. That moment, where Knight looked directly at the camera. Then the barman turned his back, and Knight angled his body around the drinks.

'Pause here, please, Tom.'

Lowe pointed at the screen. 'This is the moment when Knight had the opportunity to place the poison into Cliveden's drink. You will note that moments before – Tom, if you could rewind – Knight appears to note where the CCTV camera is. He then ensures that he positions his body in such a way that the drinks are no longer visible by the camera, for the eleven-and-a-half seconds when the barman's back is turned. You can press "play" again, Tom, thank you.'

The footage rolled on – to the point of confusion where the drinks almost got knocked over, Knight's hasty save, and then the short, inaudible conversation between him and Cliveden while they sipped their drinks. Lowe stopped it once both men had left the pub.

'I would now like to call Reginald McNally.'

The barrister-turned-landlord made his slow way into the witness box, walking with a slight limp, hunched over like a tree that had spent centuries in the wind. Away from the dusty confines of the pub and under the full glare of the court lights, he seemed out of place – Adam had to remind himself that this was once his natural environment.

After McNally was sworn in, Lowe began by asking him about his current occupation. McNally confirmed that he had been landlord of the Old Nag's Head for just under ten years. Under Lowe's questioning, he agreed that it wasn't a busy establishment, and business had been gradually slowing for a number of years – 'Perhaps because I don't serve cocktails or hummus and flatbreads on bloomin' planks.' There was a ripple of laughter around the court for that one.

'But you haven't always worked in hospitality, have you, Mr McNally?' said Lowe.

Good, thought Adam – Lowe wasn't going to skirt around the fact of McNally being disbarred.

'No, before I took over the Old Nag's Head I was a barrister. I practised for twenty-four years.'

'And did you leave the profession by choice?'

McNally sighed and looked at the ceiling. 'No, I was disbarred for misconduct. After accepting bribes, which I did because I was severely addicted to alcohol.'

'And are you addicted to alcohol now?'

'No doubt,' said McNally, with perfect comic timing. 'But I

am sober, and have been for nine years, if that's what you mean.'
A few titters from the public gallery.

Lowe smiled along. 'A recovering alcoholic who runs a pub –
that's unusual, isn't it?'

McNally shrugged. 'Not really,' he said. 'When you're around
drunks all day, it certainly takes the glamour out of wanting to
be one yourself.' More laughter.

'All right,' said Lowe, once the mirth had died down. 'Let's
move on to 13 March 2023. You were working in the Old Nag's
Head, alone, that day – correct?'

'Correct.'

'And not long after you opened at eleven, James Knight – the
man in the witness box – arrived. Correct?'

McNally took a long, performative look at Knight. 'Correct.'

'And had you ever seen Mr Knight in your pub before?'

McNally frowned, gave a good impression of someone thinking about the question carefully. 'In my pub? Not to my recol-
lection, no. But I have an absolutely terrible memory for faces,
I'm afraid – forget 'em almost as soon as I've seen 'em.'

Oh, McNally was a wily old goat. He knew what would be
coming in cross-examination – he'd be asked why he hadn't recognised Knight as a former client. But he was setting the ground
nicely for a believable denial.

'And can you describe Mr Knight's demeanour?'

'He seemed rather agitated. He was sort of shifting from foot
to foot as he waited for me to pour his drink. Like he was nervous, or something. But I should say that sort of behaviour is
not entirely unusual, among the kind of punters who order a
whisky before midday.'

'I see. And after Mr Knight had drunk his whisky, what happened then?'

'He went and sat at a back table. There was no one else in the pub but he chose the table that is furthest from the bar. I got the hint. He didn't want to chat. Now, that is unusual. Generally, the drinkers who come in alone first thing are the ones who want to prop up the bar and tell you their life story.'

'Thank you, Mr McNally. Members of the jury, if you turn to document 22 in your bundles, you will see a diagram of the layout of the Old Nag's Head, which I am now also showing on the screen. Mr McNally, is this table – marked with a cross – where Mr Knight chose to sit?'

'Yes, that is correct.' Adam squinted at his own diagram. It was indeed some distance from the bar – although still within eyeshot.

'After Mr Knight sat down, what happened?'

'Nothing much. I just left him to it. I actually thought he'd gone at one point because I looked over and he wasn't at his table. But he was definitely sitting down by the time the other man arrived.'

'This other man being DI Cliveden. Had you seen DI Cliveden in your pub before?'

McNally whistled through his teeth and turned his palms upwards. 'Sorry, I can't be certain – my memory and faces . . .'

Under the desk, Adam clenched his fists. McNally wasn't exactly lying – he'd said he 'couldn't be certain' – but he wasn't telling the whole truth either. A desperate man, with nothing to lose, Tony had said. He supposed someone who had already been disbarred would have no qualms about misleading the court.

'All right. Had anyone else arrived or left between Mr Knight's arrival and D I Cliveden's arrival?'

'Not to my knowledge, no.'

'Thank you. So, we know that D I Cliveden entered the pub at 11.53 a.m. and the two men greeted each other at the table. Did you get the impression that they knew each other?'

'I wasn't paying them a huge amount of attention if I'm honest.'

'But is there anything you recall about their body language?'

McNally sighed. Lowe was willing him to say something of substance, but he was reluctant. 'They shook hands, I remember that. So I would say it was relatively formal between them.'

'O K. And then Mr Knight came to the bar to order more drinks?'

'Yes, he ordered a pint of Stella and a Coke. I made some comment about the Coke, which he said was for his companion – just making conversation – and I asked if his mate was a recovering alcoholic too. And the accused – Mr Knight – said it was worse, he was a police officer.'

That might have got another laugh in other circumstances, but in the context of the murder trial, it sounded sinister. Some of the jury looked over at Knight in the dock, disgust on their faces.

'Mr Knight paid in cash, I believe, and you turned your back to him so you could get the change out of the till?'

'Yes. He paid with a fifty-pound note so there was rather a lot of change to get.'

'And did you notice that Mr Knight had anything in his hand at this time, other than the fifty-pound note?'

'Not that I noticed.'

'And his demeanour – was he still "agitated" as you said before?'

'No, in fact he was incredibly calm.'

'I see. And did you witness Mr Knight place any substance into either of the drinks at the bar?'

'I didn't, but like I said, for some of the time he was there, my back was turned.'

'When Mr Knight returned to the table and spoke with DI Cliveden, were you able to hear any of their conversation?'

'I had put the speakers on by then, so not really, no.'

'Not really? Does that mean you heard some?'

McNally shifted. 'From what I could tell, they were discussing some kind of business deal. I heard the word "shipment".'

Adam looked over at the jury. There was some furious note-taking going on, presumably because this chimed so well with what Paula Brook had said about the text messages relating to drugs. He realised the judge was looking hard at the jury too, her icy gaze taking in their faces as they listened to McNally's evidence.

Lowe continued: 'Were you able to hear what this shipment was?'

'I was not, no.'

'And did the body language between the two men remain cordial throughout the meeting?'

'I would say so, yes. It was a fairly short conversation. After they had finished their drinks, they left.'

Lowe moved on to some tedious details about McNally's process for collecting and hot-washing glasses. Adam knew it was necessary – it was so the prosecution could explain later why no trace of the poison had been found on the glass.

But when he looked over at Jonathan, he realised his pupil master wasn't listening at all. On his open laptop screen was not the brief on McNally that Adam had carefully prepared, but an email, which he seemed to be reading over and over again, from his wife.

Don't bother coming home tonight, you cheating scumbag. I found the thong in your suit pocket so I can assume it belongs to yet another woman who can offer you a bed tonight. How could you do this – AGAIN?

Adam looked from the email to his pupil master, who was practically comatose. He did not look like a man who was ready to cross-examine a key witness.

41

'Mr Taylor-Cameron?' the judge prompted, blinking at him disdainfully. 'Do you wish to proceed?' Lowe had finished his evidence and everyone in the court watched Jonathan expectantly.

'Ah, yes, thank you,' said Jonathan, getting unsteadily to his feet. It couldn't be the first time he'd received an email like that from his wife, and Adam watched him snap back to an expression of smug composure like a mask. But that didn't change the fact that he had barely been listening to McNally's testimony – and it showed.

'Now Mr . . . er . . . McNally . . .' He cast around blindly. 'You say you heard this . . . conversation, but were you really close enough?'

'I didn't say I heard it,' McNally snapped back. 'I said I caught snippets. I've already said – I wasn't close enough to hear it all.'

'And, er, you say you didn't see Mr Knight put anything in either drink?'

'That is correct, yes,' said McNally, his voice terse.

Nisha turned to Adam, her eyes wide with horror. 'Do something!' she mouthed.

Adam grabbed his notebook, scribbled a question, ripped it

out and held it out to his pupil master. At first, Jonathan tried to swat him away like an irritating fly but then, perhaps realising he was out of other options, he grudgingly took the note. Adam felt the spotlight beam of the judge's stare on him.

Jonathan unfolded the paper, read it, and half smiled. He looked up and seemed to have got some of his old vim back.

'Mr McNally, you say that you had never seen Mr Knight in your pub before?'

'Not that I can recall.'

'But had you ever seen – or, indeed, met – him in any other context?'

McNally swallowed. 'I have, er, since been made aware that I, in fact, represented Mr Knight as his barrister. Many years ago.'

A murmur of astonishment went round the court. Even Lowe looked astounded, and he started scribbling furious notes to his own junior and solicitor.

'So Mr Knight is a former client? And yet, you did not recognise him?'

'I have, er, a terrible memory for faces and . . . as I am now aware, it was more than ten years since I had seen Mr Knight . . .'

Adam pressed another hurriedly scribbled note into Jonathan's hand. His pupil master almost laughed when he read it.

'But, Mr McNally! The case in which you represented Mr Knight was rather a memorable one, wasn't it?'

'Well, if you mean it's the reason he has been in prison for the last decade then . . .'

'I mean memorable for *you*. Because wasn't it your final case, before you were struck off?'

'Yes, it was.'

'And you didn't remember your very last client? Or think it

was strange that he was having a drink with the key police witness who'd provided evidence against him? The same police
witness he'd accused of framing him?'

'As I have already said, I have a poor memory for faces.'

'I don't think that's it, Mr McNally. I think you wanted the
police, and this court, to think that you had no connection to
this crime. That you were no more than an innocent bystander.
But is it not true that you, too, had the opportunity to poison
DI Cliveden?'

'No!' McNally's sunken cheeks, usually a ghoulish pale
yellow, were flushed. Adam scribbled another note, pushed it
across the desk to Jonathan. The judge was watching him like
a cat watching a spider.

'Could we please show the CCTV from timestamp 11.54,'
Jonathan said. The officer did as he asked, winding the tape to
the moment before the drinks were almost knocked over, before
pressing 'play'.

'Does this moment not afford you the opportunity to –
undetected – put a substance into DI Cliveden's glass of
Coke?'

McNally watched, then smiled nastily. A rat that had found a
drainpipe to shimmy up. 'That "moment" which lasts less than
two seconds, according to the timestamp?' he hit back. 'You'd
need remarkable sleight of hand to pull that off. Sleight of hand
that, sadly, I don't have.' He held out his wizened hands in front
of him. They trembled convincingly – the unmistakable toll of
years of alcoholism.

Jonathan spun back round to Adam, as if expecting another
note. Adam was out of ideas. He shook his head. Realistically,
it was unlikely McNally had poisoned Cliveden. But hopefully,

his weird connection to both Knight and Cliveden was enough to put doubt in the minds of the jury.

'No further questions,' said Jonathan, and sat down. The judge looked right past him, at Adam. Her eyes had something close to approval in them.

'We'll take a recess now for lunch,' she said. 'Everyone back in court by half past two, please.'

The tone changed in court that afternoon. From the thrills and spills of McNally's testimony they moved on to hard scientific facts. Lowe had purposefully saved the evidence relating to Cliveden's actual cause of death until last, Adam presumed, because it was what he believed most conclusively pointed to Knight being the perpetrator. He was tightening the net.

'I call Dr Vivian Chong.'

Dr Chong was the Crown's expert forensic pathologist, who had also carried out Cliveden's post-mortem. She was petite, sharply tailored, no-nonsense. First she explained how her team had initially tested for a natural cause of death, including stroke, but the autopsy had not revealed damage to the brain which would have been consistent with this. From there they'd moved on to blood tests and stomach-content examination, and that was how they'd discovered the presence of botulinum toxin.

'And I want to be really clear about this,' she said, cutting Lowe off sternly when he opened his mouth for another question. 'I have seen a lot of nonsense in the press about how DI Cliveden was killed with "Botox". He was killed by botulinum toxin. They are not the same. In the quantities in which it is administered, Botox is perfectly safe – even if, aesthetically, it can be a mistake.' Her eyes lingered on the female juror with long raven hair extensions and a motionless forehead, who looked like she hadn't experienced a genuine facial expression for years. There was some tittering from the public gallery.

'Quite so,' said Lowe. 'So we are talking here of a dose of botulinum toxin that is far higher than what is generally commercially available?'

'Correct,' said Dr Chong smartly. 'Botulinum products – such as Botox – are extremely tightly regulated. But we do know that there is a black market for unlicensed versions of Botox. Someone with connections in that criminal underworld would feasibly be able to procure these in large quantities and combine them into a fatal dose.'

'Is it possible that DI Cliveden came to be infected with this toxin by accident?'

Dr Chong shook her head. 'Not to the level at which it was present. He had an unusually high amount in his bloodstream – far higher than the amount we'd expect to see from someone who had become infected with botulism by, for example, eating naturally compromised food.'

'And you are certain that he ingested the poison, rather than, for example, inhaling it or being injected with it?'

'Yes, because of its presence in his stomach.'

'And can you explain how the poison brought about the end of his life?'

Dr Chong went on to explain in much more scientific language the same cause of death that Lowe had so emotively narrated in his opening statement. The poison had gradually paralysed Cliveden's cells – until his respiratory system had stopped working too.

'It is very unusual for botulinum to cause death in this

manner,' Dr Chong added. 'Because there are many effective medical interventions. But in this case, the dose was extremely high which caused a rapid reaction within the victim's body. The actual cause of his death was choking.'

'And on the basis of DI Cliveden's stomach contents, are you able to say how the poison was delivered?' Lowe asked.

'Not precisely, no,' Dr Chong replied, going on to explain the processes for analysing stomach fluids. Some of the jury looked vaguely queasy, but the judge seemed fascinated. 'What we can say is that it was almost certainly in a drink which DI Cliveden unwittingly consumed, because our tests show he had not eaten solid food within the previous nineteen hours.'

'Earlier we heard from DI Cliveden's wife that he was on a diet whereby he would only eat and drink in a window from midday until 8 p.m. and fast the rest of the time. Do your conclusions reflect that?'

'They do, yes.'

'And is there a window in which the poison must have been administered, to have caused DI Cliveden's death at 14.42pm on 13 March?'

The court seemed to hold its collective breath. This was the key question.

'We believe he would have ingested the poison between ten and two hours before his death,' said Dr Chong, with razor precision. 'So between the hours of 4.45 a.m. and 12.45 p.m.'

'And we know that DI Cliveden was at home with his wife, who claims he did not eat or drink anything, until at least 8 a.m.,' said Lowe. 'So we can potentially narrow that window further, to 8 a.m. until 12.45 p.m.?'

'I think that would be fair.'

'Thank you, Dr Chong.'

Cross-examination from Jonathan was brief – just enough to confirm that Dr Chong could not say that Coke was the only liquid Cliveden had consumed before his death. He pressed her on the window of opportunity, but she refused to budge. Sensing he was getting nowhere, Jonathan sat down. They still had Dr Alice Pettigrew, their alternative expert, to come. But she was going to have to be incredibly convincing to counter the quiet certitude of Dr Chong.

The judge turned to Lowe. While she had looked briefly animated listening to the gruesome details of Dr Chong's autopsy report, her mask of studied reserve had returned. 'I believe that concludes your case?'

'Yes, Your Honour. The prosecution rests.'

'Very well.' It was nearly 6 p.m. and the jury were weary. They had already sat through five days of evidence, and several of them looked less than thrilled when the judge instructed them to return at 9 a.m. the next morning for the start of the defence case.

Lowe gave the defence team a friendly wink and a wave as he left court for the day. Jonathan refused to wave back, pouting sulkily.

'I'd never tell him to his face, but the old chap has done a fucking good job,' he muttered. 'We're going to need a miracle.'

42

It was day six and the public gallery in Court Number One had never been busier. It was the first day of the defence's case, which in normal circumstances meant the headline act – the defendant in the witness box. Adam looked at the eager, prurient faces of the spectators and felt half pleased that they were going to be disappointed.

In their morning conference in the cells, Jimmy had been adamant – he wouldn't be taking the stand, just as Jonathan had advised. Nisha's opinion about that decision was written all over her face, but she didn't say anything. They had no choice but to stick to the plan now.

'Mr Taylor-Cameron, do you wish to call your client to the witness box?' the judge asked, once court was assembled.

'No, Your Honour. My client is waiving his right to give evidence.'

Angry whispers could be heard in the public gallery. Natasha Cliveden audibly said, 'What the hell?' to her FLO. Ed Lowe, with a stack of carefully prepared questions in front of him, looked like he didn't know whether to laugh or cry.

Only the judge was impervious. 'I see,' she said. 'And I

assume you have advised Mr Knight about the adverse inference the jury may draw from his failure to give evidence?'

Jonathan inclined his head. 'I have, Your Honour. And I will expand upon this in my closing statement. My client does not believe he has anything to add to his case by giving evidence, given that he does not dispute meeting DI Cliveden.'

'Very well. We shall move on.'

There was a rapid exodus from the public gallery before Jonathan's first witness was shown in. He was Dr Rohan Douglas, who had led the police team that had analysed the forensic evidence. Or, as the defence needed to show, the lack thereof.

'So what forensic evidence were you able to recover from the Old Nag's Head that specifically linked James Knight to the poisoning of DI Cliveden?'

Ruddy-faced, red-bearded Douglas babbled away about fibres and fingerprints, his voice dreary, his lexicon impenetrable.

'Hang on,' Jonathan interrupted him. 'Forgive me – does all that not simply show that James Knight was present in the pub? Something we already know, and do not dispute?'

'The forensics back that up, yes,' said Douglas.

'Oh, what a relief!' crowed Jonathan. 'The forensics confirm the CCTV and eyewitness accounts. But do they add anything new? I ask you again – did you find anything that proves DI Cliveden was poisoned in the pub?'

Douglas was not one to use three words when he could use 300 instead. He droned on about the role of the SOCO team – scene of crime officers – before concluding: 'There were challenges that meant they did not recover all the material we would have hoped.'

'So you didn't find any glasses in the pub that showed traces of poison?'

'We vigorously analysed every glass using a combination of—'

'Is that a yes or a no, Dr Douglas?' Jonathan interrupted him.

'No, we did not.'

'And did you find any traces of poison anywhere else in the pub?'

'The SOCO team took multiple samples from a variety of surfaces—'

'YES OR NO, Dr Douglas?'

'No, we were unable to on this occasion.'

It went on like this, with Dr Douglas trying to lecture the court on the intricacies of forensic science as Jonathan pressed him to confirm that they had also not recovered any vessel that could have been used to transport the poison, or any trace of botulinum at Knight's address. It was no wonder Lowe hadn't called Douglas for the prosecution, thought Adam. Not only did he have no material evidence to share, he had also bored the whole court to tears.

Concluding his questioning, Jonathan sat down looking satisfied. Lowe got to his feet to cross-examine.

'Dr Douglas, is there a reasonable explanation for why your team were unable to recover any trace of botulinum from the Old Nag's Head?'

'Yes, that's what I've been trying to say,' replied Douglas, with obvious relief. 'Given the time taken for post-mortem examinations to be carried out, the suspect was not apprehended until more than forty-eight hours after the victim's death. By the time the SOCO team arrived, the glasses had been through a hot dishwasher several times and the pub routinely cleaned.'

'So the fact that you did not find traces of poison at the pub does not rule out the possibility that the poisoning took place there?'

'It certainly does not.'

Point made. But surely, 'not ruling out a possibility' still introduced a hefty dose of doubt? It depended how much the jury had made up their minds already.

After Dr Douglas, there was a break for lunch. It was much needed by the jury, some of whom had had visibly drooping eyelids during his tedious testimony. In the afternoon, the defence would be calling Dr Alice Pettigrew – their star witness. Adam felt nervous – he realised he hadn't heard from Dr Pettigrew in months. He'd sent her an email a couple of weeks before the trial had started, but come to think of it now, he'd never got a reply. With everything else that had been going on he hadn't followed up – and Nisha had separately confirmed the professor was definitely attending court. Perhaps he should have double-checked. Jonathan hadn't met Dr Pettigrew before, and if she wasn't as good as his pupil master hoped, Adam was sure he would get the blame.

After a dry baked potato in the canteen, Adam spotted Dr Pettigrew, lingering in the lobby, accompanied by a clerk, as he made his way back to court. She gave him a tight smile and opened her mouth as if to say something, before glancing at the clerk and thinking better of it. Adam knew it was her first time as an expert witness, so she was probably just nervous. He gave her a thumbs-up as he filed past her and into court.

Dr Pettigrew was sworn in, and Adam was pleased that

standing in the witness box she looked the part in an elegant beige trouser suit. He tried to relax as Jonathan's questioning began, and Dr Pettigrew elaborated convincingly on her qualifications and expertise.

Conscious that the jury had had quite enough of science, Jonathan got to the point quickly.

'Dr Pettigrew, do you agree with the opinion of Dr Vivian Chong, that the poison was administered within a window of ten to two hours before DI Cliveden became ill and died?'

This was it. The big moment. Dr Pettigrew was going to say that the window was actually much bigger, and that was going to open up the next line in their defence. Jonathan would introduce the CCTV footage from the Old Bailey corridor, showing Cliveden receiving a coffee before the tape cut out. Then he was going to recall Chief Inspector Paula Brook, to ask her if the police were aware the rest of the CCTV was missing, and why it hadn't been investigated. Nisha, Jonathan and Adam had wargamed it meticulously at chambers last night. Just as there was no evidence to conclusively prove that Cliveden was poisoned at the Old's Nag Head, there also wasn't any to show that he definitely wasn't poisoned via the coffee. Dr Pettigrew's testimony could blow open the whole case.

Adam watched her expectantly. She took a deep breath, and then, to his surprise, she looked directly at him. Was he mistaken, or was that an apology in her eyes?

'I'm afraid that I do agree with Dr Chong.'

Adam thought that he must have misheard. He glanced at Nisha, who looked just as confused as he was. Jonathan, meanwhile, ploughed on without even registering her answer.

'So what revised window would you give?'

'I'm sorry, I think you misheard me,' Dr Pettigrew said tentatively, as Adam's stomach flipped in astonished horror. 'I agree with Dr Chong, that the poison most likely was given ten to two hours before the victim's death. I have to apologise, because a few months ago I did tell your colleague' – she shot another, regretful look at Adam – 'that I thought the window could be much wider. But actually, since then, I've reviewed the literature and I have concluded that although he may have started to show symptoms if the poison was administered outside of that window, it is very unlikely his death would have been so rapid. I tried to call, I'm sorry' – another desperate glance at Adam – 'but I assumed as I'd been summoned to court you'd want me to come and give my expert opinion anyway.'

Jonathan's mouth was flapping open and closed like a fish. He stared helplessly at his notes, then furiously at Adam. Ed Lowe's junior stifled a laugh.

'So you mean to say there is no chance – *no chance at all* – that the poison could have been administered after 12.45 p.m.?' he finally managed.

'In science we don't like to deal in absolutes,' said Dr Pettigrew. 'But yes, I think it would be very unlikely, give or take a few minutes.'

Jonathan was lost for words. It was a defence barrister's nightmare scenario – your own witness turning against you. Dr Pettigrew was pained by his disquiet, and tried to fill the gaping silence.

'It is very unusual, though,' she said, unprompted. 'To die of botulism. The symptoms are distinctive and medical interventions are highly effective. If the victim had still been alive by the time medical teams arrived, then he almost certainly would have survived. It makes it a very strange choice for a murder weapon.

'Even as his respiratory system failed, he'd have needed something to actually choke on to guarantee death, which the murderer couldn't have been certain he would receive . . .' She was thinking aloud, but no one was following what she was saying. All eyes were on Jonathan, who looked like a man who had completely lost the plot.

It fell to the judge to take control of proceedings. She interrupted Dr Pettigrew's rambling thoughts sharply.

'Mr Taylor-Cameron, do you have any further questions for your witness? I am conscious of the time . . . and I'm not sure it is aiding your case to continue.'

'No, thank you, Your Honour,' Jonathan bumbled. He looked grateful that she'd put him out of his misery.

Ed Lowe's cross-examination was punchy and jubilant. He'd been handed a gift he hadn't known was coming – another scientific expert to corroborate the prosecution evidence. But it still felt like it took an eternity for the court session to end – with Adam knowing exactly how much of Jonathan's anger was coming his way.

True enough, they had barely cleared the doors of Court Number One when his pupil master erupted.

'How the *hell* could you let me be caught with my pants down like that?' he fumed. 'Do you realise how fucking stupid I looked?'

'And how bad it was for Jimmy's case,' chimed in Nisha, whose chummy attitude to Adam had evaporated.

'I'm really sorry – I had no idea. It's the complete opposite of what she told me in York,' Adam said helplessly.

'She said she tried to call you! How can you not have called her back – on something this important?' Nisha demanded.

Adam felt like he was falling off a very tall building. That unknown number, which had kept calling him. He'd assumed it was something to do with the mystery envelope and had ignored it. But it must have been Dr Pettigrew. And his voicemail, which his mum had told him was full. He'd planned to clear it, just as soon as the trial was over. How could he have been so foolish?

'I-I don't know what to say,' said Adam. 'This is totally my fault.'

'Yeah, it is,' said Nisha furiously.

Jonathan pressed his balled fists to his eyes.

'What the hell are we going to do tomorrow?'

43

During their short, depressing conference in the cells, Nisha had tears in her eyes as she explained to their client that the case they'd been going to run was now up in smoke. Jimmy looked uncomprehendingly from her face to Adam's. 'So that's it? You've nothing else you can argue?' he said.

'The fact that there are no forensics is still pretty damning,' said Adam lamely. Jonathan just tutted.

Afterwards, as they made their way from the subterranean dungeon to daylight, he let his real feelings be known.

'What does it even matter anyway?' said Jonathan. The cynicism he'd had when he'd first been put on the case, but which had gradually been worn away during the thrill of the trial, was back with a vengeance. 'We all know he's guilty. You can't defend the indefensible.' Nisha stalked away towards the exit, not bothering to say goodbye.

'Well, I've wasted enough time on this case,' said Jonathan, looking at his watch. 'But you'd better be working all night, boy, to try and dig us out of the hole you've got us in.' And with that, he was gone too.

Adam trudged back to chambers, a deep gloom settling on

his shoulders along with the rain, which had finally arrived to break the oppressive heatwave. He went straight to the pupil room, fired up his laptop, and opened his ring binder. They'd failed Jimmy Knight, and it was all his fault. Although he'd studied the evidence until he'd known it by heart, he thought he might as well go over it again. Maybe, just maybe, he'd find some inspiration for a new defence.

There was a soft knock at the door. 'Come in!' Adam called. He was surprised when he saw Rupert standing there.

'Oh, hi,' Adam said, a little sheepishly. The locked-door incident with Emma was still fresh in both their minds.

'Look, I don't know what the hell is going on with you and Emma,' said Rupert, unsmiling. 'But she asked me to give you this.' He held out a small brown Jiffy bag.

'Thanks,' said Adam, taking it, confused. 'But listen – I promise you there's really nothing going on. Emma's been telling me some stuff that relates to our case that she wants to keep confidential.'

Rupert sighed and picked up an old tap, which had inexplicably been dumped in the pupil room. 'Sure, I believe you,' he said. 'But that's the problem. She doesn't tell *me* stuff.

'I'm not sure how long I can keep doing it,' he added mournfully, fiddling with the tap. 'I don't think she trusts me.'

'I don't think she trusts anyone,' said Adam. 'But give it time. She's brave enough to try, and that's got to count for something.'

'Yeah, maybe,' said Rupert. He changed the subject. 'I heard you had a bad day in court?'

'Just a bit,' Adam said, with a bleak laugh. 'Hence why I'm here . . . trying to salvage something – anything.'

'Well, good luck,' said Rupert. 'Isn't it your tenancy vote in . . .'

'Four days, fifteen hours and twelve minutes? Yeah, it is,' replied Adam. The pressure of Knight's trial would have been bad enough without knowing his own professional future was also hanging in the balance. After today's events, everything was looking very bleak indeed.

'Double good luck then,' said Rupert, but his voice was couched in concern. 'I'll leave you to it . . .'

As soon as he was out of the room, Adam ripped open the package from Emma. He had no idea what it could be, so was inevitably surprised when a memory stick and a scribbled note on lined jotting paper fell out.

He picked up the note first.

I had the same hunch as you about the CCTV. I took the tape and got our cyber team to have a go at cleaning it up. The good news is they were able to recover the footage and – I'll let you see for yourself what they found. E.

Adam's hands were trembling as he plugged the memory stick into his computer. In light of Dr Pettigrew's testimony about the poisoning window, technically it shouldn't have mattered whether Cliveden had drunk the coffee or not. But had Emma discovered a silver bullet?

He pressed 'play'. The tape ran as he'd seen it before – Cliveden striding in, Abi proffering the hot drink. Then, as Cliveden turned towards the court, coffee in hand, a smartly dressed court official – Adam squinted at the screen, and thought it was an usher he recognised – intercepted him. There was a brief exchange of words, then Cliveden handed the usher the coffee cup and shrugged. He continued empty-handed into Court 3, while the usher went the other way, and dropped the cup into the nearest bin.

Adam slumped back in his seat, dumbfounded. The mystery coffee, that he'd spent months stressing over, had been confiscated before Cliveden had had a chance to drink it!

So Raquel couldn't have killed Cliveden. And Emma, who'd risked so much to help him, surely wouldn't have done. That left only McNally unaccounted for – but Adam knew he was clutching at straws. Had Jimmy really killed Cliveden after all?

There was another knock at the door, and Adam's temper bubbled up uncontrollably.

'What is it?' he snapped. Couldn't he just be left in peace?

The door opened gently, to reveal a shy-faced Georgina, a mug of hot tea in her hand.

'Sorry, Adam,' she said, with none of her usual sass. 'I just thought maybe you could use this.' She held out the tea.

'Thanks, Georgina,' said Adam, puzzled. A cup of tea was actually exactly what he needed, and he took it gratefully. 'Why are you being nice to me?'

Georgina frowned. 'What do you mean? It's just what friends do.'

Adam didn't know what to say. He'd never had a 'friend' quite like Georgina.

She perched on the end of one of the broken desks, balancing herself just so like a cat, so that it didn't collapse one way or the other on its wonky legs.

'Well, you'll be pleased to know that the Knight case is

fucked, and it's all my fault,' said Adam. 'So there's absolutely no chance of me getting tenancy now.'

Georgina's brow furrowed. 'Why would I be pleased about that?'

'Er . . . because it means you get a clear run? Means you don't need to worry about your little sabotage attempts anymore.'

Georgina looked wounded. 'What sabotage attempts?'

Adam was starting to get worried about the direction this conversation was going in. Was she for real?

'Well, like, you've been scooping up about ninety per cent of the work that's come in over the last month, leaving me with the dregs . . .'

'Adam, I was doing you a favour,' said Georgina quietly. 'Everyone could see how much time this case was taking up, how stressed it was making you . . . I just wanted to take some of the pressure off.'

'Oh,' said Adam, awkwardly. He was struggling to see what her angle was here – she must have one, surely?

'Look, Adam . . . I know this stupid tenancy thing is meant to make us compete with each other but I'm just really hoping we both get in. Chambers wouldn't be the same without you.'

Adam was speechless. All this time, he'd thought they were rivals.

'Anyway, I better leave you to it,' said Georgina, getting to her feet. 'What's your strategy?'

'I don't know,' said Adam, running his hand through his dark hair. 'I'm out of ideas.'

'There's CCTV of the alleged poisoning, right?'

'Yes, but I don't think it can help us. I've watched it so many times.'

'It's worth watching it again,' said Georgina. 'Remember that arson case I had a few months ago? The CCTV seemed to show my client among the group of hooded lads – it really did feel open-and-shut. But I watched it and watched it and then I realised – his white trainers. They weren't there. But they were in another frame, walking away from the crime scene – but not towards it. And we got him off. Obviously Rory took all the credit for that one,' she added, with a laugh.

'OK,' said Adam, looking at Georgina as if seeing her for the first time. 'Thanks, Georgina.'

Once she was gone he cued up the CCTV footage from the Old Nag's Head with little enthusiasm, and pressed 'play' for what felt like the millionth time. He watched the sequence – Jimmy arriving, ordering a drink, sitting down. Now came the boring bit that Adam usually whizzed through – Jimmy hanging around by the door, presumably watching the street to see if Cliveden was coming. In the spirit of leaving no stone unturned, he decided to sit through it.

Adam watched as Jimmy stood by the door like a sentry. He had his back to the camera, but the bulkiness of his shoulders and the narrowness of the doorway made it impossible to see the street beyond. Adam remembered how McNally had said in his testimony that he'd thought Jimmy had left the pub at one point. Flicking to the diagram of the pub layout in his ring binder, Adam realised why. The doorway wasn't in eyeshot of the bar, which was round a corner. So anything could have happened here, and McNally wouldn't have known.

Adam leaned forward with renewed interest. He slowed the footage right down, hoping to see something, anything. There wasn't much to see – he was cross with himself for falling for another stupid theory.

But then, suddenly, he spotted it. He wound back, pressed 'pause', zoomed in. There was something, right in the corner of the screen, just beyond where Jimmy was standing. A shadow, and then an almost imperceptible movement. What was it? Adam rewound again.

It looked like a strand of long blonde hair.

44

'He met someone! Jimmy met someone, who he must be trying to protect! If he did this, he didn't do it alone.'

Adam was breathless. It was the morning of the eighth day of the trial, and he'd had to run to catch up with Jonathan who was heading into court. His pupil master took in his sweaty face and mussed-up hair like he was looking at a particularly disgusting bit of chewing gum stuck to the bottom of his shoe.

'What on earth are you talking about?'

'It's all there, in the CCTV. You have to watch it really slowly but it's clear. He goes to the door to meet someone, and they have long blonde hair.'

Adam had been up all night, watching the footage over and over. It was only a tiny clue, but it was a clue all the same. Jimmy was unmistakably having a conversation with someone shorter than him, who lurked out of shot. Only a flick of their hair gave them away.

'So what?'

'Haven't we asked all along: how did Jimmy plan all this? How did he get his hands on the poison? Well, he didn't. Someone else did.'

It had, of course, occurred to Adam that both Raquel and Emma had long blonde hair.

Jonathan wasn't smiling. 'I don't see how this helps us at all,' he said coldly.

'We need to talk to Jimmy and get him to explain!' urged Adam. 'Maybe he did put something in Cliveden's drink, but had no idea what he was doing?'

'Not possible,' said Jonathan curtly. 'The prison van is running late apparently. There's not going to be time for a conference today.'

'OK, well, we've got to resubmit the CCTV instead,' said Adam desperately. 'I've got all the details of the timestamps here, we've got to show the jury—'

'No,' said Jonathan flatly. 'This ends now. I'm resting our case, and then it is in the hands of the jury.'

'Jonathan, we can't do that!' said Adam, horrified. 'We'll lose!'

'I. Don't. Care.' And with that, Jonathan turned on his heel and marched into court.

Ten minutes later everyone was assembled. Knight looked flustered as he was brought in – he must have been taken straight through from the prison van, so hadn't had time to compose himself. He nodded to the judge as he sat down, but she returned his gaze with decisive indifference.

'Mr Taylor-Cameron, you may begin.'

Jonathan stood. 'Your Honour, I have nothing further to add. I believe we are in a position to move to closing statements.'

Disquiet in the public gallery, and surprise among Lowe and his underlings. The judge raised an eyebrow.

'I have here on my schedule that you had further witnesses to call.'

'There has been a change of plan, Your Honour, in light of the rather surprising testimony yesterday.'

The judge was regarding him severely. 'Are you quite sure?'

Adam couldn't bear it. This was their last chance, their final shot at truth and justice, and Jonathan was about to blow it. He thought fleetingly of tenancy, how badly his desire for it burned and how much it would sting to lose it. Then he thought of his father, dying alone in a prison cell. A moment later, he was on his feet.

'Your Honour, if I may . . .' he began, as Jonathan wheeled round to stare at him with unmitigated outrage.

'What on earth do you think you're doing?' he hissed, but Adam ploughed on regardless.

'Your Honour, I beg your permission to recall the case officer, and show the CCTV from the Old Nag's Head to the jury again.'

'Adam. Sit. Down.' Jonathan was apoplectic. What Adam was doing was completely contrary to all protocol, and the scandalised reception his unexpected intervention received in court reflected how shocking it was.

'Mr Taylor-Cameron!' cried the judge, over the growing hubbub of whispers echoing around the court, as she attempted to restore some order. 'This is most irregular – is the defence team in agreement here or do you need to speak privately with your junior?'

'Your Honour, I can assure you that Mr Green's request very much does not reflect the defence team as a whole – I have no intention of reintroducing the CCTV.'

Adam was still on his feet. He'd gone so far now – he couldn't give up. 'Your Honour. Please. In the interests of fairness. Of justice,' he said. 'There's something in the CCTV the jury should see.'

The judge paused. She looked pale and furious, and, momentarily, ruffled.

'I will only consider requests for resubmission made by the leader in the case, as convention dictates,' she said curtly, when she had regained her composure. 'Mr Green, your request is denied. Please sit down.'

Adam was suddenly aware of the sheer volume of people staring at him. Some of the jury were smirking uncomfortably, others looked shell-shocked. Ed Lowe seemed embarrassed by association. Jonathan looked like he wanted to slap him, Nisha's face was full of concern. He glanced at the public gallery, a sea of hostile faces, and to his surprise, he saw Georgina there. She looked like she might cry.

You could hear a pin drop as he slowly took his seat again. The judge acted like nothing had happened. 'Mr Lowe, are you ready to move to closing speeches?'

'I am, Your Honour.'

Lowe got to his feet, turned to the jury. His face was open and imploring, his language simple and to the point. He reminded them of the terrible price Grant Cliveden had paid for being a public servant, the horrific circumstances of his death, and the ongoing pain of his family and loved ones.

Then he got to the meat of his argument. 'What you are being asked to decide upon today, ladies and gentlemen, is the facts of this case. They are disputed by the defence, but they are not disputed by science. You have heard the defence's own expert witness agree that DI Cliveden was poisoned between 8.45 a.m. and 12.45 p.m. on 13 March. The only time he ate or drank during that time was in the Old Nag's Head, with the accused, James Knight.

'This same James Knight, you have heard, spent a decade behind bars after the brave police work of DI Cliveden brought him to justice. That's a decade he spent nursing a dangerous obsession with the victim, and planning how he would take revenge. Because Jimmy Knight blamed all the ills of his life — from his imprisonment to the tragic death of his teenage son — on one thing. Not on the crimes that he himself had committed, but on the man who caught him.

'Less than two weeks after he regained his freedom, James Knight arranged a meeting with DI Cliveden under false pretences. DI Cliveden's commitment to his work and his calling as a police officer meant he could not resist the false offer that Knight made him via a burner phone. Having lured him to a deserted pub, Knight slipped illegally acquired botulinum toxin into his victim's drink, knowing the frightening and painful death it would cause just a few hours later.

'The defence will tell you this didn't happen. They will try and distract you with excuses and irrelevant detail. But they have not offered an alternative explanation for how DI Cliveden met his death.

'And that is because they don't have one. Even the defendant himself did not want to tell you his side of the story, and, crucially, did not want to put himself through cross-examination. That's because he knows that his one lie — "It wasn't me" — would be immediately undone by the mountain of facts that disprove it.

'James Knight was a danger to the public ten years ago, when Grant Cliveden caught him and ensured he was sent to prison.

He is a danger now. He has proved he will kill, and he will trample on our cherished societal norms, because of his own sense of personal grievance. Do not let him do it again. You must find him guilty.'

Lowe sat down. It was a good speech, and Adam had seen some of the jurors nodding along. But there was no triumph on Lowe's face, no smug satisfaction. He looked, if anything, a little weary.

Jonathan got to his feet with scant enthusiasm. He laid his notes on the lectern in front of him; Adam's stomach clenched when he saw how it was a mess of red pen, whole swathes of it crossed out. After Dr Pettigrew's last-gasp surprise, there was little left for Jonathan to say. His pupil master cleared his throat, stalling for time.

'Ladies and gentlemen, I told you at the beginning of this case that James Knight is not an appealing person.

'I know that. He knows that. You probably know that. So how could it benefit him to give evidence, here in this trial?

'All he would have been able to do is confirm things you already know.

'He does not dispute that he has been in prison.

'He does not dispute that he disliked the victim.

'He does not dispute that he met the victim, and had a drink with him.

'What case could he possibly bring you? No, all he would do is open himself up to the prejudices you may already have, and yes, we do all have them. I should know – my first wife was part Welsh!'

Jonathan's attempt at a joke fell flat, but he carried on undaunted. Adam felt like he could hardly breathe. He wanted to jump up and push Jonathan away, scream at the jury to acquit – but he was frozen to the spot.

'It was ever thus,' Jonathan was continuing pompously, 'that things are not always as they seem. So today I appeal to your common sense, to your decency. Can you be sure, beyond all reasonable doubt, that Jimmy Knight killed Grant Cliveden? Was there really no one else – no one – who had both the opportunity and motive to poison him within that crucial window?

'Do you not think that a convicted armed robber may have had another way of sending their victim out of the world than through the subtle art of poison? How, for example, did Mr Knight get hold of this highly toxic and incredibly expensive substance, in quantities large enough to kill, and also manage not to leave a trace of it on his person or property? How did this man, who left school at fifteen, know with certainty the exact dose that would kill, when the experts say that death from botulism is vanishingly rare? The prosecution say we have not offered an alternative explanation. But there are things that they have not explained either.

'My learned friend speaks of facts. But really, in this case, there is only one fact that matters. Did Jimmy Knight kill Grant Cliveden? This is not a fact, it is little more than a theory that has not been proved – not by the forensics, not by the CCTV, not by the half-hearted and incomplete police investigation.

'When you re-examine the evidence, or lack thereof, in your deliberations, I have every faith that your common sense will prevail and you will agree with me – where the prosecution says there are facts, there is doubt. And if there is doubt, you must acquit. Thank you.'

Jonathan sat down, without a glance at Adam or Nisha. His pupil master had given it the best he could in the circumstances, Adam supposed, but there was little substance. If only he'd found the CCTV earlier.

All eyes now turned to the judge. While she couldn't tell the jury whether to convict or acquit, her directions were crucial and would shape their deliberations. If you knew what to listen for, you could often get a hint of what the verdict would be from the judge's summing up.

Charlotte Wickstead was silent for some time, her eyes cast down. She wasn't making notes, simply composing herself and thinking the case through. Finally, she lifted her head, and addressed the jury, her voice clear and unflinching. First, she gave her legal directions – which Adam had never seen a judge do with as much eloquence and clarity. He started to see what a formidable opponent she must have been, when she was still at the Bar. From there she moved into a balanced summary of the cases presented by each of the advocates.

'The issue at the centre of this case,' she continued, 'is whether James Knight is the only person who had both the opportunity and motive to poison Grant Cliveden. As you know, it is not for Mr Knight or his legal team to prove that he is innocent. It is the job of the prosecution to prove that he is guilty. It is not enough that he is the most likely suspect. He has to be the *only* suspect. You should consider carefully whether the prosecution has presented enough evidence for you to be satisfied you are sure that he is.'

A few jurors in the back row caught each other's eye. Up in the public gallery, a sea of hostile faces began to murmur among themselves. Jonathan at last turned to look at Nisha and Adam, and a slight smile was playing about his lips. Against all odds, they'd had a summing-up that might just work in their favour. The judge clearly didn't think the prosecution's case was as strong as it could have been. Now all they could do was hope that the jury agreed.

45

Jonathan's smile didn't last for long. By the time the jury had been sent out and everyone else had filed out to the Great Hall, it had been replaced by a grimace of pure wrath.

'Don't you *ever* pull a stunt like that again,' he shouted at Adam, not caring who heard. 'Although, if I have anything to do with it, your days at Stag Court are numbered. How dare you? Do you not realise how that looked? What untold damage you could have done to our case?'

'Jonathan, I'm sorry, I really believe that the CCTV would have helped – all I want is for the truth to come out,' Adam said, trying not to think about the coveted tenancy which seemed to be slipping through his fingers like water – or the fact that Jimmy Knight could once again be imprisoned for a crime he hadn't committed.

'We are not dealing with the truth, we are dealing with the law!' roared Jonathan. 'I can't bear to look at you anymore. I'm going to my club.' He turned to Nisha. 'Text me when the verdict's in – I can imagine it won't take them long to find our boy guilty as sin.'

Once Jonathan was gone, Nisha put a motherly hand on

Adam's shoulder. 'Are you sure you're all right, Adam?' she said. 'You've been a bit . . . all over the place these last few days – are you coping with the job?'

'Yes, I'm fine,' Adam said, more crossly than Nisha deserved. He already knew he'd screwed up – he didn't need her cooing over him like a concerned mother.

'Look, I was too hard on you yesterday,' Nisha went on. 'It's not your fault about the expert. You can't change the facts. But today . . . Adam, I know we all wanted Jimmy to be innocent but we can't let what we want cloud our judgement.'

So Nisha was giving up on Knight too, thought Adam. He bade her a quick goodbye, while he could still keep the tears that were pricking the backs of his eyes under control.

On his way back to chambers, all of Adam's worst fears about himself felt like toxins in his own veins, frazzling his nerves and blurring his vision. He was too impulsive, not dispassionate enough; he didn't know how to play the game; he'd failed, not just himself, but his client too. After all his hard work, after trying to keep his past in a box and his roots under the radar, it was manifestly clear that he still didn't belong there. With his own pupil master now against him, and Jimmy's fate hanging in the balance, it now looked less likely than ever that he'd get enough votes to secure his tenancy. Could he honestly say he'd impressed anyone over the past year? He hadn't even impressed himself.

But worse than that was the gnawing fear that an innocent man could be about to go to prison. And it would all be his fault.

When he reached Stag Court, Adam headed straight down to the basement. If he had any chance of salvaging his relationship with Jonathan, the Kavanagh case was it. There were several boxes that he'd been putting off for weeks because they were so complicated, and because the documentation was all in French. But he couldn't afford to delay any longer. He needed a miracle discovery to save the Kavanagh case where he'd failed with Knight.

Adam switched on the fluorescent overhead light and got to work, his eyes straining over the tiny text. Luckily, he had done an additional French course alongside his law degree at Oxford. He'd always been aware that being a good student wouldn't have been enough for someone like him – he'd needed to be excellent. And the extra coursework had been a convenient excuse to get out of parties. But what he'd learned during those three years of study hadn't extended to technical medical vocabulary, and he found himself reaching for Google Translate to help him with some of the trickier words.

He typed countless obscure phrases and complicated clauses into Google Translate, puzzling over its bizarre suggestions and trying to unravel meanings like code. The work was boring and painful and tedious and difficult, which made it feel like an appropriate penance.

Every time Adam thought about going home, he remembered the look on Jonathan's face when he'd asked the judge directly to reintroduce the CCTV. Just one more box, he told himself. Maybe the answer would be in there.

When it came, it looked as unremarkable as every other piece of paper he'd examined over the last three months. It was a document just three pages long, stapled together, stamped with the logo of a Swiss clinic and signed at the bottom with Kavanagh's signature. Adam dutifully wrote it out in English – and couldn't believe what he was reading.

'Full tests carried out' . . . 'efficacy of medicines well below clinical standards' . . . 'high chance of negative side effects' . . . 'recommend destruction of entire batch' . . . The phrases jumped off the computer screen and smacked him in the face. All this time Kavanagh had said that he'd had no idea the medicines he'd sold were faulty. But here it was in black and white, with his signature at the bottom. He'd had them tested and knew that they were something between useless and downright dangerous, but he'd sold them anyway.

It was like a bomb going off in his head. Jonathan had set Adam this painstaking task in order to find Kavanagh a lifeline that proved him innocent — instead he'd found solid proof that he was guilty. Adam pushed the laptop away and staggered towards the staircase back up to chambers. He wasn't one to drink in the office, but right now all he could think of was the bottle of Scotch under his desk in the pupil room, a gift to Jonathan from a client that he'd handed on to Adam because it was 'too cheap'.

Emerging from the depths of the basement, Adam looked at his watch — 9.30 p.m. It was dark outside, casting the chambers corridors into gloom, but there was one light still on. Of course, it was Bobby Thompson's. Adam decided he had nothing left to lose. He knocked on his office door.

'Come in.'

Adam stepped into Bobby's carefully curated oasis of calm. His tastefully minimalist desk light was on, illuminating the papers fanned out neatly in front of him.

'Adam. Here late again. What can I do for you?'

'What do you do if you find out your client is guilty but he still wants to plead innocent?'

Bobby looked at Adam over his reading glasses. 'You know the answer to that. Is this the Knight case? The jury are already out, aren't they?'

'No . . . it's Kavanagh. He insists he had nothing to do with the fraud but I just found a document that says he absolutely did. But maybe – he forgot, or something? It's just a mistake?' He wasn't even convincing himself.

'Adam.'

'I know, I know. But if Kavanagh won't change his plea, then Jonathan is going to have to leave the case – and, as he keeps telling me, it's the most important one he's had for years.'

Bobby sighed. 'Adam, however important this is to Jonathan and his bank balance, justice must come first. This isn't an American courtroom drama. You can't just bury that document. You don't need me to tell you that you have a duty to tell Jonathan, and that Jonathan cannot lie in court. I'm afraid that if Kavanagh insists on pleading not guilty, then his association with this chambers has reached the end of the road.'

Adam stared at his shoes – newly shined, just as his mother and Bobby had suggested. 'Jonathan is going to hate me,' he said quietly.

'That may be so,' said Bobby briskly. 'But that's better than hating yourself for doing the wrong thing.'

'I feel like I just can't get it right,' said Adam. 'I had a whole idea of what being a barrister was going to be and I keep falling short.'

Bobby looked at him sternly. 'Why did you want to be barrister in the first place, Adam?'

Adam thought for a moment. Becoming a barrister had been such a driving ambition for so long now.

'Probably sounds childish now, but I wanted to make the world a fairer place. When I was a kid something happened to me – which made me want to be there, for people in hopeless situations,' he said. 'Then you came to our school and you said, "The law is the way we protect each other against injustice." And I knew it was what I wanted to do.'

Bobby gave him a gentle smile. 'You seem to have remembered that speech very well. Far better than I could. But what I generally say when I give those talks is that while the principles of our justice system are noble, without people within it prepared to fight for them, those principles will be lost.'

Adam remembered it well: 'We have a legal system,' Bobby had said. 'It takes work to make it function as a justice system as well.'

'You're a fighter, Adam,' Bobby went on. 'From what I've heard, you fought tooth-and-nail to get the fairest result in the Jimmy Knight case. So don't count yourself out too fast.'

Adam shrugged. He was out of things to say.

'Look,' said Bobby. 'If there is one person who would abhor to have a miscarriage of justice on her conscience more than anyone else, it's Charlotte Wickstead. She was your judge, so be in no doubt Knight has had a fair trial. If the verdict comes back guilty, you may need to get used to the fact that perhaps he did do it, after all.'

Adam couldn't tell Bobby why, but deep down that was what he feared most of all.

46

He'd known Jonathan would be apoplectic when he told him about what he'd found in the Kavanagh boxes, but Adam was still unprepared for the full force of his temper.

It was like standing beneath Vesuvius mid-eruption. Jonathan's first question was, 'Have you told anyone else about this?' and when Adam confessed that yes, he'd spoken to Bobby, it provoked another howl of rage.

'How dare you? HOW DARE YOU? My case, and you go mouthing off to the biggest goody two-shoes in here. You've left me absolutely no choice, Adam . . .'

Jonathan veered between ranting and practically sobbing over what he saw as the injustice of it all. He had not only been wronged, he had been robbed – of the bumper payday he saw as rightly his.

'So what happens now?' Adam said, once the screaming tantrum had begun to ebb. 'Do we have to make what we've found public?'

'Oh, God, no,' said Jonathan tersely. 'Charles is already going to want my guts for garters – no good giving him a reason to burn this chambers to the ground too. No, if he won't change his plea – and knowing Charles as I do, he won't – then we merely step away from the case citing "professional embarrassment". He finds another legal team, and unless they take it upon themselves to translate every last foreign document' – he glared at Adam – 'then they will remain uncompromised, and able to still defend a not-guilty plea.'

'So Kavanagh could still get away with it?' asked Adam, shocked. Amid his own worry about tenancy and his pupil master's meltdown, it had been tempting to forget that in the middle of this case was a man who had flogged medicines to the NHS to be used on seriously ill patients, in the full knowledge that they might make them more sick, or even kill them.

'If that's what you want to call it, yes,' said Jonathan bitterly. 'And his lawyers will get paid handsomely for the pleasure.'

'But he's guilty!' said Adam. It didn't sound like justice to him.

Jonathan rolled his eyes. 'What did I tell you? We're lawyers, not detectives. Why couldn't you have just done your job, Adam?'

Adam opened his mouth to say that that was exactly what he'd thought he *was* doing, when there was a knock at the door. It was Tony, brandishing a brief.

'You expecting your verdict this side of the weekend, boys?' he said gruffly.

'I do hope not,' said Jonathan theatrically. 'The longer I don't have to think about that cursed case, the better.'

'Good, then you can spare your pupil to go down to Highbury Mags.'

'Anything to get this waste of oxygen away from me,' said Jonathan.

Tony ignored him. 'Think you know the old girl, Adam: it's Gloria Wooders.'

'What's she done this time?'

'Trying to smuggle chicken fillets out of Tesco in her bra. Yes, real chicken fillets. I wish I was joking.'

In the cells at Highbury, Adam found Gloria, the ageing call girl he'd represented no less than four times now, massaging her back. She was heavy-set, with breasts that spilled from her faded blouse, hair dyed a particularly violent shade of orange, and a toothless smile.

'I've seen your handsome mug in the papers, sonny,' she said with a wink. 'Thought you'd be too busy and important for the likes of me.'

'Never,' said Adam, with a smile. 'What happened this time, Gloria?'

'Oh, you know about the problems with my back,' she rasped, in her smoky drawl. 'Can't carry a shopping basket anymore, can I? So I just slipped the meat up there for safekeeping while I had a mooch around the shop, and I suppose I must have forgotten about it.'

'Gloria. Is that *really* what happened?'

She burst out laughing, which quickly turned into a hacking cough. 'Worth a try, weren't it? Just say I'm guilty if that's what you think's best, pet – and try and keep me out of the slammer.'

The magistrates accepted Gloria's guilty plea, as well as Adam's argument that as Gloria had no money, and was stealing to eat, a fine or costs would be inappropriate. Instead, she was handed a conditional discharge, on the understanding that she would not reoffend in the next six months.

'You've got to stay out of trouble this time!' Adam told her sternly afterwards, as she gave him a tobacco-inflected kiss on the cheek in gratitude. He was going to miss all this. The merry-go-round of repeat offenders and magistrates' courts was poorly paid and gruelling, but to be able to help someone like Gloria – completely on her own in the world, with only her own wits to rely on – made it all worthwhile.

If he didn't get tenancy at Stag Court, maybe he'd be able to get a spot somewhere else, at a less prestigious chambers. Lots of pupils who didn't get taken on straight away did a third six-month pupillage elsewhere, and were still able to forge successful careers. But Adam knew that for him, it wouldn't be that simple. Thanks to the Knight trial, his failure was already writ large. And it wasn't just a case of 'not being ready', as it was for many wannabe tenants. Gossip spread fast around the Bar, and he doubted if there was a single barrister in London who didn't know about his outrageous attempt to overrule his pupil master live in court. Who'd want to take him on now?

'You fancy treating an old girl to a slap-up lunch then, Addy?' said Gloria. 'Seeing as they confiscated my chicken and all . . .'

Adam had pulled out his phone, as he had at every available opportunity since the jury had been sent out in Knight's case. He was about to tell Gloria he'd treat her to a McDonald's, when he saw the message, which caused him to stop dead in his tracks.

'I'm sorry, Gloria, we'll have to raincheck that,' he said. 'I've got to be at the Old Bailey in an hour. It's the Knight trial – the jury have reached a verdict.'

47

Adam had never seen Court Number One so packed. Word had travelled fast that the verdict was in, and the press benches were stuffed with hacks practically sitting on each other's knees in their eagerness to be in the room when it was delivered. The public gallery too was bursting at the seams. In the family benches, Natasha Cliveden sat stony-faced, her golden hair fanned out over the shoulders of her cream blazer. The whole place thrummed with a kind of nervous energy.

Knight was brought in and took his place in the dock. Dressed in the same suit he'd worn for the whole trial, he exuded a coolness that Adam knew he'd never have been able to manage in the same position. If he was remotely nervous about the fact that the rest of his life hung in the balance, Jimmy didn't show it. The stage was set.

Necks were craned as Raquel summoned the jury, like an MC introducing the main event. Those twelve men and women had gone from being spectators to the stars of the show. They picked their way to their places carefully, steadfastly ignoring the sea of eyes that took in their every move.

The jury had chosen as their forewoman a matronly woman

in her sixties, who wore a polka-dot skirt and had the air of a retired headmistress.

'And have you reached a verdict on which you all agree?' the judge addressed her imperiously.

'Yes,' she replied evenly, smoothing her gaudily patterned skirt.

The judge nodded to Raquel. She got to her feet: 'Would the defendant please stand.'

The air crackled as Knight did as he was told. Every rubbernecker packed into that courtroom was watching him, willing him to be sent down. Adam wondered if there was anyone else saying a silent prayer that he wouldn't be, and a glance at Nisha's nervous face told him he wasn't alone in rooting for Jimmy.

'On the count of murder, how do you find the defendant – guilty or not guilty?'

There was a pause that seemed to stretch like a gaping jaw. The forewoman fidgeted, looked down at the small piece of paper clutched in her hand. She didn't look at Jimmy when she finally opened her mouth to speak – addressing herself directly to the judge.

'Guilty.'

Everyone had said it was an open-and-shut case, but even so, there were gasps in court. The whole world had purported to 'know' that Knight was a murderer, but here it was, officially confirmed. It was vindication for the public and media frenzy, but Adam struggled to believe it was justice.

Jonathan sighed and slammed his notebook shut. Nisha made a strangled sound that was something like a sob. But Adam's eyes were fixed on Jimmy, who, still standing, was breathing heavily, his nostrils flaring.

'This wasn't supposed to happen!' Jimmy yelled, his words bouncing off the austere walls and shocking the court into sudden silence. Fists balled, a vein throbbing violently in his forehead, he was staring directly at the judge.

'James Robert Knight, you have been found guilty of the murder of Grant Cliveden, whom you poisoned on 13 March of this year,' Wickstead continued coolly, as if he hadn't even spoken. 'Sometimes a pre-sentencing report is ordered – but in this case I see no reason for one. It is clear that a set-term sentence will not satisfy justice when the life of a frontline officer has been taken. I have no choice therefore but to pass a whole-life order. You are sentenced to life in prison, with no possibility of parole. Take him down.'

'No!' Knight was screaming now, as the stony-faced guards clapped his handcuffs onto their own wrists, and manhandled him from the dock. The journalists were scribbling furiously, unapologetic glee on their faces. This would make a hell of a headline. Boos and jeers were gathering momentum in the public gallery, while at the side of the court Natasha Cliveden was frozen, her face white. Knight thrashed in his restraints – almost as if he could change the verdict if he could just get himself back in the dock – but his handlers were too strong for him. As he was pushed and jostled out of the door back towards the cells, the judge looked away.

Once he was gone Wickstead restored order to the hysterical courtroom. The jury were thanked and discharged before she ran through various other formalities to bring the trial to a close. But Adam couldn't follow any of it. He felt completely numb. All he could picture was Jimmy's desperate face as he was led towards the hopelessness of a life behind bars. Jimmy had trusted them; he'd really believed they'd get him off. But they'd failed him. Not once, but twice had this man been let down by the so-called justice system.

Adam got to his feet and trailed Jonathan and Nisha out of court, nodding half-heartedly at Lowe and his team on the way. He wasn't sure if any of them were ready to face Jimmy, but he and Nisha followed Jonathan down to the cells anyway, none of them daring to break the stony silence.

The version of Jimmy they were confronted with in the cell was like none they'd seen before. He'd always been so composed, so resilient, but here he was, face streaked with tears and his shoulders shaking. He stared at the table and didn't seem to hear Nisha's hurried words about next steps, until she told him that she'd get working on his appeal immediately.

'No,' he said firmly, his head snapping up. 'What's the point? This was my best chance. I won't put myself through that again.'

Jonathan and Nisha exchanged a look.

'Mr Knight, you have nothing to lose,' said Jonathan. 'What else are you going to do for the next thirty years of your life? Might as well have a stab at an appeal.'

'Fuck you,' growled Knight. 'You thought I was guilty from the start. With you . . . I was never going to win, was I?' He tailed off, like he was realising an uncomfortable truth for the first time.

'If you mean I tried to warn you, then yes, you may remember that I advised against a not-guilty plea,' said Jonathan nastily. 'But you'll have plenty of time to think on that, during your life sentence, won't you?'

Jimmy did not reply.

48

Up in the Great Hall, Nisha bade Adam and Jonathan an unenthusiastic goodbye. She couldn't bring herself to tell Jonathan it had been a pleasure working with him, or any other similar nicety, so she just managed: 'Perhaps we'll see each other again.' To Adam she said: 'Good luck.' He could tell she doubted if he'd last at the Bar, and he didn't blame her.

Adam was about to ask Jonathan if they should walk back to chambers when his phone rang. It was Tony.

'Did you hear the Knight verdict?' Adam asked tentatively, braced for an onslaught.

'I did,' he said gruffly. 'I'm sure your ridiculous conduct didn't help. A guilty verdict was always likely, but it didn't have to be such an embarrassment.'

Adam swallowed. 'Tony, I can explain—'

'Haven't I told you? I'm only interested in what you've got to say if you're telling me you won, or you've made us some money. Anyway, for however long you are still a part of these chambers, you are going to work. I'm emailing you the brief for a drunk driver at City Mags. And Adam? Do try not to fuck it up.'

As Tony rang off, Adam turned around to see if Jonathan

was still there, but unsurprisingly, his pupil master was nowhere to be seen. The hall was still bustling with people; lawyers and clerks hurrying to courtrooms, families of defendants and curious spectators chatting about what they'd seen. There was even a group of school children in fluorescent tabards being shown around. Adam had never felt more alone.

The brief from Tony pinged through on his phone. The hearing was set for two hours' time at City, fifteen minutes' walk away. There was no point going back to chambers, which was in the opposite direction, so Adam headed to the Bailey canteen with his laptop, to prepare for the hearing as best he could.

But once he had set himself up at a corner table, armed with Divina's peculiar version of a cappuccino – 'Milk frother is broken, so is normal milk, and we no have chocolate powder so I put on couple of Smarties instead' – he found he couldn't concentrate. His mind kept going back to Jimmy Knight. Bobby had said that in the event of a guilty verdict, Adam would need to face the fact that perhaps Jimmy was, actually, guilty. But he couldn't do it.

He knew why the jury had reached the verdict they had. Jurors, like most people, liked simple explanations. The prosecution had offered the simplest version of events – all they'd had in defence was a load of complicated theories about flawed police work.

But Adam couldn't help feeling that there wasn't a simple explanation to Cliveden's murder. Perhaps – just perhaps, Adam allowed himself to consider – Jimmy was involved, but there was no way he'd acted alone, and it certainly hadn't been his plan. The blonde hair on the CCTV surely proved that. There had to be a better explanation – which meant there must be something they'd missed.

Adam started to leaf through his bulging folder of notes and documents relating to Knight's case, which he'd taken to carrying around like a weird comfort blanket. Glancing up briefly, he noticed a familiar statuesque figure approaching the coffee counter. Without her wig, Judge Charlotte Wickstead looked more human somehow, but the angular profile and undeniable mystique made her instantly recognisable. She ordered an extrahot soya latte with an extra shot. Adam smiled to himself. Good luck getting that out of Divina.

He turned back to his notes, finding himself drawn to the pages relating to the phone found in Jimmy's property. No one had offered a satisfactory explanation for what 'S699' meant, the code which the sender of the texts had evidently used to get Cliveden to trust them. Had they made a mistake by not pursuing that further? Adam squinted at the page. And then there was that mystery number, wasn't there? Two calls made to it the night before the murder, and one on the morning before Cliveden died. They'd never been able to trace who the phone had belonged to, and with so many other confusing details from the phone evidence to follow up, they hadn't tried that hard either, because it had seemed slightly irrelevant. But that was before Adam had found the CCTV, and the possible involvement of another person. And before he'd had the wake-up call about the dangers of missing phone calls.

Judge Wickstead was still haggling with Divina about how to make up her coffee.

'No. No soya,' Divina was saying. 'I can put semi-skimmed in the microwave? Or maybe you prefer . . . this salad?'

Adam watched her for a minute. Bobby had said that she'd hate to have a miscarriage of justice on her conscience. If they could find any ground for an appeal for Jimmy, then surely Wickstead would support it.

On a whim, Adam pulled out his mobile, and punched in the number from the evidence document. The person whose unregistered phone it was had almost certainly ditched it by now, and if for some reason they hadn't, they'd be mad to answer a random call. But you never knew, it had to be worth another try.

To his surprise, it rang. And to his even greater surprise, at the exact same time, a piercing ringtone echoed around the canteen. Obviously a coincidence, he thought, until he became aware that Judge Wickstead, who had been haggling with Divina at an increasing volume, was suddenly rummaging in her designer handbag.

The phone kept ringing, both in Adam's ear and in the canteen. Then the judge pulled out a handset from her bag, and it wasn't the bright pink iPhone with the pug case that he'd clocked on the first day.

It was an old Nokia.

It looked like a burner phone.

The judge pressed a button and the ringing – on Adam's phone and in the canteen – stopped dead.

He stared in disbelief, not knowing what to make of what he had just seen. It didn't make any sense.

The judge looked around, almost automatically. She was about to turn back to Divina, when she suddenly noticed Adam, file open, phone in his hand.

She looked him dead in the eye, and didn't blink. Her face was impassive, without a flicker of fear.

Adam had his explanation all right – and it was about as complicated as it could get.

49

Adam gathered up his things and practically ran out of the canteen. His mind was racing almost as quickly as his heart. Suddenly, he remembered something Dr Alice Pettigrew had said in her evidence, which had got lost amid the drama of her changing her opinion.

'Even as his respiratory system failed, he'd have needed something to actually choke on to guarantee death . . .'

He knew the CCTV footage of Cliveden's death by heart. Which meant he remembered vividly that it was the judge who had suddenly proffered a cup of something to the barristers trying to revive the dying police officer.

Adam suddenly knew exactly what had happened but he still felt as if he understood nothing. And he certainly had no idea what he was going to do about it all.

So he went to City Magistrates', making his way straight to the public waiting area where he called the name of his client, Mr Bartlett. He shook hands with the sharply dressed City Boy with a chirpy Essex accent and a set of Audi car keys clutched in his hand and nodded while he listened to the 'exceptional hardship' his client would face if he was disqualified from driving – which seemed to largely revolve around missing the stag do of someone called Jonno which was due to take place next weekend. 'Oh, and my missus is pregnant,' he offered at last. 'About to pop, and she don't drive.'

Adam felt like he was in some kind of trance as he took his place at the bench, and made Mr Bartlett's case, playing up the effect it would have on his girlfriend and unborn child. The three magistrates might as well have been three gargoyles, and if you'd asked him five minutes later to pick them out of a line-up he wouldn't have been able to do it. It was like listening to someone else as he robotically appealed for them to be lenient, all the time thinking of Wickstead, her phone, and that look in her eye.

When the magistrates came back and said that they'd accepted his case, and Mr Bartlett's disqualification from driving would be suspended because of the undue hardship he'd suffer, Adam didn't even have the energy to feel elated. It was a win and he needed every one of those he could get, but nothing seemed to make sense anymore. He walked out of the magistrates' in the same fugue state, pausing for just a minute to check his phone.

An email notification flashed up.

From: C. Wickstead
Subject: <no subject>
Come and see me in my chambers asap, thanks.

That was all. Adam didn't know if it was the right thing to do, but he needed answers. Immediately he broke into a run towards the Old Bailey.

*

The court was starting to empty out for the day by the time he arrived. Barristers and solicitors were heading for the Tube, while defendants were being taken back to prison in a succession of armoured vans that were starting to drip out onto the streets. Adam had never been to judges' chambers before. He had to ask for directions from a security guard, who directed him right up to the very top floor.

A gloomy staircase led to an even dingier corridor, which he proceeded along, adrenalin pumping a drumbeat of fear through his veins. He had no idea how this was going to go.

At last he reached a polished mahogany door with gold trimmings, and knocked.

'Come in.' Her voice was cold as an arctic wind.

Adam stepped inside. Charlotte Wickstead, in a sleeveless black shift dress with her icy-blonde hair loose around her gym-sculpted shoulders, sat at an enormous antique desk which was almost as neatly arranged as Bobby's. But while his office was a temple to minimalism, hers felt like a library in an old country house. Every wall was given over to bookshelves, which from floor to ceiling were crammed with handsome leather-bound volumes. Her Hermès handbag had a special stool all of its own. The only light came from a skylight high above her head, through which the late-afternoon sun was draping the judge in a sort of ethereal light.

'Thank you for coming, Mr Green,' she said, gesturing for him to sit down. 'Can I get you a drink? Water? Or something stronger – Scotch?'

'No, I'm all right, thanks,' said Adam, determined not to let his guard down.

Wickstead folded her hands in front of her, flashing her long crimson nails. She let the silence stretch – she had called the meeting, but she wasn't going to be the first one to blink.

'You wanted to see me?' Adam said at last. It was clear they both knew what he had discovered about the burner phone – but who was going to be the first to admit it?

'Yes,' she said. 'I wanted to say you should be proud of how you fought for your client. You did everything you could for Mr Knight, even when it meant putting yourself at risk. And that's what makes a good lawyer.'

Adam regarded her warily. 'That's it?'

Wickstead held his gaze. 'That's all I wanted to say,' she said. 'But I assume that you may have some questions for me.'

She was right, he had so many – he hardly knew where to start.

'It was you, wasn't it? On the CCTV, at the pub?' Wickstead didn't say anything. But nor did she deny it or shake her head.

'You planned this, then roped Knight in so you didn't get your hands dirty. Were you meant to fix the trial so he got off too?' Adam's voice rose as he got angrier, but Wickstead didn't flinch. 'You're a judge for God's sake – how could you do this?' He shocked himself with the ferocity of his outburst.

Wickstead sat in silence for a beat or two, then got to her feet. She paced up and down, stilettos clacking on the wooden floorboards, as she spoke – as if she were questioning a witness in court.

'You found out rather a lot about Grant Cliveden during the course of this trial, didn't you?' she said.

'Well, yes, and none of it good.'

'Quite so.'

'He was corrupt. He stole drugs and money for his own

personal gain. Framed innocent people to make sure his pay-masters never got caught. Used his popularity in the police to move whistleblowers sideways. Hell, he probably murdered Jimmy Knight's son. But surely, he shouldn't have been *killed* for that – he should have been brought to justice.'

'In an ideal world, yes,' said Wickstead. 'But we don't live in an ideal world, do we? You talk of justice. Well, what justice is there in all those innocent men who got sent to prison because of Cliveden's lies? What justice is there in the gangs he so cynically helped, who continue to tear communities apart with the blight of misery, drugs and violence? What justice is there in the mockery he makes of the hard work and sacrifice of the many thousands of brilliant, honest police officers he purported to serve alongside? What justice is there in—' Her voice caught and she suddenly turned away. 'Well, you know the depths to which he sank.'

Adam couldn't believe what he was hearing. 'You're saying he deserved to die?'

Wickstead stared out of the window. 'Adam, do you know how incredibly, magnificently the human cogs that make up our fragile legal system work to keep it on track? You must have seen enough by now to know how chronically poorly resourced, over-worked and understaffed we are. And yet, thanks to the dedication and sacrifice of individuals – from the police on the front line, to the defence solicitors trekking to police stations in the middle of the night, to the court officials juggling incredibly complex caseloads and making sure everyone gets their day in court, all for little pay and even less thanks – against all the odds, justice is still done.

'And then someone like Grant Cliveden comes along. Poison

in the heart of the system, and unless something is done the rot spreads and spreads. It imperils everything that the rest of us are striving to do.

'Our priority must be justice. It caught up with Cliveden in the end.'

Adam felt nauseous. Here was a member of the highest echelons of the judiciary, talking about cold-blooded murder as if it were simply a point of law to be haggled over.

'What about Jimmy? Did you tell him you would protect him? Because you didn't, did you? First you sent him Jonathan, who you must have known wouldn't fight for him. And then you stopped the resubmission of the only evidence that would have proved he didn't act alone.'

The judge turned her glassy eyes towards him. 'I have no idea what you are talking about,' she said loudly, as if anticipating a third party listening in to their words. Did she think he was recording her or something? 'But your pupil master is a good lawyer. Particularly if you are looking for someone who will follow the expected script and not lob in any unexpected curve balls.'

'I knew it,' said Adam. 'You fixed it. Or you thought you could, but it didn't go to plan.'

'I cannot fathom what you might be suggesting,' said the judge airily. 'You must see how impossible it would be to "fix" a trial, as you say. A judge cannot control the jury, as you well know.'

'All those decisions that went in our favour . . .' Adam was talking more to himself now than to Wickstead. 'I bet Jimmy never thought he'd even get caught – did you tell him he'd get away with it? But then when he didn't, you promised you'd do your best to protect him. But you didn't. And now he'll spend the rest of his life in jail and you'll—'

'Adam, sometimes people do things for a bigger cause. They know the risks, but they decide some things are more important.'

It still didn't make sense. 'But you're a judge! There must have been a million things you could have done to punish Cliveden, without having to murder him . . .'

The judge stared right through him. 'Adam, be careful what you are accusing me of. As you say, I am a highly respected judge. You are a pupil barrister who proved yourself to be far too close to your case, given your emotional outbursts in court.' She paused, ominously. 'Perhaps it is the weight of your family history, causing you to see conspiracies where there are none.'

Adam recoiled as if she had slapped him. So she knew. And she was trying to use the information to threaten him. He was overcome with the desperate urge to get as far away from Wickstead as possible.

He got suddenly to his feet. 'I'm sorry, you'll have to excuse me.'

The judge watched on with surprise but he was already heading for the door.

'Adam!' she called after him, and for the first time she seemed like she was losing her formidable control. 'Adam!'

Her voice echoed down the corridor after him, but Adam didn't look back. He just ran.

50

Phone call

'Adam, sweetheart, hi. Did you . . . did you get my letter?'

'Yes, I did . . . Mum, it's a hell of a lot to take in.'

'I know, darling . . . and you've no idea how I fretted about whether to send it or not. Do you wish I hadn't? I've tried so long to keep this burden from you, but you kept asking and asking, and I started to think – maybe keeping this from you was doing more harm than good.'

'Honestly, Mum, you were right to tell me. But you should have done it sooner. You didn't need to carry this on your own, all these years.'

'It was my decision, to cover up what happened. Mine alone. You must see that I couldn't tell you, especially when you were so young. Then you were doing your exams, and doing so well at uni, then this pupil thing . . . I thought it would be wrong to make you live with the lie.'

'Mum, I know you were just trying to protect me. But – God – I've spent my entire life wondering about that night. And all this time you knew exactly what happened.'

'Adam, I always told you your dad was innocent. And you knew him, you loved him. You must have known that he couldn't have been guilty of a hit-and-run.'

'No, Mum, I didn't *know*! I *believed* he didn't, but I wanted to be able to *prove* it too. Because I so desperately wanted him not to be what the world said he was. A killer. A drunk. Who mowed down an innocent child then killed himself rather than face trial!'

'I told you, Adam, it doesn't matter what other people think . . .'

'Of course it matters! And it matters most of all to you! Don't you think I don't know how those nasty glances and the whispers and the backs turned ate you up inside? I might have been young but I saw how you buried the shame of it all. Even now, just the mention of his name makes you shrivel up. And you know what, to protect you, I tried to bury the past too. I was so scared of it coming out again because of what it would do to you. Terrified. I would have done anything to stop you having to go through all that humiliation again.'

'That humiliation, Adam, was my punishment. I deserved it, because of what I chose to do. But you were just a little boy – you didn't. So yes, I tried to put it in the past, and build a new future, so you could be free of it.'

'I get it, Mum, I do. But how could I ever be free of if when it was hanging over us like a black cloud? You never wanted to talk about it. Not at all. If we even came close to it you'd change the subject. Do you realise how hard that was, for me?'

'I know, Adam. But I wouldn't even have known where to begin. It was bad enough, losing the only man I'd ever loved, and finding myself having to raise a child on my own. For everyone we knew to think he was capable of such a horrific crime. I prayed and prayed to know he hadn't done it. And then the letter from that *woman* arrived – and then I wished that I didn't have the proof after all.'

'Did you really have no idea, Mum? All those years – that he had a second family?'

'No, I didn't, Adam. Your mother's a silly old mare. I thought he loved us – and only us. So many years, Adam, and I never knew.'

'That letter she sent you – it proves Dad was innocent. He wasn't behind the wheel that night – she was. He wasn't even in the car. You should have handed it over to the police – cleared his name.'

'And leave those children without a mother? Two little kiddies, and another one on the way? No, enough tragedy was caused that night. And your dad was dead. Clearing his name wasn't going to bring him back.'

'What about the parents of the child who died? Didn't they have a right to know? A right to justice? Mum, are you still there?'

'Don't think for a second, Adam, that I'm not haunted by that every single day of my life. The choice I made – what it meant for that family. I still don't know if I did the right thing. But maybe it's possible to do the wrong thing for the right reason.'

'You should never have had to go through all this, Mum. Aren't you angry with Dad – for what he did?'

'I was. I was really angry. But maybe you remember, I could never stay angry with your dad for too long. On his good days, he was the kindest, funniest, most generous person I'd ever known, and God, Adam, I loved that man. I always knew, from the start, that the good days came at the expense of the bad ones. He was flawed and messy, he drank too much, he took too many risks. He could be selfish, he could be totally irresponsible. And his lies. How he lied. For him, it was easy as breathing. I always said it would get him into trouble one day. I just never imagined quite how much.'

'He shouldn't have killed himself. He was innocent; he could have proved it.'

'He did a desperate thing. The pain he must have been in . . . it haunts me every day. All I can think is that maybe he didn't see himself as innocent, Adam.'

'You don't have to be a good person to be wrongly accused, though! The law is meant to protect everyone – good and bad alike. No matter how many mistakes they've made. Maybe Dad didn't think he was innocent. But he was not guilty, of this crime. The truth is worth fighting for, isn't it?'

'It's not always so black and white, is it? The truth is complicated – people are complicated, too.'

'So everyone keeps telling me.'

'Adam, you've worked so unbelievably hard to get to where you are. If I could take away the pain that this caused you, I would. I know it's not easy, and you'll always feel it. But my only wish is that you don't let it hold you back from embracing this amazing future that I know you have ahead of you. That's why I'm telling you all this – because I want you to move on, in whatever way you can.'

'I'm not sure if it's much of a future, Mum. Everything has gone wrong – I've made so many stupid mistakes. They're never going to give me tenancy.'

'Rubbish. They'll be mad if they don't take you. And I'm not just saying that because I'm your mum. I am so proud of you. Nobody believes in fairness like you do. You see the good in the people the world would want to write off. You see an obstacle and you just smash right through it. And you never, ever give up – so don't start now.'

'Thanks, Mum. It means a lot.'

'It's all true. And you know, once you've got your tenancy you'll really be able to put your mind to finding a nice girl-friend. Now, do you remember Janice Goldenblatt, who ushers at the synagogue on Friday? Now she has a lovely daughter, and Janice has in her mind that she'll marry a doctor, but I think a top barrister would do . . .'

51

Adam hung up the phone and flopped back on his bed, heavy with exhaustion. It was Friday night and he'd arrived home to the letter from his mother, before he'd even had time to properly process his conversation with the judge. So many revelations in such a short period of time; his brain was struggling to cope with it all.

He'd always thought proving the truth would be the biggest hurdle. But actually, he realised now, what you did with the truth once you'd proven it was even less straightforward.

His dad was innocent. For as long as he could remember, he'd hoped and believed that he was. That should have been enough, but he'd wanted more. Why had he pulled on the end of those strings? He was left now with a hollow feeling. His father wasn't the person other people had said he was, but he wasn't who Adam had thought he was either. The price of knowing the truth was having to carry more secrets, and it weighed heavily; his mother had kept them for years, and it would be a betrayal of both his parents unless he did the same.

And Judge Wickstead was guilty. But that meant Jimmy was, too. Adam had fought so hard for his client, searching for a truth that was never there. What was he meant to do with this appalling information?

Wearily, he shoved away the detritus of trainers, books and takeaway menus that had gathered on his bed, and crawled under the duvet fully clothed. He probably should have been worrying about what lengths Wickstead might go to in order to keep him quiet. Or examining his feelings about the fact he had a secret half family for whom his father had sacrificed everything, assisted by his mother who'd helped cover up a terrible crime. He should at least have been freaking out about the tenancy decision on Monday. But it was as if a year's worth of difficult clients, endless paperwork, office politics, confusing protocol and constantly looking over his shoulder had hit him all at once. The secrets, the lies, the threats, the doubt and the sheer injustice that had accompanied his journey through the broken system felt like weights he could no longer lift. He curled into a ball, and let sleep carry him away.

Opening his eyes to the shrill tones of his alarm on Monday morning felt like waking from a coma. Adam couldn't remember the last time anxiety hadn't had him in its grip on waking, but perhaps he was just all out. He showered and dressed slowly, and made himself a strong black coffee, knowing there was no rush to get to chambers. The Stag Court barristers were meeting at 10 a.m. to discuss his fate – and Georgina's too. And that was one conversation neither of them could be a part of. They had to let the hard work of the last twelve months speak for itself.

Adam flicked through his phone as he munched a bowl of Coco Pops. A short text from Rupert: Good luck mate. One from his mum, who had recently mastered emojis: They wd b mad not 2 take u!!!! followed by four fingers-crosseds, three starry-eyes, six hearts, an inexplicable engagement ring, and Champagne glasses clinking, which Adam thought was a tad premature. Finally, to his surprise, there was a text from Georgina.

Here's to us, AG – we did it! Whatever happens, we can say we survived one seriously hardcore year at Stag Court. Keeping everything crossed for both of us – you really deserve this. G x

He smiled despite himself.

It was a beautiful morning, bright and crisp with a hint of autumn in the air, so Adam decided to walk all the way to chambers. As the chaotic noise and pungent takeaway smells of Holloway gave way to the handsome mansions and leafy boulevards of Islington, he pondered the question of what to do about Charlotte Wickstead for the umpteenth time. Should he tell the police what he knew? Would anyone believe him if he did? He still didn't understand why she would risk her career, her reputation, and her integrity to rid the world of one bad apple. His mind wandered back to his mother, colluding in his father's lie to protect the children of a woman she should have forsaken. Before he did anything, he needed to speak to Jimmy. Perhaps his former client would finally be honest with him.

Through the rabbit warren of Temple's streets Adam went, passing by the spot where Emma Owens had stalked him in the dark. He realised he hadn't heard from her since the verdict. Rounding the corner of Pump Court, chambers finally loomed into view – he hoped not for the last time. He found Tony on the steps, smoking a cigarette.

'There he is,' Tony said with a slippery grin when he spotted Adam. 'Big day for you, son. Could finally get to call this place home.' He took a drag on his cigarette. 'Or get told to sling yer hook, I suppose.'

'Thanks, Tony, I am aware,' muttered Adam.

'Well, you're early. The ladies and gents are still talking through your various successes and, er, failures – which may be why it's taking some time. Go and sit with Georgie in the lobby. I'll call you when they're ready.'

Adam stepped past him, trying not to inhale an entire faceful of tobacco smoke, and headed to the tastefully upholstered greige sofas in the chambers waiting area. There he found Georgina, legs crossed around each other like a pretzel, looking more nervous than he'd ever seen her before.

'Hi,' he said, taking in her pale face and the way her nails were digging into her balled fists. 'How're you feeling?'

'Like I want to be sick,' said Georgina. 'You?'

Adam managed a brittle chuckle. 'Same here. Though I'm not sure there's been a day of pupillage when I've not felt like that,' he told her. 'So I guess it's a fitting way to end things.'

She gave him a tight smile. Adam could see that she'd poured her heart and soul into her pupillage – just like he had. Now that the moment of truth had arrived, it was borderline unbearable.

'Has anyone given you a hint?' she asked him.

'Not a thing. You?'

She shook her head. Chatting to Georgina made Adam feel calmer somehow. But with so many troubling thoughts battling for his attention, he couldn't think of anything else to say. They lapsed into silence, the only sound the ticking of the clock above their heads, counting down the seconds until their fate was sealed.

Adam had never known time go so slow. Surely, he thought, Georgina must be a shoo-in. So if they were taking so long to decide, it must be because there were barristers who strongly felt he didn't deserve a place, but maybe a handful who were arguing to give him a chance . . .

The clock hands inched towards quarter to twelve, when suddenly the door to reception flew open. Adam nearly shouted out in surprise – because standing there in her figure-hugging suit and towering heels was Raquel.

'Are your barristers in their AGM?' she demanded of Daisy on reception, in the same intimidating bark that Adam had got used to in court. 'I have a note I need to deliver urgently.'

Daisy tried to protest, offering to pass it on, but Raquel refused, insisting that she must hand-deliver her mysterious note herself. 'And it can't wait,' she added sniffily. Adam tried to catch her eye, but Raquel steadfastly refused to look in his direction.

Realising she was powerless to resist, Daisy nodded helplessly.

'What the hell is that all about?' Georgina asked, as Raquel stalked towards the conference room. Adam wished he knew the answer.

Moments later, Raquel was sweeping past them again, note successfully deposited. Georgina and Adam caught each other's eye, baffled. But they didn't have much time to ponder the bizarre intervention, because minutes later Tony was looming over them, his wide grin showing a flashing gold tooth.

'Miss Devereaux, Mr Green – they're ready for you.'

The short journey from reception to the conference room felt like walking to the guillotine. Adam's legs were jelly, his breathing was fast and shallow. Tony ushered them into the room, where twenty-five barristers sat around the glass table, faces as blank as their bland corporate clothing. Adam tried to catch Jonathan's eye for a clue of what was coming, but his pupil master looked away.

Bobby cleared his throat. 'Adam, Georgina, thank you for joining us. As you know, we have been discussing the progress you have both made during your twelve months of pupillage.

'Firstly, on behalf of all of us at Stag Court, I'd like to thank you both for your hard work this year. Pupillage here isn't easy, and we don't intend it to be. We want to push you to your limits, and we have been impressed by the vigour with which you have faced the challenge.'

Adam snuck a glance at Georgina. He could tell that, like him, she was desperate for Bobby to get to the point.

'As you know,' the senior KC continued, 'we usually take on one new tenant every year. And there was one pupil who chambers believe will be an excellent fit here, thanks to their unfailing tenacity, talent for advocacy and prodigious work ethic. Congratulations, Georgina. We'd love to welcome you on board.'

At last, the other barristers started to smile as they broke into applause. Georgina beamed back at them like a kid on Christmas morning, unable to contain her elation. Adam felt a perverse rush of joy for his rival, which was instantly replaced by a tingling sensation of shame and disappointment. He was suddenly very aware of how he was standing, the fact that he was lurking on the edge of Georgina's triumph. Was he meant to just leave?

But Bobby wasn't finished yet. Once the applause had died down, he cleared his throat one more time.

'This year, however, there wasn't just one pupil who shone. Adam Green's dogged determination, creative thinking, respect for the principles of justice and loyalty to his clients impressed not just his colleagues here, but also other people he has worked with throughout his time as a pupil barrister. For this reason, we have decided to offer not one but two spots at chambers this year. Please join me in offering your congratulations to our second new tenant, Adam Green.'

Adam was stunned. He could hardly take it in, even when Georgina wrapped her arms around him and whispered through tears: 'We did it!' But that huge smile on Bobby's face was real, as was the hearty wink from Rupert, and the enthusiastic applause from the other barristers. There was, however, one person who wasn't clapping. Jonathan was sitting with his arms folded, looking like he'd swallowed a particularly sour lemon. Getting a tenancy spot without the support of his pupil master seemed like an impossible miracle.

Adam was still in a daze as someone cracked open a bottle of Champagne and pressed a glass into his hand. He felt as if he was floating above his body as a succession of juniors and KCs came to shake his hand and tell him congratulations. Rupert slapped him on the back, Georgina chinked her glass with his. Bobby laid a fatherly hand on his shoulder and said simply: 'You deserve this, Adam.'

The buoyant atmosphere of celebration went on for about an hour, during which time Adam was astonished to find that he retained the ability to smile and make small talk almost like a normal person who wasn't going through the most transformational experience of their life. Eventually the hubbub of chatter died down as people drifted off back to their desks. Adam drained the last of his Champagne, and was about to head off too, when he heard a voice behind him.

'You were almost out, you know.'

Adam spun round and found himself face-to-face with Jonathan. He hadn't realised he was still there. There was a strange smile playing on his lips.

'I'm sorry?' said Adam.

'You're not as good as Georgina, you must know that,' his pupil master said with deliberate cruelty. 'And when I told them all the clangers you'd made with me, the rest of chambers were not inclined to take you on.'

His words stung. This was meant to be the happiest moment of Adam's life, and here was Jonathan, scribbling all over it.

'But they did,' said Adam slowly, trying to keep his voice even. 'So that's all that matters.'

'Well, yes, but if it was me I think I'd always be wondering if it was really my own merits that got me here, or just the intervention of a powerful ally?' Jonathan shot back nastily.

The same doubt had been lurking in the corners of Adam's mind ever since he'd heard he'd got in. He knew Jonathan wouldn't have advocated for him, so who had? He'd presumed Bobby, but now he wondered how that could possibly have been enough.

'Personally, I have no idea what it was about your abysmal performance that impressed her,' Jonathan continued. 'But it's got you the job.'

Adam's brow furrowed. 'What do you mean?'

'See for yourself.' Jonathan gestured at a folded piece of paper that still lay on the table, before exiting the room without a backwards glance. Adam picked it up, his hands trembling.

The paper was thick and glossy, headed with the name and address of the Honourable Charlotte Wickstead. The letter itself was just two lines of scribbled handwritten text followed by a looping signature.

I have never seen a pupil barrister perform quite like Adam Green. I trust that you at Stag Court will recognise that he is a true asset to your fine chambers, and I hope to see him as a fully qualified barrister in my courtroom very soon.

Adam dropped the paper like it was a hot coal. It wasn't just the content of the letter that had caused the hairs on the back of his neck to stand up.

It was the handwriting. He'd seen it before. Scrawled on an envelope, left in his pigeonhole, containing a secret and a threat.

52

There had been a time, at some point in the early part of the trial when everything seemed to be going surprisingly well, that Adam had truly believed that one day he'd go for a drink with Jimmy Knight.

From the beginning, Adam had felt an affinity with this particular client. One wrong turn, or having a mother who wasn't as lionhearted as his own, and he could have been in the same position. Perhaps, in another life, they could have been friends.

Adam had pictured them one day sipping frothing pints and toasting freedom. But that would never happen. Jimmy Knight was a murderer, and he was serving a life sentence. And so Adam found himself once again in the airless room in Belmarsh the day after the tenancy decision.

Just as when he'd visited before, Knight was in his grey prison tracksuit, slumped in his chair. But this time the fight had gone from his eyes.

'How are you, Jimmy?' Adam asked, although he knew the answer wouldn't be good. Jimmy just shrugged. 'Why are you here, Adam?'

'You weren't honest with us, Jimmy,' said Adam, as gently as possible. 'I know about Charlotte Wickstead. Did she put you up to all this?'

Jimmy stared at Adam for a very long time. 'Whatever you think you know, you don't understand,' he said eventually.

'Then help me understand, Jimmy,' said Adam imploringly. 'I can go to the police with this information, maybe we can use it to get you out, or at least reduce your sentence. But you need to be honest with me, properly honest this time.'

The mention of the police got Jimmy's attention. 'Don't you go grassing about this,' he said, eyes flashing. 'No one put me up to anything. I wanted Cliveden dead, and I killed him. I'd have done it with or without her.'

Adam shut his eyes briefly. It had been what he'd been expecting, and what he'd been dreading. All the way to Belmarsh he had been willing for Knight to tell him the impossible: that he was really innocent, somehow he'd been tricked, and he wanted to fight for his freedom with an appeal. It was too much to have hoped for.

'Why, Jimmy? You spent ten years in prison because of that man, and now you're going to spend the rest of your life there too. Was it worth it?'

'It was worth the risk,' Jimmy said, as matter-of-factly as if he was talking about the weather. 'There was a chance I'd have got away with it. And he needed to pay for what he did. You know that scumbag murdered my son. And all because he was too scared of the truth getting out.'

'Jimmy, what happened to Marcellus is tragic. But how can you be sure Cliveden was responsible?'

'Oh, I'm sure all right. Or at least I was when he turned up to the Old Nag's Head after that text message I sent him. S699. You lot never worked out what that meant, did you? Well, it was the beginning of his number plate. That police officer, Emma Owens, wrote to me and told me. She reckoned if he was driving that night his gang would be holding that over his head, and he'd think it was code. She was right.'

No wonder Emma hadn't wanted to admit to knowing about Marcellus's death.

And why she'd been so desperate to try and prove Jimmy's innocence. She didn't want to have had anything to do with a murder.

'So you killed him for revenge. But how does Wickstead come into it?'

Jimmy scrunched up his face, he didn't want to answer.

Adam lowered his voice, desperate. 'Please, Jimmy. You owe me this. I'm trying to work out what to do about it all – you can't just ask me to do nothing and then not explain why.'

The prisoner's face softened. 'You need to know, Adam, that I was the one who put that poison in Cliveden's drink. Me – only me. I am the killer. And I'm the one who'll serve the sentence. So don't go thinking you can try and get her to take the rap for it. Because I will never, ever testify against her.'

'But you couldn't have done it without her!'

Jimmy nodded. 'That's true. She planned it, she got the poison. Her cousin is a chemist or something. She worked out how much we needed, and she brought it to the pub. We chose the Old Nag's Head because old Reg McNally, who was my barrister once, used to take me there for a drink after court when his old man ran the place. He told me then it would always be a pub criminals loved because of the blind spots on the CCTV.

He said he'd rather die than take over running it so don't blame him either, cos I had no idea he would be there.

'She came and dropped the poison off at the pub — and I suppose somehow you worked that out already.'

'It was only a glimpse. I guess she didn't know the CCTV blind spots as well as you.' Adam couldn't keep the bitterness from his tone. 'You might have given Cliveden the initial dose of poison, but it wouldn't have killed him without something further to choke on. It was Wickstead who made sure he got a drink when it became clear the botulinum was taking effect. I bet that wasn't just water either. What did she do, slip some cod liver oil or something in there, to make sure he choked?'

Knight ignored the question. 'Adam, I know what you're thinking. Nothing gives anyone the right to take a life, right? And I lied about it too, so I made a mockery of you and Taylor-Whatsisname and your whole precious justice system. But guess what. Sometimes the system — it don't work. And believe me when I say the world is a much fairer place without Grant Cliveden in it. As for trying to get away with it and the judge trying to help me with the trial — well, I served ten years behind bars because of him, and I lost my beautiful boy. So we both reckoned I had paid my dues already. The jury had other ideas, but that's OK. I'd rather be in here and Cliveden dead than walking around free in a world with him still in it.'

Jimmy leaned back in his chair and looked at Adam, as if daring him to disagree. His story was mad, his justifications defied logic. And yet, to Adam, it made a weird kind of sense.

'Fine, you made your choice,' said Adam. 'But there's something I still don't understand. Why did Wickstead agree to help you? I know she was on to Cliveden's corruption, but how do you go from there to murder – and why are you still protecting her now?'

To Adam's surprise, Jimmy smiled. There was a faraway look in his eye.

'This goes no further, Adam.'

'OK . . .'

'I mean it. If you ever try to get me to say it on record, I'd rather die than betray her.'

'What is it?'

'All right. Me and her – we go way back. She grew up round the same ends I did. Back then she weren't the Honourable Charlotte Wickstead, mind – she was plain old Charlie Wicks.'

'Bloody hell.' Wickstead should never have been allowed anywhere near Knight's case. If anyone found out, it would be a scandal.

'She didn't get stuck in the shit like I did, though – she moved away, made something of herself. I never knew she went into the law, but I wish I had. Maybe we'd have been able to expose Cliveden earlier, together. But we weren't in touch and it might have stayed that way. Until he killed Marcellus.'

Adam was confused. 'Why would that make her want to kill Cliveden?'

Jimmy looked at Adam with a sad smile.

'You don't think I came up with the name Marcellus on my own, do you?'

53

So Charlotte Wickstead was Marcellus Knight's mother. Adam sat in stunned silence, trying to absorb the news.

'Hold on. I thought his mum was a junkie?'

'She was, yeah. That's why they took him off her as soon as he was born. It damn near broke her. That's when she left – went up north. I think it was too painful for her to stay in touch, so she didn't. Me and Marc – we never saw or heard from her again. I wouldn't have stopped her seeing him, but I suppose she thought she'd let him down already, and she didn't want to disrupt the life I built for him. I only knew she'd cleaned up and made something of herself because a few years later she started sending me envelopes of cash for Marcellus. Small at first, but they got bigger over the years. I put them all in a savings account in the hope that one day he'd go to uni. And he did and all.' Jimmy couldn't help beaming with pride.

'Even when you went to prison – she never came back for her son?'

'She didn't know. She weren't in touch with anyone from the old days. My brother tried to find her when I got sent down, but of course she'd changed her name by then. Marcellus went and lived with him and his wife instead.'

Adam was dumbfounded. 'She never tried to find out what happened to her own child?'

Knight grunted. 'It's easy for you to judge her, but I don't think anyone judges her as harshly as she does herself. Yeah, some might say it makes her a bad mum. But I'm not so sure. It was all just too painful for her, so she had to check out. She sent the money, did what she could, while preserving her sanity. I can forgive her that.'

The silence between them stretched, as Adam tried to process what he was hearing.

'So how did you two end up getting to this point together?'

'About a year ago she was on to Cliveden. Knew that he was planting evidence and all that. When she started looking into his historical cases, she found out what had happened to me. She was horrified, frantic, couldn't believe her son had been left without a parent. Obviously, she tried to find Marcellus – but it was too late. And like me, she just knew. Only one person could be responsible.'

'So she came to you.'

'Charlie Wicks came to see me, yes,' said Jimmy. 'You won't find any record of Charlotte Wickstead in the prison logs.'

Adam put his head in his hands. It was such an audacious, outrageous story, and yet also the only plausible explanation. Wickstead had tried to buy his silence by intervening on his tenancy, but was he really prepared to be bought so cheaply? Surely, in the interests of justice, he had to speak out – even if her involvement would be nigh on impossible to prove.

As if he could read his thoughts, Jimmy leaned over the table towards Adam.

'Look, Adam, I'm spending the rest of my life behind bars. Cliveden's murder is not going unpunished. His family don't have to wonder what happened to him for the rest of their lives.

'And Charlie – she's a good judge. One of the best. Say nothing and she'll continue to fight for fairness, to stop monsters like Cliveden, every day of her life. She already lost her child twice over. Don't take this away from her too.'

A year ago, Knight's impassioned plea would have left Adam cold. He'd wanted to be a lawyer so he could impose order on the world. But if his pupillage over the last twelve months had taught him anything, it was that the law was a very blunt instrument for determining between right and wrong.

There was a short silence, and Knight rubbed the feather tattoo behind his ear. Adam had spent enough time with him to know he did this when he was anxious.

'Jimmy, that tattoo . . .'

'What about it?'

'My dad had one just like it. He said it stood for freedom. It was a reminder for him not to fall into any traps.'

'The lag that inked it on me said some similar bullshit.' Jimmy chuckled at the irony. 'Didn't work for me though, did it? Did it work for your dad?'

'No, not really.'

A flicker of sadness passed over Jimmy's face. 'Freedom . . . so many people take it for granted. I sure as hell did before I went to prison the first time. I vowed I would never risk it again. But that was before there was something worth sacrificing it all for. And if you look at it like that, I'm not in a trap at all, am I?'

A crime happened, someone paid the price. Did it really matter *who* paid it, or simply that the price was extracted, somehow? Did justice really come down to the simple binary of guilty or not guilty? Even if you thought it did, written into the choice was the assumption that no one was ever, truly, innocent.

As he shook Jimmy's hand for the final time, Adam already knew that what had passed between them would never leave this room.

One way or another, justice had been served.

Epilogue

Junior barrister Adam Green stood on the steps of Bexley Magistrates' Court and looked at his watch with a start. It was nearly half past five, and that meant one thing – he was late.

Court had overrun because the magistrates had scarcely believed what they were hearing. It had taken all of Adam's composure to explain that yes, his client had meant to thrust his genitals through the letterbox, but no, he hadn't known that the letterbox in question belonged to the outraged older gentleman who had called the police. It had been, in fact, an ill-judged attempt to rekindle his relationship with his ex – who lived next door.

He broke into an awkward power-walk towards the station, quickly checking his phone as he did so. An email flashed up on the screen.

From: Jones, Tony
To: All-Users-Stag-Court
Reminder of tonight's networking event – 6pm. DO NOT BE LATE.

There was also a text message from his mum.

Hi Ads! ☺ Just a reminder to send Grandma flowers for her birthday. If you wanted you could pop into the florists on Stapleton Street. There's a new girl there, she's very pretty, Jewish, and according to Judy, SINGLE! Just a thought!!!! Xxxxx

Some things never changed.

Adam got to the station just as a train was pulling into the platform. Finding himself a seat, he put his headphones on and stared out of the window. He didn't need to pick up the copy of the *Metro* that was on the seat next to him, because he'd already read the news forensically that morning – just as he had ever since the Palmerson Inquiry had begun. The nation had been gripped by the wide-ranging inquiry into police corruption, but Adam had more reasons than most to be enthralled. The inquiry had begun after Judge Charlotte Wickstead had recommended it, following 'inconsistencies' that had emerged about Grant Cliveden's conduct during the trial of Jimmy Knight. Yesterday's key witness was a certain Reg McNally, who had testified to multiple meetings between senior police officers, including Grant Cliveden, and known gang leaders in his pub. Cliveden's once-gleaming reputation had certainly had a makeover, and the press were enjoying the fall of their one-time hero almost as much as they had relished finding the culprit for his murder. Rumour had it that Natasha Cliveden had pulled her children out of school and fled to the Dominican Republic – nominally to escape the glare of publicity generated by the lurid revelations about her husband, which had included the exposure of his affair with an unnamed court clerk whom he had gone on to blackmail. But, Adam noted wryly, it was interesting that the Dominican Republic didn't have an extradition treaty with the UK.

He tugged his winter coat tighter around himself and hurried on from Victoria to Temple and through the twisting lanes towards Stag Court. He could hear noises emanating from the 'networking event' before he saw it, the sound of plummy banter and chinking glasses spilling out of the open windows of the ageing building.

Hoping he'd be able to sneak in late unnoticed, Adam bounded up the steps. But before he went inside, he paused, as he always did these days. It didn't get old seeing his name stencilled in black on the board that listed which barristers practised at Stag Court.

He was about to push open the polished black door when suddenly it was flung open from within. Tony stood behind it, his face an angry red tomato.

'You're late!'

'Yes, I know, I'm really sorry, but . . .'

And then to Adam's surprise, Tony's face softened and he gave him an indulgent wink.

'I'll let you off this once, sir, because I know you had a good result with the Partridge case this morning.'

Adam thanked him and hurried inside, before Tony could change his mind. It wasn't every day His Grumpiness deigned to give out a compliment.

To his surprise, on his way to get the drinks Adam found himself actually doing some networking. More than a year into his tenancy at Stag Court, he knew a decent proportion of the invited solicitors now, and lots of people wanted to chat to him about Grant Cliveden. Had he known that the national treasure was actually a national disgrace all along? Adam smiled and nodded and confessed that he'd had 'an inkling'.

Someone had put ABBA on in one of the upstairs offices and

it sounded like networking was rapidly turning into karaoke. Adam was suddenly aware of how sober he was and excused himself from the group to go in search of booze. In the conference room he found a jumble of bottles on the table – and an enormous red-wine stain on the beige carpet, which someone had inexpertly tried to cover with a copy of *The Legal 500*.

Adam grabbed a beer and headed out into the corridor. Bobby and Catherine Jordan were standing at one end and when they saw Adam, to his surprise, they beckoned him over.

'Adam, just the man,' said Bobby, an eyebrow raised. 'We were just talking about one of your erstwhile clients. Charles Kavanagh.'

Even the name was enough to send a shiver down Adam's spine. Kavanagh's sneering, bullying face swam into his mind. The sheer cruelty of what he had done – exploited seriously ill people for profit, knowing he could make them sicker – was still one of the worst crimes he'd come across at the Bar.

'What about him?' Adam asked.

'The verdict came in today,' said Catherine. 'You just missed your pupil master actually. He had a few choice words on the subject.'

With everything else that had happened in the last few months, Adam had forgotten that Kavanagh had found new legal representation and was still pleading his innocence. He hadn't followed the trial at all – though he imagined Jonathan had.

'And?' he said, looking from Catherine to Bobby.

'Not guilty,' said Bobby, with a grimace.

Adam felt a stab of revulsion. With his power, his money, his lies and his total disdain for the dignity of others, Kavanagh had managed to bulldoze his way out of the punishment he richly deserved. But if he'd learned anything from the last year, it was that the legal system didn't always work the way you thought it should.

'Just as well Jonathan left before you got here, because he was rather upset,' said Catherine archly. 'I daresay he will find something – or some*one* – to cheer him up, though.'

Adam let his unease settle as the two KCs moved on to talking about the set that had represented Kavanagh and the case they had run. It wasn't fair – but he'd just have to learn to live with that. Then, over Bobby's shoulder, he spotted Georgina, and before he could help himself his face split into a wide smile.

'All right, Adam,' she said, sidling up to him. 'I heard you've been fighting for the rights of Postman Penis. What a shining example of our noble profession!'

Adam grinned and let her tease him for a bit longer. He didn't mind her jabs anymore, and anyway she was the one person he wanted to tell about the note that he had in the pocket of his jacket.

It was a thank-you gift from Emma Owens, whose name had been cleared and career restored thanks to the inquiry into Cliveden. She was adamant that none of it would have happened without Adam sticking his neck out in court, and had insisted on doing him a favour in return.

He'd known immediately what to ask for – and that's why he had the names and addresses of his half siblings, traced diligently by Emma, carefully folded in his pocket.

But that could wait. For now, he just wanted to chat and laugh with his friend, and enjoy the novelty of, for the first time in his life, almost feeling comfortable at a party.

Sorry – networking event.

Acknowledgements

My thanks go to: Emily Fairbairn for weed-whacking through my cerebral detritus to find an intelligible story. Emily Griffin for her incurable belief in me. Anna Dixon, Lizzie Barroll Brown and Sally Mulberge, my three wise humans (with better gifts). To Lesley Land, who would have been my first reader (I miss you deeply). OJ Glenton for your omniscience and guidance. Gilly Greenslade for your rapier wit. Sarah Willingham for your unfiltered habit of holding me to account. Joanne Koukis-Robinson, Gudrun Young KC and Sarah Fawcett for housing (and remembering) my best stories from the Bar. Malcolm Bishop KC (my professional hero). Jeremy Brier KC for being the funniest person I know. Simon Conway for being just extraordinary in every sense. Helen Warner for starting it all off, Queen Liz for being my cheerleader, Sacha Judd for sense checking, and Susanna Reid for your inspiration. Martin Ahearne for keeping me sane in lockdown. My colleagues at 2 Hare Court for their enduring patience and support. And to all my family (Bob in particular) for their unconditional love, especially my mum (aka Marjorie), whose limitless kindness and mindfulness have deprived me of a decent autobiography.

DON'T MISS
THE NEXT ADAM GREEN MYSTERY

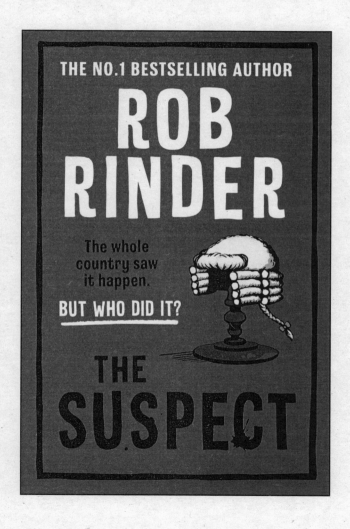

THE NO.1 BESTSELLING AUTHOR

ROB RINDER

The whole
country saw
it happen.

BUT WHO DID IT?

THE
SUSPECT